A NECESSARY MADNESS

JENNIFER JENKINS

OWL HOLLOW PRESS

Owl Hollow Press, LLC, Springville, UT 84663

A Necessary Madness

Library of Congress Cataloging-in-Publication Data
A Necessary Madness / J. Jenkins — First edition.

Summary:
Voices inside Ebrielle's head pull her into one bad situation after another. When she discovers that the strange whispers may be the key to uncovering a plot to destroy her homeland, she realizes they could prove her loyalty to her people…or lead to her undoing.

ISBN 978-1-945654-96-1 (paperback)
ISBN 978-1-945654-97-8 (e-book)

CHAPTER ONE

A HANGING OFFENSE

The large ruin stones overlooking the valley of Freeland called to me nearly every night. Some in Freeland feared the ruins, but I'd spent a great deal of my childhood playing among the black boulders of this meadow and felt an irrational sense of ownership. A pull, of sorts, that made each visit a relief. A pull that grew stronger every day. A pull that confirmed my gradual slide into madness.

Moonlight reflected off the low fog that parted around me as I approached my favorite ruin stone. I didn't bother smoothing down my skirts as I stretched out onto the rock. Lacing my fingers and tucking my hands behind my head, I exhaled and took in the colorful night sky.

Wisps of pink, green, yellow, and even a little blue snaked among the stars. I'd been told sky dancers were the spirits of those who'd passed on—family who had chosen not to follow the way of the stars into the next life, but instead lingered among the living.

As childish as it was, I sometimes imagined my mother whenever I saw a streak of vivid blue, her favorite color. I stared up at the countless stars and let time bleed into the periphery as my anger toward the woman who loved me so well, and not nearly enough, built to a crescendo. I had to look away.

We weren't supposed to speak ill of the dead. So I never talked about her.

A random thought came almost as a whisper to my ears.

I should go to the barn. The voice was just a little off, as though the pitch didn't quite match the cadence of my mind. I closed my eyes to the stars and willed the thought away.

The whispers were the second proof of my deteriorating sanity. They were different than the pulls and often came as random thoughts that almost always led to trouble. I couldn't tell anyone about them because I didn't truly know if they were the product of my own rampant curiosity or if I was just sick of mind. Usually, these intrusive thoughts preceded a good eavesdropping. Up to now, my strange intuition had led me to any number of hiding places from which I'd always come away with some juicy morsel of knowledge. It was no secret that I had a talent—Father would more likely call it a curse—for obtaining information. Thanks to my observations, I'd wager I knew more about the workings of Freeland than most.

A chill rolled along my skin and I sat up and rubbed warmth back into my arms. The barn was the last place I should go at this late hour. What I ought to do was sneak back into my home before my father learned of my absence.

Go to the barn first. The whisper nagged again. A light wind cut through the meadow, rolling out the fog and causing the high grass around my ruin stone to tickle my skin.

I planted my feet on the ground and balled my fists, battling the whisper's power over me. Curious by nature, once a suggestion entered my head, the possibilities of what I might learn if I followed the prompting ran wild in my thoughts. It wasn't that stopping by the barn would be out of my way—I'd have to pass it to get to the back door of my home. But for what purpose?

My peace destroyed, I left the stones and retraced my steps through the woods, down the path that led to my family's holdings. Moonlight struggled to reach the forest floor, but I knew this trail as well as I knew my own home and had little trouble finding my way.

When I emerged from the woods at the rear of our property, gravel *crunched* beneath my slippers and mountain wind tugged at my clothing. The barn blocked most of my view of the house, and again I froze in indecision. It was late, and it didn't make sense to visit the barn without a reason.

I gathered my skirts into fists.

Barn. Barn. Barn.

Setting my jaw, I ignored the mental whisper and walked away from the barn toward the house.

A cold energy seemed to seep inside my very bones. My head grew dizzy.

Barn!

I stopped and closed my eyes, but the dizziness only intensified and the world began to tilt.

Curious, I took a few experimental steps back toward the barn door.

My vision righted, my head cleared, and heat seeped back into my limbs. I shivered and glanced around the gravel courtyard, searching for some logical reasoning for my body's reaction, certain I was broken in a fundamental way.

Father claimed I could beat the temptation to spy with enough will power. But he didn't understand. No one did. I didn't have words to explain how these whispers, these urges, had grown over the years. Morphed from simple curiosity into a monster I didn't understand and now couldn't defy.

What kind of eavesdropper arrived *before* the people they were spying on? How could I be curious about something I didn't even know existed? How could I possibly know that something would happen at the barn at this late hour?

Never had the whispers been so strong. So... *insistent*. I knew how crazy that sounded. No jury would believe that the trouble I'd caused in Freeland in my short seventeen years was the fault of the voices in my head. Poor defense, indeed!

With shaking fingers curled around the handle of the barn door, I darted a glance over my shoulder to make sure I was alone. With a turn of the handle, the large door creaked open. I stepped inside, catching my breath as the now persistent wind beat upon the weathered wood in gusts that whistled through every crack in the old walls.

Though the room was blanketed in darkness save the moon-lit glow coming from an unshuttered window, I navigated obstacles in the crowded space with ease. Horses nickered from the four stalls, annoyed at having their rest disturbed. I reached out a blind hand as I passed the final stall where my mare, Millie, stood and her soft nose nudged my palm with a puff of exhaled breath warming my fingers.

"Not a word, young lady," I whispered, before scratching her neck and walking to the back of the barn where most of the farming tools were kept. I came to the ladder that led up to the hayloft and paused.

Up! urged the whispers in my mind.

I could turn back. It wasn't too late.

But even at the thought, a new wave of dizziness took over and the world tilted. Hands gripping the ladder, I gave in to the force prodding me onward, and climbed. I couldn't help myself.

Besides, I wasn't a *complete* victim of the proverbial devil on my shoulder. As much as I didn't like the feeling of losing control, I *was* curious and I *did* love the information I learned from these strange encounters. The urge to unearth whatever secrets would be shared here tonight doubled, as though the rotten side of me knew my conscience had flagged this as a bad idea.

One shaking hand over the other, I climbed the ladder, cursing my skirts as they tangled underfoot. I hadn't reached the final, highest rung when a familiar jolt of adrenalin sent my heart racing and raised goose bumps along my arms and the back of my neck. A warning shot, telling me there wasn't much time.

Something would happen here tonight… something I needed to witness.

I flew up the final rung of the ladder and dove behind the hay bales piled to the ceiling of the barn. With harvest in full swing, the loft was filled with winter feed for the stock. The old wood groaned and bowed with my added weight.

My breath caught as the barn door eased opened, and the weak light of a lantern illuminated the contours of my brother's face.

Voices drifted up to me.

"It's so dark, Gavin."

Hearing my best friend Marianna's voice was the last thing I'd expected. Gavin usually met his three rowdy friends in the barn at night to play cards, using one of the old apple barrels for a table. They gambled coins if they had them, but more often chores, leather belts, favorite knives, and humiliating dares were their preferred currency.

I liked those card games and the crude jokes and harmless mischief they produced. My brother's grandest smiles always materialized in this barn. Smiles I didn't often see since our mother's passing two winters earlier.

Gavin held the lantern aloft and surveyed the barn from the open door. I sank back behind the hay just before his eyes traveled up in my direction. Only then did Gavin take Marianna's hand and lead her inside, closing and bolting the door behind them.

He hung the lantern on a nail by the door and pulled Marianna to him. One arm wrapped around her slender waist and the other held her hand against his chest. He hummed a deep lullaby our mother used to sing to us as they slow danced on the dirt floor.

Marianna laid her head against his chest and willingly followed his lead, as though dancing with a young man alone in a barn at night was a common occurrence for her.

Was it? Had she and Gavin been here before? It certainly seemed like it.

She fit so well in his arms. Her long dark hair hung loose down her back, free of its usual pins. Her dress was cinched to accentuate a slim figure. Shy Marianna, who quietly worked in the bakery owned by her councilman father, who often wore streaks of flour on her forehead and clothes, who'd made mud pie castles with me down by the river when we should have been headed home after kinder school, pushed up on her toes and pressed a kiss to my brother's cheek.

Gavin probably didn't even realize he had stopped humming, his feet no longer carrying them back and forth in the dance. He threaded his long fingers through the thick hair at the nape of Marianna's neck and leaned down.

I leaned too, my head hanging slightly over the edge of the loft, caught in the spell of the moment, mesmerized by the passion I had no idea existed. I couldn't blink fast enough, certain my eyesight was somehow altered. Marianna had *never* mentioned a fondness for Gavin! And there wasn't a chance her father would approve of her cavorting with Gavin Fields alone in a barn in the middle of the night.

A low groan sounded from the boards beneath me.

Gavin's lips met Marianna's.

A *crack* accompanied a slight vibration beneath my knees. I stifled a gasp and inched back away from the edge—back to the middle of the loft where the floor already bowed from the weight of the fall harvest.

Oh no.

It happened in the space that exists between heartbeats. Just as the floor gave way, I jumped, my arms looping around one of the rough rafter beams as the loft floor fell out beneath me. The wood and bales crashed down on top of my father's prized plows, a painful clanging nightmare.

Marianna's scream harmonized with Gavin's shouts. The horses whinnied their panic, and as ashamed as I was to expose myself, my own cry joined the chaos.

"Run for help!" I heard Gavin say.

The light traveled nearer until it stopped fifteen feet below me. "Hold on, Ebby!"

With fingers cramping and forearms aching as I clutched at the rafter beam, I glanced down to find Gavin frowning up at me.

"I'm s-sorry," I stuttered.

"You can be sorry once you're on the ground. For now, just don't let go."

Oh, the shame. Father would be furious. No, worse—he'd be so disappointed.

"I'm slipping!"

"No, you're not." Only Gavin would argue with me at a time like this. "Though falling might not be a bad idea. If you break both of your legs Father might feel bad enough to spare your life when he sees what you've done to his barn."

My cramping fingers numbed. I couldn't hold on much longer. The hay would break some of my fall, but Gavin wasn't exaggerating the possibility of breaking bones if I fell from this height.

Finally, the large barn door swung open and three shadowed figures rushed into the dark space. The alarmed voices of Marianna's father and Gavin's best friend, Wesley Smith, filled the barn as they made their way toward the wreckage below me, before a booming, "Ebrielle Ann Fields!" thundered through the doorway behind them.

I closed my eyes and tilted my head up to the rafters, praying that if I did happen to survive this fall, my father wouldn't kill me.

And Wesley Smith! Of all of the young men in Freeland Marianna could have petitioned for help, she had to bring him? She may as well have led a hungry wolf through the door. He'd never let me hear the end of this one.

My father shouted, "The ladder, Gavin. It's still intact!"

I shook my head. Tears formed in my eyes as my arms slipped until my fingers were grasping the edges of the beam. One by one, they peeled off. Just as the ladder was hoisted from the wreckage on the ground into a vertical position, I fell. I clawed at the air, catching a rung of the ladder with one hand only to lose my exhausted grip. Skirts flying up around my head, I braced for impact.

Strong arms broke my fall, but my weight and momentum carried us both to the ground, landing between two bales of hay. The arms around me tightened and a deep voice that I knew almost as well as my own brother's rumbled against my cheek.

"Are you hurt?" asked Wesley.

Shaken and shocked, I abandoned all inhibition and pressed my forehead into his chest and shook my head. No, I wasn't hurt.

"You've really gone and done it now, haven't you, Ebby Ann?" His tone wasn't scolding. If anything, concern smoothed all the usual roughness from his voice.

His hand moved a fraction and brushed the bare skin of my thigh. He froze and my mouth flew open in a mortified, silent scream. My traitor skirts had flown up around my waist, splayed out around me, somehow everywhere yet nowhere necessary.

My father, the governor of Freeland, cleared his throat, and Wesley practically shoved me away from him as we both untangled ourselves enough to find our feet.

"I thank you for your assistance, Wesley, but I will handle things from here," Father said.

I didn't need a lantern to see Father's disapproving face.

"My pleasure… ah, I mean, I'm happy to be of assistance, Governor."

With one look, Father sent me back to the house, but not before Marianna's father shouted, "Your children are out of control, Fields!"

I ran all the way to my bedroom. Our housemaid, Hannah, burst into my room and took one look at my tears before batting away my shaking hands to help with the laces of my dress. She muttered a nearly inaudible, "Not again, child," and helped me into bed.

When Father and Gavin finally entered the house, slamming doors punctuated their raised voices.

With the adrenaline of listening long passed, my own self-loathing settled over me like a storm. I'd failed to control myself. Again. It seemed as though my constant failure was as inevitable as summer bowing to fall. Every day the sun a little weaker. The leaves a few shades darker. My resolve to ignore the whispers in my head as desperately futile as the day before.

Why couldn't I control myself?

BY MORNING. I'd only slept in patches. My head felt as though Wesley had used it to pound horseshoes in the smithy. When I finally gathered courage enough to face my father, I adjusted my skirts and ran my fingers through my hair. As hay and my hair were essentially the same color, I double and then triple checked to be sure that all evidence of my night in the barn was gone before braving the stairs down to the kitchen.

Dust moats danced on the sunlight filtering through the open window. Bunches of drying herbs hung from a line that ran the length of the kitchen. Hints of peppermint and dill competed with the scent of a fresh loaf cooling on the still-warm cast iron stove in the center of the room.

Hannah worked at the chopping block. Her red curly hair seemed to defy her age. No matter how hard she tried, no bun or hair wrap could tame it. "Which was it this time?" she said, not bothering to look up from her work. "Roof top? Tree?"

"Hay loft." I sighed and snatched a potato from the top of the stack she was working and used a dull knife to peel the stubborn skin off its back. Hannah accepted my confession with a nod, and we peeled potatoes in reflective quiet until Father entered the kitchen wearing one of his best coats with his hair combed back to reveal his handsome, dark features. It was a Tuesday, which meant he would spend the day in meetings instead of working alongside his men in the fields. "Ebby, I'd like a word in the study."

I set my half-peeled potato on the counter and nodded, my throat suddenly dry.

IN HIS STUDY, Father sat in his high-backed chair. Behind him a large bookshelf occupied nearly the entire wall. We didn't own enough books to fill it, but clusters of the precious volumes sat with a few of my mother's framed samplers and trinkets. I quickly looked away from the reminders of the past and focused on my father.

The sunlight coming through the window cast shadows around his face, emphasizing his disappointed features. He put his hand to his brow and massaged his temples. He held this position when he spoke to me, like my crimes had given him a permanent head throb.

"Eavesdropping again?"

I bowed my head, my mouth and lungs uncooperative in my attempt at speech.

"Ebrielle Fields?"

I winced at his soft words. "Yes, Father."

He pulled a metal key from his coat pocket and inserted the filigree end into a strongbox that sat at the corner of his desk.

The key turned, and I was suddenly struck with the familiar pull that often compelled me to the ruin stones near my mother's grave, as though a warm needle pierced my middle and a thread guided me toward the box. This feeling differed from the cool insistence of the whispers that led me to the barn. But it was also, somehow, the same.

Father removed a letter from the safe. The fancy wax seal was broken, the folds worn as though it had been read several times. He looked out his window, deep in thought, and then tapped the point of the letter once on the desk, as though it were a gavel sealing my fate.

"While your brother is repairing the hayloft, you will spend the next three weeks helping Marianna in their family bakery. It is the least you can do for the poor girl."

My head jerked up. "What do you mean?"

"Your brother went to Councilman Miller early this morning to apologize. He's been planning for weeks to ask the stubborn man for the right to court Marianna." A muscle in Father's jaw flexed and I couldn't be certain if his anger was directed at Gavin, Councilman Miller, or me.

"Needless to say, Gavin's been refused."

A lump of dread formed in my throat. This was my fault. I'd let the whispers overpower me again and, in turn, hurt two people I loved.

Father seemed to have second thoughts about opening the letter because he fiddled with the seal and then placed it back in the strong box. The moment the key turned, the warm pull within me vanished.

I was losing my mind and suddenly furious about it. My lips pressed together, my jaw locked in defiance. I might be going crazy, but I wouldn't give into these compulsions any longer. I'd fight back and find a way to close my mind to the whispers and pulls, gain control over myself.

I was a Fields, after all. And a Fields was nothing if not stubborn.

Chapter Two

Words

Three weeks later

I'd always been fascinated with words. Amazed that a series of sounds strung together could create meaning, instill passion, instruct, insult, uplift. Words had the power to testify of things that were true, to sway opinion, and even ignite change.

I'm told it was the silver tongue of my great-grandfather who inspired a group of craftsmen to migrate from Brennan, the region's largest and wealthiest province, to this valley. Dozens of men left their lives behind and journeyed over the mountain to settle this isolated area nestled in the joint of two massive mountain ranges—a valley that hadn't been occupied for hundreds of years. Great-grandfather's words must have been laced in golden silk to inspire such sacrifice.

I walked through town on an errand for my father to deliver a letter to one of the field bosses. When he'd handed it to me this morning, I'd remembered the letter in Father's strongbox and my strange reaction. As much as I wished to know what the letter contained, I hadn't had any compulsions since that night, and hoped to keep it that way.

The letter in hand was smaller, the paper less fine, and if it was meant for a field boss, it didn't concern me.

As I traversed the bustling main thoroughfare, a familiar red feather waved at me from the hat of a man standing at the end of a small strip of shops. The man turned a corner, his long red feather trailing after him. I didn't need a special prompting to want to follow Joe Ford, but there it was, like a cool breeze brushing damp skin. The sensation, whether real or imagined, produced memories of the barn, giving me pause until I rationalized the difference. Going to the barn had made no sense. This was another matter entirely. The thoughts in my head telling me to follow Joe didn't belong to the madness. Did they?

The traveling storyteller had spent the last year in Freeland, and I'd learned long ago that he only wore his red feather when he planned to spin a good tale. And wherever Joe Ford told stories, a few of my father's more handsome fieldworkers usually followed. Besides, I wasn't expected in the bakery to help Marianna until noon. No harm could come from the detour.

The tree. Be quick.

Rubbing away the flutter of excitement in my stomach, I tucked father's letter into the pocket of my skirt and set off to follow Joe Ford. Keeping pace with his string bean legs was impossible without running, so I grabbed my skirts and jumped a low fence to cut behind an old ivy-covered cottage. Fumes off a vat of boiling wool and dye assaulted my nose as I hurried past. I kept to the hedgerow bordering Freeland's fields until I reached the old oak tree.

The tree had become a favorite of the storyteller's, and I knew he'd be here with the same certainty that I knew Father loved his crops. Men from the fields came for the shade and would each pay him a hay-penny to tell his latest story while they shirked their work and passed around water skins. In a province like Freeland where hard, honest work was the highest virtue, not many held great respect for the storyteller. But I couldn't help but admire him. Anyone could swing an ax or dig a hole. It took a master of words to convince people to forget their troubles for a time and dream of greater things.

I knotted my skirts and scampered onto my favorite forked branch and nestled in. Gavin didn't hand out praise very often, but he once said I climbed trees like a squirrel. Father was quick to remind me that climbing trees and dangling from rooftops while eavesdropping on Joe's stories was nothing to be proud of. He said my unique talent for sneaking around didn't benefit anyone in Freeland and that I ought to use my time serving the needy or tutoring at the school instead of embarrassing the family with my idleness. "You are a Fields," he'd say. "Hard work is in your blood!"

Apparently, God forgot to mix in the self-sacrificing portion of my Fields blood—either that or I was a changeling switched at birth—because here I sat, a little girl no longer, but still climbing trees to hear bedtime stories.

I shivered as the wind whispered through the amber-colored leaves, blowing my wild hair into my face. The uncomfortable tugging in my stomach abated the moment I settled onto the branch, but the burning of my conscience took its place. What would Father think if he found me like this?

A distant bell chimed eleven long tolls, and within minutes, Joe arrived and twenty tired, smiling men rested in the shade of my tree, oblivious to my presence. I tucked my heavy skirt around me just in case they chanced to look up.

Joe stepped to the base of the tree, welcomed by friendly jeers and applause. "What will it be today?" one man called.

Joe, ever the master at commanding his crowd, held up his long, knobby hand. Everyone quieted, rapt with anticipation.

"The wealthy and the wise have always claimed there is no such thing as magic." Joe raised an eyebrow, daring the crowd to contradict him. "Yet there are rumors among the provinces to defy such claims. Rumors," he lowered his voice for impact, "that if proven true, could turn the peace of our region to ashes."

The fieldworkers leaned in, as if to receive a secret.

"Two hundred years ago, Rsham the Terrible, emperor of the north, ruled the southern provinces. At that time, the valley of Freeland carried a different name, and these lands still sat abandoned by the first dwellers.

"Under Rsham's oppressive rule, a rebellion broke out and the people of the Southern Provinces fought to regain their freedom from Rsham's tyrannical rule. But the imperial army easily squashed the rebellion. Hundreds of southern resistance fighters were executed for treason in the streets of what is now Brennan.

"The spirit of the rebellion was snuffed out until new hope for an end to Rsham's tyranny came in the form of a master blacksmith who mined his own oar from the mountains near his forge." Joe gestured to the high peaks to the north in whose shadow the valley sat. "A forge built in the abandoned valley we now call Freeland."

I sighed in disappointment. Instead of knights riding out to rescue kidnapped maidens or fairy queens battling dragons, I'd risked another lecture from my father to eavesdrop on a dumb history lesson I'd heard a hundred times in kinder school.

Joe continued, "Some say the blacksmith's blades were ten times stronger than any other, with metal so pure it shone on moonless nights. The iron was not iron at all, but a metal forged from enchanted ore blessed by heaven itself.

"Years passed. The blacksmith worked both day and night and produced one hundred swords. When the rebellion swelled again and Rsham's forces marched south a second time, their weapons shattered under the blades of the famous One Hundred who fought with bravery at the head of the resistance."

I leaned back in my tree.

I knew the rest of this story by heart. The mighty blacksmith was killed in the final battle of the revolution when Rsham's army was pushed out of the southern provinces. The legendary swords of the One Hundred were lost—scattered and sold off to buy food and supplies to rebuild the provinces after the devastation of war. Some claimed they were buried in the mountain. It was almost unheard of to find one of the magic swords of the rebellion. No one could ever replicate the metal of the blacksmith martyr.

"Tell us a story we haven't heard!" one of the men shouted, earning the mumbled agreements of Joe's audience.

A slow smile stretched across Joe Ford's face. I had the distinct feeling we were all cattle that had unknowingly been corralled in a pen. He had us right where he wanted us.

"What I'm about to tell you could change the course of history among the provinces."

Joe had my attention.

"In the last ten years, talk of a new sword has turned up in the underground markets of Brennan. Some say the duke paid a king's ransom to obtain it. The metal matches the magical quality of the One Hundred swords of the rebellion but lacks the famous blacksmith's signature inscription." A pause. "This is no fable, friends." The red feather in Joe's hat danced as he spoke. "Someone has learned to replicate the blade. Three have been found, all bearing the new craftsman's signature."

One of the fieldworkers shouted, "Tell us the inscription!"

I rolled my eyes and lay back against the tree. If I were telling this story I would have helped it along with some action. Maybe a good kidnapping of the sword maker's virtuous daughter, or perhaps the sword stolen by an evil sorcerer with the power to destroy the Southern Provinces.

"Each of these swords is inscribed with the word *Purgo*," said Joe Ford. "Rumor has it the duke of Brennan will pay a bounty of ten thousand gold pieces to the person who delivers the mysterious blacksmith."

Only a group of men would be foolish enough to believe Joe's words about magical swords and an enormous bounty for their creator. Joe's story continued, but my attention was seized by the distant approach of a man cutting through the tall wheat field. I knew that walk. Knew the gentle yet determined sway of the large man's arms, even though his features were silhouetted.

Father.

The workers should be in the fields. What would Father say if he discovered me trapped and treed like a raccoon without escape?

Even though I knew it wouldn't help my reputation and I hated to draw such embarrassing attention to myself, I didn't want Joe or the workers to get in trouble.

"Joe!" I whisper-yelled.

All heads traveled up the tree to where I perched in shame. Most of the men smiled at me, others gawked. Face reddening, I pointed toward my fast-approaching father in the fields.

"On your feet, boys," Joe called to the bunch, and within seconds the space under the tree cleared and Joe Ford was whistling down the lane with the jingle of coin in his pocket and a hat noticeably lacking a red feather.

The men passed my father on their way back to the fields with heads bowed. Father didn't lecture them. His presence was enough. When the last man passed, Father turned back to follow his men but paused and spared a long glance over his shoulder at my tree.

Though the leaves had thinned with the approach of winter, the foliage was still dense enough to camouflage me. Somehow, I had a feeling he knew I was there anyway. I gripped the letter in my dress pocket he'd asked me to deliver. If I didn't hurry, I'd be late to help Marianna in the bakery. The letter would have to wait until after.

I climbed down the tree and ran all the way back to Freeland's market street—grateful at least that I hadn't been caught eavesdropping by my father again.

AN HOUR INTO helping at the bakery, my hand unconsciously wandered to my stomach to smooth down the invisible wrinkles of my jerkin. All this accomplished was getting flour on my dress.

"Will you roll out the next batch, please?" Marianna asked, her voice lacking its usual warmth, her eyes cast downward. She'd been like that every day I'd helped her.

"Mari." I frowned. I'd become something of an expert at apologies over the last few years thanks to my many exploits gone wrong—sometimes it seemed I spent more time apologizing than actually living—but there were only so many ways to tell your best friend you're sorry for ruining her life. "What more can I do to make this right?"

She lifted a corner of her apron and blotted a would-be tear before it could fall. She'd been doing that on and off for the last few weeks too. Ever since her father had formally declined my brother's request to court her. "None of this is your fault, Ebby. Gavin and I did this. Not you."

"There must be something—"

"You can roll out the dough, please." Mari's tone was always kind, making my guilt all the more painful.

I threw a small handful of flour on the worktable and snatched up a mound of raised dough that Marianna had set aside. With a little finessing, the sweet dough would soon become two dozen perfect honeycakes. My favorite.

"Seriously, Mari. Let me redeem myself somehow." I paused, subconsciously digging my fist into the dough. "I could speak to your father."

"And tell him what, exactly?" Marianna's whisper was so much worse than a shout. Whispers equaled submission and I didn't want her to give up yet. I'd seen her and Gavin. The thought that I'd robbed them of something so special made me ill. "Nothing will change the fact that I was with Gavin in the barn that night. Father doesn't like anything done out of order."

"Yes, but if I hadn't been in there, if I hadn't ruined things," *again*, "then you and Gavin would already be courting." I didn't mention how he could be taking her to the Harvest Festival dance tomorrow night. That would be like rubbing salt in the wound.

She peered at me from the corner of her eyes. "All right. Fine. There's one thing you can do."

I leaned forward, pressing my palms into the table on either side of the dough. "Anything."

"Tell me how you knew Gavin and I would be in the barn."

I froze. *Anything but that.*

How could I confide something that I didn't even understand? Mari was older, smarter, and prettier, and her manners were always perfect. Every time I stepped a toe out of line, my father would lament that "Marianna would never eavesdrop on a council meeting" or "Marianna would never show up to church with leaves in her hair."

Despite Marianna representing everything my father would have liked in a daughter, everything that I lacked, I considered her my best friend. She was kind and considerate, and I couldn't stomach her thinking even less of me than she already did.

"Nothing?" she asked sadly. "You really won't tell me?"

I sighed. "I just had a… a *feeling* I should go to the barn that night."

Marianna shook her head and handed me the rolling pin. She didn't believe me. But what more could I say?

"You shouldn't be wasting your concern on me and Gavin," she mused. "You have other things to worry about."

Again. Considerate. No wonder everyone preferred her. But I did wish she hadn't brought the conversation around to me.

I rolled out the dough a little harder than necessary. "If you're referring to the matter of my seventeenth birthday tomorrow, I wish you wouldn't."

Eligible. Was there ever a scarier word? Though few girls ever married until eighteen or twenty, it was still a terrifying prospect. It meant that I should be *looking* and that boys—men—should be *looking* at me as well. What man would want a girl with the hem of her gown covered in mud from the latest escapade? More to the point, which of the mindless young men of Freeland could ever tempt me into a permanent attachment?

No, this was one birthday I was not excited about.

THAT EVENING. JUST before sunset, Wesley Smith held his hand out to me with thumb extended, a glint of mischief crossing his smiling face. It might have been a pleasing smile to the untrained eye, but I knew Wesley like I knew a sore throat or a bout of indigestion. I glanced over to my dancing instructor, a stern and stout woman Father hired to help prepare me for my ascension into womanhood and… eligibility.

"Must I?" I put all my soul into a pleading pout but was met with a roll of the eyes as the instructor signaled for the musicians to play their steady one-two-three beat.

Wesley and I hadn't spoken since the incident in the barn, due in large part to my determined avoidance of him. Gavin, my usual dance partner, could hardly stand to look at me, let alone dance with me. That afternoon, he insisted he wouldn't make it back from the fields in time for my lesson. When I suggested to Father—in the most penitent, disappointed voice I could muster—that we should perhaps cancel, Wesley's name was readily supplied.

"It isn't decent!" I'd exclaimed. "I'm not seventeen until tomorrow!"

"You've grown up together, child. You're practically brother and sister," Father had admonished. "Though it is entertaining to hear you worry about propriety for a change."

Gavin had snorted into his soup at that comment. He didn't smile often these days, so I didn't mind that it was at my expense as much as I normally would have.

And thus, here I was, toe to toe with Gavin's childhood friend and my childhood tormentor. Wesley and I were like two peas forced to share the same pod. No, that wasn't quite right. We were more like two horses forced to share the same trough—and he was constantly drooling in the water and leaving those nasty floaty things behind. Even though he was practically a man now, my family had sort of adopted him, leaving me no choice but to "endure it," as my father continually chided.

"I won't bite, Ebby." The deep rumble was out of sync with the boy I ran amuck with through the fields and ruins of Freeland. His voice, no matter how old or how tall he became, would always be the squeaky high-low of his younger years in my mind. Of course, back then I'd also always teased him about his big teeth and ears, but he'd grown into them somehow.

The music played around us, and the instructor tapped out the rhythm with hands firmly planted in the folds of her ample waistline.

Holding my breath, I set my hand in Wesley's and glanced up, up, up into his charcoal eyes. I'd expected his hands to be slimy or sweaty or some other kind of awful, but they were almost... nice. Warm, dry, and so large that my hand disappeared when his closed around mine.

Perhaps this wouldn't be so terrible after all. Wesley and I had a history of playing tricks that I often ended up on the bad end of. But how rotten could Wesley be with the dancing instructor only paces away?

I set my other hand on his shoulder and paused at the feel of hard muscle beneath his worn shirt. With the time Wesley spent in the forges, I knew he was strong, but actually touching him was a different matter entirely.

What if I let my hand slip lower down his arm? Not out of any romantic notion, just sheer curiosity. My cheeks warmed and I flinched when he took me by the waist, startled from my bizarre train of thought.

So far, so good. I tried not to think about that night at the barn. His bare hand on my very bare thigh.

His dark hair still wouldn't sit properly on his head, but what appeared awkward and unkempt as a child passed for rugged and roguish as a twenty-year-old about to finish a very promising blacksmith apprenticeship.

The dancing mistress said, "Lead her through the first set, dear."

Did she just wink at him?

The steps came fairly easily to me. The mandolin and cello harmonized in the corner, a pleasing tune. Though I wouldn't have bet a soggy biscuit on Wesley's dancing ability, his movements were smooth and controlled, his grip on me never too firm nor too light. The scent of smithy smoke that usually clung to him had been replaced by a fresh scent, and his fingernails were clean. He must have scrubbed his hands and face and changed into a clean shirt after working the morning in the forges.

On any normal day, I would have found these details amusing—would have teased him for the effort he'd put forth—but today they just made me *aware* of him, somehow.

He leaned in, breaking the barrier of my personal space with his rumbling whisper. "I have a secret." His breath smelled of mint leaves. His eyebrows danced on his forehead, baiting my curiosity.

"Congratulations," I said, as dryly as possible.

"No, seriously. It's a good secret. Practically earth-shaking."

I moved to step in the wrong direction, but Wesley tightened his hold on my waist, gently pulling me along with him in the dance before my instructor noticed the error. He, more than almost anyone, understood my love of information… a love developed after my mother's passing when I never wanted to be ignorant of the world around me again… a love that turned quickly to *need* the moment I realized a secret was about to be shared.

"Are you planning to tell me this *earth-shaking* secret?"

Wesley slowly shook his head, his smile as wide as a proud cat after a successful mousing. "You'll hear all about it tomorrow night. The whole town will."

I frowned. "And you're telling me this now to…?"

"Cause you pain, of course." He moved away from me as the final strains of the music died. He bowed with arms outstretched at his sides, as though he were a troubadour who had just finished acting the part of a gallant hero in some theatrical.

He did not receive any applause from me.

The dancing mistress clapped her hands twice. "And now the Romandeau, if you please."

Both Wesley and I visibly startled. He obviously hadn't expected the lovers dance either. It would be played exactly one time at the festival—the dance saved for one's most preferred partner at the close of the evening.

The cello began its dramatic introduction, a solo melody so beautiful I'd always closed my eyes while listening from whatever rooftop I happened to be observing the dance from that night.

Wesley quickly pulled his hand from his coat pocket and stepped up to me. His brows knit together just slightly, his motions just a hair delayed. He cleared his throat, all humor gone from his face.

I stared at the patch of bare skin visible at the base of his neck as his hand reached not for my waist, but for the side of my ribcage.

"Just a little higher, Mr. Smith," the instructor said.

A breath. Then he raised his hand until it was level with my bust line. The heat of his hand warmed my bodice, the light pressure of his touch demanding all of my attention.

"Relax your arms, Miss Fields. You're far too tense."

No kidding. I wanted to snap at the woman.

I took a steadying breath, and let my arms relax, essentially hugging Wesley's hand to my side. In this dance my arms were meant to hang at my sides as I let my partner lead me through the simple steps.

"Chin up, Miss Fields. You're to meet your partner's gaze."

Did Wesley's fingers tighten? Was he as uncomfortable as I was? Probably more.

Knowing there was only one way to get this experience behind me, I raised my gaze up past his chin, his firmly set lips, his nose, until our eyes locked. His were a swirl of deep black and silver, not unlike the metal he worked in the forges.

For a moment, I forgot to be embarrassed by his touch, forgot the strains of the melody swirling around us, and was swallowed up by the depth of his attention.

A muscle in his jaw flexed just a little. Was that a smile?

Wesley's hand guided me with gentle pressure as we danced. The movements were simple, requiring me to spin twice with Wesley's hand running the length of my back. Every time we came back to our starting position, it seemed we stood just a little closer than before. We watched each other, barely blinking. Forgetting to breathe.

When the music stopped, Wesley dropped his hand and took a step back, still holding my gaze.

Then something light tickled my collar bone, and when I brushed it away, that same something dropped into my decolletage… and started the climb up my chest.

"Curse you, Wesley!" I shrieked, catching my toe on a chair and toppling to the floor with a fabric-ripping slide.

I had no idea if the spider was still on me, but I knew one thing for certain: I would kill Wesley Smith the next time we were alone.

"That was *almost* nicely done," the dancing mistress deadpanned. "Just need to work on the ending…"

Wesley moved to help me up, but I yanked my arm out of his reach, giving him the look of a feral cat.

Wesley's smile slipped only a fraction. He took way too much pleasure out of his role as my tormentor. Bowing to my instructor, he and his wolfish grin left without a word.

Wesley, six years earlier

Every time Ebby turns her head, every time her hand shoots up into the air to answer one of Master Henry's questions, her two yellow braids sway along her back.

Never have braids ever tempted a boy as much as Ebby's tempt me. They hang down past her shoulders, pooling on my desk, practically begging to be given a good firm tug. Really, I have no choice.

I gently lift the two thick plaits in my hands, careful not to pull before I feel them. They are smooth and soft. My mother's hair is short, and I've never felt a girl's braided hair before.

I'm ashamed that I like it. Especially the tiny free curl just below the ribbon. It reminds me of corn silk, without the stickiness. For the briefest moment, I wonder how that lock of hair would feel against my cheek.

Next to me Isa Woods snickers. "Do it!" He mouths the words, nodding like the bucktooth fool he is.

Heat fills my cheeks. The boys would laugh me home if they knew what I was thinking. Isa's minor encouragement is all the coaxing I need.

I jerk down, hard and fast.

Ebby whirls, her hand flying through the air, her body spinning to throw all of her weight into the attack. Her eleven-year-old hand connects with my cheek with a loud slap.

That is what makes teasing Ebby so irresistible. Her over-reaction. Sometimes I feel it is my duty to teach her patience through my pestering.

I rub my pulsing cheek, smug and proud, as Master Henry marches down the aisle toward us. Before Ebby has a chance to protest, he grabs her by the wrist and yanks her from her seat.

I feel myself stand as he marches her down the aisle and opens the back door to the freezing winter snowstorm outside. "You will stand outside my classroom until you learn to behave yourself."

"But Master Henry—" The door is shut before she can even defend herself.

Ebby's woolen coat and crocheted mittens hang from the sidewall by our desks.

"She's going to freeze out there, sir," I say.

Master Henry turns on me, a man who will not be questioned. "Would you care to take her place, Wesley?" His gray eyes narrow, making me feel small, and I want to melt into my chair.

"No, sir."

I watch the back door for the remaining hour of class, not catching a word of Master Henry's lesson. Outside the howling wind taunts me. And when the bell rings to signal the end of our daily lessons, Master Henry trudges to the back of the class and throws open the door.

I secretly hope Ebby has been resourceful enough to find shelter and warmth for the duration of her banishment, but she hasn't. Two inches of snow pile on one shoulder and the top of her head. She stands with hands tucked into her armpits and her whole body trembles, but she appears not to have moved even an inch.

She scowls up at Master Henry, defiant as ever.

"Class dismissed." Our teacher grimaces and walks back to his desk.

It is Stock who snatches up Ebby's coat and mittens and runs them back to her. She thanks him, looks over at me—a tear or perhaps melting snow running down her cheek—and then runs toward home.

CHAPTER THREE

FALLING SHORT

On the morning of my birthday, I awoke with a sickly feeling in my gut. I couldn't shake the sense that something wasn't quite right. I threw back the covers of my bed and the moment my feet hit the cool wooden floorboards, a quick stab of needle-like pain lanced my middle and an invisible pull dragged me to stand directly in front of my wardrobe.

I opened the cabinet doors and frowned at the cluster of dresses hanging there. The strange lure to the dresses didn't subside, and I didn't have any idea why I'd been drawn to this spot.

"What do you want?" I asked the needle and thread tethering me to the wardrobe. The idea that I was suddenly *talking* to my wild impulses caused goose flesh to dot my arms. I slammed the doors of the wardrobe, and though the painful pull beckoning me to the wardrobe flared hot again, I left my room at a run.

Gavin stepped from his room into the hallway at the same time ahead of me, and I slowed. He hesitated and then nodded before passing me.

I took a moment to collect my breath, grateful that the sensation of a needle lancing my gut had diminished to a slight ache. Perhaps I could resist the next whisper too. Two forms of madness. If I could fight one, I could surely fight the other.

A hopeful smile stretched across my face as I followed Gavin into the kitchen. We all preferred eating there instead of the more formal dining room. Father didn't take any kind of stipend for his work as elected governor. None of the councilmen did, even though the title of councilmen was passed down from father to son and sometimes to son-in-law. The council elected a governor from its ranks every five years, and Father had occupied the seat since I was in braids. He always called it a mantle of responsibility, not a privilege. We lived in the same home as his parents. The home my great-grandfather built with his own two hands.

Mother used to call the jumble of narrow passageways, tiny receiving parlor, and squeaking floorboards her castle. She'd added a flower garden in the front of the house and grew little white daisies along both sides of the front walk. Father teased her, calling them her "little weeds" even though he weeded the flower garden himself for her on top of his other duties. I pushed the thoughts of flowers and imaginary castles away. Anything that reminded me of *her* was like touching fire.

"Breakfast," Hannah said, setting fresh bread on the wooden table beside a bowl of steaming porridge.

"I'll eat on the road, Hannah." Gavin avoided my gaze while adding, "I finally finished repairing the hayloft. Father says we'll see rain late tonight and tomorrow, so I'm to restack the bales with some of the field hands before the Harvest Festival." Gavin grabbed the bread and saluted Hannah in thanks before heading out the door.

"Breakfast," Hannah said again, gesturing to the single place setting at the table.

I sighed and dropped into the wooden chair. "Will you eat with me, Hannah?" What a pathetic creature I was! Begging for

Hannah's company when the woman likely had a million other things she needed to be doing.

"'Tisn't every day a girl turns seventeen." Hannah gave a sharp nod. The old chair scraped against the floorboards as she pulled it out.

"I was beginning to wonder if everyone had forgotten." Again, pathetic. If a person could drown in their own self-pity, I was in serious danger.

Hannah snorted. "With your coming-of-age coinciding with Harvest Festival, I don't think it would be possible to forget. It's all everyone's talking about. Seems right proper for our beloved governor's daughter to gain her wings, so to speak, on such a day as Festival." Hannah leaned in conspiratorially and whispered, "Some say it's an omen. That you're meant for greatness." She wiggled her eyebrows. "Perhaps a prosperous marriage."

As though the only possibility of greatness from a girl of seventeen was to be achieved by marriage. I sighed. "I doubt Father would agree with any such rumor."

I wrapped two hands around my middle. My shoulders curved inward as though to support the weight of the pain that settled in my heart.

I should have a mother today.

She wouldn't be here to help me get ready tonight. She wouldn't be able to tell me how to respond to a man's advances or how to avoid making an absolute fool of myself in the dancing circle. My memories of her dimmed with every passing year… but not the anger, nor the regret of opportunities wasted. Those were mine for keeps. A permanent memorial.

Hannah patted my hand, discerning the direction of my thoughts. "I'll be right back." She pushed away from the table with another scrape of chair legs.

I dragged my spoon through the bowl of thickening porridge in a figure eight design, barely bothering to glance up when Hannah reentered the room.

"I should wait for your father, but men never seem to appreciate this sort of thing."

I looked up and my mouth dropped open. Deep blue fabric draped over Hannah's arms as though she carried one of the rivers of Freeland.

Standing abruptly, my chair rocked backward. I walked to her in something of a trance while snippets of memories flew before my eyes. Memories of mother sitting in her rocker, sewing coats and other items for the refugee children who migrated to our little valley. The memories flickered and changed to a time when the vigor of her rocking slowed to an occasional creak and the thick wool material for the coats was replaced by beautiful blue fabric I wasn't allowed to touch. Her practiced hands laying each meticulous stitch as she rocked back and forth as her time in this world ticked away with each motion and her sickness tore her slowly apart.

The sickness no one wanted me to know about.

Mother knew she was dying and concealed it so well. Everyone knew but me. I could have used the weeks and months leading up to her death to say a proper goodbye—to really show her how much I loved her and would miss her—if only she had allowed me the chance. Instead, I'd been reduced to a handful of days, and the shock still kept me off balance.

Omissions really were the worst kind of lies.

Reaching out, I allowed my fingers to run along the soft and expensive blue cloth.

"It was for me." I blinked back tears. From the moment I was old enough to wield a needle and thread, Mother taught me to sew my own clothes so she could devote her time to helping the needy of Freeland. I'd seen this fabric, touched it with longing, but never asked to use it. It had been mine all along.

"She bought the fabric the day after the physician discovered the tumor." Hannah's soft voice cracked as she placed the heavy fabric in my arms. "She spent every free moment on this gown, knowing that if she couldn't be there for your coming of age, this dress might hug you in her absence."

A knot formed in the back of my throat. I dropped my hand and stepped back, suddenly needing to be anywhere but here.

Hannah dabbed her eyes with the edge of her apron, clearly not sensing my distress. "I had to tuck the hem a few inches. Since you both looked so much alike, your mother assumed you'd match her in height." She smiled her famous crooked smile. "She was a smart woman, but misjudged that one, didn't she?" She tapped the end of my nose, confirming just how childish I was to her.

I looked down at the most beautiful gown I'd ever seen and wondered what my mother would think if she could see me now. Would she be disappointed that I wasn't *measuring up?* It seemed that everyone I loved felt that way about me.

HANNAH INVITED AN old friend of my mother's to help her get me ready that afternoon. Together they pulled, curled, twisted, and braided my hair until I was certain I'd lost half of it as a casualty of war. The result was simpler than the process suggested: a braid crowning my head with the rest of my long blond hair curled in loose ringlets down my back.

The dull ache in my gut from the morning still gnawed at my middle. It could have just been nerves, but either way, I was determined not to give it my attention.

Hannah tucked a few sprigs of blue forget-me-nots into the braid while her friend worked the fastenings of the blue dress. I couldn't stop running my hands down the front of the flowing skirt. Fabric this soft demanded to be touched. Even if doing so made my stomach churn with anger… and guilt.

A mirror was brought forward just as Hannah clasped a long golden chain around my neck. My mother's chain, with her rose quartz pendant hanging just above the dress's square neck-line. It brought a little more attention to my bust than I was used to but completed the look perfectly.

I blushed at my own reflection, feeling…truly pretty. For the first time in my life. Perhaps tonight wouldn't be so bad after all.

A light knock sounded outside my door. "She's ready, Governor," said Hannah. She winked at me as my father pushed open the door. His massive body filled the doorway and when his gazed settle over me his eyes almost instantly misted over.

"Ebrielle" was all he managed for a few moments, and then, "You look just like her." He cleared his throat and a genuine smile chased away the shadows of pain. "When did you grow up? How did I miss it?" He closed the distance between us and folded me into one of his smothering hugs.

"Watch her hair!" Hannah cried.

Father stepped away, clearing his throat to regain his composure. "I was hoping for the chance to speak with you before I left for the Harvest Festival. I've actually been meaning to say something to you for quite some time." He looked out at the setting sun visible through my window and grimaced. "It's getting late, and that sky concerns me. Hopefully the clouds will hold until after our dance." He cupped my cheek in his giant, calloused hand. "Can we talk tomorrow at breakfast?"

"I'm not going anywhere." I smiled at him, reveling in this moment of peace between us, while at the same time, wishing I could change into one of my normal dresses. Every moment I wore it made me think of my mother, and I wasn't prepared to confront my anger or my deep regret where she was concerned. It may have been two years, but the bleeding wound wasn't ready to heal.

At least Father seemed pleased. I couldn't remember the last time he wanted to speak to me, just me, when I wasn't in trouble for something. He hesitated before leaning down to kiss my forehead. "Tomorrow morning then."

CHAPTER FOUR

AN EARTH-SHAKING SECRET

arvest Festival always began at the amphitheater—a grassy bowl large enough to hold a small army. Torches lit long aisles sloping down to the stage at the bottom. All of Freeland gathered for a council meeting that preceded the food and dancing. I'd always been sent home with Hannah for the dancing portion of the evening (usually after stuffing as many honeycakes in my pockets as possible). Tonight would be different. Tonight, I was a woman.

The annual council meeting was a tradition that extended back to our very first year in the valley. A symbol that this was the people's province and that every resident—man, woman, and child—shared a claim to Freeland, even though many flocked to our growing province every year.

Hannah, Gavin, and I walked through the line of torches toward the bottom of the hill with our traditional mats tucked under our arms. Normally I would have received only a passing glance from the gathering crowd, but today I felt the stares of the general assembly. I clutched the skirts of my blue dress, channeling Mother's strength, and looked straight ahead.

"Where is Wesley?" Hannah asked, rolling out her mat on the ground. "I don't want him sitting alone."

"He's coming," said Gavin, scanning the crowd.

Wesley's family had always been close to ours. Our fathers were boyhood friends. Ever since his parents passed last winter, he didn't have anyone but us to sit with at the council meeting. I shivered at the memory of that awful day when black smoke rose from the beautiful Smith home.

It had been an especially cold winter. Gavin, Wesley, and a few of their friends had taken a weeklong hunting trip to help bolster the meat supply for some of the widows and elderly in Freeland. Wesley had returned to the charred remains of his home and his parents' caskets ready for burial. My father didn't let him see their remains. Poor Wesley couldn't have prevented the accident, but I knew he blamed himself for not being there to save them. As if his presence could have stopped the greedy fire.

I wore black to the funeral. Wesley wore, and still wears to this day, a bracelet of pink braided fabric taken from one of his mother's dresses. A token of his loss.

Marianna's polite laughter made Gavin's head whip around. He tracked her every movement as she walked down the sloped path with her mother to sit with the other families of the councilmen, who were seated on the stage. Marianna's mother frowned when her daughter rolled out her mat only two feet from Gavin.

I couldn't fight off the smile that crept along my lips at the sight of Gavin sitting perfectly straight and staring at Marianna as though he were a love-sick puppy. How had I missed their connection before?

Just as Father took the stand, Wesley plopped down between myself and Gavin, nudging him even closer to Marianna. He winked conspiratorially at me as he tucked dark clumps of hair behind his ears. His hands were black and calloused, and his threadbare dress clothes unkempt as always. Perhaps Wesley intentionally dressed in rags to deter the many girls in town who found him attractive. Or perhaps he planned to leave town with some of the passing tradesmen heading to the coast of Sea Port. Maybe he was training to become a pirate and had to wear out his clothes to fit in with his roguish new shipmates.

Or—I sighed at the boring likelihood—perhaps he was just a dirty young man who spent too much time in the forges.

"Nice of you to dress up," I whispered.

This earned me a smile, instead of the sneer I was hoping for. "Nice of you to notice me, Miss Fields." Wesley wiggled his brows, and I fought back the urge to poke him in his charcoal-colored eyes. He still hadn't apologized for the spider, and I certainly hadn't forgiven him.

Hannah must have guessed the direction of my thoughts. She cleared her throat, a universal warning she used to keep me in line in public. I scooted as far away from Wesley Smith as possible as the crowd hushed with a subtle wave of Father's hand.

"Fifty years ago, a small group left Brennan to settle Freeland. Our latest census shows we now have three thousand and thirty-six citizens. As Governor and Councilman of Agriculture, this is my report."

His deep voice carried easily over the crowd. "We've had a tough growing season this year, but our workers managed to yield acceptable numbers. We've harvested sixteen thousand bushels of grain, ten thousand bushels of barley, four thousand sacks of cotton, ten thousand five hundred pounds of beans and lentils…"

Father and his workers didn't provide all the food for Freeland. The Stock family raised livestock, and every boy old enough to wield a bow went hunting in the foothills for wild game when they weren't fulfilling their duties in town. Every household also managed a small garden, pickled their own vegetables, and dried their own fruit. We were an industrious group, welcoming refugees from the other four provinces so long as they were willing to work and keep our laws.

After giving his report, Father sat down and shook the hand of a councilman seated next to him as the crowd applauded. I couldn't help but smile. Hundreds of workers broke their backs to help him feed our people, but no one could manage Freeland's fields as well as Father. Everyone looked up to him, and not just because of his stature.

I was a different story. It was no secret that "poor Governor Fields" had an unfortunate, wild daughter who preferred climbing trees and eavesdropping on other people's business over learning to embroider doilies.

The councilmen took turns reporting the status of their industries, including Seth Moorly, the elderly blacksmith under whom Wesley apprenticed. By the time Father took the stage again, night had fallen and the torches burned bright. The air smelled moist, like the rain Father predicted wasn't more than a few hours off.

I yawned, trying my best not to let the lightning bugs lull me to sleep.

"We'd like to thank you all for your attendance. We are so…" Father's gaze caught on something over the head of the audience and his speech died on his tongue. A ripple of gasps and murmured voices filled the crowd. I looked around, sensing people's unease, feeling it roll into full panic.

Soldiers. At least twenty sat astride warhorses at the top of the hill. Torchlight distorted the faces of the statuesque men. The metal of their armor and livery glinted in the flickering light. A dark horse at the front of the formation yanked his head against the reins of his master, while the rest of the horses stood in a perfectly still line along the perimeter, blocking our only exit.

We climbed to our feet.

Robbers? No, too organized. Invaders? Possibly, but wouldn't there be more men than these impressive few? And who would bother invading our inconsequential province? We were just a group of farmers trying to stay out of the politics of the other provinces.

The rider of the spirited horse seemed too young for his command. Gold stitching and corded tassels adorned his riding cape. He dismounted from his tall black steed and walked down the grassy slope to the stage with a confident, brisk stride.

I took an involuntary step behind Wesley. He looked over his shoulder and raised a quizzical brow. "Using me as a shield, Ebby?" He flashed a grin. "Glad to know I make you feel safe."

I swatted his arm. "Hardly! I just figured if we were attacked, better you than me." He put his hand to his heart in mock pain, his eyes dancing like they always did when he played a practical joke on me.

He leaned closer to me. "I knew your father planned to make the announcement tonight, but I doubt he expected them so soon."

And then I remembered. Wesley's earth-shaking secret.

Most of the crowd had risen to their feet by the time Father's voice boomed over the fearful chatter. "Everyone will please take their seats." Reluctantly, the people of Freeland obeyed Father's order. "Allow me to introduce Lord Theodore Kent of Brennan, son and heir of His Grace, the duke of Brennan. Our council has anticipated his arrival for these past few weeks. He brings with him exciting news from our neighbor province."

My jaw fell open. This was impossible!

First of all, Freeland had never, in its short history, officially associated with Brennan. Secondly, and only slightly less alarming, how did *I* not know about their arrival in advance?

The crowd settled, but some, myself included, couldn't relax with those men peering down on us. Lord Kent and Father exchanged a few private words, and for one brief moment, Father glanced up at me, a frown evident on his face. He offered a grim nod and stepped aside for Lord Kent to take the floor.

"As your councilmen well know, I'm here on errand from Duke Terrence Reginald Sebastian III as an ambassador to the people of Freeland." His voice carried a refined lilt of superiority, but his smile seemed to soften his aristocratic tenor. "We have agreed to open trade between our provinces. As a token of friendship, I am commissioned to escort a handful of your best tradesmen to Brennan for the Festival of Masters where the provinces gather every year to share the products of our respective trades. I have a list, supplied by this esteemed council, of the individuals who will be included in our historic company."

Another hum of excitement passed over the crowd.

"Please don't let our arrival disrupt your plans for the evening. I understand tonight is not only a celebration of your annual Harvest Festival but also the coming of age of your governor's daughter. Governor Fields has honored us with an invitation to attend tonight's festivities and we will happily accept. I will make my rounds tomorrow to personally invite those chosen to accompany me to Brennan the following day."

I knew I didn't have a right to feel betrayed by Father. He was the governor, after all, and had to put the people of Freeland above all else, but something about the situation gnawed at my middle as Lord Kent bowed and the council closed with the excited chatter of the audience. People around them speculated who would be included in the handsome lord's company.

Who indeed?

CHAPTER FIVE

RAIN

Gavin dusted the seat of his trousers as Wesley helped Hannah to her feet. "I can't believe your father knew this was coming and didn't breathe a word about it," she said.

Wesley plopped his arm over my brother's shoulder. "You should've seen Ebby's face. I don't think she's been so surprised by a piece of news in all her life!" He grinned at me, and I looked away. Was his memory so short or did he not know me at all? It seemed I was spending a good portion of my day not looking at Wesley Smith.

Gavin shook his head. "I just don't understand why Father's suddenly so anxious to cooperate with Brennan. Lord Kent seems all airs and politics, and dresses like he's never known a day of hard labor in his life."

We reached the top of the grassy bowl and made our way over to the food tents where Father planned to meet us. In the background, musicians tuned their instruments, preparing for the dance that would soon begin. Each note sparked my unease. We walked past tray upon tray of cheeses, roasted apples, breads, nuts, and so much more. I found the honeycakes at the end of the row, Marianna guarding them with her arms crossed as though hugging herself.

"Are you well?" I whispered, surprised by her uncharacteristic show of nerves.

She nodded and grabbed my arm, dragging me away from Gavin, Hannah, and Wesley to stand beneath a tree festooned with glowing white lanterns. "Do you think Gavin will be sent with the company heading out to Brennan?"

"What makes you say that?" I asked.

"He is the governor's son and heir to the councilman's seat. Don't you think he's an obvious choice?"

I honestly hadn't considered it. But Marianna made a fair point.

"I don't want him to leave me," she whispered. "He'll meet someone else. He'll move on."

"He loves you. He'll find a way to convince your father."

"Not if he's on the other side of the mountain."

Father reached the others under the food tent. His lips formed the words *Where is Ebby?*

"Listen"—I grasped both of her arms and gave them a slight shake—"Gavin loves you. He'll find a way."

I left her under the tree and returned to the accusatory glare of my brother in the food tent. He stood statue-still with one of Marianna's honeycakes halfway to his lips. I knew he wanted to grill me for information, but our father didn't give him the chance.

"Are you ready for this?" Father asked with arm outstretched.

Not even remotely. I nodded reluctantly.

Glowing torches surrounded by glowing faces bumped and nudged me as we sliced through the tide of lifelong acquaintances. Glittering laughter met me at every turn. Surely a portion of tonight's gaiety was because of Lord Kent. I heard his name mentioned over and over again as we navigated the crowd. Curiosity was a fuel to the flame of enjoyment, and I knew this because I had felt the warm buzz of that feeling countless times before. I'd felt it almost every day I could remember, in fact.

The crowd pushed back, creating a clearing in the center of the town square where more lanterns were strung from ropes running from points around the perimeter to a tall pole at the center of the square. In the background, shops sat off the paved road with candles lighting each window. The musicians quieted, and Father ventured into the square, abandoning me on the cusp of the crowd. Hannah took hold of my hand and whispered, "You'll do just fine, dear. Forget all of these people and only think about the steps."

Easily said. I nodded.

Directly across from where I stood, on the other side of the square, my eyes widened to find Lord Kent staring. I quickly looked away, but our gazes tangled again when I dared glance back.

Father reached the center of the circle, and just as he began to speak, the familiar pull that I'd felt that morning lanced through my core, causing my knees to buckle in surprise. I took an involuntary step backward and bumped into Wesley. His strong hands clasped my shoulders, and his chin hovered near my ear. "Where do you think you're going?"

Father raised his voice so the entire town could hear him. "Today, my daughter, Miss Ebrielle Ann Fields, turns seventeen years old. I present her as the newest maiden of Freeland, and as her father and in keeping with custom, claim this, her first dance."

The tugging in my stomach practically insisted I run in the direction of home and father's fields.

Not now!

"It's going to be fine, Ebby." Wesley's whisper tickled my ear. "I haven't told you yet, but…" He cleared his throat. "You look… nice."

Was it my imagination, or did his fingers trail the skirt of my dress?

Fighting the pull with all my strength, I took a shaky step forward. Then another. Father waited for me in the center of the square with one hand outstretched. It was tradition that a Freeland girl danced with her father or brother for her first official dance. Everyone in town would watch, and when my first dance ended, it was customary for every eligible man in Freeland to claim a dance with me before the night ended.

Sweat trickled down my back by the time I finally reached him at the center of the square. With a strong nod from my father, the musicians launched into a steady one-two-three beat. He took my waist and I his shoulder, and we were about to take our first step of the dance when a distant horn blared three distinct times.

A distress signal.

The anxiety swarming around in my stomach from not following my instinct to run toward the house flared again. The music stopped. The crowd rumbled with a mix of curiosity and fear.

One of Father's field workers cut through the crowd, eyes wide with panic. "Flood!"

Time seemed to stop for a moment. Though two massive rivers forked around Freeland, they rarely flooded their banks this time of year.

Father gaped for a beat, then found his voice. "Two groups. One to the East River, one to the West."

People in the square scattered, shouting and running in every direction. Father took off at a sprint toward our home and the East River, shouting orders for Gavin, Wesley, and several other men to follow. Very few people rode horses to Harvest Festival—the stock animals were saved for work in the fields and lumber yards—so men were reduced to running.

I stood frozen in the center of the square. A single droplet of rain met my cheek. People ran in every direction, off to ensure their homes were safe or to help fill sandbags. The tugging sensation in my stomach still pulled at me. Had it been trying to warn me of the flood? Or was there something else? Something less noble?

Whatever the cause, I didn't have the legs to follow. Another droplet of rain connected with the sleeve of my dress and an unfamiliar voice pulled me from my shock.

"I've ordered my men to help with the flood, but I can't join them until I know you are well and cared for, Miss Fields." My gaze traveled upward, along the muscled lines of a pure black stallion to the man seated in its saddle. I couldn't decide if he was that large, or if the horse only gave that impression. The bright blue of Lord Kent's eyes was noticeable even by the light of the lanterns burning around us. It was a blue that, if I wasn't careful, I could lose myself in. The same blue of my dress.

A dress that would soon be ruined if I didn't get home before the full brunt of the storm.

Lord Kent's brow furrowed. "I know we haven't been properly introduced."

"No, we haven't." I stared but couldn't help myself. I wasn't used to seeing a man with such fair features and fine clothing.

"Where do you live? Please let me take you home." He held out his hand, as if to pull me up into his saddle.

Home. The needle and thread that pierced and pulled me in that direction flared hot again. "I'm sure my father needs you more than I do, my lord." I didn't mean to be rude, but this was hardly the time for chivalry.

"And yet, I can't in good conscience leave you standing in the center of this square in that beautiful dress with a rainstorm fast approaching." He held out a hand for me to take. I glanced up once more into his handsome face and turned away to start for home.

Lord Kent battled his horse to keep even with my slow pace. "I can join them faster if you'll ride with me." He trotted ahead and reined in his beast to block most of the lane, forcing me to stop. "Are you afraid?" he asked, frowning.

"Of course not." *I've just never ridden a horse with a strange man before.*

Not wanting him to think me a simpleton and not wanting to waste another moment over something as unimportant as my cowardice, I gritted my teeth and accepted his outstretched hand.

He pulled me up to sit sidesaddle in front of him and kept a firm hand on my waist as he nudged his war horse forward into a gallop. "Which way?" he shouted over the wind.

"Only a half mile down this road. Turn left at the third lane."

The rain came down in full force, pelting the bare skin of my arms and face.

"Hold on to me." Lord Kent gathered the reins in one hand, and with the other, tugged his cloak around to cover me and offer shelter from the rain. Startled by the intimacy of sharing the warm space, I had to remind myself to breathe. His clothes carried the scent of campfire and pine from his travels. The jostling of the horse forced me to wrap my arm nearest him around his waist. Though I hesitated at first, I eventually gave in to resting my head against his chest as well. Butterflies danced around the tug in my stomach, confusing my curious need to get home with the forbidden thrill of resting in the arms of a handsome stranger.

His hold on me tightened as the horse slowed to a stop on the graveled path only minutes later. I didn't notice the sheets of rain outside my cloaked sanctuary until Lord Kent dismounted and helped me down. He held tight to my hand as we raced past mother's flowers on to the covered porch.

I tugged my hand free of his and wiped the water from my face. "Thank you for your help," I panted.

"Thank you for accepting it." A dimple formed in his cheek when he smiled and bowed. "Until tomorrow."

He adjusted his cloak and jogged down to his horse. The beast stood with nostrils flaring, its legs locked at attention, prepared for his master's quick mount. In a skitter of gravel, Lord Kent shot through the front yard, down the lane, and onto the road that led through the fields to the East River.

I stared after him, my hand pressed to my cheek, still slightly warm from the heat of Lord Kent's chest.

CHAPTER SIX

LETTERS

It was the warm tug in my stomach that brought me back to my senses. I pushed through the door and was standing in front of Father's study in a matter of seconds. My hand paused on the latch.

What was I doing?

I shouldn't be here, invading my father's privacy while he was out fighting to save Freeland's homes. I jerked away from the door, but a physical need to enter the study overwhelmed all rational thought. I fumbled for the latch. Desperate to obey whatever had pulled me toward this spot, I nudged open the door with shaking hands.

What was wrong with me?

I went straight to the desk and reached for the letter I'd seen Father hold weeks ago during my last lecture. It lay open on his desk, no longer safely tucked away in Father's strongbox. Father must have been reading it again before he left for the festival.

Goose bumps raised on my forearms. Because *somehow,* I'd known, even back at the dance, that I could gain access to it again.

I reached out with shaking hands. The moment I picked it up, the need within me vanished.

I gasped in relief, my chest heaving, finally able to draw a full breath.

Not wanting to be caught lingering inside Father's study, I grabbed my wet and battered skirts and bolted from the room, slamming the door shut behind me. I didn't stop running until I reached my room and lit a candle by my bedside. I knelt on the ground, my elbows resting on the bed and unfolded the letter that didn't belong to me with shaking hands.

Dear Governor Fields,

It is with great pleasure that I invite your daughter, Miss Ebrielle Fields, to join His Grace and I for the Festival of the Masters this coming fall and winter until the mountain pass opens again in the spring. I understand Miss Fields lost her mother two winters ago. My heartfelt condolences to the family, etc.

I daresay Miss Fields will benefit from my esteemed tutelage in all things refined while she enjoys her stay with us in Brennan. His Grace and I trust that our hand of friendship is pleasing, and that you share in our hopes for strengthened ties between our provinces.

With warm regard, etc.,
Duchess of Brennan

I read the letter three times, expecting the lines on the pages to say something different.

Thinking back to the morning after I destroyed Father's barn, I remembered the way Father held this letter in his hands as he stared out the window. Was this what he wanted to speak to me about at breakfast tomorrow? Was I to be sent away?

A door shut in the house and I startled, dropping the letter to the bed. Footsteps groaned along the old floorboards leading up to my room.

"Ebby?" Hannah asked with a knock. "Are you here and well?"

It took two tries to get my voice to function properly. "Y-yes. I want to be alone."

Hannah remained quiet for a moment, then said, "I understand." Another long pause. "I'm going to help Widow Haws down the road. I'll be there if you need me."

"I'll join you." Anything to feel useful and take my mind off that letter.

"I'll mostly just be holding her hand. Her property isn't in any danger. She just doesn't do well with this type of excitement," said Hannah.

"I should go and help Father then."

"Help him by staying put. Once his teams have the floodgates diverted, there will be little else they can do tonight besides sandbag."

We both knew I was worthless when it came to hefting the forty-pound bags.

"Hannah?" I asked before she could leave. "How did the rivers flood their banks? The rain hadn't even begun to fall when we received word."

"Run off from a mountain storm. I'm told your father ordered the floodgates shut yesterday and one of the field bosses failed to do his job. The governor will be livid when he comes home."

The rivers of Freeland brought life to our valley. A series of dams and diversions controlled the flow of water to crops for irrigation. The province relied on my father's knowledge of clouds and weather to control the water—a responsibility Father took very seriously.

As Hannah's footsteps retreated down the hall, a queasy idea entered my head. In a daze, I walked over to the wardrobe I'd been avoiding and pulled out the dress I'd worn the day before. Shoving my hand into the pocket lining, I found the letter I was supposed to deliver for Father the day before. I'd been distracted after listening to Joe Ford and nearly getting caught perched in the old oak tree.

Oh no.

I unfolded the note and walked over to the flickering candlelight.

Floodgates on East and West rivers must be closed tonight. Storm coming.
-Fields

Was it possible that my innocent diversion at the oak tree could result in something so terrible? *All for a stupid story about magic swords.*

I had to make this right somehow.

Without stopping to change my dress or grab a cloak, I sprinted down the hallway and returned the duchess's letter to Father's study. Then I bolted out the door to the barn. I reached Millie's stall and quickly bridled her, not bothering with a saddle. I climbed a step stool and threw myself onto her back.

"Let's go, girl." I nudged her out of the barn in slippered feet. The rain still poured from the sky and clouds blocked any light the stars and moon might have provided. When I finally reached the main road, I nudged Millie into a trot, not trusting myself to travel any faster on the muddy road without a saddle.

One of my slippers fell off, but I kept moving, desperate to reach my father at the West River to see if I could be of some help.

I'd ruined everything and had to find some way to make this right.

After a few minutes on the trail, the sound of hoof beats caused Millie to shy over to the side of the road. Men's voices carried to my ears, muted by the rain and the splashing of hooves. Millie carried us under the overhanging branches of a tree painted in inky black shadow. The branches scraped across the back of my neck, snatching at my dress and hair like greedy fingers.

"Gavin? Is that you?" I said, fighting to gain control of Millie. The dark figures came close enough for me to make out two men on horseback.

"Ebby?" Gavin exclaimed. "What are you doing out here?"

"I… I have to help." How could I explain? I'd allowed the whispers to distract me. This flood was my fault. Everything was always my fault. And now Father had the opportunity to be rid of me, and he was going to take it.

I covered my mouth with the back of my hand to muffle a sob.

"Ebby?" The rumble of Wesley's voice confirmed the identity of Gavin's companion.

I couldn't break down now, not in front of Gavin and Wesley. Still tangled in the branches of the tree, I swung one leg over Millie's back and slid off the horse, wincing at the sound of ripping fabric before dropping to the muddy road with only one slipper.

Another sob racked through me. I grabbed Millie's reins and pulled her along behind.

"What are you doing?" Gavin said, exasperated. "Father doesn't need a sick daughter to think about on top of the flood."

I snorted. The edge of my voice turned brittle. "He won't have to think of me for long."

"She's speaking nonsense," grumbled Wesley. "Probably devastated her night was ruined."

I stopped walking, wincing as a rock stabbed the underside of my foot. "I don't care about the stupid dance!" I was well and truly sobbing now, my ugly tears mixing with the rain. "Tonight. The flood. It's all my fault." I took another step in the direction of the West River. "I have to help."

"You need to get her home, Gavin."

But it wasn't Gavin who dropped to the ground beside me. Wesley took hold of my arm and yanked me over his shoulder like a sack of grain. "Stop!" I cried, but he ignored me, throwing me up onto my horse as though I weighed next to nothing. Then he handed Gavin the reigns and slapped Millie's hindquarters to get her moving at a trot.

I could have jumped. I certainly thought about it. But the adrenaline was draining from my body and rational thinking slowly took its place. There really wasn't anything I could do to make this nightmare go away, and maybe if I had thought about it for five seconds before riding out in the rain, I could have avoided this scene.

I looked back at Wesley, who had mounted his horse and followed us with stoic determination, the firm line of his mouth barely visible in the low light. His rough kindness surprised me.

Would I miss him when Father sent me over the mountain?

Probably not.

We reached our barn and I slid off Millie before anyone had the chance to help me. Water weighed down the fine fabric of my blue dress. Mother's careful stitching was ripped open in several places, including a big gash connecting the skirt to the bodice. I clenched my fist in the fabric, lifting the hem out of the mud even though it was already thoroughly destroyed. My aching, bruised feet had me limping to the door of our home.

I could tell by the way they silently followed me to the porch that both Gavin and Wesley sensed I wasn't well. But they had no idea the extent of my loss. I'd failed Father. And I'd destroyed my mother's final gift in the process.

I walked directly up to my room, removed the remains of my mother's dress, and grabbed the note I'd been asked to deliver the day before.

"Ebby! Your clothes!" Gavin scolded as I limped down the hallway wearing only my undergarments. In my arms I carried the folded ruin that was my blue dress with the note resting ceremoniously on top. I pushed open the door to Father's study and placed both the dress and his undelivered missive on the floor by the hearth where're I knew he'd see them, then turned and marched back to my room.

AT BREAKFAST THE next morning I sat at the edge of the chair with a stick-straight back. Hannah brought bread and tea, but I could not eat. My guilt was a monster that had kept me up all night. Father drained his mug, picked up his fork, and paused with mouth hanging open when he noticed my stare.

"You aren't going to say anything?" I sounded so childish. Pathetic. I knew he'd spent much of the morning in his office. He'd seen the dress and the letter I'd failed to deliver. I could only imagine the frustration he must feel. That frustration would double if he knew eavesdropping on Joe's story had been the distraction that led to my latest, and maybe greatest, failure.

I paused.

Not Joe's story, but this demonic curiosity—the seductive whispers and pulls that always seemed to be the root of my problems. I had wondered if the source of the mysterious voices was evil. There was no room to doubt it now.

I swallowed hard. "The flood was my fault."

Father rubbed his brow. A muscle in his jaw ticked. Then he looked away, staring at a piece of floral embroidery framed with care on the wall. Mother's work.

"You remind me so much of her. Every day, I can't help but think that if she were here, she'd know what to do. How to handle..." He cleared his throat, collecting his composure, then leveled a gentle yet piercing look in my direction. "Whose name do you bear?"

I swallowed. I'd received countless lectures in the past. But none began this way. "I bear Grandmother's name."

"My mother's name. What other names do you bear?"

"I don't understand."

He removed his hand from his forehead and looked me directly in the eyes. "Answer the question, Ebby."

"I bear M-Mother's middle name, Ann, and I bear the family name, Fields. I bear your name, Father." A cold sweat lined my hairline. I hadn't actually spoken Mother's name since the day she passed. The day I'd been avoiding her because I was too angry to come home.

"The name Fields was entrusted to me by your mother. She received the name from her grandfather who came with the first group of travelers to settle this valley. Our records describe him as an intelligent, hardworking man who turned the earth and helped our people grow crops to harvest and store for the difficult winters. He worked hard to earn his name. The sacrifices he made provide us with the Fields title and the respect of Freelanders still today."

My eyes itched and my throat constricted. I had to look away.

"Every word that escapes my lips, every deed I perform, be it good or ill, is tacked onto your great-grandfather's sacred name. I honor it for your mother." I winced out of habit. "I honor it for Gavin. I honor it for you, Ebby Ann."

He didn't need to say any more. I stared at the space just above his head, fighting the threat of tears I was too stubborn to shed, and nodded. "I'm sorry, Father." Failing to meet his expectations wasn't new for me. But this calm declaration sounded like some sort of military surrender. I pictured my father, the elected governor of Freeland, riding his black horse to the top of a grass-covered hill bearing a white flag and a thick frown.

Panic, real as rain, stretched its ugly fingers around my throat. Why couldn't he just yell at me? Yelling implied he still held hope for my reform. What I saw in his face was something very different than hope.

What I saw was defeat.

Nothing could be more terrifying.

He must have sensed my fear because Father's stern expression softened. "You saw the letter from the duchess," he whispered. Not a question.

My cheeks burned and I nodded.

"When that letter arrived, I didn't want to send you. I even wrote a response declining the offer." He wrung his hands in his lap. "It wasn't until the incident in the barn that I finally made my decision."

I gawked at him. This was really happening! He'd written to the duchess. Was Hannah packing my bags already? Would I be expected to leave with Lord Kent and his men tomorrow with the rest of the tradesmen?

I whispered to hide the tremor in my voice. "You're sending me away. You don't want me anymore."

Father's brow wrinkled as he reached for my hand. "You know that isn't true, Ebby."

Somewhere buried beneath my anger and shame, I did know that no matter what I did to disappoint him or tarnish the name of Fields, Father would always love me. My head and neck grew hot. My nails dug into the table like anchors to keep me from jumping to my feet. "I know I've been a disappointment, but give me another chance. If I mess up again you can lock me in the cellar and tell people I died. Just please, please don't send me away."

No matter the geography lessons I'd received growing up, Brennan and the other Southern Provinces were foreign to me. I'd read of their obsession with class distinctions, among other eccentricities, but facing them in person was another matter. Refugees from other provinces came to Freeland every summer, each with a different tale of hardship. Why would I want to leave?

Father leaned forward, resting a calloused hand on mine. "It's not forever, Ebby. Only a few months. The duchess's offer is a great honor. And…" He looked away. "I'm not sure I know how to help you anymore. It's time to try something different, and with the Festival of Masters, you'll be able to travel with your own countrymen. Gain new perspective and see more of the world outside our small province."

Was he trying to appease my humiliation or his own guilt?

I nodded tightly, willing my tears back. Unable to swallow or even breathe around the shame welling in my throat.

"Please excuse me." I pushed back from the table and all but ran to my room, throwing myself at the bed.

I lay perfectly still, looking up at the ceiling as if it were a giant map of the Southern Provinces. I'd heard that Sea Port to the west was filled with devil worshippers who used dark magic and swam naked for luck. Vikehand was almost a complete mystery to me, but one refugee had told me about giant animals that could eat a girl my size in one bite. It was even further north than Brennan, our closest neighbor over the mountain. All of the Southern Provinces shared the same language and holy texts, but otherwise had very little to do with each other.

I cursed my favorite curse and huffed in anger because being angry hurt less than feeling sorry for myself. It didn't matter how pretty the packaging of Father's words.

He was sending me away.

CHAPTER SEVEN

FAREWELL

Hannah knocked on my bedroom door. "May I enter?"

I groaned. "I'm not really in the mood for company."

She pushed open the door and didn't bat an eye at the furious scowl I cast in her direction. "That's exactly what I told Lord Kent when he came to call after dinner."

"Hannah!" I sat up, heat instantly filling my cheeks. Had she really dismissed my first ever caller without even telling me?

She laughed with her head back, sending her red curls in every direction. "I'm only kidding, child. Lord Kent did come, but only to discuss travel arrangements with your father." She picked up the brush from my vanity and seated herself on the bed. Hannah's hands were as the clock in our sitting room: steady, slow, and ever moving. Sometimes I pretended to mind when she gathered my hair and settled in to work the brush through my tangles.

She used to joke that it was her way of keeping me from running off, but we both knew this was the easiest way for me to confide in her if there was something on my mind… something I might have told my mother, if she were here.

After a minute or two of silence, Hannah finally nudged me into conversation. "He is handsome."

"Who?" I pretended ignorance.

I had been so focused on the prospect of being sent away that I'd forgotten about Lord Kent and his rather intimate escort home last night. Forgotten that *he* would be leading the company back to Brennan. Fear and anticipation warred within me at the thought.

"Did you know he asked Gavin to join the company also?"

Selfish hope surged within me. I'd feel so much better if my brother traveled with me. It would make the journey less like a punishment and more like a diplomatic mission. But poor Marianna, who had predicted this invitation, would be devastated.

"What did Gavin say?" I asked.

"Turned him down on the spot. When Lord Kent tried to change his mind by explaining Brennan would provide him the society of nobility from the other provinces, Gavin actually cut him off."

Nobility. Brennan was known for their love of social hierarchy, but Freelanders hated that word. It was an insult we threw around when someone got a little too high in his saddle.

Hannah continued, "Gavin told him that given the flood and other… difficulties, it would be impossible to leave Freeland at this time." I could only assume Gavin considered his unsettled match to Marianna the *difficulty* in question.

"Your father depends so much on Gavin, I doubt he would have let him leave, even if he wanted to."

"I am another matter." I tried to make the comment sound light as air, as if the rejection didn't carry any sting.

Hannah's hands stilled on my hair but didn't speak.

I understood perfectly. There were no words to combat a truth that stared you in the face.

I usually stayed in after Hannah brushed my hair, but on this night, my last night in Freeland, I slipped out of the house for one last walk through town.

Shame.

Loss.

Heartache.

Every footstep carried a different emotion. I was losing my family all over again. But where my mother was taken against her will, my father was sending me away by choice. He might love me, but he didn't want me.

As I ambled through the cobblestone streets, my feet automatically carried me to some of my favorite hiding places. The old hutch behind the bakery, for example, had always been something of a sanctuary. Tonight, the scent of meat pies and warm bread wafted into the air, convincing my full stomach that one last honeycake was absolutely necessary.

Marianna wasn't in the shop, but her cousin Lisbet offered me the little cake free of charge. "A going away present," she said.

I cringed at her words, turning it into a nod of thanks as I accepted her gift. Was my exile a topic at every dinner table in Freeland tonight? What would Marianna say? She'd probably be grateful that I wouldn't be around to jeopardize Gavin's chances with her father. I gave the small cake to a child I passed on the road.

Twilight settled over Freeland and instead of heading home, I traded the main road for a foot trail through the woods that bordered town. I picked a withering sunflower and, one by one, tore off the petals as I followed the familiar path that bent along the outskirts of town toward the ruin stones.

I came to a divide in the trail and paused at the sound of metal striking metal. Freeland's forges were only about a hundred yards from my favorite meadow, and only one person worked in the smithy at this late hour.

Without thinking, I turned down the path I'd taken countless times. Every time I'd walked it in the last year, my heart always broke as I stepped through the final copse of trees to see the hastily built cabin atop the remains of what had been one of the nicest homes in all of Freeland.

Wesley shared the two-room cabin with his father's oldest friend, Seth Moorly. Since Wesley wouldn't inherit his father's title as Councilman of Freeland's metal workers until he turned twenty-one, Seth had stepped in as steward until Wesley completed his apprenticeship and came of age. I struggled to imagine Wesley sitting in a place of distinction in the councils of Freeland in less than a year. Heaven help us!

The forges built by Wesley's father and grandfather stood only a stone's throw from the point where his family porch had once been. Light from a single brazier flickered as the rhythmic pounding of hammer on metal rang out into the night. No doubt Wesley was working on a new sword.

Though my meadow called to me, I followed the path toward the brazier pavilions.

Sparks flew with every blow. Wesley focused on the hot metal with startling intensity, as if forcing the red ore to submit with his eyes alone. He turned the glowing metal over and over again, striking without hesitation between blows. Just above his thick smithy gloves, forearms corded with muscle caught the dancing light. I wasn't used to seeing his arms exposed. I let my gaze follow the length of those arms to powerful shoulders whose definition could be easily seen through the thin, sweat-soaked tunic he wore. Despite his substantial size, Wesley appeared surprisingly graceful as he worked, like pounding metal was as natural as picking up a piece of bread and taking a bite.

I settled in to watch him work, resting against one of the log columns supporting the roof of the pavilion. I didn't worry that he would catch me watching; his eyes were only for his work.

His eyes.

I couldn't see his face under all the soot and smoke, but I could see his eyes. The whites caught the light and contrasted against the masculine, soot-covered planes of his face.

Just like Father's comment about me suddenly becoming a woman, I couldn't remember the day Wesley turned into a man. But looking at him now, with his thick arms manipulating the hot ore, I knew I'd somehow missed it.

The hissing steam of Wesley's doused blade awakened me from a trance. Dim stars dotted the young night. A chill rolled over my skin. How long had I been sitting here? How could so much time pass without my notice? If Wesley caught me lurking around the smithy at night, he'd want answers.

What excuse could I offer him? *I came to say goodbye and lost track of time watching you work. By the way, your eyes are quite nice.*

He'd laugh me all the way home.

I backed away from the pavilion. If I hurried, I could reach home before night matured to full darkness. Halfway down the path, I spotted Lord Kent heading in my direction. I leapt behind a prickly bush before he spotted me. I couldn't be certain why I reacted that way, but watching Wesley work had been like stealing a private conversation between him and his precious blade. Perhaps I was ashamed. But it wasn't as though I'd committed a crime. I'd seen him in the smithy a hundred times before tonight. I was a Fields, for heaven's sake, not some deviant.

But it was too late. I was stuck in that cursed bush until Lord Kent safely passed. I didn't really remember telling my legs to follow him. I instinctively found the perfect listening place in a thick cluster of bushes, well hidden from the smithy fire and the road.

If Lord Kent had business with Wesley, it meant an invitation to Brennan! My stomach knotted with hope. As annoying as he could be, Wesley was like family. I'd take any grain of mercy I could get at this point, even if it meant the patronizing company of my brother's friend.

"Wesley Smith." Lord Kent extended his hand.

Wesley wiped his dripping brow with his forearm, smearing some of the soot on his face before closing the handshake. "Lord Kent," he said with a curt nod before resuming his inspection of the blade.

"Governor Fields said I might find you here. I assume you know why I've come."

Wesley picked up his hammer and went back to pounding his metal. I mentally tsked his rudeness.

"I want to personally invite you to join our company tomorrow," shouted Kent. "We've heard rumor of your talent with a hammer and anvil. Our blacksmiths have had hundreds of years to perfect the craft. They could teach you techniques that would change your life in the forges forever."

Wesley set aside the hammer. I thought for sure he'd jump at the chance to work the winter making swords. It was his favorite thing in the world, even better than annoying me. When he finally spoke, I didn't like the words.

"I cannot leave my apprenticeship with Mr. Moorly. He needs me here."

First Gavin wasn't going, and now Wesley?

Lord Kent interrupted my self-pity. "Seth Moorly is joining us. He agreed to travel with us this afternoon."

Wesley's eyes widened and a scowl darkened his features. He hesitated, but then shook his head. "I'm sorry, sir. But I simply can't leave Freeland." He placed his blade back in the fire and pulled off a glove to shake Lord Kent's hand. Only Kent didn't release Wesley's hand right away. "The festival is a great place to sell your wares and gain a name," Kent said, glancing over at the small cabin that Wesley called home. "If you happen to change your mind, we're meeting in front of the Fieldses' barn at dawn."

Wesley cocked his head to the side. "Why meet on the southern side of Freeland when your company's traveling north?"

"Gentlemanly courtesy. Miss Ebrielle Fields is departing with us, and I want to make this as easy as possible for her. I'm afraid she's in for a rough, dangerous journey across the pass with the winter coming in early. We all are."

Wesley's eyes grew even wider. His jaw fell open. "Fields is letting his only daughter travel to Brennan alone? With Gavin declining, I assumed she would, too."

Lord Kent frowned. "She's not going alone. I'm quite capable of looking after her, Mr. Smith. She'll be safe by my side."

By his side? I blushed at his choice of words.

Wesley pulled his gloves back on. "Safe journey." He turned his back to Lord Kent as he pulled the blade from the fire and began his pounding again.

Lord Kent frowned. "Good night, Mr. Smith."

THE FIRST LIGHT of morning warmed my cheeks and kissed my eyelids. The smell of baking bread wafted through the cracks in the door while horses whinnied and men shouted in the stable yard. Hannah entered to help me dress and finish packing the last of my things. Lord Kent had informed us that I wouldn't need to bring a full wardrobe, and that his mother had already commissioned several gowns for my sojourn in Brennan. I was only to bring clothes for the journey over the mountain. When there was nothing left for me to do, I set my shoulders to the door.

"I can do this." My legs must not have heard my announcement because they didn't budge. My mouth went dry. Panic turned my heart to flapping hummingbird wings. What if I *couldn't* do this? No amount of pretend courage could change the fact that I was destined to disappoint my family, and maybe even disgrace the name Fields while in Brennan if the cursed whispers and pulls overtook me again.

Somehow, I managed to leave my room on numb legs. Outside, a crimson sky rose behind Freeland's fields in the east. The eerie beauty couldn't fool me. Father always said God tried to warn us before he sent bad weather. The angry sky meant the weather would be merciless on this first leg of our journey. I forced the doubts from my mind, but fear left deep footprints.

Ten Brennan soldiers in boiled leather and chainmail waited outside our stables. Their eyes followed Hannah and me across the courtyard as they sat astride warhorses better suited for battle than a long journey. The long swords on their belts and bows on their backs probably should have given me comfort. They didn't. They represented a need to defend ourselves from robbers and the wild beasts of the mountain.

My sweet mare, Millie, stood saddled and packed, lazily whipping her tail back and forth. I stroked her chestnut neck with shaking hands. "Don't be scared, girl. I'll get us through this," I whispered.

Some of my dread melted when I spotted a familiar red feather bobbing among a throng of my fellow Freelanders preparing to make the journey. When lanky Joe Ford caught my eye, he winked and turned to speak to one of Freeland's master glass blowers.

With Joe and myself, there were a total of nine Freelanders making the journey, including my brother's friends Isa and Stock. Master Moorly walked over to us with a slight limp. He removed his hat, revealing a bald crown framed by graying hair. "Please, don't worry, Miss Hannah. I'll look after her." The master blacksmith had an easy smile that somehow brightened his eyes. I'd been told that Master Moorly would act as my official chaperone and protector over the course of my stay in Brennan. He was a kind old man, though I didn't know him half as well as Wesley did.

"Thank you, Seth. Be sure to look after yourself as well. Freeland will miss its best blacksmith these coming months."

Hannah turned to me, her tentative smile causing crow's feet to wrinkle around her eyes. "Be strong, Ebby. Remember who you are."

I fingered Mother's rose quartz pendant hanging around my neck. *How could I ever forget?* Hannah had insisted I wear it, that it was a way of bringing a piece of Freeland with me. She couldn't know it felt more like a choking device than a comfort. I would remove it and the memory of my mother as soon as we made camp that night.

When Father approached us, I was too hurt to look at him, so the ground met my gaze instead.

"You have a red morning sending you off. You know the clouds better than anyone on this journey. Trust your instincts. I'll miss you every day."

My lip quivered and I closed my eyes against the tears that threatened to spill over.

Father gently took my chin and I lifted my eyes to meet his. "I've trained you not to think much of ranking or status, but as the governor of Freeland's only daughter, you will be seen as a person of rank in the Brennan court. An ambassador of Freeland." His smile slipped. "The politics of the provinces are shifting. Keep your friends close, your ears open, and do your best to learn everything you can from the duchess."

I had a feeling we weren't only talking about ladylike manners. "I'll do my best, Father." I swiped at my running nose, certain that a true lady never would have done such a thing with her bare hand.

Gavin walked up and I braced myself for the usual coldness he'd shown me since the barn. Instead, he leaned down and kissed my cheek. "You are far too pretty." He studied me with a grimace, as if contemplating how a well-aimed mud pie might improve my face.

"I'll miss you, too." I smiled but turned away before my emotions slipped away from my careful control. How odd that he would be the hardest to leave behind. He couldn't even stand my presence lately, but shared loss and blood made him my longest, truest friend.

Final goodbyes were offered around the yard as I mounted my horse. Lord Kent exchanged a few final words with Father then, with a swirl of his black cape, swung up onto his horse. He trotted forward to my side. "Are you ready, Miss Fields?"

"As I'll ever be, my lord."

Smile lines gathered around his blue eyes. "Master Moorly and I will see to your every comfort on the mountain. There is no need to fear."

A blush rushed to my cheeks, defying the cold morning air. I looked down at my hands gripping the reins. "Thank you, my lord."

Seth Moorly and I traveled with Lord Kent at the head of the caravan of craftsmen. I allowed myself to look back only once. Father and Gavin stood shoulder to shoulder, two pillars of strength whose protection I'd always taken for granted.

Will I ever see them again?

I shook my head at the strange thought. After all, I'd only be gone a few months.

We passed dark windows and smoking chimneys on our way out of Freeland. No one spoke over the rhythmic clopping of horse hooves. It seemed as though the rest of the world stood frozen in a peaceful hold in time, and I was the only one in motion, forced into a change not of my choosing.

As we left the shops of town behind us and climbed the foothills, I looked up to find a man blocking the trailhead. He sat astride a tall horse with another horse tethered at his side. A long black cape and hood concealed his body and shadowed his face. A leather baldric stretched over one shoulder down to his opposite hip. I gripped my reins hard to keep from dropping them. It was as though a trigger went off in my brain, sudden and frightening. All the warmth of my body seemed to leak away and whispers filled my head, firing off a litany of hissed warnings.

I'm not ready for this adventure!

I'm just a frightened little girl.
This is too big for me.
Turn back! I should turn back!

The irrational voices repeated like an echo bouncing off the walls of my mind and violent chills curled my shoulders forward. I gripped the pommel of my saddle with the hand not holding the reins.

The man didn't lift his head to face our company until we were upon him. Just as I contemplated yanking the reins to head home, the rider's familiar face came into view. My fear dissolved to chagrin, for the black figure was not a man at all. He was only a very large boy in a cloak.

Wesley.

"Do you have it all, m'boy?" Seth asked his apprentice as we approached.

Wesley nodded. "All the tools the horses could carry, sir." The poor packhorse was laden with bulging saddlebags and a long wooden box fastened to its back.

I must have looked childish, cowering in the back of the group like a frightened mouse. I nudged Millie forward to gain my place at the front of the group, hoping Lord Kent hadn't notice me leave his side, praying Wesley wouldn't see me for the coward I was. I sat a little taller in my saddle and waited for Wesley to hand the packhorse's lead rope over to the master blacksmith and be on his way.

But he didn't.

"Lord Kent." Wesley inclined his head toward the young leader of our company. "I'd like to reconsider your offer."

Lord Kent returned the bow. "You are most welcome, Mr. Smith. Come, ride with me." He gestured to a place at his side.

"Thank you, no. I'll join my friends in the rear."

Our procession continued again, Lord Kent and I at its head. "I'm curious, Miss Fields. Did you ask Mr. Smith to join us today?"

What an odd question. "No, my lord, I didn't. Why do you ask?"

"I'm just trying to understand what changed his mind."

"Changed his mind?" I feigned ignorance. I'd never been good at acting as though I didn't know something when I did—it was part of the reason I got into trouble so often.

"Yes, he declined my offer last night, and I wonder what made him reconsider."

"Loyalty to Master Moorly, I'd guess," I answered honestly.

His bright blue eyes studied me for a long moment, and I had to look away. "Maybe," he said. "It's not that I'm complaining, Miss Fields. I'm told Wesley Smith is considered a very gifted craftsman. Between you and me, he and Master Moorly are the most valuable assets of this company—second only to you, of course."

I inclined my head, accepting his compliment with a shy smile. When I reached back to grab my water skin, I noticed the sour look on Wesley's face. Was he frustrated that Master Moorly had joined the company? Did he really feel such an intense sense of obligation to the man? Honestly, I didn't really care that he didn't want to be here. His presence was almost like having a brother with me on this journey. We didn't have to like each other to be allies.

Wesley, five years earlier

I sit waiting, crouched low to the ground, resting on the balls of my feet. The trees around the ruin stones are thick, making the hiding spot perfect. The stones are alive today, but I am the only one who can feel it.

Ebby is the Ghost on the Mountain and it's hardly fair. Even though she's surprisingly fast for a little runt, and she hides like a shadow in the woods, she's still no match for Gavin and me.

Sometimes I let her see me, and then wait until she's within a few strides of me before I start running. She'll track me for a mile before giving up. No matter that there are other kids in the woods; I am always her most desired target.

"You're it!" Something connects with my back, and it's just enough to throw me off-balance. I crash face-first into the scrub oak, unable to protect my face from the branches that scratch my skin.

Her high-pitched scream trails behind her as she runs away from me. She knows she's made a big mistake. Knows that I'll track her down till my dying breath, if necessary.

CHAPTER EIGHT

AN OBNOXIOUS "PROTECTOR"

The red morning didn't disappoint. Wind whipped our faces and cold air bit at the tip of my nose. I occasionally closed my eyes and ducked my head, trusting Millie to carry me where I needed to go. The trail through the foothills of Freeland carried us into a forest of mixed pines and firs. The stately evergreens shared the hills with wild maples and aspens whose leaves had turned vibrant shades of red and yellow a few weeks ago. Now only a few survivors clung to their branches with the last of their strength.

Lord Kent tried to pass the time asking questions about home and my life as a governor's daughter. I think he wanted to find something in common, as he too was the child of a province's ruler. It didn't take long to discover how very different our childhoods were. Except for the past two years as a soldier in his father's army, he spent his life with tutors and servants. Judging by the way he carried himself, I guessed he was at least five or six years my senior. I couldn't believe it when I learned he'd only just celebrated his twentieth birthday, that only a few months separated him and Gavin in age.

I was but three years younger than Lord Kent, yet he seemed a grown man. A leader of men. I'd never felt so immature in all my life.

Despite the biting chill, the day passed quickly with Lord Kent for company. By nightfall, my legs ached and my cheeks burned red from the wind. "Make camp!" Lord Kent called to his men and the Freeland tradesmen when we reached a meadow just before dark. I'd barely halted my horse when Lord Kent hopped off his tall black mount and came to my side. He reached up and, without asking if I needed help, took me by the waist and lowered me from my saddle. I wasn't used to having someone besides Gavin or Father help me. Gavin had never been so gentle and often made the joke that I was so heavy he could hardly support my weight. In Lord Kent's arms, I floated, and when my boots touched the rocky soil, his hands lingered at my waist and the corners of his mouth stretched into a pleased expression.

I should have thanked him but couldn't seem to find words, so I bobbed a quick curtsey instead. Grabbing Millie's reigns, I turned and all but slammed into the wall that was Wesley's chest. He steadied me, gripping my shoulders. "Still glad you chose this?" he asked, staring after Lord Kent with a scowl.

Again, I was speechless. Didn't he know about my banishment from Freeland? He must assume I'd chosen this fate. My shame lifted at the thought. How would I act if this journey had been my choice?

"Absolutely," I said, stepping out of his reach. When we were younger, he'd only touched me as an excuse to put spiders in my hair.

"Good." His chin jutted out a fraction. He offered a quick nod and walked away to help the Freelanders gather firewood.

That night there were two fires.

Wesley and I sat with the Freeland camp while the Brennan soldiers warmed their hands around a fire twenty yards away. Lord Kent attended his horse in the middle of the two camps. Ever the diplomat.

"That was a nasty bit of weather, eh, Ebby?" said Isa Woods as he whittled away at a small block of pine. Isa was another councilman's son. His father oversaw the lumberyard in Freeland. He'd joined Gavin and Wesley in our barn more than once to lose at cards. I liked him, though many fathers in Freeland guarded their daughters from his roguish charm.

I nodded. "With that milky sheet of clouds ringing the sun, we should have seen rain. Tomorrow will be better," I said. "Father always says 'a red sky at night is a plowman's delight'."

Isa stared at me with his big blue eyes. "You can predict the weather like your father and brother?"

I shrugged. "Father and Gavin base Freeland's livelihood off their cloud readings. They're much better than I am."

Samuel Stock, the last of Gavin's friends, settled in next to Wesley. Stock, like Wesley and Gavin, had what we liked to call the Freeland build. He towered over Isa and could likely lift him over his head without trying. He had thick dark hair and the shadow of a full beard to match. He always seemed so much older than Gavin and Wesley, even though he was just barely twenty-one. He'd had to grow up faster than the others, being the only one old enough to inherit the title of councilman.

"The storm warnings sent by the governor have helped my men and I to save our herds many a time," Stock said.

Isa smiled at Stock, as though some joke hid behind his lips.

"What?" said Stock, in his formal, flat tone.

"Nothing," said Isa, still smiling.

Stock calmly took Isa's hand, causing him to drop his whittling block, and bent back two fingers.

"Owww! Okay, okay!"

Stock let go, still calm as a summer breeze.

"I just think it's endearing, the way you talk about *your men*." Isa dropped his voice an octave to imitate Stock's deep baritone. "You've gotten so serious since you became council-man. You used to be a little fun. Now it's 'my workers' this and 'my men' that. Relax." He playfully slugged Stock in the shoul-der.

"Not all of us can eat off our father's spoon. I can't afford to piss away my life like you do. Even Gavin and Wesley have grown more responsible than you. All you do to fill your time is chase skirts and play drinking games." He glanced at me and grimaced slightly. "Sorry, Ebby."

I waved away his apology. They'd always seen me as one of the guys. An extension of my older brother.

Isa stopped his knife mid stroke, eyeing his friend. "A man could get offended by such accusations, Stock."

"But you're not," said Stock, his words muffled by the mug at his lips.

"No, no I'm not." Isa smiled and returned to his whittling. "But honestly, *Councilman*. It wouldn't hurt *you* to chase a skirt or two."

Stock rolled his eyes. "I'll get around to it."

Wesley left the circle after the meal, and the rest of the Freelanders broke into relaxed conversation. After a while, I glanced over to Lord Kent, who pulled a curry comb out of one of his packs. He hadn't so much as warmed his hands by a fire and night was setting in fast.

I scooped a helping of venison stew into a bowl and carried it over to where Lord Kent stood brushing down his horse.

"You should eat something," I said. The wooden bowl warmed my fingers, chasing some of the night's chill.

Lord Kent looked up at the sound of my voice. His gaze un-settled me. Always so piercing and direct. He tucked the brush into his saddlebag and walked around the dark horse with a smile tugging at the corner of his mouth. "You're kind to think of me."

In one graceful move he accepted the bowl and somehow managed to secure my hand to the crook of his elbow. In Freeland it was customary to ask for permission before escorting a girl, so his bold gesture took me by surprise. My cheeks warmed as I noticed the curiosity of the men seated around both campfires. Every eye seemed to be on us.

"Why do you stand apart from your men?"

"I suppose I'm in love." He winked at me.

I tried to tug my hand free of his arm, but he pinned it to his side before I could and laughed. "With my horse, Miss Fields. He's a magnificent animal."

The heat of my blush could have started a fire.

"I've embarrassed you," he said, his eyes wide with sincerity. "Please forgive me."

I cleared my throat. "Nothing to forgive, Lord Kent." I didn't want him to know how much his words affected me. Innuendo and flirting were as foreign to me as Brennan itself. I didn't even know how to translate this language.

We reached the Freeland fire and men made room for Lord Kent and me to sit. Conversation died for several awkward moments before Joe Ford turned to me and said, "I understand you got in a spot of trouble for listening to my story, Miss Fields."

I froze. He had no idea the amount of trouble his tale about the magic sword had caused. That by following him, I'd inadvertently caused the flood. Even more humiliating, did he know I sat at this campfire as an outcast instead of a guest?

I prayed not.

"I never had the chance to thank you for warning me that day," he continued.

"It was nothing," I said, still not quite able to meet his gaze.

"Well, I won't forget it, Miss Fields. I owe you a debt."

"Consider it paid. I've robbed you of enough stories over the year you've spent in Freeland." The fire jumped and popped as it devoured the wood.

Wesley sat down beside me. "I'm surprised you were included on this trek, Mr. Ford," he said. "Governor Fields has you working in lumber, right?"

Joe set down his whittling. "Yes, but I never planned to settle in Freeland. I served my time in the lumberyard only for the experience of living in a new province. I am a storyteller, and my place is on the road."

I glared at Wesley, like he was the bearer of bad news, then looked back at Joe. "But you can't leave. We won't have a proper storyteller in Freeland if you go."

A smile cracked the side of Joe's mouth. "I've seen the way you watch people, Miss Fields. The trick to great storytelling is in observing the world around you. With enough practice and enough life experience, you'd do the job just fine."

Isa Woods snickered under his breath. To be honest, the idea of captivating a crowd like Joe was more than a little appealing, but it was the farthest thing from appropriate for a woman in Freeland. My father would die of shame, and while people might sit around and listen to my tales, they'd never respect me for my talent.

Lord Kent left us once he finished his bowl of stew, seeming content to eat and watch rather than engage in conversation. Though no one remarked on the young lord's presence, the Freelanders seemed to relax in Kent's absence.

"Give us a tale, storyteller!" Isa Woods called to Joe.

Joe rubbed his hands together conspiratorially. "I happen to know some delicious tales about this mountain pass." He turned to the person on his left. "Have you ever heard about the wild spirits of Mount Brennan?"

Apparently, it was a good tale, because everyone jumped at Joe's offer. Everyone except Wesley. He stood and held out his hand to help me up. "Master Moorly would like a word, Miss Fields."

I let my eyes roll. "Just a minute, Mr. Smith, I want to hear the story." I always hated calling Wesley "Mr. Smith." It never tasted right on my tongue, but in company it was appropriate.

"Please." It was his eyes that changed my mind. They were begging me to listen to him, just this once. *Fine*, I thought, moving to my feet. "Don't start without me, Mr. Ford. I'll be right back."

Wesley gave me another one of his looks and led me toward a blanket hanging over a tree branch and staked down at the corners. Inside the triangular shelter, Master Moorly snored like a bear. A few paces away sat a modest looking, fully enclosed tent.

My gaze jumped from the tent to Master Moorly then back to Wesley. "I thought you said Master Moorly wished to speak to me…"

Wesley mumbled to himself about having to do everything. Then he cleared his throat. "Your father asked Master Moorly to see that you spend your evenings away from the campfire and the habits of the other men."

I pointed to Master Moorly and crossed my arms. "Clearly, *he* doesn't mind that I listen to Joe's story before bed." I turned to walk back to the fire, but Wesley caught my arm.

I stared at his hand and looked up into his face, daring him to keep his hold.

He tugged at a lock of thick, dark hair behind his ear—a nervous habit he'd carried with him from childhood. "I'm saying that you shouldn't be out taking food to men in the dark. Or taking them by the arm every other minute. Or staying out late in a camp full of drinking men. Kent had you by the waist, Ebby. The *waist*."

Now my cheeks reddened. "That was innocent. Lord Kent was helping me off my horse. In case you've forgotten, it's customary to take a man's arm if it is offered."

"Did he offer his arm, or did he take yours?"

How intently had he been watching me? I decided not to dignify the question with a response. "What else can I do but stay by the fire? Would you rather I wandered in the dark alone?"

"A valid point. That is exactly why your father asked that I construct this tent every night." He gestured to the tidy structure. "I moved your bedding and supplies inside. You can thank me later, if you like."

He folded his arms across his chest, a smug look of victory on his face. I wanted to kill him, but once I considered the lengths he had gone to make certain I was cared for, my anger changed into something more like surprised gratitude.

"You… you built this for me?"

He rubbed the back of his neck and pretended to look toward the horses. "Sure, I mean, we're practically family, right? Gavin would throw me in the well if I let something happen to his little sister."

"If this is for me, where will you sleep?" I looked over at the lean-to, completely occupied by the mass of Master Moorly's large body.

"Don't worry. I'll be close. I think you should get some rest. We have a long day tomorrow, and the sun will be up early."

"But I want to hear Joe's ghost stories." I hated that I sounded like a child begging her father to stay up past bedtime.

"Trust me, Ebby. They'll give you nightmares. Ask him to tell you the stories once we're in Brennan, and not actually *on* the mountain." He ushered me inside before I could argue. When he unfolded his own bedroll on the ground directly outside my door, I almost choked on the thin mountain air.

"You're sleeping *there?*"

"You can rest easy, Ebby. I'll keep the wolves away."

"Are you referring to the four-legged or the two-legged species?" I grumbled.

"Both." His wry smile reminded me of our childhood. I closed the tent flap so I didn't have to look at him.

CHAPTER NINE

GHOSTS ON THE MOUNTAIN

Wesley's breathing turned steady and deep minutes after his head hit the pillow. I probably should have followed his example. My body certainly could have used the rest. But at that moment, Joe Ford was telling a story that I didn't intend to miss.

I stepped over Wesley's broad chest with a blanket tucked under one arm, careful not to disturb the fallen leaves he'd gathered for extra padding. I'd had plenty of training in the art of sneaking about. He didn't even stir as I crept around the side of my tent.

I couldn't risk anyone telling Wesley or Master Moorly that I'd returned after they bedded down for the night, so I walked in a wide arc, well beyond the light of the fire. I climbed a boulder fifteen paces away from the circle of men. Though I didn't benefit from the warmth of the fire, I could hear Joe's words perfectly in the still, moonless night.

"It's been said when your ancestors left Brennan to settle Freeland, there were seventy who made the journey. Several never made it off this mountain alive. Some say wolves as big as moose carried them away in their sleep. Others say a mighty gust of wind pushed them off a cliff to their deaths. There are even rumors of a wild people who inhabit these peaks and feed on human flesh."

My fingers numbed, and my body contracted into something smaller than it was. Less of a target. Coiled to spring and dart away from danger.

"We may never know what happened to those travelers, but it's suspicious that they disappeared so close to ancient tribal lands of the Inute."

"The who?" Isa asked.

Joe Ford turned his head to Isa and scoffed. "Surely you know of the first dwellers of the Valley of Freeland?"

"Of course I do," said Isa, smiling. "I just didn't know they had a name."

"We don't know much of their history, but most scholars agree that the ruin stones in your foothills are all that remain of the Inute's temple."

"But what does this have to do with those travelers?" Stock asked. "Didn't the Inute population die of a plague of some sort?"

Joe Ford nodded. "A disease brought to the Southern Provinces from foreign soil. Those who survived the plague left the valley and integrated with other travelers and the Inute magic was diluted over the centuries through their posterity."

Isa leaned over to Stock and asked, "Did he just say *magic*?"

"Oral tradition tells us the ancient people who inhabited this region had a strong connection to the spirits of the dead. If they chose, they could converse with them in various ways." Joe paused, smiling at the men surrounding the campfire. "The only problem, not all of the spirits were good."

I looked over my shoulder toward the dark forest at my back, wishing I could sit a little closer to the fire.

"Ancient writings tell of multiple accounts of spirits, good and evil, possessing the bodies of innocent victims. They used the bodies of the living to exact revenge and fulfill unfinished—even sinister—tasks from their unresolved lives."

For several moments, only the occasional crack and pop of the fire could be heard over the cold breeze.

Joe's voice caught as he stared into the hypnotic flames. "Something happened to those travelers. Possession can do horrible things to a person, boys. Things they would never do themselves. I've seen it with my own eyes. Men who were once sound of mind reduced to mumbling nonsense in the streets, driven mad by the voices inside their heads. Voices that might compel a man to jump off a cliff, or go without food, or do any number of awful things."

I practically fell off my rock.

"How do you know if you're being possessed?" asked one of the Freelanders.

I considered the strange urges I'd had since my mother's passing, urges that had grown over the past two years or so. Was it possible that a spirit had compelled me to the barn? Had it led me to the hayloft, knowing I'd fall? Was the flood a product of my forgetfulness, or had a dark spirit intentionally distracted me, compelling me to follow Joe Ford instead of delivering the letter?

"I've never been possessed before," said Joe. "I'm told most people can't hear spirits, but every now and then, someone inherits the gift of connecting with the world beyond this one. Once a dark spirit knows you can sense it, others gather, like the crack in a dam that allows more and more water every minute until the dam breaks entirely."

"They go mad?" one of the men offers.

Joe nods. "There is likely Inute blood in all of us, boys. It could happen to anyone..." He leaned in toward the fire, his voice dropping for emphasis and his face distorted in harsh shadows. "Especially on this mountain."

The chill of night crawled along my skin. Cold fingers, grasping at me. Reminding me that I was alone, away from the protection of the men and fire, practically begging some roaming spirit to take over my body.

Joe continued to weave his tale of one such possessed traveler, but I'd heard enough. I stumbled back to Wesley and my little tent. The hairs on my neck and arms bristled as a light breeze traveled over them. I listened for sounds that weren't there, praying Joe's story was just another fable cooked up to scare young children.

At the tent, I jumped over Wesley and got in my bed, shivering. I burrowed under a patchwork quilt and willed my imagination to quiet. It didn't seem like I'd been asleep for more than a minute when the nightmares began.

I fought my way along a narrow mountain ridge. The wind howled, beating upon me with ruthless force. Translucent hands shoved against me, voices ringing in my ears. Numbing. Singing a haunting song. Promising to rip open my skin and fill me until there was no room left in my body for *me* to reside.

Something touched my arm.

My eyes shot open. I tried to scream, but a hand covered my mouth. I thought for sure a man-eating savage had come to take me away, until I noticed the hand belonged to Wesley.

My arms found their way around his neck and I hugged him as I cried. "I'm so glad it's you. I'm so glad it's you. Don't let them take me, Wes. Don't let them force me out." I wasn't exactly sure how I ended up in his lap. He rocked me like a child, soothing my fears.

"I'm here." His voice held a strange echo, maybe because my ear was pressed to his chest.

Darkness and more darkness.

I WOKE JUST before sunrise with my arms wrapped around my own shoulders. They felt achy, like I'd been hugging myself all night long. I instantly thought of Wesley and the fading memory of nightmares. Was it all a dream? If he really had come and held me, I'd die of humiliation. Still, if he hadn't, then why would I ever dream about Wesley as a comforter? He was the exact opposite. Why didn't I dream that Lord Kent had swept me up into his arms, like in the old stories Mother used to tell me as a child? At least that might have made some amount of sense.

I shook my head, ready to forget last night's horrible stories and the terrifying dreams that followed. I shivered into a clean riding dress, donned my heavy wool cloak, and pulled the oversized hood up to cover my hair and protect my ears from the morning chill. Pushing and pulling at my pack and bedroll, I managed to recreate the compact load Hannah prepared for me yesterday.

I stood back and observed my work with a small sense of pride. Now I just needed to fasten my pack onto Millie's saddle. Lifting with my legs, like Father taught me when I helped carry bags of seed, I swung the bag back and forth until I had enough momentum to send it out of the tent. No more than a second after the pack left my fingers, someone groaned on the other side of the tent wall.

I poked my head out to find Wesley lying in front of the door with my pack and bedroll resting precariously on his middle.

"You're up early, Ebby. All packed, I see." He spoke with a slight grunt as he hoisted my bag from his lap.

"Sorry, Wes. I forgot you were playing guard dog."

He turned his head to the side, as if he couldn't decide how to take my comment.

I changed the subject. "How were things out here?" I flinched at the sight of his frosted, red nose.

"Fine." The air smoked with his breath. He pulled a wool shirt over his head and tamed his wild thick hair with a winter cap. "How did you sleep?"

"Fine," I lied.

"No scary dreams about giant wolves or soul-taking spirits?"

"H-how?" *Please tell me it was a dream. Please!*

"I heard you talking in your sleep. I told you not to listen to those ghost stories. But have you ever listened to me?" He shook his head, almost as though he felt sorry for me.

Why would I ever dream about Wesley Smith?

WHEN THE REST of camp had packed their gear and dowsed their morning fires, Lord Kent helped me into my saddle, then mounted his own with a gentleman's grace to address the company. "If we travel this properly, the trail will take us to Brennan in about eight days' time. We'll break twice a day: high noon and sundown. As long as we're on this mountain, I am your commander. If any man has a problem with that, let him leave now."

Wesley exchanged a quick glance with Stock and Isa. Something heavy passed between them I couldn't quite interpret. Then his thickly lashed eyes sought me out, as if he'd somehow sensed my unease from a distance. There was a warmth in his gaze that said, *We'll be fine, Ebby* in his own rough way.

I looked down at my hands. Wesley's shifting moods had me completely unsure of how to interpret anything he said or did. I liked it better when he teased me all the time. Then, at least, I knew where I stood.

When no one objected, Lord Kent nudged his horse forward and we began another long day on the mountain. Apart from the constant wind, the weather seemed to approve of our passing. Cold hands and cold cheeks were the worst of the first few days. Whenever a gust curved through the pass, I closed my eyes and prayed it wouldn't send us off the edge of the narrow trail. Every night I slept in the tent adjacent to Master Moorly, and every night Wesley unrolled his bed directly in front of my door while the older blacksmith snored away.

We reached the peak of our journey on the third day. Here, at the mountain's summit, the thick evergreens thinned until the trail turned to rock—rock underfoot, a rock wall to our left, and a sheer rocky drop off to our right. Lord Kent and I sat on a saddle blanket eating our lunch of dried meat, not bothering to speak over the howl of the vicious wind. As usual, I turned to the clouds for company.

A milky sheet of crystals stretched from horizon to horizon as though we sat in a windy celestial waiting room blanketed by the stillness of heaven itself. A perfect ring of wispy clouds framed the sun. To the untrained eye, this might appear to be just a magical painting from Mother Nature, put on display for our own enjoyment.

But I knew better.

"Lord Kent?" He didn't hear me, so I tugged on his sleeve. "Lord Kent!"

He held up a finger for me to wait then untied the clasp of his cloak. He flung the heavy cloak over both of our heads, creating a temporary shelter that muted the roar of the wind.

"Yes, Miss Fields?" he asked with his usual butter-smooth voice. For a brief moment I forgot everything but the warmth of him so near me, the two of us feeling isolated under his cloak. It reminded me of our first meeting in Freeland. I was suddenly back on his horse, protected from the rain with my cheek pressed to his firm chest, wearing a beautiful dress.

"Miss Fields?"

I blinked back to the present, ashamed that I was so easily caught in his spell. "We're walking into a blizzard," I said, remembering my purpose. "We need to find shelter before it hits."

He stared at me for several seconds, like I'd left my mind back in Freeland. "How can you know this?"

"I'm a Fields. We know the weather!" Then I quoted another one of Father's weather rhymes. "A ring around the sun or moon brings rain or snow upon you soon." He gave me a look that proved his doubts. He just sat there, wasting valuable time while there were preparations to be made.

"We need to act!" I wanted to shake him.

He shook his head. "We're going to ride. If the storm gets wild enough, we'll pull to the side and wait it out. It's all we can do."

I didn't know what to say. Lord Kent underestimated the storm. He underestimated my judgment. People would suffer because of it. "I don't agree with you," I said, not as bold as I would have liked.

"I know you don't, Miss Fields, but it's my call." Under the cloak, I couldn't see his expression, but it wasn't hard to catch his condescending tone.

I pulled the cloak off my head. The rush of wind blew my hood back, but I didn't care. I needed to warn Wesley and the Freeland men. As I turned to run, Lord Kent grabbed my wrist, yanking me back to his side. "Where are you going?" he yelled over the wind. I must have looked like a fish out of water gasping for air as my lips failed to form words. I couldn't believe his boldness. I looked down at my wrist and back to his face. He loosened his grip, as if remembering himself.

"I am going to warn the Freeland camp," I yelled over the wind.

"Remember, Miss Fields. I am your commander. Your people must abide by my rules."

I nodded, and practically ran into Wesley as I turned. I'd been doing that a lot lately.

"What's going on here!" he yelled as he grabbed me and pulled me behind his back.

Sir Kent's eyes darkened. "Not your business, Smith." He walked away from us to rally the rest of the men. "Mount up!" he called.

Wesley whipped me around. I began to feel like a rag doll Marianna and I used to fight over when we were still in braids. "What happened? Why were you under that cloak with Kent?" he yelled, but I could barely hear him over the roar of the wind.

I grabbed his collar and yanked him down to my height. "I told Kent that we're in for a nasty storm. I thought we should find shelter. He disagrees."

Wesley looked up at the sky, as if straining to see what I saw. He looked back down to me, pulled my hood back over my head, and said, "We have to follow Kent, but I'll keep my eyes open for a shelter along the way."

I nodded and ran over to my horse. Ignoring etiquette, I struggled onto her back with my own strength—a sight Hannah would have fainted to see. We rode in groups of two along the narrow trail with Kent as my usual traveling companion at the front of the caravan. After only traveling a few yards, Lord Kent reached across the narrow divide separating us for my hand. My gaze snapped up to meet his. Was this his way of offering an olive branch? I inclined my head, indicating my acceptance of his gesture. There was no use fighting with him. I knew the weather, but he certainly knew the mountain.

Time passed and the wind died down to an almost perfect stillness. The energy of the whole company seemed to relax in their saddles. Everyone except me. Father always spoke of the eerie calm that settled in before a big storm. I gripped my reins with more vigor and looked back to Wesley. He gave me the reassurance I needed with another simple, tight nod. Isa and Stock flanked him with the same trusting expressions.

The road narrowed to the point where we had to travel single file. A paralyzing chill rolled up my back as I leaned over the edge of the skinny trail. I couldn't see the bottom of the ravine, but I could see the tops of giant pines hundreds of feet below. I leaned forward in my saddle and led my mare as far from the edge of the cliff as possible.

Then the first snowflakes fell.

CHAPTER TEN

DIGGING TO BRENNAN

At first the snow was beautiful. The crystals danced down to us, floating without the wind to push them in any particular direction. As their volume increased, so did their speed and purpose. What began as a magical gift from nature turned into the evil work of the mountain spirits.

It wasn't long before several inches of snow covered the narrow trail. We walked into the storm like white sheep to the slaughterhouse with only a few feet separating us from the cliff's edge. My horse lost her footing time and again. The snow came down so thick I couldn't discern the edge of the cliff from the whiteness in front of me. Only the wall of the mountain beside me kept us from falling to our deaths as I had Millie walk as close to it as possible.

I looked back to ask Master Moorly or Wesley if we should stop but couldn't see them through the snow. Flecks of black from Lord Kent's horse twenty paces ahead were my only reassurance that I wasn't completely alone on this mountain.

My timid horse's ears stood on high alert and she grumbled and huffed her complaint with every other step. I leaned forward in my saddle and did for her what Mother used to do for me when I was scared from a bad dream. Voice shaking, I sang:

The silent sweet of thistle wheat
Is swaying in the fields.
And I, dear girl, will morrow bring,
A new bonnet of shells.
I'll lay them out and sound them out,
Till morning's come and gone.
And show you, dear, the magic there,
In every precious song.

Every time Millie calmed, her footing would falter, and I'd have to sing the melody all over. I sang the lullaby until my throat was raw. It might have been my imagination, but mingling with the high-pitched cries of the wind were softer, ghostly calls beckoning me to join them off the cliff.

Somewhere in the white darkness a crack like twenty of Stock's whips sounded. Millie halted, and a moment later a giant flow of rock and snow tumbled just in front of my horse's front hooves.

My mare reared. I struggled to grip the horn of the saddle but failed. My head connected with the side of the mountain as I was thrown. The muted whinnies of a terrified horse ricocheted through the pass. My vision came and went, but it didn't really matter. There was nothing to see beyond the white curtain of cold. Warm blood rolled down my neck and back. Men shouted words too foggy to understand. I used the rock wall of the mountain for support as I struggled to my feet. My legs shook like a newborn calf.

"Millie!" I screamed. "Millie!!" I fell to the earth, sinking deep into the dense snow. On hands and knees, I crawled until my hands felt the edge of the cliff, hoping for any sign of her in the white storm.

But she was gone.

Already on my knees, I prayed that she didn't feel pain. I prayed for the rest of the men in our company, and I didn't feel one part guilty about praying for myself.

I crawled back to the wall, shaking so hard I could hardly clasp my gloved hands together. Lord Kent had been right in front of me. Did he share Millie's fate? Did the others?

Slowly moving forward along the path, I came up against a sloping wall of snow and rocks I didn't dare climb. An avalanche had blocked the way, and there was no sign of Lord Kent. I retreated a few paces, head throbbing, and curled in on myself against the mountainside.

Snow flew in every direction. I lost feeling in my fingers and toes. I needed to move to get my blood flowing, but my vision tilted from side to side whenever I tried to stand. A cloud of despair almost wholly encompassed me when I saw the black of a cloak and felt a gloved hand on my shoulder. I knew who had come for me even before making out his face.

Wesley scooped me up without a word. Stock moved to help him, but Wesley waved him off. They trotted back down the trail, away from the small avalanche of snow and rocks blocking the path. My head pounded. Blood still trickled down my neck. The dizzy white world spun, even with my eyes closed.

"Lord Kent... Millie." My mind struggled to find the proper words.

Wesley brought us through a wide fissure in the side of the mountain. It wasn't a true cave, rather an opening that led into a greater, three-walled cavern. Inside waited the rest of our company, including horses and ten soggy-looking Brennan soldiers. They all rose to their feet at the sight of us.

"The way is blocked," Wesley announced as he laid me down by a blazing fire. "There's been a small avalanche. We'll have to wait until the storm passes."

"But Lord Kent!" one of the soldiers demanded.

"We don't know if he made it," Stock said, voice low. "No sign of him on this side of the block."

I forced my eyes open long enough to say, "You must save him, Wes."

Wesley unfastened the clasp of my damp cloak and replaced it with a thick blanket. I murmured a quiet thanks, too tired and cold to feel uncomfortable with his unusual attention. Master Moorly tended to the cut on the back of my head. My eyes drooped, like some imaginary force had roped my lashes and forced them closed. I didn't fight the sleep or the memory that followed me into my dreams.

My brother was a miserable seeker. He didn't have the patience for quality searching. Instead, he ran all around as fast as his legs would carry him, never taking the time to root out the really good hiding places.

I hadn't meant to hide with Wesley, but we were both drawn to the same lilac bush. It was late spring, making the shade and the scented flowers a perfect place to enjoy the long wait for Gavin to find us.

When I first realized Wesley was there, I showed him my back and tucked under the branches. For the first ten minutes or so, neither of us spoke. But when it was clear Gavin wasn't coming, Wesley broke the silence.

"What do you want from life, Ebby?" he asked.

I sucked in a deep breath of lilac and sighed, drunk on the aroma. "I want my parents to be as proud of me as they are of Gavin." I tensed, realizing my mistake the moment the words slipped out of my mouth. You didn't just go around confessing embarrassing things to Wesley Smith.

Wesley must have been in an odd mood, because for once he didn't laugh at me.

Intrigued, I asked, "What do you want, Wesley?"

It was quite a while before he rolled over and looked me right in the face. At fourteen he had a smattering of freckles that ran along his cheeks and nose. He'd already been working in the forges with his councilman father for a few years. They owned the largest home in Freeland. Wesley's ancestors had been wealthy even before they left Brennan to settle in Freeland. It showed in his clothes and his arrogant manners. I couldn't imagine him ever wanting for anything.

"I want to be taken seriously. To be needed and important like my father."

I woke up in the night, thinking about the memory.

I'd never forgotten Wesley's face as he confided in me that afternoon. With all our bickering and teasing, from that day forward, I knew we didn't have to like each other to be fierce friends.

IN THE WEAK morning light, men took shifts digging though rock and snow while I stayed in the cavern with the horses. With a half-burnt stick, I lazily drew pictures in the dirt. Anything to distract myself from the loss of Millie and my worry for Lord Kent.

My head felt like Hannah had used it to beat out the kitchen rugs.

I didn't hear Wesley come back from his shift until he hovered directly above me. "You miss home already?" he asked. His eyes seemed heavy and his body swayed from fatigue.

I looked down at my drawing with mild surprise. I had subconsciously drawn a picture of my home: the big wrap-around porch, the shuttered windows, and even the lines delineating Mother's flowerbeds. "Don't you?" I asked.

He shrugged and sat down beside me, leaning back on his palms. With his parents gone and his family home burned to ash, I supposed he'd been homesick for more than just a few days.

"The road is almost clear. Lord Kent is working on the other end. We've been communicating with him for the past hour."

"How?" I sat up on my knees. "Is he all right?"

Wesley picked up my drawing stick and balanced it on his palm. "I suppose he had a cold night. That will teach him not to trust a Fields on matters of the weather." He smiled to himself.

"Hold on," I said. "Did you just pay me a compliment, Apprentice?"

He drew a few fancy letters on the ground with the tip of the stick then smeared it with his gloved hand before I could make out the word. "You have to be good at *something*, Ebby, or no one would ever keep you around." He rolled his eyes.

I knew he was only joking, but he didn't know I'd been sent away and his words hit uncomfortably close to the mark. "I'm so relieved Lord Kent is well," I said, changing the subject." I'd been afraid to consider the small chance of his survival. It had seemed as though the avalanche had hit right where he should have been.

Wesley didn't look up from his drawing. "I don't understand why you care as much as you do."

"He's human, Wesley. Of course I care. It could have been any of us out there in the snow. What if he'd been carried off by the avalanche?"

"It would have been his own fault."

My mouth dropped open. "I can't believe you just said that!"

Wesley gave up his drawing and stabbed the center of the circle with the stick. "You lost your horse and almost your life! If it weren't for a crevice in the mountain, we could have died in that storm. You warned him about the weather, Ebby. He chose not to listen, and it almost killed us." He pulled the stick from the earth and threw it across the cave.

I took a moment to calm down before resting my hand on his arm. "He should have listened to me, but he doesn't deserve your spite."

Wesley climbed to his feet and scowled at me. His words were quiet, but intense. "Shall I go and take another shift so you can see your hero sooner?"

My hero? "What is wrong with you?" I shouted and regretted it instantly. Placing a hand to the side of my head, I moaned. Wesley crouched down beside me, hovering as if he wanted to help.

Excited voices bounced along the stone walls of our shelter. Wesley straightened with hands balled into white-knuckled fists, staring past me to the men who trickled into the cavern.

Stock dusted the snow from his hair as he approached us. "Kent wants to get moving before another storm comes. Says we don't have supplies enough to linger."

Wesley glared at the cavern opening. "I'll put you on my supply horse, Ebby," he said without looking at me.

"Fine," I grumbled. *But I'm not going to like it!*

I followed Wesley to the far corner where his large horses waited on restless legs. There was nowhere for them to graze but there had been a half-frozen pool of runoff in one corner where the horses could drink and recover their strength.

Wesley loaded the smaller horse with his tool pack, and instead of fastening the long wooden box across its back, he folded a woolen blanket and draped it over the horse. I felt sorry for the poor animal that now had to bear the weight of both Wesley's iron tools and my body. Of course, once I saw the bulge in Wesley's arms as he hefted his thick saddle onto the larger horse and then lifted the long wooden box to sit on its muscled hindquarters, I decided the larger horse was no better off.

"What's in the box?" I asked, my curiosity beating down the anger I felt toward him.

"Some things I plan to sell at the Festival of Masters," he said, tying the box to the back of the saddle. The horse stamped its hooves, protesting the weight of its new load.

We were quiet after that. Neither one of us wanted to discuss Wesley's financial situation or his need to rebuild his family home back in Freeland. Perhaps that was why he'd come. Not for Master Moorly, but for himself. He needed the money.

Wesley turned back to me and released a breath that puffed white in the cold. "Ready?"

I adjusted my hood, my head throbbing, and pulled my heavy cloak more firmly about me. "I can mount a horse without your help, Wesley Smith."

Wesley stepped aside and gestured toward the packhorse. "Be my guest, my lady." His smile held a degree of taunting that I found oddly comforting.

Even this smaller horse was larger than Millie. And without a saddle stirrup, it wouldn't be an easy feat. Still, my pride was on the line, and I wouldn't give Wesley the satisfaction of knowing I needed him for such a menial task.

I ran at the horse, planning to plant my hands on its back and swing my leg over the side. Just as I jumped, the horse took a nervous step forward. The graceful mount I'd intended diminished to an ugly flail as my body connected with the saddlebags. The bump on my head pulsed and ached.

Wesley snorted and I could have sworn I heard the word "stubborn" muttered under his breath as he walked over to my side. I turned to face him, prepared to return any cutting comment he made with two of my own. But a different kind of smile greeted me this time. Nothing taunting about it.

"May I please help you?" he asked, his voice a deep rumble, both familiar and strangely new.

I nodded.

Wesley took my waist and just as he was about to lift me on the horse, Lord Kent came up behind him.

"Miss Fields!" His blond hair disheveled, his eyes wild. "Miss Fields." He said my name again, this time with reverence. "When the snow broke, I didn't know if you'd been taken. I spent the night in agony. I'm so relieved to see you safe."

Wesley snorted and practically threw me into the saddle with an irreverent bump.

The squeak that escaped my lips was unwanted and rather ugly. Wesley went around to the other side of the horse, adjusting straps and meddling with clanking iron tools.

Lord Kent came right next to the mare and stroked her neck. "I'm sorry, Ebrielle," he whispered.

I blushed at his use of my first name. No one called me Ebrielle, except perhaps Father when he was angry.

"Never again will I overlook the ability of a Fields." He took my hand without asking. I cringed knowing Wesley could likely see. "Can you forgive me?" Lord Kent squeezed my hand in both of his as he pleaded with the full intensity of his light eyes.

I nodded, fighting the heat that rushed to my cheeks. He should have listened to my warning, but how could he know the extent of a Fields's ability for reading the weather? Besides, it felt wrong to have such a man pleading for the forgiveness of an unworthy exile like myself.

Kent released my hand and looked over to Wesley. "If you think the beast will tire, mine can easily carry two."

Wesley yanked hard on a leather strap. "She'll be safe with me." I heard the accusation in his words, but Lord Kent didn't seem to notice.

CHAPTER ELEVEN

BRENNAN

Wesley and I spoke in nods and grunts for two full days. He led my horse along the narrow trail, set up my tent every night, and tended to Master Moorly's needs. It seemed he never had a moment's rest. My pride wouldn't allow a word of thanks to pass my lips, even though the guilt weighed heavily upon me.

At one point, the terrain was so rocky we had to dismount, tie the reins to the saddles, and trust the beasts to follow us on their own, because the risk of them falling was too great. Lord Kent had come to me and insisted I accept his help over the more treacherous sections.

Isa had wrinkled his nose at Lord Kent's concern. He'd known me his whole life and seen me scamper up boulders and trees with the other children of Freeland in the foothills. He used to bleat my name, *E-h-h-b-y,* whenever we played because he claimed I climbed like a mountain goat.

On the morning of the final day of our journey, we emerged from the steep mountain trail and looked down through the heavy mist of Mount Brennan. The valley was five times the size of Freeland, with lands so flat Father might have dropped to his knees with envy. At the very center of the valley, a lone hill rose from the earth. It was a dark mound among the colorful fields. A bleached white fortress crowned the top of the hill, like bones sticking out of a mound of dark soil.

As I looked out on the vast province below, I wondered why my ancestors ever left.

"Pretty amazing, isn't it?" Joe Ford appeared at my side standing so thin and tall that I feared he might blow away with the wind.

"It's incredible," I agreed. Neither of us tore our eyes from the valley below.

"I haven't forgotten about the favor I owe you," he said.

"It really wasn't anything—

"There's a place called the Talk About."

Something warm stirred within my gut.

"It's a place where storytellers and wanders like myself meet in the late hours of the night. If you ask one of the servants from the fortress, they'll tell you how to find it." Joe glanced back toward the men breaking down camp. He hiked his small pack and bedroll up on his shoulders. "If you ever need me, my door is open to you." He started down the mountain, not bothering to wait for the rest of the company. "Ask for Jeffery," he turned to add.

"Who's Jeffery?" I shouted against the wind.

"Jeffery is my Brennan name." He stopped and looked once more toward the men of our company. "Best to keep that between you and me." He winked. His smile curled like a vine around a beanpole as the red feather of his hat whipped in the breeze.

I watched him go until he was lost to the forest that bordered the city, wishing I'd had the nerve to ask him to elaborate on his mountain ghost story. Would I ever see him again?

"What was that about?"

I startled and sputtered. "Oh, Wesley. Don't sneak up on me like that!"

Wesley had his arms crossed in front of him, examining me with a bit too much scrutiny. "Strange that the storyteller left before the rest of us. Seems sneaky."

I rolled my eyes. "You're always looking for the worst in people, aren't you?"

"And you're constantly blinded by the good in them. Even if they only possess a small amount of it."

I smirked. "I have no trouble seeing your flaws, Wesley Smith."

He grumbled under his breath then asked, "So what did he say to you?"

"Nothing. Just wished me farewell and a pleasant stay in Brennan," I lied. I didn't need a lecture from Wesley. It wasn't like I would actually go to this Talk About place.

Wesley dumped me on his packhorse and stalked ahead to his own mount. He double-checked the lead rope connecting our two horses and then we were off. The closer we moved to the city center, the larger everything appeared. After passing through acres of farmland with a smattering of country homes, we approached a towering wall that ran the whole perimeter of the city.

With a nod from the guards at the gate, the company crossed into what seemed to be a new world. Two-story buildings lined the streets, all pale with dark wood trimming the windows, doors, and gables. Smart-looking ladies wore rich gowns, their hair piled in elegant twists on top of their heads while another street over, children in rags played without shoes. The smell of warm bread wafted from bakeries while crackling sausages from a street griddle made my mouth water.

Traffic from carriages and pedestrians made the journey through the city slow. Ahead of us, I had to raise my head to see the highest turrets of the fortress. The ride sloped upward as we approached the tall granite walls. Chains rattled as an iron portcullis opened its black mouth to allow us entry into the inner courtyard. Were we really walking into the belly of the giant monster with its ten-foot spikes for teeth? Had I reins, I might have turned back then and there. But on we marched, a willing sacrifice.

Several Freeland craftsmen in our company dissolved into the crowd outside the walls of the fortress to secure lodgings. I continued onward with Wesley, Master Moorly, Stock, and Isa who were all considered guests of noble rank and were invited to stay at the fortress with me. Lord Kent had explained that Brennan recognized the title of councilman to be the closest thing to nobility Freeland could claim. Since Isa, Stock, and Wesley would soon inherit the title and Seth Moorly currently held Wesley's title until he came of age, they deserved to be treated accordingly. Wesley and his friends had rolled their eyes at the announcement, but what could they do? They were all guests of Brennan and didn't want to offend their hosts.

Inside the belly of the beast the walls sparkled, blinding me when the light caught the quartz in the granite stone. The courtyard spread out into a perfect square with walls three stories high. Three! A grand fountain surrounded by formal gardens invited the eye at the very center.

The fortress itself consisted of a central building with an east and west wing connected at right angles. Stone statues of ungodly animals rested on pedestals and granite shelves: lions with eagle wings and lizards with whipping forked-tongues and bear bodies. All of the macabre beasts seemed to watch me as we approached the center fountain.

Above us people in fine clothing lined the second story terrace that wrapped around three of the four walls. Women wore dresses with full skirts and sleeves that draped like water and men wore bright colored tunics and high boots. At first glance, they all appeared happy and welcoming, but when I looked past their stiff smiles, I thought I saw something else. Maybe their eyes twitched in irritation because of the brightness of the court-yard. Maybe not. I tended to read too deeply into things.

Lord Kent handed the reins of his horse to a stable hand with strict instructions for the animal's care and then walked past Wesley to help me down from my horse.

"You are all most welcome here at the fortress." He gave my hand a slight squeeze before resting it in the crook of his el-bow. As usual, a flurry of nerves jumped inside my stomach at his touch. "The duke and duchess will be anxious to meet you all, but introductions will be delayed until you're settled. Then my father can personally thank each of you for accepting our invitation." He clapped twice, and a handful of servants rushed toward our group.

A small, mousy woman in an angular bonnet and white apron approached.

"Anna and I will take you to your quarters, Miss Fields," said Lord Kent.

Wesley stepped in and offered his arm. I had the distinct impression he wanted to yank me out of Lord Kent's hold. "Master Moorly has asked that I see Miss Fields to her room, if you don't mind, my lord. He has some instructions he would like me to pass on before we settle in."

Lord Kent glared at Wesley for just a moment before a smooth smile returned to his young lips. "Good of you, Smith." He dropped my arm. "My father will be eager for my report." He turned to me and added, "I'll see you all soon," before he bowed and left us.

The woman with the angular bonnet led us through the huge double doors at the center of the fortress where a skylight in the ceiling drew our attention upward. Burning incense tastefully muted the damp smell. Sandalwood, if I wasn't mistaken. We walked deeper into the fortress, past the entry and into the larg-est room I'd ever scene, filled with plenty of seating, art and tapestries on the walls, and ceilings three stories high with giant exposed wooden trusses. We took the east corridor and eventually climbed a grand staircase, passing dozens of doors and walkways before stopping at an unmarked white wooden door.

Anna humbly cast her eyes to the ground as she held the door open for us. I didn't dare cross the threshold, fearing my dirty riding boots would spoil the pristine marble floors. Wesley nudged me, and I, like a good horse after gentle encouragement, crept forward.

My gasp caught in my throat. The white floor seemed to rise up the white walls, providing the illusion that I was floating in a cloud with misleading dimensions. The only real color came from a vase set on the table in the heart of the room filled with a bouquet of deep red roses.

I blushed at the site of them and inadvertently used Wesley as a shield.

"What's going on here?" Wesley raised his voice.

Anna startled. "Is something wrong, sir?"

"Who sent these flowers?"

"They were a welcome gift arranged by Lord Kent," said Anna. She looked to me for help, and I could tell she didn't understand. I moved in front of Wesley and rested a hand on his chest. "I don't think the roses mean the same thing here," I whispered.

Wesley pushed my hand away. "That's no excuse. He knows better, I swear he does."

I turned to poor Anna to explain. "In Freeland, when a man gives a woman red roses it means he intends to marry her. Unless an agreement has been reached in advance, it's seen as an extremely forward gesture."

Wesley didn't waste another breath on words. He walked over to the marble table, snatched the offending flowers from their vase, and flung them out the open window into the courtyard below. He huffed out of the room before I could protest. Whatever instructions he meant to pass along were left unsaid. I glanced around at the pale maid who now pressed a hand to her chest. Offering a shaky grin and feeling more bewildered than ever, I said, "We've had a difficult journey."

I DID MY best to cover up the parts of me that the bubbles of my bath didn't reach as Anna massaged lavender soap into my scalp and Madam Hold, the head housekeeper, rattled off my schedule for the next few days. Madam Hold was a round woman with angular opinions whose deep voice rasped as though she'd accidently inhaled smoke from a cook fire.

When I asked if we could possibly meet to discuss this at a later hour and insisted that I could bathe myself, the old woman batted away my concerns with a wave of her hand. "Your first official visit with the duchess is scheduled for the day after tomorrow. The lessons you receive after that visit will depend upon your performance at tea with Her Grace."

"My performance?" I asked.

"During your stay with us, you may expect lessons on comportment, courting, dining, and of course, dancing. It is the duchess's wish that you be trained in all the necessary skills of a lady of culture and refinement."

I sank lower in the bath, just in time for Anna to dip a bucket into the water. She held it aloft and asked, "Are you ready, miss?"

Not remotely.

THE BATH WATER carried a brownish tint when I left it. Though it was early evening, I was too tired to dress for dinner. Anna helped brush out the many tangles of my hair as I sat in my night dress by the fire.

"You don't talk much, do you?" I said, trying to catch the maid's gaze in the mirror.

Her cheeks colored some, but she didn't remove her eyes from my hair.

"We haven't had a chance to get to know one another. I'm Ebby." I didn't offer my hand because her fingers were tied up.

Anna face reddened. She curtsied and continued her work.

Was this another Brennan custom? No talking to the help? If this woman was going to attend me over the entire winter, I needed to get to know her.

"Anna's a pretty name. What's your surname?"

Anna pretended not to hear me.

"Please *say* something."

She looked at me in the mirror then looked away. "I'm not permitted to talk when working, miss."

"Why not?"

"I'm common." She looked back down and fiddled with my hair again, only this time with less purpose.

Was this really how the Brennan nobility functioned? My disbelief must have registered on my face because she eventually dropped her hands and stared at the floor. "Would you like me to go now, miss?"

"No, I wouldn't like you to go. That is, unless you want to."

She shook her head. Her lip quivered.

I turned around to face her. "I don't know what you're used to, but in Freeland my maid was one of my closest friends. In fact, I think my family preferred her company to mine on several occasions."

A smile peeked around the corner of her mouth.

Encouraged, I soldiered on. "I might just die without someone to talk to for the next few months."

I turned back around, not wanting to make her too uncomfortable. She eventually returned to doing my hair. "My name is Marta Featherbee," she finally said in a quiet whisper.

"I thought your name was Anna."

She shook her head again, this time with more confidence. "When Lord Kent doesn't know your name, he calls you Anna or something common like that. I know better than to correct him."

I blinked. Twice. I couldn't imagine Lord Kent acting so cold and impersonal with anyone. "Thank you for your help, Marta Featherbee."

She curtsied a "you're welcome" and left me with a plate of food and a promise to see me at first light.

I hoped she was joking.

I burrowed into a down pillow in a bed as big as my room back in Freeland. My eyes had only been closed for a second when two solid knocks sounded on the door.

I sat up and patted my hair to smooth down the unruly flyaways that were my constant battle. "Come in."

The knocks sounded again.

I straightened my nightdress as I went to the door. "Hello?" Who would be calling at this late hour?

I pulled on my dressing gown and a pair of slippers, and opened the door a crack.

At first all I saw was a bright bouquet of pink roses. The boy holding them had two letters in his mouth, a bag hanging on each arm, and a sweet roll in his spare hand.

"Can I help you?" I asked.

He mumbled something incoherent around the paper in his mouth.

"Um. Why don't you come in?" I opened the door wider and the boy shuffled in, barely seen over the flowers. He set the vase on the vanity and took the envelopes from his mouth.

"Sorry 'bout that." He examined the water rings on the letters and frowned. "I hate making two trips when I can do it in one."

The sandy-haired boy couldn't have been a hare's twitch older than eleven, but he took my hand and kissed it. "My name is Simon Right, and I am at your service." He made a sweeping bow. I had to bite my bottom lip to keep from laughing.

"The stable hands said you were a beauty, but the bards could never have prepared me for your charms. You're an absolute vision, Miss Fields." He offered me one of the letters. The ink was smudged in several places.

I was careful to grip the corners as I unfolded the letter, but was only rewarded with four odd words.

Bring me the Freeland blacksmith. –Duke

I held it up for the boy to read. "I don't understand."

Simon slapped his palm to his freckled forehead. "I'm an idiot." He offered the other letter. "This one is yours."

I held it up to the light of the fire to read.

Dear Miss Fields,

I apologize for the forward gesture. It is the custom of Brennan to offer a beautiful guest flowers upon arrival. I meant no offense and would love to make it up to you.

Every year, to celebrate the commencement of the Festival of Masters, the duke hosts a hunt for all his honored guests. My father and I would be honored if you would join us for this tradition tomorrow.

Since your horse was lost in the journey here, Father would like to offer you one of our mounts as a show of friendship. Your maid will provide you with the important details.

Until tomorrow,

Theodore Kent

P.S. Hopefully this bouquet is to your liking.

Theodore. I wanted to giggle—something I never did. I'd never received flowers before coming to Brennan, if you didn't count the dandelion Isa gave me when I was six years old, which I didn't. As Lord Kent said, it was only a custom, but I still appreciated the kindness.

"I assume this belongs to someone else?" I refolded the first message and handed it back to Simon. "I think it involves Master Moorly, Freeland's regent councilman representing our blacksmiths."

Simon bounced on the balls of his feet. "The duke always requests a private audience with the blacksmiths who arrive for the festival."

I instantly thought of Joe's story about the blacksmith with the magic hands, or magic metal, or whatever he told the field-workers. Was it possible that the duke was really looking for the man who could make the Purgo blade? I wished I had paid closer attention to the story. I was sure if I asked him, Joe would tell it to me again.

That thought triggered another.

"Simon," I asked, "have you ever heard of a place called the Talk About?"

He shuffled his feet and then, like a shy fox being lured from its den, said, "It's the storytellers' lair. But you don't want to go there, Miss Fields. It isn't a safe place." Simon took a bite of his sweet roll and picked up his things. "Has anyone ever told you your skin shines like the sun on a fair day?"

"I, um… well, no." Simon was young and just trying to flatter me. But I'd never been labeled as a beauty before, and didn't know what to do with the compliment.

I thanked Simon for the delivery and closed the door, doing my best to push away the curiosity seeping into my bones.

Why would Joe invite me somewhere that wasn't safe? And stranger still, why would the duke want to talk to all of the blacksmiths? I thought about finding Joe and pressing him for the truth behind the Purgo but quickly banished the idea. It had been a child's story. Something cooked up to entertain a crowd of tired men in need of a good distraction and to line Joe's pockets with coin. That was all.

Besides, I wasn't here to delve into the duke's business, or further my habit of eavesdropping. I was here to make a lady out of myself, to be an ambassador and prove that I was worthy of my family name. Swords and storyteller dens were not my business.

Ever so slowly, a familiar imaginary needle pierced my gut.

I reached for the door and paused, wondering how my hand had found the latch without my permission.

An entirely different story of Joe's filled my thoughts. A tale of ghosts on the mountain and wandering spirits. I swallowed, taking a painful step back. A movement that seemed to make the air around me heat, and my muscles tighten.

Please, no.

I'd hoped that leaving home would cure me of this strange compulsion. This unrelenting impulse that got me into so much trouble. If these really were spirits, it seemed they weren't confined to any one location.

I shook my head, working my lower lip in my teeth. Unlike the promptings that came as whispers to my conscience, these pull impulses were more internal. The strange thing was, this feeling, this *urgency* didn't feel like an evil spirit at all. It was a need deeper than any hunger I had ever felt before. It belonged to me, somehow.

Needle and thread. Piercing, pushing, pulling. Guiding the thread into place to build something new and wonderous.

Images of my mother sitting on her rocker on the front porch of our home rushed to the forefront of my mind, forcing me to look at the strange sensation in a new light. Did I really know for certain that the tugging in my gut was bad? Hadn't it been the whispers that led me to the barn and distracted me from delivering my father's message about the floodgates? I'd assumed the pull was bad because the whispers that invaded my thoughts seemed to lead to trouble. But were they the same? Could the tugging pull in my gut be my own intuition?

How could I know if I didn't explore the possibility?

Even though I didn't understand it, the idea of ignoring the invisible call to action seemed more dangerous than noble. I made a decision, then and there, that I'd simply call this familiar pull in my gut exactly what it was. A pull. No more thoughts of spirits. I wouldn't try to understand it. Since it felt right to follow my gut, I would follow.

Besides, I wasn't a prisoner confined to my rooms, I was a guest. No one would judge me for taking a look around the place. I lifted a lantern from an elaborate hook by the door, checked it for oil, and turned the latch, praying that I wasn't lying to myself.

Praying that this feeling inside me could be trusted.

Wesley, four years earlier

I wait outside Gavin's house sitting on the porch swing. My bouncing foot creates a frantic rhythm on the weathered floorboards. A bead of sweat rolls down the center of my back and I have to pinch the bridge of my nose and count backwards from one thousand to keep from pounding on the door.

I need to get to the river before I melt into a puddle on Gavin's porch—to cool off both my body and my temper.

Where is Gavin? He said he'd be out just as soon as supper ended.

Shouts erupt from inside the house, one voice high in pitch, the other high in volume. A door slams and quick footsteps thump toward the front door.

I jump to my feet as the door is pulled open. Finally!

But the hem of a skirt deflates my hope.

"In case anyone cares," Ebby leans inside the house, "I'll be off disappointing everyone by the East River!" She slams the door with two hands to create a loud boom that makes even me flinch.

Ebby whirls around and launches herself in my direction, sending us both toppling over the edge of the porch and into a bush.

"Gah!" she yells. "And they say I sneak up on people!"

We disentangle ourselves from a jigsaw puzzle of adolescent limbs, and I give her an extra shove off me for good measure. "Where is Gavin?"

Ebby scowls. "He left an hour ago." She looks back to the house and frowns. "Smart boy."

Typical Gavin not to wait for me. By now he is probably already down at the river with Isa and Stock. Gavin would never own up to it, but his work is easier than mine and he always finishes first. He also doesn't have a perfectionist for a father, always breathing down his neck, melting down his work if it carries even the slightest imperfection.

My father is completely impossible to please.

Ebby starts walking, and I follow. She's going where I'm headed anyway.

"Where exactly are you going?" I ask when I notice Ebby take a turn down River Lane. It is one of the oldest roads in Freeland and cuts a direct line dividing the north and south parts of town. You can travel it in a straight shot from the banks of the West River to the banks of the East River.

"Where I go is none of your business, Apprentice." Ebby's two braids bounce behind her. Tempting as always.

"You better not be headed to the rope swing." Gavin and the boys will not tolerate the company of a thirteen-year-old girl. Our time at the rope swing is exclusive. Sacred even. It's the only time the four of us, all sons of councilmen, can escape our duties in Freeland and pretend our biggest responsibility is besting each other for distance into the water. Stock, the oldest of us by more than a year, has set a record that the rest of us are determined to beat.

"I'll go where I please."

"Your brother will be—"

Ebby spins around and stabs a finger into my chest. "I don't care what Gavin thinks. I'm going to the river."

I walk a step behind her, distracted from my own frustrations. I think back to the ruckus I heard at the Fields home and wonder if perhaps Ebby might understand me more than Gavin. If she were a boy and older, I might even prefer her to him.

Gavin really is a little too high on his good-boy horse every now and again.

I shake the thought away and kick the back of Ebby's shoe just at the perfect moment to send her stumbling. Then I sprint by her. "Beat you there!" I call over my shoulder.

Because I know she can't beat me. And she knows it too.

I secretly hope she comes to the rope swing. But I would never tell her that.

CHAPTER TWELVE

COMPELLED

I let the pull lead me through the sleeping fortress. After multiple turns, two flights of stairs, and one slippery encounter with the polished marble floor, I found myself drawn to a set of large stained-glass doors standing ajar, inviting me in.

I lowered my lantern and looked over my shoulder, straining to hear sounds that might prove I wasn't alone. The fortress slept in heavy silence. Carefully, I pushed open one of the large doors, cringing at the whine of the hinges before slipping inside.

My meager light wasn't strong enough to fill the space, but as I walked the perimeter of the room with lantern raised, I nearly wept at the discovery. Every wall held shelves from floor to ceiling with hundreds, maybe thousands of volumes. The smell of ink, paper, leather, and dust beckoned me forward. Never had I seen so many books in one place.

The pull dragged me past dozens and dozens of red, brown, and blue leather covers. I let my fingers trail along the spines, wishing I had time to explore the library in greater detail. Reading wasn't so different from eavesdropping. It came with the thrill of observing the world undetected and free to interpret as I wished.

I came to the back wall of the room where two freestanding shelves stood apart from the rest of the more formal displays. On the backside of the shelves, unseen from the door, were stacks of wicker baskets filled with what appeared to be discarded old scrolls and ledgers. I surveyed the stacks and was drawn to a basket at my left, just below eye-level.

Though the room had been cool only moments before, a bead of sweat rolled down my spine. With hands trembling and the pull in my stomach cresting into tight pain, I set down the lantern and rummaged through the basket, certain I had officially lost my mind.

My fingers couldn't move fast enough. In my manic search, I noticed the scrolls and ledgers bore the same tight, neat penmanship. A man's script. When I dug to the bottom of the basket, my fingers grazed a brown leather-covered book with a haphazard, hand-sewn binding.

The moment I lifted the book from the basket, the pain and hungry need in my gut vanished. Panting and flushed, I returned the original scrolls and ledgers to their places. Then I scooped up the book and tucked it under my arm before grabbing the lantern and bolting from the library.

With the pull gone, common sense returned. I'd just stolen something from the duke's fortress on my first day as a guest in his home. Not to mention I was wandering around in my nightdress and dressing gown! Why hadn't I considered that before leaving? What if I had run into someone? How had the pull blinded me to something so obvious?

After a handful of wrong turns, I finally found the corridor leading to my room. Closing the door, I practically threw myself on the bed and held a hand to my rapidly beating heart as candles flickered around the room thanks to an unknown draft of air. Only when I'd calmed down enough to trust that I hadn't been followed did I blow out all of the candles around my room save one, and carried it and the stolen volume back to my bed. I untied the string of leather securing the book and cracked the spine. I didn't know what I expected to find, only that it must be important to warrant such an urgent search, compelled by my pull.

By the light of a lone candle, I searched the inside cover for an inscription or date but found it blank. I turned the yellowed page and the sight of the neat script on the first page had my heart racing again.

June 10th

As the youngest of ten sons, my inheritance has long been divided. I don't mind the prospect of gaining a profession and earning my way in the world. I choose to see it as an adventure rather than a necessity born from desperation. I am the only member of my family with the gift, *and that good fortune sustains me. My mother is convinced it will help me find my way in the world, as it has for so many of our ancestors.*

I recently acquired a position as a scribe in the fortress. I plan to work my way into the duke's good favor, retaining my noble title without a coin to back it.

My employ thus far has consisted mainly of drafting deeds of property. The duke is confiscating land belonging to old farming families in Brennan and granting them to young lords in return for their continued support. On paper the arrangements seem legitimate: the deserving lord gains land and title, the ignorant farmer gains the wisdom and backing of a lord, and the duke gains his support.

I remained happy in my ignorance until yesterday when I was given the task of delivering one of my righteous notices to a wheat farmer and his only daughter. The farmer stared dumbfounded at the duke's seal while his daughter, Charlotte, wept silently. When she walked me to my mount at the edge of the property, I wiped her tears with my own cloth. Her forced smile and glistening eyes made me want to march back to the house and rip apart the duke's order.

I confess, Charlotte intrigues me. Though the social order of Brennan forbids it, I am compelled to know her better…

"MISS?"

I sat up and the book clattered to the floor. I looked up to find light filtering in through the window and Marta standing in my doorway carrying a tea tray.

"I didn't mean to startle you, Miss Fields. It is time to dress for the hunt."

When I said nothing, she held out the tray in her arms. "I… I brought tea."

"Of course." I stood and nudged the leather book under my bed with all the innocence of a criminal. "Please come in."

As she set down her tray across the room on the dressing table, I scooped up the book and hid it underneath my feather mattress.

"You must eat and dress quickly this morning, miss. The nobles are gathering in the courtyard soon."

After twisting and tugging my hair and cinching me into a deep gray riding habit, Marta picked up a brightly colored red sash.

"What's this?" I ran my fingers along the sash, amazed by the quality of the fabric.

"Every lady is given a different-colored sash to be tied about her waist," Marta explained. "They are meant to be favors."

"Will I be expected to give it to someone?"

"It is tradition," said Marta.

"What does it mean?"

"Same as any favor, I suppose. It means you fancy the man you give it to."

Marta tied the blood red sash. It stood in bold contrast to my gray riding habit. Every time I saw that color, I thought of the roses Lord Kent gave me. "Could I have a different color, please?" I asked.

Marta bit her bottom lip and shook her head. "I'm afraid it's too late for that now."

Though I admired Lord Kent, I wasn't ready to announce my interest in him to all of Brennan. Especially in red!

THE COURTYARD WAS filled with at least thirty horses, most of which had riders mounted and ready. I was surprised to find that nearly half of the group assembled were ladies.

Lord Kent looked up from a conversation with a heavily tattooed man with multiple piercings lining his ears. He excused himself—much to the tattooed man's frustration—and approached, beaming, with outstretched hands.

"Lovely as always, Miss Fields." He took one of my hands and kissed it, not noticing that the man with the piercings had followed him to my side.

"My lord, another word?" said the stranger.

Lord Kent rolled his eyes. "We've concluded our talks, Kilsom."

"I have more to say on the matter." He reached for Lord Kent's arm. "You can't just expect us to sit back and let you—"

"Not here!" Lord Kent yanked his arm free. The skin around his collar flared red.

I flinched and the tattooed man closed his eyes in frustration. "Please forgive me, madam." He bowed in my direction then to Lord Kent added, "Please tell your father I insist on another audience," before he walked away.

There it was again. The swirling flutter of nerves dancing in my stomach. The pull that combined miserably with my insatiable need to know everything. Evil spirit or not, if I didn't learn how to curb this impulse, Father would never want me back.

"Now that we're alone," Lord Kent cleared his throat, "I want to apologize again for the flowers. It was inexcusable." He took my arm.

"It wasn't your fault, my lord. The customs in Freeland and Brennan are clearly different."

"Indeed." Lord Kent led me over to a groomsman who held the leads of both Kent's prized black stallion and a smaller mare of matching black. "She is well broken, but possesses just enough spirit to keep up."

I reached out and let the horse smell my hand, and then bent to softly blow at her nose so she could really get my scent. The horse dipped her head and I ran my hand along her regal neck, struck with loss, thinking of Millie and the thousands of times we'd carried on this same ritual. "What is her name?" I asked.

"You may name her whatever you like, my dear. She's yours."

I looked up at that, shocked. "Your letter mentioned a horse, but I assumed it would be a loan."

"A gift in compensation for your lost mare." He bowed.

It was silly and more than a little embarrassing, but I couldn't help the glisten of tears that filled my eyes. My throat tightened. "Thank you, my lord. That's quite a gift."

Lord Kent kissed my hand. "It brings me joy to see you so happy, Ebrielle." He gestured to the saddle. "May I help you up?"

I stroked the mare's cheek once more and nodded. "Yes, please." In a moment, I was astride, and I nodded my thanks to Lord Kent after adjusting my long skirts. Beyond him, a large man with rust colored hair, a full belly, and full beard mounted a large white horse.

"My father," Lord Kent said, now seated atop his own horse. "I'll introduce you at the picnic. He's looking forward to making your acquaintance." Lord Kent flashed me a handsome smile and I couldn't help warming at his attention.

The duke led us all through the portcullis and beyond the fortress walls, his horse passing wind with every other step for the first quarter mile. I had to admit, the pairing of horse and rider was too perfect. I assumed it was the duchess who rode next to him. Her dress fluffed and bounced in rhythm with the slipping wig atop her head—a regular cupcake with frosting. She looked over to her husband with a pained smile and wild eyes that screamed unease.

Lord Kent and I followed, falling in line with—to my great surprise—Wesley and a young woman with long dark hair pinned to flow over one shoulder and thick lashes that framed her eyes like black fans. Her full lips were tinted a deep red to match her lavish riding habit.

Wesley was so deeply focused on the dark-haired beauty that he started when my horse fell into step beside his. "Ebby! What are you doing here?" he asked in a whisper.

Was that disappointment I heard in his voice?

Lord Kent made the introductions. "Miss Ebrielle Fields, may I introduce Lady Georgiana Kent. My sister."

It took me a moment to find my voice. I blinked, then leaned forward in my saddle to offer an awkward, seated bow. "An honor meeting you, my lady."

Her laughter was musical. "My brother failed to mention he was a twin, I take it."

A twin! "He did." I glanced over at Lord Kent, who offered me an apologetic shrug.

After introductions were made, Wesley leaned toward me and whispered, "I wasn't expecting you."

"Do you think I'm incapable, Wes, or is it my company that vexes you?" I said, trying to smile in an attempt to mask my hurt feelings.

He shook his head. "I know you can keep up, Ebby. It's the *hunting* part of the hunt I was thinking of."

"Oh… that."

Wesley knew me all too well. I loved to ride and explore the woods. I used to beg Father to let me join him and Gavin on their hunting trips. When they finally let me come, I tried extra hard to prove my ability. All day I scouted scat trails and antler rubbings, quiet as a falling leaf until we came upon our prey. Father, Gavin, and Wesley each had their bows drawn and aimed toward a family of deer nibbling at the tall grass in a clearing.

I screamed for the deer to run before I could stop myself. I couldn't bear to see the poor family lose a father, brother, or even possibly a mother. I'd only just lost my mother, and death of any kind caused me pain.

"I might just linger in the background at the end."

I caught Lady Kent's smirk before she smoothed her red lips into a sympathetic smile. "That's a shame." She reached out and touched Wesley's forearm. "Hopefully not all of the Free-landers are unequal to the sport."

That vixen! That snake! That…

I stopped mid mental attack to realize something so obvious it might as well have spat on my shoe. Yes, Lady Kent seemed a spiteful young woman, but that wasn't what truly bothered me. Could I really be jealous? Why should I care if the duke's daughter fawned over Wesley? He was like a brother.

I nodded to Wesley and Lady Kent and nudged my horse onward to catch up to Lord Kent, telling myself not to look back. We traveled for miles out of the city and into the densely forested foothills until the trail opened into a meadow. The sun took pity on the field, making it exceptionally warm for this time of year. Servants waited with big blankets and mounds of food.

Lord Kent helped me down from my horse and led me to sit on one of the blankets. When Wesley and Lady Kent joined us, I inwardly groaned as she dropped gracefully to the blanket and arranged her skirts in a fan around her. I couldn't help comparing my homespun flaws to her perfect manners and appearance. Slouching, I tried my hardest to disappear as the others pulled at twisted butterbread and ate berries with sweet cream.

"Aren't you hungry, Miss Fields?" Lord Kent asked as he plopped an especially large blackberry into his mouth.

I grabbed a piece of butterbread and pulled off a small portion. "Yes, thank you. I was just… lost in thought."

Lord Kent examined me with one raised brow.

To be honest, I'd been distracted by the stares Lady Kent gave Wesley. I could spot a girl on the hunt as well as anyone.

"Leave the poor girl alone, Theo. Not everyone can keep their thoughts while carrying on intelligent conversation," said Lady Kent.

Wesley stifled a laugh. The traitor! By laughing, he was taking a side, because the line between Lady Kent and I was officially drawn. She was far prettier than I could ever dream to be. Why did the woman need to lower me further by questioning my intellect? What did I do to inspire such venom?

I almost choked as Lady Kent continued. "*You* don't seem to have trouble multi-tasking." She turned to Wesley, her womanly figure curving in a painfully perfect way. "I hear you have quite a talent in the forges. My father tells me you have a brilliant mind for your work."

Wesley paled as he swallowed hard, making an unseemly gulping noise in the process. "I'm only a smithy, Lady Kent. We're known for our metal, not our minds."

"Yes, but I'm told you are a master, even on the cusp of finishing your apprenticeship."

He accepted the compliment with a nod and went back to his meal.

At least Wesley was humble about his skill. No one could fault him there. I had always appreciated humility. Father was like that—determined to be common despite his skill and status in Freeland.

Lord Kent leaned toward me, his lips tickling the hair around my ears, distracting me from Lady Kent and the quiet conversation she was now having with Wesley. "I have a surprise for you, Miss Fields," he whispered. "A gift."

I turned wide eyes to him. "Another?"

"I don't know how you celebrate birthdays in Freeland, but here in Brennan, we give gifts."

I blushed again and stole a quick glance at Wesley to see if he'd witnessed another one of my silly reactions, but he was too deep in discussion with Lady Kent. I wondered why their voices had lowered, but I couldn't divide my attentions from Lord Kent without being rude.

"My birthday was two weeks ago," I said.

Wesley and Lady Kent burst into laughter. What could she possibly have to say that would make him grab his gut?

Lord Kent held out a small box tied with a blood red bow. I immediately thought of his roses and my sash. Was there some subliminal message in the wrapping, or was I just being silly?

I accepted the box and brought it down to rest in my lap. "Thank you, my lord."

"Theodore," he corrected, his light brown hair falling forward into his face.

"Theodore," I said, as heat creeped into my cheeks. I held the box with reverence, unused to receiving gifts from a man. A part of me worried that by accepting he might expect some measure of devotion or commitment in return.

He must have sensed my hesitation, because he frowned when I pulled my eyes from the red ribbon.

"Is everything all right, my dear?"

"Of course." I made sure to smile before pulling at the red ribbon. My hands shook as I lifted the lid from the box. Inside were the most beautiful combs I'd ever seen.

"They're made from seashells." Lord Kent answered my question before I could ask.

Seashells! The colors of the shells moved as I balanced them in my hand. Purple turned silver and light blue before my eyes.

"They're beautiful, my lord."

He took one of the combs from the red-ribboned box and tucked it behind my ear. His fingertips lightly traveled down my neck before he reached for the other comb. "They were made by a Sea Port artisan in Brennan for the festival."

"I don't know how to thank you."

He fastened the other comb to my hair. "Happy belated birthday, Ebrielle."

"My lord and lady." We turned to see a bowing man in livery. "Your father asks that you present your guests."

Lord and Lady Kent exchanged a glance. Something brief passed between them. A silent communication that, I supposed, came naturally for twins.

Lord Kent stood and offered me his hand. "Shall we?"

Wesley and I walked sandwiched between the Lord and Lady Kent around the perimeter of the meadow. Talk in the clearing quieted as we passed. Heads turned in our direction.

"We're the duke's guests, Ebby," said Wesley under his breath. "Stop wringing your hands as though you're walking to the gallows." I quickly dropped my hands to my sides. I hadn't even noticed my outward display of nerves. Did I always have to be so transparent?

The duke sat at a small table that had been transported out to the meadow for his comfort. His wife, the author of the letter that brought me here in the first place, had left him to converse with a group of ladies on the other side of the clearing.

We stopped before the duke and Lord Kent said, "Father, may I present the lovely Miss Ebrielle Fields and future councilman blacksmith, Mr. Wesley Smith of Freeland."

The duke nodded to accept our bow and curtsey but didn't bother to stand. "You both are very welcome." He ran his fingers along his thick russet beard. "It is no small feat to coax a Freelander from his side of the mountain."

My tongue seemed too large for my mouth. Thankfully, Wesley saved me from having to reply.

"We are honored to accept your invitation, Your Grace."

"When will you inherit your full title, lad?"

"I will complete my apprenticeship in late summer, Your Grace."

"Until that time, you work under Master Moorly?"

Wesley nodded. "Yes, Your Grace."

The duke studied Wesley for an extra beat, his eyes narrowing. "And you find him a competent master of the trade?"

"No man could replace my father's training. He was the finest master of metal I've ever known, but Master Moorly is a competent craftsman and teacher, Your Grace. I'm honored to train with him."

"I heard about the fire that claimed your father," said the duke. "A great tragedy."

Wesley bowed his head in what appeared to be agreement and thanks.

I caught myself staring between both the duke and Wesley, wondering at the strange line of questioning. I wouldn't have suspected the duke to pry into the dealings of a mere smithy—even one set to become a councilman of Freeland. There was something intelligent in the duke's golden-brown eyes. Something that betrayed a strategic mind.

The duke turned his attention toward me, and I willed myself to stand a little taller. "And how does the governor of Freeland fair?"

"My father is very well, Your Grace. I thank you." I bobbed another quick curtsy.

"Hmmm." He tilted his head a fraction to the side, as if deciding what to make of me. "I've heard stories about your father's stature. Either they are grossly exaggerated, or your mother must have been a rather small woman."

"Father," Lord Kent started, "that is hardly—"

The duke cut him off with a single raised hand.

Color heated my cheeks, but I was determined not to be cowed by the important man. "My father is very large, indeed, Your Grace. Mother, before she passed, was also known for her height." I waved a hand in front of me. "As you can see, the trait did not pass to me." *I don't measure up,* I mentally added.

"Not in the least," the duke agreed.

We were excused and returned to our blanket, my face still hotter than a July day spent working the fields.

When the duke left his table to mount his horse, many of the company followed his example. It took the duke three tries before he was able to swing his heavy leg over the white steed. The poor animal sidestepped with the added weight, and I couldn't blame him. Once mounted, the duke addressed the crowd of nobles. "Return to this meadow for the measuring at sundown. The winner will be announced at dinner this evening. That should give you ladies plenty of time to favor your beau." He looked directly at me. Lines around his eyes wrinkled to crow's feet in what I assumed was a smile. With his thick red beard, it was difficult to tell.

I inclined my head in a soft bow and he turned away.

The clearing erupted with life. Shouted wagers harmonized with flirtatious laughter. Some of the men already wore the colored sash of their lady and others, it seemed, did their best to earn it with pledges and promises indiscernible in the buzz of voices.

Lady Kent and Wesley were on their horses when we reached them. To my surprise, Lady Kent had a quiver of arrows and bow strapped to her back. Many of the women, including the duchess, would stay with the blankets and berries, and of the few women riding, only Lady Kent carried a weapon. Her yellow sash was still secured around her waist. I relaxed some, but knew it was only a matter of time before Wesley wore it across his broad chest from shoulder to hip. *Oh Wesley, you poor fool.* Any thought of staying behind vanished. I'd not prove myself a coward in Lady Kent's estimation. I'd show her and the rest of the hunting party what Freelanders were made of.

While Lord Kent checked his horse's hooves, I retrieved my riding gloves from the saddlebag of my horse. As I stuck my hand into the glove, I cut my knuckle on an unexpected piece of paper tucked into the cuff of my glove. Blood smeared the tight letters of my name, written in red ink. I turned away from the men and broke the smooth wax seal. My fingers couldn't move fast enough. Who would place a letter in my glove? And how did it get there without my knowledge?

It was hard to read the cramped writing with hands shaking, so I didn't trust my first glance. *"Go home."*

I turned the letter over, hoping to find some clue of the sender, but the card was completely blank. Who would send me such a thing?

"Miss Fields?"

I literally jumped—both feet inches off the ground, jumped. I pushed the paper up my sleeve as I turned around to find Lord Kent fighting a grin. "I think we're ready."

The edge of the paper tickled my wrist. Was someone else trying to bully me? Or perhaps it was just a prank. I only arrived yesterday. Even I couldn't make enemies so fast.

"Ready for an adventure?" Lord Kent whispered, taking my waist to lift me into my saddle. His buttery smooth voice sent a ripple of chills up my spine. My response lodged somewhere between my chest and throat, so I settled with a nod. I had a distinct feeling I was in for quite a ride.

Chapter Thirteen

The Hunt

It wasn't long before the hunting party divided into smaller groups. A handful of nobles headed in one direction with the duke while Lord Kent, Wesley, Lady Kent, and I left the trail we'd been following to weave deeper into the dense forest. Snapping twigs and huffing horses provided little distraction from the red-inked letter. I appreciated our forced silence. It meant not having to endure Lady Kent's rude jabs while giving me time to sort out the questions buzzing in my head.

Whoever planted that letter had to be a member of the hunting party—narrowing down my search considerably. But who?

After at least an hour of travel through the untamed forest, the ground sloped into a gully, giving us a rare break in the trees and view of the opposite ridge. Lord Kent held up his fist, signaling for us to stop, then pointed toward the ridge in the distance where a herd of deer dropped down into the gully. The enormous antlers of the lead stag marked a prize I knew we wouldn't pass up. "You take the left, blacksmith. Drive them in and I'll take the right," said Lord Kent.

Before I had time to ask about my role in this plan, Lord Kent and Wesley took off with Lady Kent right behind. My "tame" mare reared, catching me by surprise before she exploded into a run and I was thrown backward. I landed hard, my breath stolen. Struggling to inhale, all I could to do was look up at the boughs of firs and listen while racing hooves sounded in the distance.

I rolled onto my stomach to find my horse gone and every muscle in my body aching. Dropping my head into my arms, I closed my eyes and caught my breath. Any moment, the thunder of pounding hooves would signal the return of Wesley and the Kent twins. I needed the time to steal my composure and lock away my shame.

I slowly climbed to my feet with no sign of the others. Looking around for a trail to lead me out of the woods, I found nothing—not even a game trail—on the pine needle laden forest floor. My only option was to follow our tracks back to the meadow where the other ladies waited.

After a few minutes of walking, a dense fog settled over the forest. The clouds had turned gray and thick, blocking the sun— my preferred navigational resource. The ground turned rocky, the tracks harder and harder to see.

I don't remember this. The whispered thought caressed my conscience, beckoning my attention. Turning to search the woods behind me, I hoped for some familiar landmark.

This is the wrong direction.

The fortress is this way.

I should definitely head this way.

I took a few steps in the opposite direction and froze. Had I just imagined the subtle and sporadic dents in the hard ground? Were they really horse tracks?

Cold kissed my fingertips, working its way up my arms until I shivered. Were these thoughts even my own?

Sit and wait. Someone will find me.

I should sit.

The whispers came just as those from the barn and again on the mountain. Illogical and each in a slightly different tone than my usual thoughts. They tumbled over each other in a rush, shattering all confidence.

Refusing to give power to my fears, I finally found a stream and followed it, trusting it would at least keep me from walking circles. Though my body ached, I knew the others would be concerned, and didn't want to cause anyone worry. After all, I wasn't some green girl afraid of the forest. I was a Fields and practically raised in the out-of-doors.

Hours passed, leaving no doubt I'd been walking in the wrong direction.

I cursed every curse I knew while tying the skirt of my dress in a knot. Pine trees were lousy for climbing, but I found a tall birch and set to work. Normally I enjoyed a good climb—much to my father's chagrin—but after being thrown from a horse for the second time in only a few weeks and walking for hours, my legs and arms trembled from fatigue. Bark cut my palms. Branches swayed under my weight. The sky turned indigo in the waning light of day as the fog thinned. It was still thick enough that my hopes of escaping the forest receded with the setting sun.

Lord Kent would have realized I wasn't behind him shortly after I fell, right? He'd tell his father and they would send out a search party. Wesley would likely blame me for getting myself lost. I could almost see his angry face in the warped bark of the tree.

I secured a footing and pushed up to grab a higher branch when an arrow struck the tree just inches above my head. I fell back, arms flailing for a moment that seemed to last a lifetime, then caught hold of the trunk again. Another arrow struck, practically splitting the first. The archer had skill.

"Who's there?" I shouted. It was getting dark. Perhaps the archer mistook me for an animal. "I'm lost and in need of help!"

Another arrow whistled through the air, connecting in the exact place my hand had been only moments before.

I hated bullies. I'd been teased enough in my childhood to know the only way to confront an enemy was head on. "Clearly you can hit me if you wanted. Take your shot or leave!" My voice sounded a lot stronger than I really felt.

When no more arrows flew, I scrunched into a ball and climbed to the other side of the tree trunk. With my body pressed to the tree and the air completely absent from my lungs, panic finally took its hold over my body. My muscles screamed from the building tension. I should've been looking, trying to spot my attacker through the fog so I could keep the trunk of the tree between us. But my limbs wouldn't obey. My eyes wouldn't even open. A bird frozen in its perch.

The night sky turned a deep gray as twilight set in to full dark and I refused to climb down the tree. Finding a thick fork of branches, I settled in for a long, cold night and waited for the sun to rise. Every now and then I startled awake, terrified that I was falling. A family of owls sang like ghosts around me. Wind in the trees whistled, bringing a chill that pierced my skin and settled deep into my bones.

When dawn finally came, delirious tears of relief streaked my face. The fog had lifted and I spotted the fortress in the distance. It couldn't have been five miles away. I knew where I was. Now all I needed was the courage and strength to climb down the tree.

I made slow progress. Climbing up was always easier than climbing down. Especially when one worried about being hunted like a tree squirrel.

The pounding of horse hooves sounded in the distance accompanied by a faint shout. Through the thick foliage of the forest, I spotted two horses and riders. I didn't move, didn't dare breathe. Was the archer from last night back to finish me off?

"Ebby!" The call came and my fears dissolved. I'd know that raspy voice anywhere.

I hurried down another few branches. "Here," I croaked. "I'm right here!"

He spotted me sitting on a low tree branch and kicked his horse into a sprint. He hadn't fully come to a halt before leaping from the horse.

I practically fell into Wesley's outstretched arms. He set me on the ground but I was so relieved to see him that I couldn't let him go. Whatever energy I had left went into wrapping my arms around his middle and burrowing my head in his firm chest. The warmth of his body burned my arms and cheeks, reminding me of the safety of home. I choked back a sob, realizing just how badly I missed my father and Gavin.

"It's all right." Wesley moved his hands up and down my back to fight off the chill. His lips pressed against the top of my head. "When you weren't there…" He cleared his throat. "The fog was so thick we couldn't find any tracks. Lady Kent joined in the search this morning. She's actually the one who spotted you."

"So glad you're all right, Miss Fields." Lady Kent looked ready to yawn from indifference.

I jerked out of Wesley's arms and smoothed down my rumpled skirts. "Sorry." Heat rushed to my cheeks despite the cold. "I didn't see you, Lady Kent."

I couldn't help glancing down at Wesley's waist to make sure he wasn't wearing a certain yellow sash. Wesley wore his same tunic from the day before, but no sash.

"Don't be shy, Miss Fields," said Lady Kent. "You've been through quite the ordeal, and I know Wesley is much like a brother to you." Were Lady Kent and Wesley already on a first name basis?

"What happened?" said Wesley.

"I… I—" I looked up the tree at the arrows lodged in the trunk then back at Wesley. *I should tell him. Everything.* But not with Lady Kent present. "My horse threw me. I couldn't find my way and climbed the tree hoping to get a view of the fortress but the fog was too thick, and then night came on."

Wesley looked haggard. He ruffled my hair. "You're never allowed to ride a horse again."

Lady Kent's brow furrowed and she turned away.

"Let's get you back," Wesley said. He swung his leg over his saddle and with one arm, hoisted me up to sit behind him.

"I'm never allowed to ride a horse again?" I teased, speaking more from shock than anything else.

"Bite your tongue and hold on."

CHAPTER FOURTEEN

THE DUCHESS OF BRENNAN

I spent two days in my rooms. I didn't need that much time to recover from my night in the woods, but I wasn't going to tell Madam Hold that. Lord Kent came to see me the first day but couldn't stay long as he was needed to help greet the late-arriving dignitaries arriving at the fortress for the festival.

On the second night, Marta left my silver dinner tray piled with more food than I could ever eat at the tea table and wished me a timid "good night."

I instantly went to retrieve the journal I'd uncovered in the duke's library. Over the last day, the entries I'd read reported mostly the mundane chores of a duke's scribe. There had been no further mention of the farm girl named Charlotte. Still, I knew there had to be a reason the pull led me to this particular book, and I was determined to discover it.

I brought the book to the table—planning to read while I ate—when a knock sounded at the door.

Jumping to my feet, the words of the red message charged to the forefront of my mind. *Go home.* The sound of an arrow *thumping* into the tree inches from my face rang in my memory.

I tucked the journal back under my mattress and crept to the door. "Who is it?" my voice shook, despite my efforts at bravery.

"Only the best of Freeland!" Isa's boisterous voice sounded on the other side of the door, and I quickly opened it.

Wesley, Stock, and Isa, my brother's closest friends, smiled down at me through the doorway, and all the shadows of the room suddenly vanished. *If someone meant to harm me, they certainly wouldn't knock first,* I chided myself.

Isa held a deck of cards in one hand.

"This is hardly my father's barn, boys," I said, pointing at the deck.

Wesley glanced down both directions of the corridor. "Do either of you see any boys about?"

Isa didn't hesitate. "Only us manly men types. Definitely no boys."

I rolled my eyes and gestured for them to enter with a sweep of my hand.

"Do you ever wonder how you managed to become friends with this lot?" I asked Stock in a conspicuous whisper.

"Daily," he rumbled. Leave it to Stock to say more with one word than Isa with ten.

They seated themselves around my tea table and Isa immediately went to work on my food tray.

"So," I said, looking down at the cards in Isa's hands. "Why are you really here? There must be a hundred places to play cards in the fortress. In fact, your own rooms come to mind."

Wesley cleared his throat. "We just wanted to check on you. When you weren't at dinner again tonight…" He frowned. "I, *we,* just wanted to make sure you are all right."

Stock and Isa exchanged a knowing glance.

I hadn't yet confessed what really happened during my night in the tree. For a moment, I considered speaking to Lord Kent about the strange message but didn't know how to broach the subject. My stomach had squirmed at the thought.

Stock took the deck from Isa and began shuffling with masterful skill. I had a feeling the big man felt more comfortable with his hands busy.

"Can I ask you all something?" I said, walking over to sit on the end of my bed a few feet from them.

"Of course," said Wesley. He looked up from arranging his hand of cards. The sun had set, forcing us to rely only on the light provided by the candles lit around my room. Wesley's features seemed darker than normal, his brown hair closer to black, his eyes deep and fathomless.

"Do you think we're welcome here?"

Wesley set down his cards. Isa, whose back was to me, turned. Stock folded his large arms across his chest. All looked at me, waiting. Somehow knowing I had news.

"What happened, Ebby?" Wesley finally said.

"It's probably nothing." I fidgeted. "Just a letter I received."

The chair scraped against the marble when Wesley stood. "Where? When?"

"I found it in my riding glove at the picnic." I went to the writing desk and pulled the red-penned message from the drawer. Even now, seeing the tight script sent a chill up my spine.

Wesley took the small, folded card from me and frowned. "Strange." He threw it on the table and Stock and Isa leaned in to read it.

"I thought it was just a rude jab against Freeland, until I was alone in the woods."

I told them about the arrows and my terrifying night in the tree. All three were white-faced by the time I finished telling my story.

"Someone tried to kill you!" Isa exclaimed.

"Not kill. Frighten," said Stock. "It sounds to me like who-ever was behind the bow had the skill to kill but lacked the intention."

Wesley hadn't spoken. He just sat there, his face pale and his thoughts his own.

"I thought about telling Lord Kent, but if someone's just toying with me, with us, I don't want to give them the satisfaction of knowing they got to me."

"You have to tell someone," Wesley said, finally waking from his shock.

I leveled my gaze at him. "I just did. And I already feel much better. But let's leave it there."

A couple of seconds passed in silence. Then Stock said, "I agree with Ebby."

The boys settled in for a game of cards that no one seemed eager to play. Wesley kept looking over at me, his grimace deepening and his worry apparent.

They left after several half-hearted games with absolutely no crude stories and without Wesley threatening to end Isa's life. I much preferred these games when they thought they were alone. Wesley turned back to me before closing the door behind him, his face a cold mask. "Lock this."

"Of course," I said.

"And you'll let me know if anything else happens?"

"Careful, Wes. You sound like you care about me."

He wrinkled his nose. "Let's not get ahead of ourselves, Miss Fields." He couldn't quite suppress a smile before shutting the door.

I TOOK MY morning meal by the open window in my room overlooking the courtyard. A light mist carried the cool air and warm scents of roasting almonds and chestnuts from the festival below up to my window. Some stalls were still being constructed, but most of the traders and craftsman were busying about the courtyard, displaying their wares in preparation for a crowd.

I glanced at the door of my chamber and pulled the pocket-sized leather-bound volume from under my skirts.

August 30th

I sneak away from the fortress whenever I can manage it, always finding an excuse to visit Charlotte's family farm. I used to spend the ride contemplating how best to break off our attachments, convinced this would be the last time I came to see her. Now I don't bother lying to myself.

She waits by a willow tree on Saturday mornings with a basket of fruit, warm bread, and preserves. I rest my head in her lap as she runs her fingers through my hair, talking about clouds and weather patterns, how the right amount of sun and rain can work miracles in the fields.

I write her bad poetry using every over-used line I can re-call. She often laughs as I recite the sappy prose, never truly believing I, a nobleman's son, can feel such passion for a farmer's daughter.

Heaven forgive me, but I do.

Two solid knocks sounded on my door and the book toppled to the floor. I scooped it up just as the door flew open and Madam Hold entered. The stout woman didn't seem to have time for smiles, but she hurriedly gave me one anyway.

"I see Marta has been here already."

My maid had come earlier with a pink gown draped over her arm and a face too sweet for me to anticipate the discomfort I'd received by her hands. I'd worn a corset before, but never anything compared to the whalebone torture device she'd laced me into. The "day dress," as Marta called it, had a square neckline trimmed in ribbon and sleeves that hugged my arms to the elbow before draping nearly to the floor. I didn't know why they called it a day dress. It was certainly not a dress I would have worn to do my daily chores back home.

Marta had also applied rouge to my cheeks, a touch of paint to my lips, and lined my eyes in charcoal. My hair was pulled up into a twist of curls.

Madam Hold looked over my appearance and gave a curt nod, as if I'd passed some sort of test. "Her Grace is anxious to meet with you before you enjoy the festival this morning with Lord Kent."

We walked along the three terraces overlooking the square courtyard. Each hall held countless arched windows supported by columns of stone. Even in my ridiculous dress, I felt small next to the grandeur of the fortress. Along the perimeter of the courtyard, tradesmen and women were beginning to sell their wares to a growing crowd. Troopers warmed up, making the bustle appear more like a hurried dance than a festival.

"The fortress courtyard is open to common merchants and tradesman during the festival," said Madam Hold, noting my interest.

I wanted to walk among them, to discover the cost of a dozen candlesticks and a bundle of herbs. I wanted to compare Brennan's potatoes to Father's, and see if Hannah told the truth when she said Freeland grew the best raspberries in the Southern Provinces. So many questions needed answering!

There were secrets down there, too. Heavy secrets I could almost taste on my tongue. Secrets that niggled in that mysterious place in my stomach. The place that frightened me. How could I learn anything wearing a tightly cinched dress with beads in my hair?

"Can we walk through the courtyard?" I asked.

Madam Hold laughed, causing her ample curves to rise and fall. "The only daughter of the Governor of Freeland in that throng?" Her chins wobbled as she shook her head. "It's far too dangerous without a proper escort."

We walked on and I let my disappointment wash over me.

"Has anyone prepared you to meet the duchess of Brennan?" Madam Hold spoke over her shoulder as we walked.

"I saw her from a distance at the hunt, but I was never formally introduced." I had thought it strange that the very person who'd written to my father inviting me to Brennan hadn't bothered to elicit an introduction. If she was to teach me manners, it was a rather poor start.

Madam Hold stopped walking. Her eyebrows knit together as she sucked in a slow breath. "Lord Kent has told you nothing about her?"

I shook my head.

She led me to a stone bench and pushed me to sit. "There are a few important things you must know before entering her chamber. The duchess is a beautiful, *young* woman. She is an *intelligent* woman. You, and everyone around you, want to be like her. If you can remember those three things, you'll do just fine."

Madam Hold's fierce gray eyes seemed to shout something beyond the simple words she spoke. I'd seen the duchess and recalled a wrinkled complexion, sunken eyes, and a nose shaped like one of Wesley's smithy hooks.

I nodded slowly and we resumed our walk. Madam Hold led me away from the windowed corridor and into a different wing of the fortress. The rooms became more extravagant. I couldn't help but marvel at the lace and feathers, the shimmering draperies, and the expensive tapestries.

A grand set of pink doors stood at the end of a long corridor. An excessively handsome footman wearing a leather jerkin over a pink doublet opened the doors upon our arrival. As the heavy-looking doors swung open a thick perfume caught in my throat, making my eyes water and my nose itch. The guard took us through the doors and announced, "Madam Hold and Miss Ebrielle Fields of Freeland."

We walked along a rose-colored rug to a dais at the end of the room. I wiped my eyes from the sting of the assaulting smells so I could look upon the woman sitting in the place of importance. Her attending women all wore fluffy pink dresses, while the duchess herself wore wedding white.

"Welcome," the duchess said in a high, wispy voice that made me feel as though ants danced on the back of my neck. She raised an appraising brow at me, eyes calculating.

Curtsying deeply, I kept my gaze fixed on the floor. "Thank you, Your Grace." I stood to find her grinning, as if I were the cause of great amusement. I looked to Madam Hold for help, but she was already halfway out of the room.

"Are you the most important woman in Freeland?" the duchess asked.

I stuttered before I found my voice. "No, Your Grace."

"Are you the most beautiful?"

"No, Your Grace." That honor fell to Marianna without question.

The duchess looked at her ladies and smiled. "Tell me, dear," her voice spewed sweetness, "since you admit that you are both common and ugly, if you could be anyone else, who would you be?"

Rage crawled up my spine like a hot wind gaining momentum over the low fields of Freeland, and then I remembered Madam Hold's words. "If I could be anyone else, I would be… you, your ladyship." The lie tasted bitter on my tongue. The ladies of court went back to their sewing, disappointed and uninterested. Not the duchess. She beamed and called her guard to bring me a chair.

"I believe I like you, Miss Fields. During your stay in Brennan, you will come to my chambers every day after taking your morning meal. I have much to learn about your home in Freeland, and you have a great deal to learn about becoming a woman of influence in the Southern Provinces."

"I'm honored, my lady." I stared at the floor again, shocked to find her so different from the letter she sent my father. A true Fields would never have accepted this muffin's insults like a broken colt. My cheeks grew hot with shame, but what else could I do?

The duchess went on to explain how the rest of my education would continue, but she was interrupted by the footman's announcement of Lord Kent. The ladies seated around the duchess stood, and I belatedly joined them. Lord Kent walked with smooth steps, the heels of this boots echoing off the marble floors. It always took me a moment to adjust to his charm. He smiled at me and offered a bow to the room.

"Good day, Mother. Ladies. I've come to collect Miss Fields."

The duchess nodded, her affection for her son obvious. "Until tomorrow, Miss Fields."

I curtsied and rested my hand on Lord Kent's arm. "Thanks for the rescue," I murmured as we left the chambers.

Lord Kent laughed out loud. "That bad?"

I nodded, pleased that I'd made him laugh.

"My dear, today is the opening of the festival. You can embroider daisies with my mother another time!"

CHAPTER FIFTEEN

THE FESTIVAL OF MASTERS

All around the courtyard, banners flew carrying the varied colors of all of the Southern Provinces. Only a few white banners of Freeland flitted among the rest. In truth, the Freeland banners were not exactly white. Our original founders were practical, and likely didn't see the value in wasting dyes on things such as banners. Ours were the color of sun-bleached wool with two intersecting blue lines from corner to corner to represent the two rivers of Freeland. Our lifeblood.

"Where to?" Lord Kent gestured around the courtyard that had been divided into sections based on the craft and the various demonstrations being given. Near a Sea Port banner, the figures of two glass blowers blurred by the heat of a furnace. Across the way, a sculptor used his bare hands to mold clay. Women under a banner of Vikehand green sat before a giant loom, weaving a colorful tapestry.

"I want to see everything."

Lord Kent laughed at my excitement. We spent the after-noon with my arm in his as we walked around the courtyard admiring the displays and craftsmen. I clapped along with crowds and gushed over the new creations while he offered nods of acknowledgement and brief words of approval. Ever the diplomat.

Dark clouds stretched across the sky, thick enough that I'd bet three honeycakes it would rain before dinner. I never thought I'd get comfortable with my hand resting in the crook of a man's arm, especially someone as dashing as Lord Kent, but by the end of the afternoon, it felt as natural as letting it hang by my side. I studied him when he wasn't looking, deciding whether I dared tell him about the notes and arrows. He had the power to help me uncover this mystery, and he'd been so considerate during my travel thus far.

We wandered outside the courtyard toward four large blacksmith tents, each bearing the color of its province. As usual, when Lord Kent approached, the crowd parted for him. The sharp sound of metal striking metal vibrated in my ears before I saw the bellows and braziers of the blacksmiths.

A giant man from Vikehand struck a glowing brick of iron. As he did, orange sparks flew in every direction. His arms were even larger than Father's. A long braided beard fell to the center of his chest. I couldn't take my eyes off the thing, afraid it might catch fire as it flipped about while he worked.

"That's Derek Bringhurst," said Lord Kent. "The finest blacksmith in all the provinces."

My gaze shot to Lord Kent only to find his crystal blue eyes already fixed on me, as though searching my face for a reaction. "How do you know he's the best?" I asked casually.

Lord Kent shrugged. "Father always buys his blades from Vikehand. Their iron is stronger than any other metal he's seen."

I almost asked Lord Kent about the Purgo blade from Joe's story, but thought better of it. As kind as he was to me, I still wasn't sure how much I could trust him. The Vikehand blacksmith raised his hammer again, but must have caught sight of Lord Kent. He paused, his chest heaving from exertion, and glared at the duke's son. Lord Kent gave the slightest nod of his head and the blacksmith turned his attention back to his work.

The other blacksmiths seemed just as unnerved by Lord Kent as the giant from Vikehand. These craftsmen were supposed to be the greatest in all the provinces. If Joe's story was to be believed, one of them had to be the maker of Purgo. The only other man I might have considered was Wesley's father, were he not in the grave. Father always said Councilman Smith's talent at the forges was unequaled.

Trumpets sounded at the main gate of the fortress, and in the span of a heartbeat, the strikes of metal and shouts of merchants silenced, freezing everyone in place. Armed guards in blue livery parted the crowd riding high-stepping horses. They were followed by the exotic man I'd seen arguing with Lord Kent on the day of the hunt. He rode the same dappled grey, wearing multiple piercings along his ears with pictures painted on the bare skin of his arms and neck.

"Who is that?" I whispered to Lord Kent.

"That'll be Sir Daily, the ambassador from Sea Port."

In Freeland we often housed immigrants from Sea Port, but I'd never seen a man quite so *colorful*. I gawked at him, a million and one questions burning through me. *Why wasn't Freeland asked to send an official ambassador?*

We approached the white tent of the Freeland blacksmiths where Lady Kent greeted us with a sour smile. "What are you doing here, Theodore?" She stuck her chin out at her brother. A challenge.

"Same thing you are, Georgiana."

Her eyes widened, and she glanced at me like her brother had just given away a great secret.

"Enjoying the festival," continued Lord Kent.

Lady Kent turned her back on us, giving her attention back to the Freeland tent. She wasn't the only girl gawking at Wesley as he worked the bellows. In shirtsleeves, the muscles of his arms were bare and the tie closing his tunic had come undone, showing a portion of his chest. Wesley didn't seem to notice his female audience, but I did. If staring was a disease, there was an epidemic in Brennan.

"Tell me more about Master Moorly, your protector," asked Lord Kent.

Master Moorly walked out with another pair of swords for the display table. Wesley eyed him like a father looking after a child. Once Master Moorly set down the sword, he turned to Wesley, almost as though he awaited his next assignment. I'd never spent much time in Master Moorly's company, but it seemed strange behavior.

"Why do you want to know about him?" I said.

"I just find it curious that your father would send you to us with only an aging blacksmith for protection. If you were my responsibility, I wouldn't let you out of my sight."

I instantly prickled. "Father trusts him." I mentally dared him to contradict the governor of Freeland. Only *I* was allowed to do that.

He opened his mouth to reply but froze when a group of Brennan soldiers broke through the crowd and nearly knocked me over trying to get to the Vikehand tent. "The duke would like a word," said the lead soldier wearing Brennan red.

Derek Bringhurst, Vikehand's giant blacksmith, crossed his arms in front of his chest, mallet in hand. I wasn't the only one holding my breath to see if the man would put up a fight. Even the soldiers shuffled their feet in anticipation.

I didn't even notice Wesley at the Vikehand tent until he stepped before the guards. "What right do you have to come and disrupt our work? The duke can't..." Before he could finish, the head soldier drew a sword and pointed it at Wesley's chest. I rushed forward, but Lord Kent's hands clamped down on my shoulders, holding me back.

"Stand back, Apprentice," said the guard.

The big Vikehand blacksmith rested a hand on Wesley's shoulder, calling him off without a word. He dropped his working belt on the table with a loud clank, tossed his braided white beard over one shoulder and walked away from the soldiers, toward the Brennan fortress. A man who would not be led.

I walked back to the fortress with Lord Kent feeling flushed. First, the letter Simon accidently delivered asking after Master Moorly. Now this more forceful summons. Was it possible the duke *was* searching for the creator of the Purgo blade from Joe Wood's story? At first the thought had seemed ridiculous, but now I had to wonder.

What if Joe's story was actually true? What would the rediscovery of the Purgo mean for the rest of the provinces? For Freeland? A nervous buzz of energy settled in that place in my stomach where the pull usually resided. Simon said the duke was interviewing all the blacksmiths. If the stories surrounding the sword could be trusted, and the duke managed to replicate the blade, that would give him unprecedented power in the region. Power that might even threaten Freeland.

I needed more information. Perhaps it was time I did a little investigating of my own? It couldn't hurt.

CHAPTER SIXTEEN

FIRST DANCE

The next afternoon, Marta lit what must have been twenty beeswax tapers, giving my room a magical quality. She massaged my temples, powdered my face, and applied a smooth color to my lips before using a hot iron rod to curl my hair. Tonight was to be Freeland's official welcome to the Festival of Masters from the Brennan court. Master Moorly, Stock, Wesley, and Isa would all be formally presented.

"Is all of this necessary?" I asked. We'd already gone through my morning toilette (as Marta called it) before I reported to the duchess's chambers to start my lessons on dining etiquette. To be asked to endure the whole routine of dressing and primping twice in the same day bordered on criminal.

Marta fitted a silver circlet adorned with white stones into my hair. I wasn't used to having my blonde locks tucked and twisted on the top of my head, but I trusted Marta to make me presentable. Never giving much fuss over my appearance back home, I'd let her do her job and leave my complaints unspoken.

Marta finished my hair and cinched me back up into the womanly shape I didn't recognize. I'd enjoyed a few hours with my stays mercifully loose after another day spent with Lord Kent at the festival. The bindings restricted my movements and made breathing a chore. With each tug of the lacings, I had to wonder if that was the point; to stifle my gender and confirm our comparative physical weakness to men. The idea made me homesick for Freeland's less restrictive customs. Next came a soft pink evening dress with off the shoulder sleeves and an elaborate neckline that left little to the imagination.

"I'm sorry to complain, Marta, but this dress seems to be missing some fabric." I rested my hands over my exposed chest.

"All of your evening gowns are cut in this style, miss. It is the latest fashion of Brennan."

She tried to place a necklace with a grand stone pendant around my neck and I stopped her. I don't know how long I sat on that chair staring at my mother's necklace hanging from a corner of the vanity mirror in front of me. Long enough for Marta to shift her weight from one leg to the other. It was a simple chain and pendant, polished both by the jeweler and by the subconscious worry of my mother's fingers over the years. I pictured that stone sitting in the deepening hollow of my mother's neck as she grew thinner in what would be her final months of life. The usual flare of anger washed over me at the thought, but this time the pain of being lied to was overshadowed by the longing for something familiar. Something that was hers.

Reaching for the necklace, I paused before allowing my fingers to touch the chain. I'd run away from home the night before her death, taking to the woods to be alone to show her and Father just how angry I was at them for keeping the true nature of her illness from me. I wasn't there when she passed.

A knock sounded at my door. "May I come in?"

Marta gave me a satisfied nod before answering the door, and I lifted the necklace from its hook, securing this piece of my mother around my neck. It wasn't the grand apology I would have offered her had she been alive, and it didn't mean I wasn't deeply hurt by her decision to keep me in the dark. But when that necklace touched my skin, a portion of my bitterness fell away.

Lord Kent stepped into the room wearing a black fitted jacket and high polished boots. His light brown hair was combed to the side, his handsome face closely shaven. His blue eyes studied me, taking in every detail of my appearance. "You're stunning."

Marta approached carrying a long white cloak in her arms. Lord Kent took it from her without a word and stepped up to drape it over my shoulders. As he fastened the clasp at my neck, I reached out and fingered the soft wool of the cloak.

"It's beautiful," I said.

Lord Kent's hands left my neck and he offered me his arm. "So are you."

WE REACHED THE grand hall to find it packed with people. Thick wooden trusses arching from one end of the room to the other supported a massive vaulted ceiling. Heavy woven tapestries lined the walls and candles flickered in five giant chandeliers above our heads.

A man wearing red livery approached Lord Kent and bowed with hands tucked behind his back. "His Grace would like a word, my lord."

Lord Kent turned to me and frowned. "May I leave you in the hands of your countrymen?" He gestured to the group of Freelanders congregated in the corner of the room. I'd been so awed by the grandeur of the great hall that I hadn't even noticed them. "I'll return to claim you before dinner is announced."

"Of course," I said. *Claim me?*

He bowed and walked away, leaving me to wander over to the Freeland corner.

Master Moorly noticed my approach and received me with open arms. "It does me good to see you, dear child. You look remarkable." He kissed my hand and patted it like a doting father.

"You look Brennan," said Isa, coming up behind us.

"I don't like my new clothes," I admitted.

"Well, they like you," he said with a wink in a low voice that no one else could hear.

I rolled my eyes. "How are you all fairing?"

"I should be asking you that question, I think." A wrinkle formed between his brows. "No more letters?"

I shook my head. "No more letters. I'm more certain than ever that it was just a prank." Even as I said this, I recalled the arrows in the tree and couldn't fully believe my own dismissal. "I miss home," I sighed, "but if being here helps Freeland build ties with this rich valley then I suppose I'm where I should be."

"Good for you, Miss Fields." Master Moorly patted my hand again.

Wesley joined us and gave Isa a brotherly slap on the back. He opened his mouth to say something, but whatever it was caught on his tongue when he saw me. His smile melted into a grimace and I returned the sour look, wondering what I'd done to upset him since he didn't seem at all pleased to see me.

Warm hands brushed against my neck as the white cape was taken from my shoulders. I rested my hands on my mostly bare arms and whipped around to find Lord Kent with my cloak over his arm.

"I've startled you, Miss Fields. Please forgive me." He made a low bow then turned to the rest of the Freeland men. "They're ready for us to take our seats in the dining hall." Placing my arm on top of his, he led me to the feast.

The head table sat perpendicular to the rest of the guests. Lord Kent pulled out a chair for me near the center of the table and took his seat to my left. Wesley took the chair to my right and the rest of the Freelanders followed down the line. A servant whisked my cape away, and I wanted to call him back but didn't dare make a scene with all of Brennan staring down the long table at us.

I examined the dresses of the women around me. They were all elegant and refined, and I supposed their necklines were as low as mine. Why did my dress feel so incriminating when a roomful of women wore a similar style? I took a deep breath and forced my hands away from my bare shoulders to the table, not wanting to act childish or make a big deal out of nothing.

"I see you're wearing your mother's necklace," said Wesley.

I groaned inside. Why was Wesley looking at my chest? I casually put one hand back on my neck, fingering the chain. "Yes."

"Did Lord Kent pick out your dress?" he whispered so only I could hear.

My anger flared and I found myself gripping the cutlery before me. I pointedly turned away from Wesley, focusing instead on the sea of strangers seated at dozens of tables in the hall while mumbling one of Mother's rhymes. They were the best remedy I knew for calming.

That's when I heard them whispering.

"The situation is under control," Lord Kent murmured to his father at his left.

I set down my knife/weapon and examined a ribbon on my dress.

"I should hope so. I've given you this task, Theodore. Need I remind you that your inheritance depends upon your success?" growled the duke.

"No reminder necessary."

Lord Kent sat forward, and though he did his best to smooth the anger from his face, his neck and cheeks were still unusually red. He glanced in my direction and caught me looking. The transformation from grimace to smooth smile was startling. He leaned down to whisper in my ear. "I must say, Miss Fields, Brennan looks well on you."

Wesley choked on whatever was sliding down his obnoxious throat, but all I could think was that Lord Kent meant to distract me. He launched into a frivolous conversation involving some of his father's guests, and the dinner passed without further incident. I did my best to ignore Wesley through it all. My thoughts kept wandering back to the conversation between father and son.

What situation did Lord Kent have under control? Obviously, something important enough to threaten his inheritance.

After the mountains of food were cleared, red-jacketed servants pulled out chairs and the lure of lively music drew the elegant crowd back to the hall where a group of musicians pulled bows over strings and smart-looking couples filled the dance floor.

The Freelanders stayed in one corner, welcoming introductions from a line of dignitaries from Sea Port, Vikehand, Cyprian, a few of the lesser territories, and of course, Brennan. Men bowed over my hand and women curtseyed. I stole looks at the dance floor while repeating the same words over and over again to each noble. "So nice to meet you... Brennan is lovely... We feel so welcome..." I prayed no one would ask me for a dance.

As if he read my mind, Master Moorly joined me as the line of well-wishers thinned. Even after our travels on the mountain, I'd had very little interaction with the man. "As you know, I've been assigned to act as your chaperone, Miss Fields. Your father has decided to allow you to participate in dancing at festivities such as this while we are in Brennan, so long as I approve the man."

"Thank you, Master Moorly. But I think I'd feel more comfortable watching." I used to love sneaking up to the roof of Jacob Tailor's shop to watch the dances in Freeland. There was something almost magical about the way men and women moved together while whispering secret things in each other's ears. Like any girl my age, I used to dream of floating across the dance floor in the arms of some handsome man who adored me. Now that dancing was actually an option, I feared making a fool of myself in the arms of a strange man with all of Brennan watching. It didn't sound appealing in the slightest.

As always, Wesley didn't announce himself. He just appeared at my side, eyeing Master Moorly warily as he spoke to me. "I'm surprised, Ebby. I thought you'd be excited for your first dance."

"I don't know anyone besides Lord Kent, and he's already dancing. Besides, I'm supposed to dance with my father or brother for my first official dance." Like an unwelcome guest, the memory of the night of the flood filled my mind.

Standing alone in the square.

Lanterns swaying above me in the breeze.

The panic I'd produced by not completing a simple task.

My mother's blue dress, ruined.

My shame at being sent away.

It might have been just a silly tradition to some, but I'd always looked forward to the rite of passage of being led out by my father for the first time.

"So, you'll refuse every man tonight?" Wesley asked.

I frowned. I hadn't really thought about it, but dancing didn't feel right at the moment. Of course, this evening was meant as my official welcome. What if my refusal to dance caused offense? "I suppose not, but who would ask me besides one of our company?"

Wesley mumbled something I didn't catch.

"My tongs." Master Moorly spoke abruptly, patting his waist as if searching a non-existent apron. "I've misplaced them again." He looked to Wesley, who stepped near the man and whispered, "They're at the pavilion, Master Moorly. I checked before we left."

The older man's confused expression didn't quite clear, but he nodded anyway.

Wesley's cheeks reddened. He cleared his throat and turned back to me as though the interruption hadn't happened. "I think you'll be surprised at the number of men who like dancing."

I paused before answering, looking between master and apprentice, sensing by the nervous shift of Wesley's feet that he didn't want to discuss the odd exchange. "I suppose we'll see."

Turning back to the dance floor, I was suddenly aware of every male in the room. Whenever a man walked in my direction, even if he stood across the great hall, I held my breath and willed him to turn before finding me. Shifting a few casual steps to side, I positioned myself safely behind the wall of Freeland men.

I didn't notice the short, middle-aged man until he side-stepped my guard and approached me with a broad grin.

So, this was to be my first dance, this stranger with short legs and long teeth.

"Miss Fields?"

Why was he whispering?

"A friend of mine said to find you."

"I think you must be mistaking me for someone else."

"*Jeffery*," he leaned in closer so no one else could hear, "asked that you meet him tomorrow evening outside the fortress. He said he's telling a new story." He paused then added, "A very important story that you must hear."

Before I could respond, Wesley stepped to my side.

"May I have the next dance?" the balding stranger asked, no longer bothering to whisper. His hand was out-stretched, his gaze expectant.

"I... I..." The truth was, I didn't trust this man, even though Joe Ford sent him. The idea of holding his hand for my first dance made me cringe.

"The lady agreed to stand with me next. Isn't that right, Miss Fields?" said Wesley.

My head whipped up to meet his uncertain gaze. There was no question that Wesley was trying to save me. But why?

"I believe I did." I turned to the strange messenger. "But thank you, sir." He frowned, bowed, and walked away.

"Wes—"

"I know I'm not Gavin or your father, and you'd probably rather hold hands with a slug, but—"

I rested my hand on his chest to silence him. He looked down at my hand, and I quickly pulled it away. "Wesley Smith, you're not my brother, but as long as you're not hiding treacle up your sleeve or a spider in your fist, you're the next best thing."

He laughed and offered me his hand. I rested mine on top of his and he gripped my fingers as he led me out toward the crowd of couples. All I could think about was Joe and his cryptic messenger. That was, of course, until Wesley placed his warm hand at my waist.

I stared at him for a moment, confused. Unlike my dancing lesson the day before my birthday, Wesley wasn't standing with me at my father's request to fill in for Gavin. Yes, he'd only asked me out of a sense of obligation, but standing with him now felt legitimate. Real.

The music started, and Wesley spoke out of the corner of his mouth. "Take my shoulder, Ebby."

"Oh!" I reached up and took his broad shoulder. Would I never be used to the mound of hard muscle he'd earned from his time in the forges? Wesley didn't laugh or make fun when I stepped the wrong way. He just tightened his hold and led on, even though his experience in dancing wasn't much greater than my own.

There were a great many things I wanted to ask him: What did the duke want from Master Moorly the first day we arrived? Why had Wesley defended the blacksmith from Vikehand? How did Brennan smithies compare to our own? How was he enjoying the festival so far?

I would have asked him these questions, but I was suddenly too shy. I assumed it was the unfamiliar way he held me as we moved. His focused gaze. The heat from his hand that permeated the fabric of my dress. His charcoal and silver eyes swirling with the light of the room. Whatever the cause, my cheeks warmed as he led me through the steps.

I danced with several other men that night, including Lord Kent, but no dance was as confusing as my dance with Wesley.

CHAPTER SEVENTEEN

THE TALK ABOUT

After dinner the following night, Lord Kent escorted me to the library where various game tables had been set up to amuse the many guests of the fortress. He'd spent the evening practically glued to my side. Wherever I went, whatever conversation I was drawn into, he made his presence known. I couldn't decide if he gave me such attention because he felt protective, or because he genuinely enjoyed my company.

Either way, he smelled of cedar and he was more than pleasant to look at.

A man cleared his throat beside us, and I nearly jumped out of my slippers.

"Excuse me." Tattoos peeked out of the collar of the man's tunic. What little skin I saw that wasn't marked by swirling lines and shapes was tan and a bit weathered. I recognized him instantly as the Sea Port ambassador that Lord Kent had argued with the day of the hunt. The hoop earrings he wore swayed with the motion of his bow. "I wondered if I might beg an introduction from you, Lord Kent. I met this child years ago, but I'm afraid she will not remember me. Her father and I are old acquaintances."

Lord Kent straightened, and with some effort, masked his annoyance at being interrupted. "Miss Fields, may I present Sir Kilsome Daily, the new Sea Port ambassador."

"You know my father?" I asked, breaking etiquette. Father had never left Freeland, and I'd remember a face like Kilsome Daily's.

"Actually," the Sea Port man twirled one of the rings on his finger, "you and I were good friends when you were about two years old. I was a guest in your home. You used to crawl up on my lap and yank on my earrings."

"You're joking!" I covered my mouth for speaking too loudly, drawing the judgmental glares of others around the vast library. I ducked my head a little. "Forgive me, but how remarkable!"

Mr. Daily threw back his head and barked a laugh. "Don't censor yourself for my benefit, Miss Fields. You sound just like your father."

Funny. I'd never heard Father do or say anything out of order.

"He and I were lads together. Shared the same mind on many of the issues facing the provinces. Freeland's lucky to have him as governor. He's the type of man people want to follow. You have big shoes to fill, Miss Fields. I expect great things from you."

You and everyone else.

FIRELIGHT FLICKERED AROUND the white walls of my room as I sat on my bed. Marta had built up the fire, braided down my hair, and helped me shed my fancy Brennan gown before excusing herself for the night.

I couldn't get Joe Ford's message out of my head. He'd said it was urgent I meet with him. Even though I knew it was insane to leave the protection of the fortress at this time of night, how could I simply ignore Joe's request?

I *wanted* to trust him. And that was almost as good as actually doing so. *Right?* I snorted at my own idiocy. How could I even entertain the idea!

Leaning over to blow out my candle, I paused thinking about the stranger in the woods who'd threatened me. The voices in my head that seemed to lead me into danger at every turn. Joe was likely the only person in all of Brennan who might believe me when I admitted my suspicions of being possessed by spirits.

I could blow out the candle and close my eyes to my problems, or I could find out what Joe had to say and perhaps get some answers.

The next thing I knew, I was standing in front of my wardrobe, pulling out the gray woolen dress I'd traveled in while crossing the mountain. I donned a cloak and gloves and pulled the hood over my head to hide my bright yellow hair.

I forced myself to stop. Curious, I placed my hand to my abdomen and closed my eyes.

Should I go?

The heat in my stomach flared to the point of discomfort. I gasped, jumping backward, knocking my head on the foot of the poster bed. In my mind, I knew what I needed to do and even where I planned to go, but could I really trust this… phantom impulse?

I shivered at the thought as I peered inside the looking glass above the room's vanity. Instead of the governor's daughter, I saw a common vagrant. In Freeland I'd always gone to great lengths to listen to Joe's stories, but never had I attempted something so reckless as this. Father would be furious if he could see me now! I paused with my hand at the door, the gentle brush of the wind at the window mingled with my own beating heart.

Was I just being foolish? Things had gone well here, for the most part. Did I really want to jeopardize that?

Suddenly, the needle-like pull demanded I leave this room, coming on in such a violent wave that my knees buckled. I thought of Joe's messenger at the ball, the urgency on his face as he tried to convince me to meet "Jeffery" tonight.

There were just too many questions that needed answering. And my gut told me Joe Ford might be able to help. I played with my mother's necklace, chewing on my lower lip. *Sorry, Father.* I swallowed down the fear that was rising in my chest—fear of the night ahead, fear that I was losing my mind and body to this strange urge—and unlatched the door.

Though I had been ready for bed, the rest of the fortress was very much alive with dignitaries from Vikehand, Cyprian, and Sea Port roaming the corridors of the vast fortress. Laughter spilled from rooms. Light glowed beneath the doorways. Guards leaned heavily on spears as they chatted with each other. When I reached the main foyer, I heard a familiar voice.

"Right this way, sir." Wesley guided a confused looking Master Moorly toward the west wing corridor.

"Are you quite sure this is the way?" said Master Moorly, his brows pinched. "I have no memory of this passage."

Wesley took the older man's arm and guided him on, despite Master Moorly's objections. "You must trust me in these matters, sir."

Master Moorly looked weary and somehow older in the low light. He nodded. "I do trust you, my boy. It's just…"

They walked out of my range of hearing, down the corridor that led to Wesley's and Master Moorly's chambers.

That was strange.

I didn't have time to think about the odd exchange, and instead took advantage of the empty foyer. I bolted through the door and down the steps of the fortress. Keeping to the shadows along the inside wall of the courtyard, I didn't stop running until

I crossed under the portcullis. "Gate closes at midnight!" one of the guards shouted.

I turned back and offered a wave, not daring to give myself away with a Freeland accent. Joe wasn't waiting just outside of the fortress wall. *What had he called that place, that storyteller's den?*

I considered turning back and taking my chances with asking the guard directions when a heavy hand fell on my shoulder. Another cupped my mouth before I could scream. "I'm a friend, Miss Fields," said a voice I recognized from last night at the banquet. "I can take you to the Talk About if you like."

That's what it's called! Some of the tension in my gut lessened.

I nodded, and he released me without another word. I followed Joe's short messenger through narrow alleyways and behind shops and homes. We turned and climbed and backtracked until my legs felt like they might fall off. The whole way I second-guessed my decision to come. But the pull in my gut persisted, and I knew I needed to trust it.

When we finally reached an unmarked red door, a sense of relief washed over me as the pull relaxed. I had no prayer of finding my way back on my own and that I was at the mercy of Joe and his friends, but at least I could inhale a full breath of air again.

The short stranger knocked three quick raps on the red door, paused, and then knocked three times slowly. After a minute, a heavy bolt dragged along the backside of the door. It inched open, but there was no one there to answer it.

"This way, miss," said the short stranger. I looked behind me, judging my chances of escaping him when he clamped his hand around my wrist and yanked me inside. The hood of my cloak fell back and a light shown in my eyes, blinding me. Several people in the room gasped.

"That's Freeland's most prized daughter you're tugging around, Stewie," said Joe. "I've met the girl's father and trust me, you don't want to misuse her."

The short man I'd been following released my hand and muttered a quick apology, then disappeared into the crowd. The rest of the men dispersed with a wave of Joe's hand. "You came." He seemed impressed.

"You said it was urgent."

He nodded then gestured for me to follow.

The room was actually a well-hidden tavern with a bar along the wall and groups of dusty tables and chairs scattered about the place. Men drank and whispered to each other in small groups. They wore rough clothing, weapons at their belts, and baldrics across their chests. Many stared at us with open curiosity as we passed.

"What is this place?" I asked.

"Welcome to the Talk About." He pulled a red curtain aside to reveal a private table. "A place where we minstrels swap stories and gather information."

I slid into a weathered chair as Joe closed the curtain separating our table from the rest of the tavern and took the seat opposite me. A lone candle flickered between us.

"Why are you so secretive about this place?" I asked. "Storytelling isn't illegal."

Joe leaned forward. "Now that, Miss Fields, depends on the story."

I scrunched my nose. Every story I'd heard Joe tell had something to do with magic or mythical creatures. Why would the duke of Brennan feel threatened by a bunch of make-believe?

"I invited you here tonight because I owe you a favor, and I have a feeling you're going to need my help in the coming weeks. Otherwise, I would not take such a risk. And while I think your province a little too in love with manual labor," he smiled a crooked sort of smile, "I was treated fairly there. Like an equal."

Joe had been assigned to work in the timberyard while in Freeland because he had no trade of his own and storytelling didn't put food in a man's belly.

"What is it you want to tell me?"

"Do you remember the last story I told before your pa almost discovered me in the fields?"

A tingling sensation ran the length of my back. "The famous blacksmith and sword?"

Joe nodded and leaned closer to whisper. "Since the Freeland Company arrived, there have been rumors that someone is interested in selling a Purgo blade in one of the underground markets."

"But I thought that was just a story."

He solemnly shook his head. "Almost every story comes from a point of fact, my dear."

I screwed up my lips, trying to remember the details of Joe's tale. It wasn't like me to forget a story, but so much had happened since my father found me hanging from that tree. "Why is this sword so special again?"

Joe looked at the ceiling and sighed. "It is *only* the stuff of legend! An exact replica of one of the One Hundred swords lost after the great rebellion from the emperor Rsham. Not to mention the missing piece to the duke of Brennan's plan to," he leaned forward and whispered, "take over all of the Southern Provinces."

I frowned. Joe was blurring his stories with reality. Perhaps he'd drunk too many tankards of ale tonight. It certainly smelled on his breath. Besides, what would a storyteller know about the duke's plans? "Isn't a sword a sword? You said the One Hundred swords were made out of a special metal, but swords are just one weapon in warfare. What makes the Purgo so special? Is it extra sharp or something?"

Joe let his jaw hang open a bit. He mouthed the words *extra sharp* like I was the crazy one in this conversation, not him. "Miss Fields, the Purgo is said to be made of the strongest metal known to man. At least ten times stronger than the iron swords your average smithy produces. The blade keeps its edge through days of fighting—the metal so pure it practically glows in the moonlight." He rested his long arms on the table separating them and clasped his hands. "The blade is stronger than armor, Miss Fields. Virtually unstoppable. And as far as we know, only one man in the world knows how to craft it."

I shook my head. "What does that have to do with me?"

"While the Festival of Masters used to be a way to bring about cooperation and friendship among the provinces' craftsmen, the past few years the duke of Brennan has used it as a cover to root out the blacksmith who produces the blade. He's been desperate to find the man ever since the rumors of a new master started popping up about three years ago. Then, within a day of your arrival, someone's shopping the Purgo. Looking for a high bidder. And with dignitaries in town from every province in the region, there's a lot of money to be made on the sale. After all of the duke's efforts to find the sword maker at the festival, the first one attended by Freeland produces the blade. Follow my meaning?"

"But the only full blacksmith in our company is Master Moorly." I had a difficult time picturing the old man as the keeper of such a secret.

Joe sat stock still for a moment before standing abruptly and pulling the curtain away. "I've another meeting with a friend from Vikehand, and you need to return before the gate closes for the night. Come. I'll walk you back."

"That's it?" I cried. "But what should I do?" A few heads turned in my direction and I pulled the curtain back to cover us.

"I'd warn Master Moorly. If he's the one who created that signature blade, he ought to lie low if he ever wants to see Freeland again."

"But Master Moorly is a Freeland Councilman. The duke can't force him to stay! My father would see that as an act of war."

Joe gave me a shrewd look and led me out of the dim-lit tavern and into the crisp autumn night air. I followed him through the twists and turns of the city. A million and one questions rested on my tongue. When the gates of the fortress came into view, he said, "Your father would do well not to get between the duke and his prize. Brennan is known for eliminating leaders who threaten its cause. It's a favorite hobby of His Grace."

"But—"

"Warn Moorly, Miss Fields. I'll be in touch."

As his back retreated into the shadows, I realized I hadn't had a chance to even mention the pull or evil spirits.

CHAPTER EIGHTEEN

SECRETS

The torches lining the corridor of the west wing casted moving shadows across the old stone walls. Water dripped from a spot in the ceiling and night-loving creatures occasionally scurried by my feet.

"Are you sure this is the way to Wesley's quarters?" I asked Marta. I'd had the good fortune of bumping into her while sneaking back to my room through the servants' quarters. When I asked her to help me, she wrung her hands together for a solid minute before agreeing to take me on this midnight tour of the fortress.

"This is the oldest wing of the fortress," she explained and stopped at a warped, wooden door, wringing her hands again. "I don't know that you should be out this late, in this part of the fortress, without a chaperone."

"Wesley is like a brother." I patted her hands. "I'll ask him to walk me back and see you in the morning."

Marta bit her lip but bobbed a curtsey. I watched her retreat into the darkness of the corridor, leaving me alone with only my candlestick to fend off the dark and dank.

Suddenly feeling ashamed of my white floors and fine draperies, I thought all the Freelanders were housed as well as I was. Wesley might have only been an apprentice, but he was still the son of a Councilman.

It was nearly midnight, but Wesley was still in his work clothes when he yanked open the door. His eyes were hooded and heavy, but widened at the sight of me. "What are you doing here?" he asked, peeking his head out into the hallway to see if I was alone. Satisfied by my lack of company, he pulled me inside and closed the door.

Alone in Wesley's private room. My father would hang us both from my favorite oak if he saw us now.

By the dim light of a lonely oil lantern, he led me to the room's only chair and held my arm until I was fully seated. It didn't seem long ago that he would have sawed off a chair's leg just to see me fall.

He crossed his arms and leaned against his bed frame and ruffled the hair on the back of his head. "What's wrong?" he asked.

"Why do you automatically assume something is wrong?"

"Why else would you be here? And let's face it, this is you we're talking about."

I rolled my eyes. "Don't be immature, Wes. I have something important to tell you."

"I'm listening."

I sighed, collecting my thoughts. "Before we left Freeland, Joe told this story about a special sword called a Purgo." I told Wesley everything I knew about the sword and how Joe had sought me out tonight. "If Master Moorly is the creator of this sword, the duke might never let him leave again. I came to warn—"

He raised a hand to cut me off. "What would your father think of your tromping unprotected through Brennan at night to listen to another one of Joe's make-believe stories? Will you never learn?"

His words stung, but I pushed forward. This wasn't about me. This was about Master Moorly. "If what Joe said is true, and Master Moorly is really making the swords—"

"He's not." Wesley refolded his arms.

"But how can you know for sure?"

"I just do!" he shouted. "Now quit prying into other people's lives. It's time to grow up, Ebby. Isn't that why your father sent you?"

I turned away from him, cheeks burning. I'd come to Wesley because I trusted him to help and wanted to protect one of my countrymen. Joe had given me this warning in payback for a favor, a favor I never would have gained had I not eavesdropped on his stories. My talents might not be completely reputable, but the pull had urged me to go to the Talk About tonight. I trusted it and I knew in my bones that I was meant to use that gift for good. All I ever wanted was to be respected by my family. I wanted them to be proud of me for who I was, strange urges and shady talents included. I wanted to be valued like the men in my life, to contribute in meaningful ways and stop feeling like a constant disgrace. Wesley knew this, knew *me*, so his words cut extra deep.

I bit my lower lip, stood, and strode to the door before throwing it open. It banged against the wall. "I'm only trying to help. You're just a... a..." Every name that came to mind pegged me at about five years old.

Not wanting to show him how badly his words injured me, I ran from the room, even though I knew it was an immature thing to do. After our dance, I thought Wesley and I might be getting past our differences. Maybe growing out of the teasing. Raising a white flag of truce to be allies here in Brennan. I was wrong.

Without noticing the scurrying creatures or the eerie dripping of water, or even the utter darkness, I ran away from Wesley and… and the truth. I slowed to a walk, thinking about Wesley's brutally honest words. What would Father think of me sticking my nose where it didn't belong? But was it so wrong to care about what was happening around me?

When I arrived at my room, I was so deep in battle with my conscience I almost didn't notice the small envelope resting on my dressing table. I studied the cramped red script with a small amount of trepidation. I recognized that handwriting… that ink.

I pulled the oil lantern from its place on the mantel and set it next to the fluffy bed. My hands shook with nerves as I pulled open the envelope and blinked. Three hurried words written in tight letters with the same red ink that marked the envelope.

You're in danger.

I shivered and turned the card over, hoping to discover some mark from the sender.

Nothing.

I stared into the black night before me, wishing I'd received this letter during the day when the sounds of birds and bustling servants could distract me from the eerie nothing awaiting my next eight hours. How could I possibly sleep knowing someone was sending me messages in the night, someone who thought I was in some sort of danger?

I mentally scanned my acquaintances, thumbing through the people I'd met since we arrived here. I knew only a handful of people well enough to have even the smallest opinion of them: Lord and Lady Kent, Marta, Simon, Madam Hold, the duke and duchess, and Mr. Daily, the ambassador of Sea Port. Why would I need to be careful with any of these people? Who would they bother deceiving me? I was just the token female of the Freeland Company. I posed no threat and served no purpose.

Setting the red-penned warning on my bedside table, I climbed into bed. My cursed mind simply would not rest. I couldn't even focus on Wesley and the way he berated me tonight. As the October wind howled at my window, I silently begged the heavens and all my ancestors that my eyes would fall heavy before my imagination turned any more shadows into haunting men writing threatening messages.

Tap, tap, tap.

I didn't mean to scream, and in my defense, the timing of the knock was less than ideal. I covered most of the scream in my down pillow. That didn't stop Wesley from practically breaking through the door. He held his light high as he took one frantic glance at me and then paced the room, as if looking for another person.

If my heart wasn't racing at fatal speeds, I could have killed him.

"Wesley Smith!" I hissed. "What in the name of all things good are you doing?" I pulled my covers to my neck to hide my dressing gown.

The truth was, I was glad to have him there, even though I was completely indecent and I was supposed to be furious with him. He approached my bed like a man approaching a hissing snake he wants removed from his garden. "Are you all right, Ebby?"

I knew it was completely juvenile, but I pulled the covers over my head. I bit down hard on my bottom lip and commanded my girlish tears to halt before they surfaced. Only when I was sure of my control did I bring the covers back down.

Wesley smiled at me, his big eyes showed all the signs of repentance. "I followed you because I'm sorry about what I said. I shouldn't have brought up your father. And I shouldn't have raised my voice at you."

I iced over, annoyed that Wesley thought my emotion was the product of his mean words. "You can say what you like, Mr. Smith. I'm used to it."

He sighed and sat at the foot of the bed. Half of me wanted to kick him and the other half wanted him to scoot closer. I wanted his comfort as much as my pride wanted nothing more than for him to leave. Pride or not, the shadows were much less threatening with him in the room.

"Ebby, I *am* sorry. And to prove it, I'll give you a confession. Think of it as a peace offering."

I kept my head turned and sang one of Mother's songs in my mind to make certain enough time passed before I gave in.

"Please, Ebby." Was that a smile he was holding back? Did he really know that my resistance was so futile when a secret was on the line?

I rolled my eyes. "Fine. But it better be good."

He took a deep breath then blurted, "Master Moorly hasn't made anything in the smithy since my parents died last year. His mind is slipping. He forgets things. Gets confused. Forgets people. Coming to Brennan seems to have made it worse."

"How is that possible?" I had noticed a few memory lapses, but surely my father knew of his health. He had assigned him to be my protector, after all.

Wesley's face turned a bit red. "Master Moorly was one of my dad's best friends. My guardian. Being a blacksmith was his life. He doesn't have anything else."

"So you help him." Realization dawned. "You've been working under his name this past year. Helping him save face."

Wesley nodded sheepishly. "Half the time he doesn't remember how to hold a pair of tongs. It's been hard." His voice grew thick. He picked at the black soot that filled the creases of his hands.

"I didn't know."

"That's why I know he didn't create the blade the duke is after, Ebby." His jaw clenched and there was a spark of fire in his eyes again. "Can you keep my secret?"

I didn't see why Wesley was so concerned about people knowing he was doing this kindness for Master Moorly. It seemed like a heavy burden to carry on his own. I rested my hand on top of his, sealing our pact. "Of course I'll keep your secret."

He nodded, the full force of his smile lightening his face, and then his eyes settled on the open note on the bedside table. The candle burning beside it gave eerie life to the frightening words.

"What is this?" Wesley snatched up the note before I had a chance to stop him. He sucked in a sharp breath. "When did you get it?"

He looked at me with a more critical eye. "That's why you were so frightened when I came in, isn't it?" He scooted closer to me, reaching out but hesitating to see if I would let him comfort me. "Ebby, I'm so sorry."

It wasn't the pull that compelled me this time. I looked into his deep eyes and something in me shifted. No, that wasn't right. Something that had always been present awoke and no amount of logic or reasoning could push it down any longer.

I cared for Wesley Smith. Not in a brotherly way. Not because he was Gavin's friend. I cared for Wesley the way crops crave rain.

I let myself lean into him, barely believing my own nerve. My head rested on his shoulder at the very moment his arm settled around me in a tender half embrace meant to provide comfort more than anything.

When he finally spoke, his voice was scratchy and deep. "When?"

"It was sitting on my dressing table when I got back from visiting your room."

Wesley slowly released me and gained his feet. I could practically see the wheels turning inside his head as he began to pace the room. I couldn't tell if he was talking to me or to himself, but a stream of words came out just the same. "Had to be someone who knew you were going out tonight. Maybe saw you leave. Red ink—rare. A warning? A threat. From whom? From what?"

The cold flagstones chilled my feet when I slid out of my bed. I padded over to Wesley and captured his arm to break his trance. "It's late, Wes. I'm tired."

He froze at my touch and looked down at my hand resting on his arm. He blinked and then looked up at me. "I'm going to fix this, Ebby."

I smiled. "I'm not your responsibility."

Head shaking, he frowned, forehead pinched in worry. "But don't you see, Ebby? Master Moorly isn't well. His responsibilities are mine, remember? Looking out for you is one of the main reasons why I came."

A responsibility.

I tried not to let the staleness of the word disappoint me. But it did explain Wesley's protectiveness during this trip. I was a duty to him. A task. Even that short connection a moment ago followed that pattern. It meant more to me than it should. More than it did to him.

"Bolt the door whenever you're in this room alone." He walked me to my door, my hand still resting on his forearm. It felt awkward there, but I didn't know how to pull it away without drawing even more attention to it.

He solved my problem by taking my hand and offering it a quick pat. "I'm sure everything will be fine."

The door closed behind him and I didn't hear the sound of his retreating footsteps until after I'd slid the lock into place.

CHAPTER NINETEEN

THE GONG FARMER

A full week passed without incident. Even when I wasn't sitting with the duchess, she constantly had me running to take tea with important members of her court or picnicking in the greenhouse with a gaggle of ladies I didn't care to know. I had dance lessons, music lessons, and even had to practice table manners with Madam Hold. Between the duchess and her son, I had very few minutes to myself.

Sitting in my room one afternoon, I picked up the journal I'd stolen from the duke's library to wind down from an exhausting lesson in elocution.

February 27th

Charlotte didn't come to the tree last Saturday. I waited for hours under the willow, detailing a list of reasonable excuses for her absence. At dusk I had no choice but to sulk back to the fortress. I've spent the whole week anticipating our next meeting, but something is wrong. I can sense it, as though a dark cloud approaches. I'd send her a letter, but she doesn't read, and I dare not risk getting her into trouble with her father.

I wonder if she would let me teach her to read.

February 28th

The duke keeps me busy with more tasks than usual, moving his political chess pieces about the province with my quill and inkwell. The boring words tend to blur together as I work: marriage licenses, nobility patents, land titles.

Today had been no different. I'd finished my assigned tasks and was depositing a stack of legal documents on the duke's desk so that he might add his signature, when a gut-wrenching pain twisted my insides and forbade me from leaving the duke's private chambers.

I've been led by the gift before. Only last year, I'd been prompted to mount my horse and take the north road while visiting my family seat. I'd found my brother thrown from a horse with his leg badly broken and in serious need of a doctor.

Today, in the duke's chambers, the urgency pulled me to a stack of scrolls. I knew them to be official communications to other provinces that would be delivered in the day's post.

I was drawn to one in particular.

Even though I'd had occasional interactions with my gift, it still amazed me how swiftly my hand landed upon a scroll bound for the province of Vikehand. I glanced over my shoulder and untied the string binding the official pages. Skimming the contents, my eyes were drawn to a list of names written in three columns near the bottom.

Charlotte's name jumped out at me, and I nearly dropped the scroll.

My eyes poured over the lines above, as my heart beat faster with every word I devoured. A number of peasant children, along with her, are to be traded as indentured servants as payment for the spring lumber shipment from Vikehand.

Before I could decide what to do, the outer door of the duke's study opened. I wrapped and tied the scroll with practiced speed, even with my hands shaking with rage. Dropping the scroll back to its stack, not knowing what else to do, I made a show of straightening my day's pages as the duke entered the room.

God forgive me, I had no choice but to bow and leave Charlotte's fate on the cursed man's desk.

I set the book into my lap and tried to calm my racing heart. This nameless author was… like me. What I'd often considered a curse, he referred to as a gift. Something he'd inherited. Something to be proud of.

I quickly read on.

March 5th

I am convinced life is nothing more than a string of choices. In the end, our intentions do not mean much, but our actions... they define us.

I stole the document sealing Charlotte's fate from the courier's own satchel. With luck, the poor lad won't know it is missing until he reaches Vikehand in two weeks. He will have to ride all the way back to Brennan and have a new copy drafted. The duke will be livid, but it buys us time.

This past Saturday Charlotte did not smile as she approached the tree with her basket. I ran to her and felt my world come into focus as she entered my embrace. Her father has taken ill and medicines aren't helping. She does not think he will last long without a miracle. I hired a physician to visit their home and see to his health.

I did not mention the duke's plans since it seemed wrong to add to her distress. However, I visited the other families whose children are included on my stolen list. It is reckless, but Charlotte would want me to. Determined to find a solution, I have arranged to meet with all the fathers (except Charlotte's) in one of the barns on the outskirts of Brennan tomorrow.

THE NEXT MORNING the duchess had to repeat her question again. "Good heavens, girl. Where is your head today?"

"Forgive me, Your Grace. I didn't sleep well last night." When my thoughts weren't consumed with Charlotte and the owner of the journal, they drifted to the mysterious red inked warnings.

Lady Kent walked into the room. Her deep purple gown rested exactly where it should, hugging her slim waist and ample curves. Her hair was all curls and ringlets with a shining silver circlet resting on top.

I found my feet just in time for the guard's introduction.

"Lady Georgiana Kent." Her name echoed off the cold stone in elegant ripples. Every lady in the hall curtsied. My gesture looked more like a stumble than anything else.

"Georgiana," said the duchess as her daughter approached us. "Do sit with us."

Lady Kent was all elegant lines as she lowered herself into the chair at her mother's side. She turned to me, her voice as smooth and enticing as it had been back at the picnic hunt. "I've spent some time this past week getting better acquainted with a few of your countrymen."

A maid handed Lady Kent a circular loom with a halfway-completed floral pattern that put my bumblebee to shame. "I'm especially impressed with your Mr. Smith."

She looked at me as if waiting for a "thank you," but what was I supposed to say? *Yes, we grow our young men with great care in Freeland. Give them lots of grains and plenty of pasture time.* A weak smile was all I could manage before turning my gaze back to my needlework.

A full hour passed. The duchess and her daughter communicated in short whispers and curt nods. They spoke of nothing beyond the weather and the bitterness of the tea. I shouldn't have been frustrated by the exchange. But I was.

If only my mother could be here, even for a moment. She wouldn't have brought me into a room filled with other people who were required to keep her company while she did absolutely-ly nothing useful. She would have put my hands to much better use, and I would have laughed and joked and even half-heartedly complained with more affection than these two showed each other.

After stealing glances at Georgiana Kent, I didn't want to admit my jealousy of her perfect skin or her full lashes. Even though I'd been raised better than to judge a person merely by looks, how could one not envy the natural way her hair framed her face or the grace with which she held herself? I found myself sitting a little taller in my chair, biting my lips to give them more pout. It was silly and stupid, but Lady Kent inspired that kind of poise. She was a true lady, the beautiful heroine of my favorite stories.

When the duchess excused me for the day, I walked back through the terrace looking down over the busy square with longing. In fact, I was so consumed with the square that I practically ran into the page boy, Simon Right, before I saw him.

"Miss Fields!" No matter how old he pretended to be, every so often Simon's true age crept to the surface. He recovered quickly from the surprise. "How is the loveliest woman in the Southern Provinces?"

I cringed under his puppy flattery. "If a person could die of boredom, I would have expired about an hour ago."

"The duchess?" he guessed.

I knew I shouldn't complain, but sometimes a person just needed to clear the air.

"What you need is a good diversion." He wiggled his eyebrows up and down in a suggestive way.

I couldn't help but laugh. "And you can offer me that?"

He put his hand to his chest and bowed. "Name your pleasure, miss."

I bit my lip and looked over the stone railing, down into the square filled with merchants and a crowd so thick you couldn't part it with a buttered knife. When I'd walked the festival with Lord Kent, we failed to reach the entire eastern row of booths.

Excited thoughts rushed through me. *The festival! So much to see! So much to learn and do!*

"The festival," I blurted, surprising even my own ears. "I want to go to the festival." My voice lifted in question at the words. I took measure of my thoughts, listening for signs of the whispers that sometimes led me into trouble, but the voices in my head had quieted, leaving only a genuine desire to attend.

Simon cocked his head to the side, no doubt trying to understand my strange reaction. Then he shrugged and said, "To the festival!" Remembering Madam Hold's warnings, I retrieved my old Freeland cloak from my rooms and pulled the hood down to hide my face.

"Anything in particular you want to see?" Simon shouted over the din of the crowded courtyard.

At home I would have done my usual rounds, passing by the tanner, tailor, cobbler, and the rest to observe the condition of things. "I want to see everything." Even as I said those words, agitation buzzed in my middle. Right in the place the pull usually resided. Was I just nervous about going into the crowded festival with only Simon as an escort? It made sense, especially considering the red-inked warnings I'd received.

"Have you ever tried a Brennan sugared bun, Miss Fields?" Simon asked.

With that one question, the decision was made for me.

Simon was the perfect guide, dodging through the crowd with practiced ease, trusting me to follow even when doing so cost me several frustrated glances from those I bowled over to keep pace with him. We passed carts of herbs and barrels of fruit and vegetables. Merchants hawked their wares while potential customers bartered. Voices blended into one overwhelming rumble, like a continuous stream of thunder. Cinnamon, basil, rosemary, and ginger root tickled my nose.

The people of Brennan looked much like those of Freeland, but there was something that set them apart. Something I couldn't quite place. Perhaps it was the deeper wrinkles lining their foreheads or the shadows beneath their eyes. Whatever it was, it made me want to keep close step behind Simon Right.

"Where do we find those sugared buns?" I turned to find that Simon wasn't beside me.

I walked through the crowd, not frantic but anxious to find my little guide. With so much happening around us, it wasn't too surprising that we'd lost each other.

I saw Joe Ford standing with his arms stretched out like a bear, snarling in a voice that carried over his small audience. He quickly switched positions to look the part of the sword-wielding knight. He jabbed at the air then jumped back from the strike of his invisible enemy. The young crowd was in rapturous awe of my friend. I smiled at Joe and he saluted me as I passed. But I still couldn't find Simon.

Halfway around the great fortress wall was a thirty-foot gap in the row of merchant carts and a smell so repugnant my eyes watered.

The man at the base of the latrine tower whistled as he worked, loading shovel after shovel of the fortress's *pleasantries* into a wheelbarrow. I had the lucky fortune of catching him as he walked his cargo to some unseen pit away from the rest of the civilized world.

I knew a higher being watched over me at all times. This was my chance to practice one of the countless lessons I'd received on goodwill and equality. "Good day, sir." I stopped and bobbed a curtsy.

The man pushing the wheelbarrow paused. He looked at me, mumbled something gruff and incoherent, and walked on.

I wasn't expecting more than a "good day" in return, but his outright contempt threw me completely off balance. For a moment, I forgot Simon and did what any sensible girl would do to a man who had slighted her: I followed him.

"Sir?" I said, slipping in some of his drippings while in pursuit.

He didn't stop, but he did turn his head.

"Sir, I think you misunderstood my gesture back there."

He carted on.

"I… I was just being friendly. I didn't mean to offend…"

When we reached his destination—a ten-foot pit half filled with waste—I had to hold my nose. He dumped his load and turned the wheelbarrow back for another trip.

I couldn't believe he wouldn't speak to me! I shrugged my shoulders. "Sorry if I caused offense." I turned to leave.

"Miss Fields," the stinky man said.

I stopped, a chill rolling up over my arms and a buzz in my gut. I took a step back toward the strange man. "How do you know my name?"

He looked around, biting the inside of his cheek as if deciding whether to answer my question. He suddenly abandoned his cart in the middle of the path and motioned me over to a quiet spot near the wall.

"You talk funny," he said.

"I talk funny?"

He shrugged. "That's how I knew it was you."

"Oh." I still couldn't believe this gong farmer even knew my name.

"I hear a lot of what goes on in the fortress, Miss Fields. People come to my side of the wall when they don't want people hearing 'em. But I hear everything, and I remember every conversation and the men who speak them."

"And someone was speaking about me?" I asked, looking around to see if anyone was watching our strange exchange.

"You're a valuable little person, Miss Fields. The only daughter of Freeland's leader." He tsked. "Lots of people talk about you."

"Oh." I wasn't sure how I felt about that.

He adjusted his cap and wiped his palms on his pants, a resigned look of sympathy on his face. "Name's Derby. Derby Hovel."

"Nice to meet you, Mr. Hovel."

"Can I give you a bit of advice, Miss Fields?" He furrowed his tufty brow. "I wouldn't wander outside the walls of the fortress unescorted, if I were you."

I swallowed, nodding when I couldn't summon my voice. He turned back to his work and left me standing alone, in the middle of the abandoned stretch of road, frightened. Why would someone speak about me in private? There were many things I didn't know about Brennan, or life in general for that matter, but there was one thing I knew for certain: I wasn't that interesting.

Simon. Where are you?

CHAPTER TWENTY

THE STREETS OF BRENNAN

Hitching up my skirts, I ran back toward the heart of the festival, my cloak billowing behind me. The unsettling buzz in my stomach had turned into violent nausea. I ran toward the front of the fortress and the rest of the market square came back to life around me. How would I ever find Simon in this crowd?

The faces all looked menacing. My vision whirled. I noticed the red of a woman's scarf, the red of a painted stall, the red-cheeked apples from a Vikehand cart—all reminding me of the warnings I'd ignored by leaving the fortress. Warnings suddenly much more threatening in this crowd of strangers.

Panic! a foreign voice in my head demanded.

But even as I felt panic take hold of me, I knew it wasn't logical. I could see the main gates of the fortress. I simply had to cut through this crowd and return on my own without Simon. He would understand.

That's when I spotted him at the other end of the courtyard. A much larger boy had him under the armpits and was dragging him out of the market square. His cries for help were lost to the thunderous crowd. I took off after them without thinking, knowing full well there was nothing I could do—with all my constricting skirts and pint-sized build—to help him.

"My friend's in trouble," I hollered to anyone who would listen. But no one paid the slightest bit of attention to me. The farther I ran from the fortress, the fewer merchant carts I encountered. Simon's shouts for help took me past the row of smithy braziers and around another corner. I sprinted to the end of the half-deserted street and halted when his shouts died. Voices traveled to my expert ears, but they didn't belong to my young friend.

"Tell me what you've heard, page. You're not the only one collecting fees for information."

Peering around the corner, I saw the bulky brute who had carried Simon off pinning him against a wall by the shoulders. The pair were surrounded by a rag-tag group of boys who appeared to be closer to my age than Simon's.

"I... I don't know anything. Was just trying to impress some friends."

The rough boy scoffed. "Liar."

Simon winced under the boy's grip.

There was a time for eavesdropping, and there was a time for action. "Take your hands off him," I shouted, running around the corner.

The group started and turned toward me, their looks of alarm turning to grins when they saw who had yelled. The shortest of the five shook a tin cup. Its contents rattled like an old snake tail Gavin and Wesley used to tease me with when we were kids.

"Where did you get the girl, *Slimon*?" said the boy holding the cup.

He had two missing teeth—one on the top left and one on the bottom right—but with his mouth closed and a good bath he might have been handsome.

"Run, Miss Fields," young Simon whispered.

"He gets a nice cozy job inside the fortress after his mommy dies, and now they give him a girl? Boys, we've got to get us a job running notes with this blue blood." He cleared some mucus from his throat and spat it at my feet.

I had a mind to ring this ugly kid's neck. He wasn't that much bigger than me, but the fear in Simon's face made me reconsider.

Often the smallest snakes can be the deadliest.

Unexpectedly, the large boy pinning Simon released him.

With face still white with either fear or lack of air, Simon walked toward me at a fast pace. "Please hurry, Miss Fields."

The group followed us around the corner, the tallest swinging two feet of rope in a menacingly casual manner. The short leader jogged alongside us and shook his cup right next to poor Simon's ear.

"Come on, *Slimon*. We can make our little bet double or nothing."

This wasn't good. They hadn't really let Simon leave. These boys were just predators playing with their food.

Three of the boys swooped in on me before I had a chance to escape.

The tall one grabbed my waist from behind and two other boys took hold of my arms. I fought against them, but my efforts were futile at best.

"Here's how it's going to go," said the short leader. "You'll roll and every time you win, we'll remove one of your debts." The boy stepped over to me with an eager grin. "But be sure to win, page boy, because every time you lose, we all get a kiss from your lady friend." He placed his hand on my cheek and rubbed it with his grimy thumb.

I jerked away, but the boy with his hands around my waist held me fast, and they all laughed.

I wanted to strangle these boys—for how they were treating me, for the look on sweet Simon's face. The poor boy was close to tears. If Madam Hold found out about this, he might lose his position. Without any family, where would he go?

At the end of the street, a boy carrying a bundle of wood passed. As I opened my mouth to call for help, he caught my eye then dropped his load and ran in the other direction. I decided then not to wait around for help that wasn't coming.

Simon took the dice with shaking fingers and rolled. I didn't know the game, but judging by the reaction of the boys, he must have done well.

"That's one down, page. You've got four more losses to make up."

Simon took the cup and chanted some wish over the lip before rolling its contents onto the cobblestone. Again, the same deflated reaction.

"Three to go, *Slimon.*"

The tall boy at my waist grew impatient. His hands slid up my sides to the base of my rib cage. It was a slow movement. One inch. Then another.

My breathing increased, and he must have noticed. He snickered in my ear. The sound was muted yet somehow lustful. He enjoyed my fear.

Again, his hands moved higher while the others focused on the game of dice. His breath reeked of old cheese and rotting egg. Simon rolled, and as everyone bent in to examine the dice, I slammed the heel of my boot down on his foot and yanked my arms from the two boys holding them. I managed to put my elbow to the nose of my hot-handed captor before the others regained their hold on my arms. The tall boy grabbed me by the middle, cursing and bleeding all over my hair and face as I struggled to free myself.

In my defense, Simon grabbed a stick from the ground and whacked a boy in the nose. With a smirk, the shortest boy kicked him in the stomach and Simon crumpled to the ground, gasping.

"It seems we have a little fighter on our hands, gentlemen," said the short leader. He pulled a rusty knife from his pocket and gently pressed the flat of the blade to my face. "You see, miss, we don't mind a good fight, especially with a pretty thing like you."

Isa Woods seemed to come from nowhere. He plowed into the group, sending me and my captors stumbling. Stock and another Freeland craftsman joined the fray, putting boys in headlocks and grabbing shirts before they could escape. Isa wrenched the largest one from me by his hair.

It was five boys against three hardened Freeland men. In under a minute, the ragtag group was being hauled to the fortress while Simon and I followed close behind.

Wesley arrived as we passed through the gate, panting like he'd sprinted a mile.

Only when I saw Wesley, with his long strides and set jaw, did I register the danger we had just evaded. My legs wobbled under my heavy skirts and my head swayed. He took me by the arm—ignoring his own righteous etiquette—and led me into the fortress behind my attackers with his hand supporting my back. Shouts erupted as we passed the courtyard.

Now they care, I thought woozily. The noise followed us up the grand staircase and through the long corridor that led to my rooms. Wesley's grip tightened with every step. By the time he released me to sit in a chair at my writing desk, my arm throbbed as blood rushed back into my thirsty fingers.

He knelt in front of me and ran his calloused fingers across my brow.

"It's not my blood."

He nodded, swallowing hard, and then his hand moved to the bracelet he wore around his wrist. The remnant of his mother's dress that wasn't burned in the fire.

The person he felt he should have been around to save.

The fabric had once been fine pink muslin but was now dingy gray and worn from a year's worth of fiddling from dirty blacksmith hands. "I just wanted to be sure." He closed his eyes and seemed to force himself to release the bracelet. The comforting smell of brazier smoke from his clothes filled my room as he paced my now muddy floor.

He turned to face me again. "Ebby." I flinched when he spoke, expecting a great deal more than the soft whisper that escaped his lips. "Why were you outside the fortress alone?"

"I wasn't alone," I started. "Simon Right was showing me the market and—"

Wesley's whisper exploded into shouts. "Why, in the name of heaven and hell, were you out in that crowd with Simon Right for protection? He's just a boy, Ebby! After those notes… You could have been—"

Wesley abruptly turned on his heel and stomped back down the corridor, leaving me reeling from the whiplash of his emotions. Without saying he was glad I was all right, he just left. In the sudden silence, I digested our confrontation. Wesley had no right to chastise me! No matter what duty he felt toward my family. Besides, we were attacked. It wasn't as if Simon and I went out looking for those foul boys. Why was I the one getting yelled at?

Wesley's shouts echoed down in the courtyard. Judging by his vibrato, someone was about to get a whole lot more than a lecture. I rushed to the window and threw back the draperies.

Wesley bullied his way to the center of a circle of men. He pushed past my attackers and went directly for Lord Kent, who must have been summoned because of the disturbance. Wesley yelled while stabbing his finger into Lord Kent's chest until guards rushed to restrain him.

Before they even reached him, Wesley released Lord Kent and stalked back to the main entrance of the fortress, likely to cool his temper in his room.

I melted to the floor, tipped my head into my hands, and silently wept as the adrenaline from the ordeal seeped away.

CHAPTER TWENTY-ONE

EVASION

Lord Kent had insisted that his father would understand if I chose not to attend the banquet that evening. After the scene in the courtyard this afternoon, I was certain most of the fortress would be talking about my encounter. It wasn't every day a guest of the fortress came through the doors covered in blood. Shaken as I was, and as tedious as the banquets could be, I didn't want to spend another evening alone in my rooms.

My hands still trembled after a rose petal bath. The water, though hot, never fully soothed my frayed nerves. Marta and I went through our usual routine of dressing, cinching, and curling. I wore a cream dress with matching slippers and curls woven around a golden circlet that sat low on my forehead. Mother's pendant rested in the hollow of my throat.

It wasn't until we were halfway through the third course of our meal that I relaxed completely. I sat with Lord Kent at the opposite end of the long banquet table as the Freelanders, but Stock's and Isa's encouraging smiles, even from a distance, brought comfort. After dinner, we moved to the great hall where musicians tuned their instruments. Before I knew it, I found myself dancing two straight sets with Lord Kent.

It was nice to enjoy a moment free of worry. When the music ended, I could hardly stand on my feet. "Thank you." I laughed through a curtsy. "But I think I need to sit for a while."

He led me to a bench along the rim of the room and took the seat at my side. "You're beautiful, Ebrielle." He spoke as though he couldn't hold his words in without bursting. "A man would never tire of your company."

A tickle filled my stomach as I fought down my first response: *"So are you."* I just stared at my hands, feeling the color rush to my cheeks.

"How is Simon?" I asked Lord Kent, now that we had a moment alone.

"The page boy is fine." Kent's tone was flat. "He's been assigned to work in a," he paused, "less desirable position for the week."

"Why?"

"Punishment, Miss Fields. For leading you into such danger."

"But I asked him to show me the festival. It wasn't his fault."

Lord Kent's eyes softened. His hand lifted and his fingertips grazed my cheek. I thought of Wesley and had to turn away.

Lord Kent shifted closer to me, the heat of his body seeping into my side. "You are a treasure, Miss Fields. And I am very determined to protect my treasures."

There had always been something about Lord Kent's manner that kept me from confiding in him. A part of me wanted to ask him if he suspected someone from Freeland was responsible for producing the Purgo, but I didn't want to create more problems for my people by discussing things I wasn't meant to know. "Is there a reason why someone might not want me here?" I asked instead.

Lord Kent froze, staring at me with his bright blue eyes. "Is this about what happened on the streets today?"

Before I could answer, Wesley approached us wearing a new jerkin and polished boots. I don't know why I never noticed how well his Freeland build looked in gentleman's clothing. Surely he hadn't worn his working leathers to all of these formal dinners. He looked like a man, and again I found myself wondering how I'd missed the day he transformed.

"Miss Fields." He bowed. "Would you care to dance?" Wesley extended his hand.

Lord Kent reached out and rested a hand atop mine. I wished he hadn't, especially in front of Wesley. "Ebrielle would like to rest a while."

Wesley's face turned a unique shade of purple. Behind him Lady Kent searched the crowd. When she spotted Wesley, she walked our way. The huntress on the prowl.

"I'd love to dance!" I all but shouted.

Lord Kent's hands melted from me as I stood to claim my partner. To Lady Kent's obvious disappointment, I took Wesley's arm and he angrily mumbled to himself as he towed me along to the opposite end of the hall.

I knew I had a lecture coming about propriety, but I preferred that to seeing Wesley captured by Lady Kent and her feminine wiles. What a good friend I was!

"That man has some nerve." He continued his mumbled string of frustration. "Thinks he's looking out for you, that has to save you from me." He shook his head. "That snake in the grass."

Once we were as far away from Lord Kent as the room allowed, Wesley kept his scowl and took my waist, finally speaking to me. "Are you determined to allow Lord Kent to court you?"

"What?" I was expecting an argument, not this.

"Are you?" His commanding demeanor softened as he awaited my answer.

"No. I enjoy Lord Kent's company, but I don't seek it out."

"You enjoy his hands resting everywhere and anywhere? You take pleasure in being paraded around like his little prize?"

I pushed Wesley away and walked over to face the wall, blinking away the sting from my eyes and waiting for my constricted throat to calm so I could deliver equally harsh words. I wanted him to feel the pain he gave me. Did he really think I could be so shallow? Didn't he know me at all?

Wesley carefully took my arms above the elbow and whispered in my ear from behind. "Ebby?" His warmth radiated like a pleasant campfire at my back.

I couldn't look at him.

"I'm sorry, Ebby. I just want you to be happy. I was wrong to…"

Turning silent when I turned to meet his gaze, he swallowed and searched my face. Desperate. Apologetic. My drive to fight back melted into something I couldn't identify. He thought of me like he did Master Moorly—just another person he had to look out for. Another helpless person who needed him.

I wanted to tell him to give me a little more credit but couldn't form the words around the lump in my throat. We stood there staring at each other without saying a word, until the music for the next dance began and he offered his hand.

On instinct, I took it, and he cupped my waist, pulling me close enough for his chin to rest on the top of my head. I closed my eyes and drank in the sensation of his touch. A place in my chest that had been vacant suddenly filled and we danced with an unspoken agreement to drop the subject.

As the song ended, I curtsied and he bowed. We faced the hall to find Lady and Lord Kent heading toward us from the opposite side of the room.

Glancing at Wesley, I noticed he watched the same scene unfold. He looked back to me. "Do you want to get some air?" He held my gaze with a magic that made my mouth dry. Was he really choosing my company over hers? Was this zing of joy in my heart caused by the small triumph over Lady Kent or was this just another attempt to keep me from Lord Kent?

I decided it didn't matter and nodded. Before our pursuers could reach us, we slipped out of the great hall, walking in silence, my arm in his, through the torch-lit corridors of the damp fortress. The world seemed different with Wesley at my side. Calm. Relaxed. As much as I wanted to slug him in the gut at times, he always made me feel at home. Like a favorite blanket.

"I'm sorry about what I said." Wesley tightened his hold on my arm. "I was just angry. There's something about Lord Kent that drives me crazy. I don't trust him."

There was no use fighting with Wesley. We weren't going to agree on Lord Kent's intentions. Not after tonight. "You're a terrible judge of character, Wes," I said, thinking of Lady Kent.

His soft chuckle jostled my arm. He rested his free hand on top of mine, sending a wild shot of heat to my cheeks. "The pot calling the kettle black, Ebby." His teasing tone was lighter than usual.

I never realized how much I loved his laugh. Huddling closer to him, I craved the familiarity of his person. I never imagined wanting to be near Wesley Smith, but here I was, longing to be closer, to be held.

Needing it from him.

As if he could sense my feelings, he stopped walking and turned to look at me. The torchlight flickered across my face while his was cast in shadow. He took one of my hands and simply held it. It was then that I realized how much I loved his hands. Large and rough, they were the hands of a man who *created*.

My heart fluttered like hummingbird wings. I should have used this time to tell him everything I'd learned. To plot. To predict. But we just stood there, alone in the corridor, saying nothing and somehow everything all at once. Letters and arrows were the last things on my mind.

Realization hit with full, unrelenting force: I wanted Wesley to kiss me. I wanted him to want me. To love me. Not because it meant beating Lady Kent or because he reminded me of home, or any other reason. I just wanted *him*.

That's when a young boy I'd never met flew around the corner, crashing into Wesley's hard shoulder. The contact sent the poor boy flying through the air and knocked me out of Wesley's grasp. I stumbled over to the boy to help him to his feet.

"Wesley the Bear!" He spoke in reverent awe. "I'm sorry. I didn't see you there." He turned to me. "Please forgive me, Miss Fields."

"Nothing to forgive. I'm fine." Not daring to look over to Wesley, I was too embarrassed to see his face after my thoughts of kissing.

"The duke would like a word with you, Mr. Smith"

Wesley and I exchanged a knowing glance. "Please tell His Grace that I will attend him as soon as I escort Miss Fields to her rooms."

"Of course, sir." The boy who was more elbows and knees than anything else scampered down the hall to deliver the message.

My rooms weren't far. Once we reached the final corridor, I turned on him. "Is it possible the duke suspects you of creating the Purgo?" I asked.

"Would that be so shocking?"

I twisted my fingers, biting my lip. "I think we should consider leaving this place, Wes."

"And go where, exactly?" The mountain pass wouldn't be safe to travel this late in the year. We both knew that. He lifted my chin with his curled finger and forced me to look up into his solemn gaze. "We'll be fine. But just in case…"

Wesley released my chin and pulled a small dagger from a hidden sheath buckled beneath his tunic. He handed it to me. "I want to you keep this." The metal clip attached to the leather sheath would allow me to conceal it on a belt or garter, if I so desired.

I frowned. "Do you really think it's necessary?"

He ran a worried hand through his dark hair. "I hope you never need it, but I like the idea of you carry one of my blades, just in case."

I pulled the dagger from its sheath and gasped at the snowy shine of the blade in the torchlight. "It's beautiful." I looked up at him. "Thank you."

He pulled me in for a hug, tucking my head beneath his chin, the motion so swift it shocked me. "Will you be all right without me?" His whisper rumbled near my ear and my cheeks threatened to set fire.

"I'll be fine, Wes."

But would *he*?

He must have sensed my rising panic because he squeezed me once more and said, "I'll see you tomorrow."

"Maybe I could visit you at the forges?" I offered, feeling instantly foolish. The lines defining our friendship were everywhere and nowhere. I would have killed for a brief glimpse inside his mind. Was there a chance he cared for me in the same way I cared for him? Or was I the responsibility who was mudding the water?

Wesley shook his head. "You stay inside the fortress. I'll find you at dinner." He left, taking a jagged, utterly confused chunk of my heart along with him.

I closed and bolted my door.

When I approached my writing desk, all the warmth from my exchange with Wesley drained away. On the desk sat a sealed letter, the familiar red ink like an icy dagger in my heart.

Wesley, three years earlier

I'd finished my duties for Father early and had headed toward the East River to meet Gavin for a swim when I saw Ebby swinging an empty bucket and kicking rocks on the lane that led to one of Freeland's wells.

During the harvest, field workers labored from sun up to sun down to bring in the crops. Ebby was likely drawing water to relieve their thirst.

Seeing Ebby with her bucket was an opportunity I had no intention of squandering. I nicked an apple from John Grower's orchard and leaned against a nearby maple to watch her approach, careful not to be seen.

If I knew Ebby at all, I was in for a show.

Ebby wore a simple dress. Her talent with a needle and thread wasn't quite as terrible as it had been two years ago, but one side of her hem was still a few inches higher than the other. Her hair rebelled against its fastenings, wispy blond locks escaping and curling at her temples.

It took me a moment to remember to chew my bite of apple.

Ebby dropped the bucket into the well and let it fill with water before heaving on the prickly rope. She always struggled pulling up the bucket. She may have been small for her fourteen years, but she wasn't helpless. She placed one foot on the edge of the well for leverage and leaned with all her weight on each tug.

I should have gone to help her. It would have been the chivalrous thing to do.

But from this angle only thin stockings covered her shapely lower legs and I couldn't compel my seventeen-year-old self to do anything but stare.

Gavin would murder me if he caught me.

And I would deserve it.

It took a while for the bucket to raise high enough to clear the lip of the well. Once in range, Ebby couldn't let go of the rope to pull it to the ledge, and she wasn't strong enough to hold the rope with one hand and grab it.

She used her foot to gently push the bucket until it swayed like the pendulum of a clock. She timed the swinging, and expertly lowered the bucket onto the lip of the well at just the right moment. Not an easy task, but she'd done it before, and she'd do it again.

Taking a moment to catch her breath, she glanced over in my direction.

I could see the tightening in her eyes the moment I'd been caught. No doubt I was the last person in Freeland she wanted to see.

When we were younger, she might have chased me with a mud pie in hand to make me pay for watching her little stunt. A part of me wished she would do just that. Instead, she growled and hoisted her bucket off the ledge with water splashing all over her dress and marched past me toward the fields.

I should have helped her draw the water. I was a cad. She thought that already. This was further proof.

I found myself walking beside her and shoved my hands deep into my pockets to keep from reaching out to help her. "You're making a mess of your dress walking in such an angry rush," I said as water splashed around her.

She scowled and tried to hold the bucket away from herself but lacked the arm strength to do it for long.

I didn't ask, just yanked the bucket from her hands. It wasn't that heavy, and I found myself proud of the muscle I'd been gaining from my time spent in the forges with Father.

Had Ebby noticed my growing strength? Was she impressed?

"Kindly return my bucket, Apprentice."

I winced. Ebby found great pleasure in reminding me of my title. Apprentice. I was already far better than the other smithies who worked under Father in the forges. My apprenticeship would continue until I turned twenty-one, regardless of my skill, but Father himself said I had the makings to become a master.

I didn't hand over the bucket.

I could see Ebby fighting an internal battle. Usually, she'd be stomping her feet by now, her face contorting in comical ways to show her anger. She reached for the bucket again but this time I lifted it over my head, taunting her with my newly acquired height.

"Fine," she huffed, folding her arms across her chest.

We walked together in silence, Ebby putting as much distance between us as the dirt road allowed. She watched me from the corner of her eye, but I wouldn't give her the satisfaction of returning her gaze.

CHAPTER TWENTY-TWO

WESLEY THE FLIRT

Love's flame leads to certain destruction. I read the new warning over and over again.

Were they talking about *my* love? Was this love supposed to be a person or something else? If this mysterious correspondent knew me well enough, they might know of my love of information. It made sense that my strange urges could lead to trouble, but "certain destruction" seemed a bit extreme.

I held up the note and re-read the hurried words. *Love's flame.*

It seemed more likely that the author referred to a person.

Wesley? Impossible. There was a much better chance the writer of these notes would assume Lord Kent was the object of my affection. We'd spent many hours together since my arrival to Brennan.

My head swirled and swayed on a wobbly axis. Surely the heroines in Joe's stories didn't have this much trouble discovering the answers to their problems. When there was conflict in a story, all they had to do was be noble and honorable and everything worked out. Good always triumphed over evil.

I knew one thing for certain: if I didn't figure out the true meaning of these warnings, something terrible would happen.

I RAN INTO Mr. Daily at breakfast the next morning. After a deep bow and a few exchanged pleasantries, he asked if I might join him for a round of cards after lessons with the duchess. It gave me something to look forward to during my lesson on the proper greetings and customs of different levels of society throughout the Southern Provinces. Since none of the nods, gestures, and curtsies would be useful once I went back to my home in Freeland, it all seemed like a monumental waste of time. When I escaped the strongly scented rooms of the duchess, I couldn't reach the duke's library fast enough.

"Miss Fields," Daily exclaimed. He stood and pulled out my chair before retaking his seat at the card table. As with everything in the fortress, the table and chairs seemed to be crafted by a master. The polish shined so brightly I could see my reflection in the mahogany wood.

Just as I accepted my hand and sorted my cards, Lord Kent appeared at my back. "You're a hard one to track, Miss Fields," he said.

Mr. Daily's jaw flexed as he laid the first card of the game. "I thought I'd see you here, Kent."

Theodore laughed to himself, like there was some joke I was missing. "The hummingbird is always attracted to the flower."

Now it was Mr. Daily's turn to laugh. "Yes, as the fox is always drawn to the hen house."

Lord Kent forced a thin smile and pulled a chair over to sit right beside me. "I hope you don't mind the intrusion." His warm breath hit my exposed shoulder as he leaned over and examined my hand. A chill crawled up my spine, slow like the patient legs of a spider.

"Not at all," Daily said in a flat tone. "Your move, Miss Fields," he said, narrowing his gaze on Lord Kent.

I scooted my chair forward and played a card, then drew one from the top of the deck.

A member of the Vikehand court called a greeting to Lord Kent. "I'll be right back," he said, crossing the room.

The edges of Mr. Daily's lips turned down into a grimace. Keeping his attention trained on Lord Kent, he spoke from the corner of his mouth. "We need to talk. Soon. Without your babysitter."

"My *what*?"

Lord Kent shook hands with the man from Vikehand and, after exchanging a few words, walked back to us and settled into the seat next me. "Whose turn?" he asked, leaning over my shoulder, so close I felt his breath against my neck.

Mr. Daily cleared his throat. "I believe it's mine." He studied me, twisted a ring on his middle finger, then played an ace of spades, winning the set.

I turned my head in time to see Wesley watching me from the doorway to the library. He seemed out of place in his soiled smithy attire. When our eyes connected, he held my gaze, his mouth set in a firm line. Last night he'd said he'd come and find me! But I didn't know how to get away from Lord Kent without drawing unwanted attention.

Wesley watched Lord Kent with narrowed eyes then turned back to me.

Later, I mouthed.

His brows knit together, and then the doorway was empty.

FOR THE BETTER part of the afternoon, Lord Kent followed me like a puppy, reminding me of Mr. Daily's babysitter comment. He asked questions about my home in Freeland and my family. He was especially interested in my father's business as governor and if he entertained ambassadors from the other provinces. His usually flattering attentions seemed tiresome today.

When Lord Kent left me to dress for dinner, I was glad to be rid of him. My manners had turned more clipped over the last few days as his constant attention began to feel more possessive and less flattering. I'd found myself subconsciously comparing his every word and action to Wesley's.

A smile tickled my lips as I opened my wardrobe to select a new dress for dinner. Tonight's dress should be special. Something that made me feel "Freeland pretty," not "Brennan pretty."

A tempting thought struck me. I rushed over to the window and threw back the drapery. Wesley had told me not to leave the fortress, but the sun was still an hour from setting. Marta wouldn't be here to help me dress for at least that long.

I bit into my bottom lip then rushed back to my wardrobe to pull out my Freeland cloak. Slipping out my door and rushing through the corridors of the fortress with hood raised and cloak whipping behind me, I crept out of the servant's entrance by the kitchens. I ran at a slight jog, unable to wipe the grin from my face. It didn't take me more than a few minutes to see the billowing smoke of the forges.

Dusk cast the courtyard in shadow, making the grotesque statues seem almost alive. As I approached the Freeland blacksmith pavilion, the sound of a young woman's laughter sent a cold chill down my legs and arms. *I know that laugh.* Veering from the path, I ducked behind a small hay pile for cover.

Lady Kent's dress was too short and way too low on her chest. She leaned over Wesley as he examined his newest sword. I wanted to shove her heaving breasts back into her dress and smack Wesley across the face to awaken him from his trance. Though I couldn't hear exactly what was said over the billows of the smithy, I could guess well enough the nature of their conversation.

"You are the finest smithy in the Southern Provinces, Wes. Your arms bulge every time you lift your metal." I could almost hear her shrill voice compliment his charcoal eyes, how they captured the light of the hot coals as he pounded his creations. She probably stared in slobbery captivation at the way the shadows played handsome tricks across the planes of his face when he worked.

Wesley's response was likely just as dumb. *"Why thank you, dear girl. I know I'm wonderful."*

I fumed while watching her make the silly comments that made him smile his quirky smile. He said something witty in return and Lady Kent practically rolled over laughing. Wesley wasn't that funny.

No one was *that* funny.

Why would he seek out the smiles of that flirt when there were respectable girls back home who would make him so much happier?

Was this why he didn't want me to visit him?

Maybe I'd misread him last night. Maybe he really had taken me away from the dance just to keep me from Lord Kent. Maybe I'd misinterpreted our moment in the hallway. He hadn't kissed me. When I thought about it, he hadn't done anything but hold my hand.

Did he still consider me his best friend's little sister? His responsibility. His burden.

Had these feelings growing between us only been my imagination?

What if Wesley thought he was in love with Lady Kent? Would she follow him back to Freeland? I shook my head, unable to picture Lady Kent pickling her own cucumbers and helping in the community. No, she'd convince Wesley to stay here. I would be forced to travel home without him. Who would inherit the blacksmith Councilman seat? Who would be Gavin's partner against Isa and Stock when they played cards late at night? Who would stand with my brother at his wedding?

I waited in the shadows behind the hay pile until, *finally,* Lady Kent left him.

Wesley frowned at me when I emerged. With hay likely sticking out of my hair at odd angles, no doubt he knew I'd been eavesdropping.

But it didn't matter.

Walking under the shelter of the smithy, I dropped onto a bench by his newest swords. I knew nothing of metal work except that Wesley's swords were special. The detail of the hilts and the smooth shine of the perfect blades were remarkable even to my ignorant eyes.

"Why are you outside the fortress, Ebby? It's getting dark. I assumed you'd be with *Theodore* or that Sea Port fellow."

"I came earlier but didn't want to interrupt your quality time with Lady Kent." If one could call that viper a lady!

He frowned, like I'd given him a piece of sour apple to swallow. "Why do you care who I see?" His voice grew a little stronger.

"You're a Freelander, Wes. You deserve a Freelander. Not some bulging basket of breasts."

Wesley folded his arms, his face reddened. "No one in Freeland interests me, Ebby. I have no one to go back to."

I wasn't prepared for this comment. I knew we were more brother and sister than... well... more. But to totally disregard my company...

I'd made a huge mistake coming here, only imagining that he cared for me. That our time together last night meant more to me than it did to him. I'd let myself dream about what it would be like to be loved by Wesley Smith. Not as a brother, but something dangerously *more.*

What a fool I was.

"What about your responsibilities to the Council and Master Moorly?" I said, more calmly. "What about Harvest Festival and spring cooking? What about the reservoir in the summer? And the fishing pond…"

"Ebby—"

"What about the color of the sky as the sun falls behind the mountain, or stealing our raspberries, or your late-night card games with Gavin, Isa, and Stock, or, or…"

I wanted to say, "*What about me, Wes?*" But pride caught the words in my throat, and I couldn't speak them. I turned to leave but he grabbed my arm before I could put any distance between us.

"Sit for a minute. Talk to me." He gestured toward the chair in the corner of the pavilion next to a giant water trough. "Please," he added in whispered afterthought.

I complied but couldn't bring myself to look at him.

Neither of us spoke, even though the tension of words unspoken hung thick in the air between us.

After several long moments passed, Wesley dragged another chair from the worktable over and placed it in front of me.

"Anymore red letters?" His voice was its usual rumbling whisper.

Even though I had, indeed, received another letter last night, I couldn't make my lips move, refusing to confide in this man.

Cold October raindrops fell from the sky, connecting with the ground in sporadic *tinks*. A shiver crawled up my arms and I pulled my old woolen cloak closer to me. The ropes woven into the seat of Wesley's chair whined as he adjusted his position.

"The duke questioned me last night."

My attention snapped to him. In my jealousy, I'd forgotten to ask about the duke's summons.

"After talking to Master Moorly when we first arrived, the duke guessed the old man's condition. He wanted to know who had been making the swords for him."

"What did you tell him?" I asked, my shame momentarily forgotten.

Wesley straightened up a bit. "I told him I had."

I sighed and gave in to the conversation. This was bigger than my pride and confused feelings. "That's actually good news."

Wesley's brow furrowed. "Why is that?"

"Joe Ford thought Master Moorly might be the maker of the Purgo. He said the duke wouldn't let Moorly leave if he discovered it to be true. At least now we know the duke won't bother you and Master Moorly anymore. I doubt he'd suspect *you* to be the maker of the Purgo." I smiled at the thought.

"Of course not." Wesley suddenly stood. He started throwing his iron tools into a wooden chest, tidying his workspace.

The jarring clangs made me flinch. "What's wrong?" I asked. "What did I say?"

Wesley didn't answer but kept working with a fury.

I rose from my chair but didn't dare approach him.

With his back turned, he spoke to me in his low rumble. "I may not wear the nicest clothing, my inheritance might have burned to the ground when my parents died, and I may not be the next duke of Brennan, but I am a good blacksmith, Ebby." He finished his task and turned, his face a mask of stone. "At least grant me that."

He walked out of the pavilion before I could say another word.

Chapter Twenty-Three

"He Lets Us Live"

I took my time walking back to the fortress, even though the rain came faster now. Every drop felt heavy against my cloak. Just before reaching the servants' entrance, a sharp pain lanced through my middle.

The pull.

Only this time it felt as though a rope pulled me instead of the usual thread. I folded in half, sinking against the side of the stone keep as a war raged in my gut. Why was it more insistent than before?

I thought back to the journal, to the young man who considered these urges a gift. Trying to breathe through the pain, I forced myself erect enough to take a shaking step in the direction of the pull. The tension eased some, and I continued walking.

This was a different feeling than I'd received when I went out with Simon to see the festival. How I had ever confused the whispers and the pull back in Freeland was beyond me. Where the whispers led me to barns and tempted me off cliffs, this needle and thread tugging sensation was more like what lead me to the journal in the duke's library. A sort of beckoning. A plea.

There was a language to these two very different urges. Intelligences that meant to help and harm me. I allowed myself to imagine that this pull that I'd detested for so long was actually a confidant. A friend. The moment the thought entered my head, a wash of truth filled me.

I was led toward the west tower. Instead of resisting the pull, I gave myself over to it and broke into a jog. The tension in my gut subsided even more. Once at the latrine tower the violent pain completely vanished, leaving me breathless and damp from both the rain and my own perspiration.

Remarkable.

I approached the gray clad man hunched over his work at the base of the tower. The squishy-squelching of shovel meeting waste was followed by a *plop* as the contents were loaded into the wheelbarrow. I gulped down my revulsion—which proved to be a bad idea given the nasty taste in my mouth.

"Mr. Hovel?" I called, not trusting my stomach to move any closer to the odorous pile. It was growing too dark to see properly and the rain still pelted the earth. I probably should have run straight back to the fortress, but the aching pull in my stomach brought me here for a reason.

Derby Hovel looked around to me with bright, unaffected eyes. He jammed his shovel in the mound of pleasantries and used his filthy sleeve to smear some of the dirt across his forehead—at least I hoped it was dirt. "Miss Fields." He pulled off his cap and offered me a shaky bow.

I returned the gesture with curtsy of my own. But what now? I'd followed the pull and expected something to *happen.* The gong farmer raised a brow at me, clearly confused why a girl would run to his tower at dusk in a rainstorm.

"Could I ask you a few questions?" I blurted.

He heaved on the handles of his over-filled cart and pushed it in my direction. "I'd be happy to help you, miss, so long as you keep up."

I matched Mr. Hovel's hurried pace. "The last time we met, you said you knew all of the business of the fortress."

"Not true, miss. I know many secrets, but not everything."

"Someone's been sending me letters written in red ink. Warnings and riddles. Do you know who would send me something like that?"

Mr. Hovel didn't seem to hear me. He just kept pushing his squeaky cart over the bumps of the cobblestone road. My mother constantly lectured me about speaking up when I spoke to my elders. I cringed at the thought—my heart still confused and tender where my mother was concerned—and cleared my throat, leaning in to repeat the question. "Letters. Warnings. Am I in danger?"

He waved me off. "I'm not deaf girl." He carted on.

I bit down on my itching tongue. After a minute or so of silence, the hope of information deflated from my wanting chest. "If you don't know, Mr. Hovel—"

"What do you know about Brennan, Miss Fields?" Mr. Hovel examined me under the hood of his furry, white brows.

I thought back to the lessons I'd received in kinder school and the scattered conversations I'd overhead my father have with the other councilmen of Freeland. "Not much," I admitted.

He growled impatiently. "Brennan relies on the taxes it collects from Sea Port, Vikehand, and even some of the lesser territories."

I jumped over one pile of Mr. Hovel's fallen cargo. *Yuck!* "I'm not sure I understand. Why does Brennan tax the other provinces? Don't they govern themselves?"

Mr. Hovel stopped at the mouth of an extra-large pit and dumped his load. "Yes," he grunted. "Paying the duke a percentage of their earnings is their way of buying peace. No one wants a fight."

We walked back to the fortress in silence. This new information rolled around in my head. Brennan was a bully that tormented others simply because it could. No wonder it was so prosperous.

"You see, Miss Fields. Not everyone lives in a 'Free-land.' I work at the base of these towers because I am a servant of Brennan. Sea Port, Cyprian, and Vikehand pay taxes to Brennan for the very same reason. We simply don't have a choice. The mountains protect your home, but nothing stands between Brennan and the coastline of Sea Port or the forests of Vikehand. If the duke gets his way and is allowed access to Sea Port's harbor, nothing will stop them from continuing their conquest of the other provinces."

"Why don't the people just vote for change? Surely this has come up in council meetings."

Mr. Hovel shook his head. "You must have left your good sense back in that lavish room of yours. We *belong* to Brennan. We work her lands, we raise her cattle, and some of us," he gestured toward the wheelbarrow, "shovel her waste."

I didn't understand. In Freeland everyone worked but everyone was well cared for. Here only some lived lives of rank and wealth, while most lived impoverished ones. How could an entire nation of people stand to be ruled like that? "What does the duke do for you in return?"

"He lets us live."

When the Freelanders first came to Brennan, I'd had the impression that no one liked us. They were polite when needed, but that was all.

And now I knew why.

If people from the other provinces didn't envy our freedoms, they most certainly resented the fact that we didn't pay taxes to Brennan. "So, you think someone is threatening me because Freeland doesn't pay Brennan taxes?" The logic still didn't quite add up. I'd been expecting Mr. Hovel to bring up the Purgo. Now I found myself more confused than ever.

"I'm not a man of the world, Miss Fields, but I do know our duke has brought you and your countryman here for a reason. And I very much doubt it's to build relationships with Freeland."

The muddy clarity of this whole business made the red letters twice as threatening. I needed more information about the Purgo *and* the duke's intentions with my people. There had to be a connection.

It was time to take matters into my own hands. And that meant using the one talent I could offer my tiny province. The one skill that I alone could claim with confidence.

Eavesdropping.

CHAPTER TWENTY-FOUR

SOMEONE IMPORTANT

In between lessons with the duchess and dodging Lord Kent, I spent the next few days snooping around the forges and observing the other blacksmiths. Staying close to the fortress, I slipped among the crowd and tents to hear any conversation that might help me discover the maker of the Purgo blade. I had a feeling if I discovered its creator, everything else would fall into place.

Meanwhile, I avoided Wesley like a spider does the heel of a shoe. My pride couldn't afford to be squashed again. Since our argument at the forges, it felt as though Wesley, my safety net, was gone. I almost laughed at how strange everything seemed. Ironic that I'd spent my whole life avoiding Wesley, and now, when I needed him most, he wasn't there.

"You look like a princess," Marta said as she untwisted the last blonde ringlet and let it fall loose on my back. For the past few nights, I insisted on looking more like a Freelander, but tonight was the first night I really felt like one. She rested a delicate halo of white baby's breath on the crown of my head and stepped back.

"I lied. You're an angel," she said.

I looked in the mirror and frowned. It had been weeks since I wore my hair down. Flowers felt more comfortable than the heavy gems of Brennan. I felt like a Fields and like my mother's daughter.

"Are you ready, Ebby?" Master Moorly appeared at my door, offering his arm. I crossed the room and took it, smiling. "You look lovely, my dear."

"Thank you, Master Moorly."

"No wonder you're breaking his heart," he muttered.

I wasn't sure if this was the lucid Master Moorly from my childhood, or the illness that had swept so much of the man I knew away.

"Excuse me?"

He patted my hand but offered no response.

At dinner I was seated next to Lord Kent, and to my surprise, Wesley and Lady Georgiana sat directly across from us. Wesley acted like I wasn't there. All meal he chatted with Georgiana, making her laugh and whispering words that brought color to her cheeks.

I stabbed a potato with my fork.

"Is everything all right, Ebby?" Lord Kent glanced between me and Wesley and frowned. He leaned in, whispering so only I could hear. "What has the rogue done?" His blue eyes flicked over to Wesley as he took one of my curls in his smooth fingers. He offered me a dimpled smile and, for some reason, I forgot the question.

"I've been thinking," he said, still whispering. "How would you feel about extending your stay? My father would be more than happy to write a letter to Governor Fields saying you'd like to stay until next fall. You need to see Brennan in all of her seasons to really know her."

He cleared his throat and leaned even closer, so close his breath tickled my ear. "I want you to love Brennan, Ebby. It's important to me."

Lord Kent used the end of my curl to trace his own lips.

"Do you need a napkin?" Wesley's curt voice saved me from having to answer.

I could tell by his tone this wasn't going to be a happy discussion.

"Excuse me?" Lord Kent released my curl, his brow raised.

"I'm sure Miss Fields would appreciate you wiping your mouth on something other than her hair." Wesley's voice had turned deep and threatening. It actually reminded me a bit of his late father.

"Mr. Smith, I can handle myself," I said, glaring at him.

Lord Kent pushed back his chair like he meant to stand, but I pulled on his arm. "Please, don't make a scene."

I must have looked pretty convincing, because the fire in Lord Kent's eyes lessened at my plea. Without breaking eye contact with Wesley, his breathing stayed heavy and his chest pumped. "For you," he said, finally turning to me as he settled back into his seat.

When conversation around the table resumed, I asked Kent about his horse and anything else I could think of to distract him from Wesley. As soon as dinner ended, Wesley stood and walked out of the room without looking back.

"I'm going to talk to him," I said to Lord Kent.

"Then I'm coming—"

I shook my head. "This is between me and him." I was done playing this game of tantrums with Wesley. We wouldn't survive the winter at each other's throats.

I expected Wesley to go to his room, but instead he stormed out the great hall and foyer, pushing open the main doors of the fortress. A gust of fall night air swept into the keep. Without a wrap for my bare shoulders, I shivered as I followed, doing everything in my power to catch up to him. I passed a group of guards in red livery who offered a confused bow as I ran by. In the blacksmith quarter, glowing fires still dotted several of the pavilions, casting gnarled fingers of light and shadow along the street.

"Wesley, stop!" Clouds formed at my breathless plea. Whirling around, surprise was written across his features.

"What are you doing out here?" He crossed the distance between us in only a few strides. "Where is your cloak?" He pulled me into the Freeland pavilion, then fastened the canvas canopy that had already been drawn around most of the pavilion. It was something many of the smithies constructed around their workspace when they closed up for the day. No one wanted their expensive tools to wander off in the middle of the night.

"What's wrong with you?" I asked.

Grimacing, Wesley stoked a fire from the coals of the forge. "*Theodore* was making a fool out of himself. I had to say something."

"Admiring me is foolish?"

He doesn't care for you.

In his eyes you're just a silly little girl.

The whispers in my head grew to such volume, I covered my ears and bent in half from the painful thoughts that were mine but strangely… not.

You'll never be good enough for him!

Just like you'll never be good enough for your family name!

You are nothing.

A weight constricted my chest, forcing the air from my lungs while fanning my anger and fear into riotous flame. Red faced, I blurted, "I thought you'd changed, but you're still the dirty boy with soot under his nails who only knows how to tear things apart. A filthy apprentice who won't amount to anything in this world."

The voices hammering inside my head died the moment the words left my lips. The release was instantaneous and I could breathe again. Only now I didn't want to.

When you grow up with a person, you know how to hurt them.

Wesley looked like I'd driven one of his own swords through his chest. When the shock left, pain etched across his face.

I covered my mouth, surprised I was capable of such cruelty. "I'm sorry. I was just angry." Pressing a hand to my chest, I felt unsure how to explain the emotions that had swept over me. "I haven't been myself..." Surely he knew I didn't mean what I'd said! I just wanted him to hurt like I hurt.

"You know what I think?" Wesley's hushed voice gained energy as he spoke.

I didn't answer. He'd stepped right in front of me, so close the tip of his boot kissed my formal slipper. I looked up into his face, at the strong lines that defined his jaw and the bottomless eyes that created a yearning inside of me more real than any pull I'd ever experienced.

"I think you've spent your whole life dreaming of living a fairytale. You're in love with the idea of someone like Lord Kent. It's made you blind."

I held my chin in the air, refusing to look away. "You're wrong."

Wesley trembled, as if a war battled inside him. Then, like a flash of lightning, he dove beneath the worktable and pulled out the long wooden box that had journeyed over the mountain with him from Freeland.

A sinking feeling filled my gut where the pull resided.

He dumped the contents at my feet. A half-dozen blades in various sizes and designs clanked to the dirt floor of the pavilion.

"What are you doing?"

Wesley dropped to his knees and triggered a false bottom on the chest. His hands moved with fury as he lifted the wooden slab. I didn't like this Wesley. He was wild and frightening, barely holding on to civility. He reached into the chest and with two hands lifted a sword from a pile of wooden shavings with metal so white and pure it glowed in the firelight. He turned it over in his hands. There on the blade was the inscription.

Purgo

I gasped, shaking my head in fear. "Oh no. No, no, no, no." I reached out and let my fingers run along the flat part of the blade. It was breathtaking. "Oh no, Wesley."

"Everything my family owned burned in the fire, Ebby. My only inheritance was my father's talent. I may not be a duke's son," he spat, "but I am not your average blacksmith either. Once I sell the Purgo I can—"

The canvas walls of the tent flew open around us. Guards rushed in from every angle. Lord Kent was at my side in an instant, pulling me away from the scene.

Wesley's eyes met mine, his pain so acute I couldn't swallow, couldn't move.

I shook my head and fought against Lord Kent's arms. Guards rushed into the tent. Wesley used the pummel of his sword against a man's skull.

"No!" I cried. But it was too late. Men attacked Wesley in a swarm. He threw his elbow into another man's face, but they held him face down on the ground before he did more damage. He struggled under their grasp and a few soldiers hit him over and over again while others kicked at his exposed sides.

"Make them stop!" I screamed. I bucked and kicked in Lord Kent's arms, crazy with fear.

Lord Kent called out an order, and the men stopped. He tried to pull me away, but I shoved him and ran toward Wesley, but the vile man hooked my arm and dragged me back.

Wesley lay face down on the ground, unconscious, with blood pooling by his nose. Kent's men picked him up by the crooks of his elbows and dragged him back to the fortress, his feet trailing along behind him.

Wesley, two years earlier

It always takes me a moment to get used to the smell in the Fieldses' barn. I wrinkle my nose at the battling aromas of fresh cut alfalfa and manure. If any one of us had a place of our own, we wouldn't be here, but as it is, the barn is the only option.

"What's your poison?" Gavin leans over the apple barrel, bumping the lone lantern in the cavernous barn. It wobbles, casting weak light around the room before Stock steadies it.

"Cards," I say. My backside is still bruised from the game of dares Isa convinced us to do last week.

"Dice," Stock says.

"Truths," Isa blurts.

We all stare. Has he lost his mind?

"What are we, little girls?" I say. "How would you even wager with a game like Truths?"

"Easy," says Isa. "The most shocking truth earns the pot."

"No," I say. Gavin and Stock nod at my objection.

"It'll be fast and painless. Just one quick game." Isa pulls out a slingshot he's been whittling for the past two months. He knows we've all been admiring it. The handle is carved to look like the coiled body of a snake. The body splits into two to make the standards of the slingshot. The snakes' tongues are the pig bladder sling.

A work of art to any teenage boy.

"One round, but I get to ask the questions," said Isa.

We all mutter our agreement and Gavin adds, "But I vote for cards after we're done." He glances at me and I nod. We are allies in everything. If I had said dice, he would have said dice.

Isa rubs his hands together conspiratorially. "If you had to choose a wife today from all of the girls of Freeland, who would you pick?"

Stock flashes one of his rare smiles. "I don't think it works that way, brother."

"You and girls. You're obsessed." I roll my eyes. "Choose another truth."

Isa waves his slingshot in our faces. Taunting us. Tempting us.

"Marianna," Gavin says with a shrug. His answer doesn't surprise anyone. He's made eyes at Mari since we were kids.

Isa turns an expectant eye to Stock. At nineteen, Stock has already been attending assemblies and other festivities. He's danced with a number of girls, but he's shy around them.

I don't even hear his answer because all I can think about is my truth.

Does Isa already know? Is this why he's offered up his slingshot? To cause trouble.

Totally something he would do.

I could lie. But I really want the prize and he knows it. No one's truth is more shocking than mine.

Isa turns to me. He can't relax the grin that's taken over his face. The dog.

"Wesley?" He lifts his eyebrows up and down.

I eye the slingshot one final time and blurt, "Ebby."

Gavin sits back and blinks at me from across the apple barrel. Stock seems equally stunned. Isa crosses his arms across his chest, proud of himself.

"My sister?" Gavin spits. A pause. Then he launches himself across the barrel. His fist connects with the side of my cheek as the glass lantern shatters at our feet, snuffing the light from the room.

I don't hit him back. The others quickly pull Gavin off me and he slams the door as he leaves.

Stock, Isa, and I sit in the dark. My cheek has a heartbeat thanks to Gavin's fist. I feel like pummeling Isa, but instead I snatch the slingshot from his grubby hands and leave without another word.

Apparently, Gavin and I aren't allies in everything.

CHAPTER TWENTY-FIVE

ASLEEP

That night as I lay on my bed fully clothed with one arm draped over my eyes, the image of Wesley beaten and unconscious haunted me. I'd been shoved into the white cage that was my room and told to stay there and wait for news.

I'd spent most of the time replaying the awful things I'd said to Wesley. I'd hurt him. Caused him to lash out and prove me wrong. I didn't really think Wesley inept. I respected his work. I respected him. The whispers had compelled me, once again, and once again I'd lost control. Was I broken? Was it possible that my access to the pull also provided other spirits access to me? Spirits like those who possessed my ancestors on the mountain…

The idea caused a shiver to roll along my skin. I'd been led to the journal, to the young man from a time before my own who seemed to experience exactly what I had. I'd come to believe that this curse really might be a gift.

However, no matter how hard I wanted to believe I was gifted, that this pull might help me in my dark hour of need, the whispers had set in motion a twister of destruction upon my life from the day it led me into the barn to spy on Gavin and Mari. It had sucked away all peace, spitting out wreckage I couldn't begin to repair.

I'd made a mess of everything.

Trying to take my mind off Wesley, I retrieved the journal from its place beneath my mattress, and opened to the fine pink ribbon I used as a bookmark.

March 10th

My meeting with the villagers, whose children are in danger of being sold, didn't go well. I suggested raising funds to pay the duke not to take their children, but many resisted the idea, saying they had other family members to consider. Some stayed quiet and mourned their children as if they were already gone.

At one point I grabbed a pitchfork and launched it across the room with enough force to pierce the wooden door. I may have angered several of the men, but I refuse to apologize for my actions.

For the first time in my life, I have found something I am willing to fight for—something greater than myself. Charlotte will not be taken from me. Whether the others plan to join us or not, I will take her away before the duke's men have a chance to cart her off to Vikehand. If necessary, I will change the shape of the world to keep her safe.

March 20th

Last night was the third meeting with the villagers. The company now varies from wealthy to impoverished, but we all have something in common: We are all desperate to leave Brennan. Our numbers have grown to fifty. By spring there will be more. Some in the group don't trust me. They don't believe an educated Brennan scribe will give up everything to start over again. But they do not know Charlotte.

The doctor is not convinced Charlotte's father will recover from his illness. I plan to ask for his blessing tomorrow. It might do him good to know that she will be cared for when he is gone. If he approves my suit, I'll tell Charlotte everything. I expect the courier to return from Vikehand any day now.

March 25th

Charlotte and I were engaged a day and a half before her father passed. Enough time for him to offer his blessing and to share the location of a storehouse filled with farming tools and seed kept secret from his new lord. Charlotte's pain is my pain. I am her only family now. It is a weighted responsibility, but one I have longed to carry since the day I first met her.

The spring thaw is taking its time, but Charlotte and the others do not have another month to wait. Seventy-five of us have chosen to leave Brennan. Sometimes I wake to the sound of my own shouts. I fear I've made a terrible mistake. A mistake that will lead many to their destruction.

The weight of my responsibility to these people is crushing. Every day, I fear, is the day the duke will learn of my plans.

We cannot trust the roads to Vikehand and Sea Port so we have decided to—

I turned the page over.

Blank.

I turned another.

Blank.

"No!" It took all of my self-control not to throw the book across the room. This author was my companion. A co-conspirator. In my mind, the scribe's survival was deeply personal. The pull had connected us by leading me to the journal. But what was the point if the author didn't finish his story? Had the gift or pull or whatever it was that possessed us let him down? Was Charlotte sold as a slave to Vikehand?

Three knocks sounded at my door before it creaked open. "Miss Fields?"

I sat bolt upright and wiped tears of frustration from my swollen eyes and adjusted my skirts. "Enter," I said.

I startled to my feet, the book sliding from my lap, as the duke himself stepped into the light of my candle. He offered a curt bow. "May I sit?" His voice was gentle, tinged with regret. He stroked his russet beard, and for just a moment, I saw a flash of an older, more hardened Lord Kent in his face.

It startled me because it was the face of lies and deceit.

I swept my arm to the chair in front of the vanity. "It's your chair." I quickly picked up the journal and set it on my bedside table, hoping the duke wouldn't recognize it as something stolen from his own library.

The legs on the chair wobbled and whined as he relaxed his large body. "You've had a difficult evening," he said.

"Your men attacked my friend. They hurt him." I winced at the memory of Brennan soldiers kicking Wesley while he lay motionless on the ground.

"I didn't mean for him to be harmed, Miss Fields. I want him to be healthy."

"Yes, you'll want him fit to make another sword. Perhaps dozens and dozens of them."

His eyes widened, and I realized my mistake. I wasn't supposed to know about the famous sword or the duke's interest in it. I changed tactics. "My father sees Wesley as a son, Your Grace. He will not be pleased to know how he was treated tonight."

The duke smiled at me like my threats were charming. "Your friend has a temper. I'm told he threw the first punch. Perhaps you should tell him it isn't wise to fight my men."

"I… I want to see him. I want to know he's all right."

He chuckled softly to himself. "Tell me, does your father know what this boy is capable of?"

"Is this why you bothered to come to my room yourself, Your Grace? You want information about my father?"

"I came in person as a show of good will. Now, *please*," he grounded out the word as though his attempt at manners pained him, "answer the question."

I didn't know what to say so I settled for the truth. "I don't know what my father suspects of Wesley's talent in the forges, Your Grace. But you can't keep Wesley here like you own him. He's heir to a Councilman's seat in Freeland."

The duke threw his head back and laughed, sending waves along the fat of his extra chins.

I rose to my feet. "What is so funny?" My hands curled into fists at my side.

He mopped his streaming eyes and running nose with a handkerchief. "What makes you think I'll have to force your friend to stay? I can pay him three times what he would make anywhere else in the provinces, not to mention he's half in love with my daughter."

He walked to the door and sighed, a smile still plastered to his plump face. "If you wish to see your friend, you may visit him in the morning. You'll find him in the infirmary on the first floor of the west wing." He turned the latch and pulled open the door. "Oh, and Miss Fields? I'd hate to see such a charming guest harmed in all this. Remember, a fly is only swatted when it becomes a nuisance."

When the door clicked shut behind him and his footsteps receded down the hall, I lunged for my cloak and swiped the candle off the mantel. If the duke thought I'd wait until morning to see Wesley, he was wrong.

I crept through the dank passages of the fortress, using the servants' stairwell and corridors to avoid the duke or his guards. The flicker of my lonely candle was the only thing that kept me from running all the way to the infirmary. The darkness outside my tiny light pressed like a weight against me, suffocating and tangible.

I reached the west wing without incident, but when I approached the door of the infirmary, two men stood guard outside the door, their eyes snapped to me and my candle. "Who goes there?" one asked.

There was no turning back. I took a deep breath and stepped closer, holding the light up to my face. "Miss Fields of Freeland," I replied. "The duke gave me permission to visit Wesley Smith." *In the morning*, I mentally added.

The two men exchanged glances then stepped away from the door to let me pass. The infirmary was lined with rows of empty beds. An oil lantern hung at the end of the room illuminating a dark form lying completely still. I dropped my candle and ran to Wesley's side. His eyes were closed and his chest rose and fell with even breath. One side of his face was swollen with deep bruising, but that was the least of his problems.

Even though his feet hung off the bed because of his height, he looked young. Too young to face a beating from Brennan guards. Much too young to create the sword everyone was so obsessed over. I walked to the foot of the bed and started unlacing his boots. "I'm sorry I said those things, Wes." Knowing he was asleep made it easier to speak. "I didn't mean any of it. I was just angry."

I pulled his boots off and covered his feet with the blanket. Seeing Wesley in such a defeated, humble state made me forget my anger. "The duke says he won't force you to stay here, but there are guards at the door." I swallowed hard. "I'm afraid we're in danger here in Brennan. You can't teach them to make that blade. It's a long story, but I think the duke's planning some kind of attack."

Sleep softened the strong lines of disapproval that I usually earned from him. "The duke thinks you'll stay in Brennan for his daughter." I paused and swallowed the lump forming in my throat. "Is he right?"

I searched his face for an answer I knew I wouldn't receive. "I think I might... you shouldn't like Georgiana Kent. She's not like you. I feel ill just thinking about her and you and..."

I sighed, resting my head in my hands, suddenly exhausted.

"Do you love her, Wes? Does she make you happy? I suppose I should let you be happy. Father always told me that caring for someone meant putting their happiness before your own. I guess I could do that for you. I suppose if Miss *Perfect* was everything you've ever dreamed of having in a companion, then I should be happy for you."

There was a quick rap at the door before it swung open. The physician hustled in. I wiped a tear from my cheek with the sleeve of my gown. *When had I started crying?*

The physician looked at me and melted into a warm smile. "There, there, dear lady. He'll mend, I assure you."

I turned back to find Wesley staring at me, his eyes alert. Had he heard everything I'd just said? Had he been awake the whole time?

"Ebby, are you alright?" he asked.

"I'm sure your little flower is just mildly wilted from the ordeal, Mr. Smith. It's my experience that one never reacts well to seeing their lover damaged." He gestured toward Wesley's body, like the rest of us didn't realize Wesley was stained with blood and bruises.

"I'm not his... I..." I don't know why I couldn't form the words to correct this blunt physician. I was *not* Wesley's lover. Wesley's brow deepened and a thin white line appeared where his lips should have been. Was he angry or uncomfortable?

"Miss Fields is a family friend, sir," Wesley grunted.

The physician raised his brows. "My mistake."

I bid the two men good night, unable to make eye contact with either, and fled to my room.

CHAPTER TWENTY-SIX

HURRAH!

Idiot.

I was a complete idiot for letting my mouth run in the infirmary. Wesley caught me spouting nonsense that I *never* would have uttered under normal circumstances. Oh, if shame had a cousin it was burning, red hot anger.

Wesley sent me a letter the following morning. Simon tapped his foot in my doorway while I reread Wesley's latest note.

Ebby,

We need to talk.

-Wesley

Simon's foot-tapping persisted. "He said not to leave your side until you write a response." Simon had finally resumed his usually duties around the fortress and seemed to take his job as serious as ever. I had no doubt the page boy would stand rooted in my room until I replied, but I was too embarrassed to agree to meet Wesley after making a fool of myself the night before.

Simon melted down the doorframe until he was crouching and then pulled a ball and five jacks from his trouser pocket. He looked over at me and grinned, letting me know he was quite content to sit there all day if necessary.

"Fine." I groaned and dipped a quill into the inkwell at my writing desk.

Wesley,

No.

-Ebby

I folded up the paper and went to apply the seal, when my conscience took hold of me. It wasn't Wesley's fault that I'd made a fool of myself. It didn't change the fact that he was in trouble with the duke.

I reopened the small letter and added a postscript.

I'll talk to a few friends. See what I can learn. In the meantime, don't hit anyone.

I sealed the letter and handed it over to Simon. "I need a favor."

THAT NIGHT. KEEPING pace with Simon would have been hard enough in trousers. In my heavy skirts, cinched corset, and flimsy slippers it was nearly impossible. "Slow down," I whisper-shouted for the third time.

I felt the pull singing inside me. Goading me onward. Working with me instead of against me.

"Nearly there." We darted through a maze of narrow streets. Even though I'd been to the Talk About before, nothing looked familiar. I'd told Marta I wasn't feeling well enough to come down to dinner. She didn't question me, only set a food tray by my bed and wished me a good night.

We reached a dimly lit courtyard surrounded by old buildings. The red door of the Talk About was in a dark corner to the right. Simon gestured to the door. "Are you sure you can get back on your own?"

I nodded even though it was a lie. Simon had taken a great risk in bringing me here without permission, especially after our last episode. The longer he was away from the fortress, the greater the chance of him being caught.

"Thank you."

Simon gave one of his grand bows with arms stretched out wide and then took off into the night like a whip.

As I stepped up to the red door, I felt extremely alone. I knocked three times fast then three times slow. It struck me in that moment as I stared at the door just how much my life was beginning to resemble one of Joe's stories.

I didn't like this fairytale.

A stout man with a bulbous nose and slanted forehead opened the door. "What do you want?"

I held up my chin, determined to show no fear. "I've come to see Jeffery."

The man grunted and let me pass. "The meetin's just getting started.'"

"Meeting?" The man took his seat in a packed crowd of humbly dressed men. All eyes were fixed on the stage where Joe stood. His attention flickered to me, and he actually looked relieved.

"Miss Fields!" Everyone in the room turned as Joe waved me forward.

I shook my head, wishing I could somehow blend in with the walls.

Joe jumped off the stage with his grasshopper legs and bounded to my side in only a few strides. "We need you." He took my arm and led me to the front of the room.

"I only came to ask if you'd heard about Wesley," I whispered, conscious of every man staring in my direction.

Joe didn't seem to hear me. "Allow me to introduce our saving grace, lads!" He helped me onto the stage despite my protests.

"Meet the Governor of Freeland's only daughter, Miss Ebrielle Fields."

For some reason, my name spawned a mass of hushed chatter in the room. Why would a bunch of storytellers and bards be interested in a person like me?

Joe cleared his throat and regained the attention of the crowd. "Many of you know that Freeland has been slow to join the Alliance in the past. Now, with their own mana councilman's heir—unveiled as the blacksmith capable of crafting a Purgo, their desire to remain neutral will not stand. The duke will want to hold the secret of the sword for himself. He'll force the Freelander to train Brennan blacksmiths in his secret art. The only way that boy is going back to Freeland is in a casket."

No. Please, no.

"We should kill the boy ourselves before he gives the duke the secret to the sword," someone shouted.

"Brennan will be unstoppable with the Purgo," called another.

"No!" I shouted, stepping forward. "Listen to me!" The angry pull in my gut that had been festering during this conversation subsided into something different. Something comforting. Encouraging.

I didn't know about any alliance, but clearly this was no storytelling den. This was the home of a rebellion. "Wesley Smith is my friend. Almost like a brother. If you ever want my father to assist in your cause you will do everything in your power to keep his adopted son safe."

Joe glanced at me from the corner of his eyes and grinned. "You see, boys. Miss Fields here is interested in helping us! She is the only one who can get close to the blacksmith. She will see that he doesn't give the duke the secret of the Purgo."

I scowled at Joe and turned my back to the crowd, dragging him by the shirt to the far corner of the stage. "You can't make promises like that! I don't know anything about the rebellion. I'm just a seventeen-year-old girl."

Father's voice rang in my head, clear as a bell, confident as the flow of the mighty rivers of Freeland. *"You're a Fields."* The sensation in my stomach vibrated confirmation of that one simple truth.

Joe frowned. "Ebby, you might not know what these men and their families have endured at the hands of Brennan, but I do. I've seen the hunger. The slave-like conditions many of them work under. It's spread to Sea Port and Vikehand. Without question, Freeland is next." He ruffled his hair. "If the duke gets that sword, we might never have a chance to fight back." He took me by the shoulders. "We need your help."

What could I say? Father had asked me to act as a sort of ambassador for Freeland. To represent him. I turned back to the crowd of men and sighed. Without Father to advise me, I could only trust my conscience.

"I'll do what I can."

Joe pulled me into a giant hug. He jumped back to the front of the stage with me in tow. "*Hurrah* for Miss Fields! Our secret weapon!"

The men shouted *hurrah!* I thought I might be sick.

Joe walked me back to the red door and put his arm around my shoulders. "You're panicking."

I nodded. "What do you expect me to do, exactly? You know I don't have any power in the fortress. Why would you lead them to think that I do?

"Because they need the hope and you need time. Just convince Wesley not to teach the duke's men to make that sword."

"And if I can't?" I didn't think Wesley would do anything that could hurt Freeland, but I also knew there were ways to make a man do something he didn't want to do.

Joe shook his head and gestured out to the crowd of rebels still deep in debate. "Then the lad might wake up with an arrow in his chest."

CHAPTER TWENTY-SEVEN

THE PLAN

Before lessons with the duchess the next morning, I pushed past the guards outside Wesley's door shouting, "The duke said I could see him!" and burst into his room. I used both hands to slam the door behind me with a gratifying boom.

"Ebby?" Wesley asked. He slowly moved one leg and then the other to rest on the ground before grunting to stand.

I forgot my embarrassment from the other night and rushed over to help him back down. "What do you think you're doing? You're supposed to be in bed until tomorrow!" I scolded.

He rolled his eyes but didn't fight me as I put my hands on his shoulders and forced him back to bed.

"I have to talk to you about your sword." My words blended into each other. "You can't let the duke learn how to make the Purgo!"

He sat up; his face noticeably closer to mine. "And what makes you think I know how to make that sword?"

"You told me you did!" Realization dawned on me. He had been angry. Maybe even mad enough to take credit for something he didn't do. "If you didn't make it, who did?"

Wesley toyed with a hole in his shirt. "My grandfather brought the secret of the Purgo with him to Brennan when he helped settle the province. He taught my father, and the secret died with him last year. I brought it to the festival, hoping to sell it for money to rebuild my family home."

I took his hand in mine and desperately squeezed. "Really? You really don't know how to make that sword?"

He stared down at our clasped hands, and I quickly released him.

"What are you not telling me, Ebby? What have you overheard?" He spoke with a gentle smile, as if trying to encourage the confession of eavesdropping we both knew was coming.

I sighed and slumped onto the foot of his bed, glancing around the room to make sure we were still alone. I told him all about Joe Ford and the alliance formed between people from the Southern Provinces. I spoke of taxes, forced labor, and even Mr. Hovel. I told him about my trips to the forges and the Talk About and my commitment to help the rebellion if I could.

Wesley didn't look surprised by any of my information, but he didn't look concerned by it either. "Freeland has stayed out of this conflict for a reason, Ebby. You should, too."

"If Brennan learns how to make that blade, the duke's tyranny will likely spread to Freeland."

Wesley thought about this for a moment then shook his head. "Freeland isn't profitable enough for the duke to bother threatening us. And even if he did, we have a mountain dividing us. He'd never be able to get his troops through the pass. It's too easy for us to defend."

"What about those warnings I've been getting, Wes? Obviously someone knows something about the duke's plans. They must have suspected your talent and Freeland's potential role in this mess." I wrung my hands together.

Wesley leaned back in his bed with his eyes closed. "What have I done?" he muttered to himself. The poor boy looked exhausted.

"Should I come back later?" I asked.

He reached out and took hold of my wrist. "Ebby," he whispered, "I need you to know that I don't care for Lady Kent." A pause. "Not now, not ever."

I froze. Unable to pull my eyes from his, feeling heat invade my cheeks and roll up my back. Did he know how much that one declaration meant to me? When I finally had the good sense to look away from his dangerously captivating eyes and focus on my hands, Wesley added, "I met with the duke this morning." His tone was light, perhaps too casual.

"And you told him you don't know how to make the sword, right?"

He nodded and swallowed hard, like something was caught in his throat. "He said I have until the end of the festival to remember."

"And then what?" I scoffed. "It's not like he can punish you for not knowing something."

Wesley released a shaky laugh. The color drained from his face. "He can if he thinks I'm hiding something."

No.

"I think it's time to make a plan to get you and the rest of the Freeland craftsmen out of Brennan," he said. "I'm afraid if I don't give him what he wants he might use you to get to me."

I shook my head. "That won't happen."

"He knows I care about you, Ebby," he snapped, kneading his fingers into his forehead.

My mouth hung open. Speechless.

"In the meantime," he went on, "I think you should see what you can find out about Brennan's plans for Freeland and the other provinces."

I nodded slowly. "You'll be watched constantly, and besides, I was always the better sneak."

He smirked before growing serious again. "We need proof to take back to Freeland that the duke has plans to harm the provinces."

It was true. If all of those years sneaking around had taught me anything, it was how to get information.

"Talk to Joe. See if he and his revolutionaries can smuggle you out," Wesley said sadly.

"You say that like you aren't coming."

"You said yourself the duke will have close eyes on me. I honestly don't know if I can escape."

I reached out and took Wesley's hand. "We're family, Wes. Family sticks together. I'm not going anywhere without you."

He covered my hand with his and smiled like he didn't believe me. But I'd prove him wrong. I gathered my skirts and headed for the door.

CHAPTER TWENTY-EIGHT

A DEADLY PROPOSAL

That afternoon, after serving my time with the duchess practicing a hostess's responsibility of planning menus, I sent Simon out with a letter for Joe Ford. I'd need his help to get Wesley and the rest of the Freelanders out of Brennan before the end of the festival. That didn't give us much time to prepare. The festival only lasted another week, but I knew those revolutionaries didn't want the duke to have Wesley any more than I did. I only hoped helping us wouldn't cost them too dearly.

Thankfully, Joe didn't waste time. His letter arrived the very next morning.

Miss Fields,

I have spent the night lobbying for the rebels to help you leave. It all comes down to this: the rebellion is willing to risk the resources it would take to transport and hide your people through Sea Port on the condition that you swear by

blood, in your father's name, that Freeland will join the re-
bellion. I'm sorry to ask this of you, child. But your request
is extremely dangerous. If you can produce a letter promis-
ing this, and sign it in your own blood before tomorrow
night, we can save you, Wesley, and the rest of the Free-
landers in Brennan from the duke. You can board a ship in
Sea Port and enter Freeland from the south, arriving in
spring. It is a long journey, but the mountain pass isn't safe
this time of year.

This is the best I can do.
Joe

P.S. Many of the rebellion feel threatened by Wesley's abili-
ties. If you choose to stay and take your chances with the
duke, be warned that Wesley will have a target on his back.
I have forbidden any action taken against him, but if out-
voted in the end, there is little I can do to protect the lad.

Three days!

That wasn't nearly enough time to make such a decision. Every time I convinced myself that it wasn't my call to make, the images of Wesley being beaten by Brennan soldiers replayed in my mind.

Joe's revolutionaries clearly didn't understand how Freeland functioned. Even if I promised Father's support, nothing happened in Freeland without a vote from members of the Council. By signing that letter, I could create more enemies for Freeland than we already had if the rest of Freeland's Council refused to help the revolutionaries. Though it nearly killed me not to act, I needed more proof of the duke's plans.

Proof I needed to obtain in the next three days.

I wrote to Isa and Stock, explaining we needed to consider leaving before the brunt of winter set in, but mentioned nothing of my involvement with Joe Ford and the Brennan revolutionaries in case the message fell into the wrong hands. I kept my head down, attended the duchess's tiring lessons, and tried to hide from a decision that never should have been mine to make.

I'd had Simon draw me a map of the fortress, showing me exactly where the duke's chambers were. When I knew Lord Kent to be busy elsewhere, I took walks through the fortress near the duke's rooms, trusting the pull to help me. I explained to anyone who asked that I desired the exercise and wasn't interested in catching a chill outside in the festival. I memorized turns and doorways and became familiar with the schedule of the fortress.

On the third day after receiving Joe's letter, I walked toward the duke's corridor again. The pull had been a quiet force over the last twenty-four hours, but today it rolled within my stomach and crackled through my veins with such urgency, I had to fight my body to keep a steady and even pace. Was it coincidence that the pull seemed to draw me to the very destination I intended to go?

Wind forced its way into the fortress through the small gaps of the structure. The pinched air echoed with the shrill aggression of a weasel in a snare, mirroring the war waging within me. Goosebumps rolled along my skin. But on I walked, winding through the maze of corridors in the opulent, drafty stone prison I now called home.

I approached the family corridor. Until today, I'd only peered down this corridor in passing to look longingly at the four doors that, according to Simon's map, belonged to the duke and duchess and their children. With the absence of a regular guard posted at the mouth of the corridor, I slowed. The long hallway appeared just as it always had: the torch light flickering off the gray stone, the bronze sculpture of a man on horseback situated on a marble pedestal at the end of the hall, the polished doors facing one another like lonely sentinels. But to my surprise, the duke's elaborate door stood ajar. Light from a blazing hearth within made the doorway glow. It was as though the room wanted me there, like I was being given a very personal invitation to all the secrets within.

Usually at this point in my jaunt, I kept going, not wanting to be obvious about my interest in the duke's chambers by turning down the dead-end corridor.

By now, I knew how the pull worked. It had led me to the duke's door. Strangely, it hadn't pulled me to the duke's door before. Was it because the door stood ajar, increasing my chances of hearing something valuable?

My shaking hand smeared down my cheek.

With my back pressed against the wall, I took careful steps down the forbidden corridor toward the duke's door.

The sound of voices made my shaking legs stiffen. I lurched forward, bolstered by the pull, closer to the door until I made out the words.

"You're failing," came the unmistakable harsh tone of the duke. I still pressed my back to the wall but peered into the room as much as I dared. Lady Kent stood with her back to me while the duke waved a fat finger in her face.

"I'm doing my best, Father." Lady Kent 's voice shook with fear. "It's just—"

"No excuses. You're good for one thing, Georgiana. One thing."

"You underestimate them." She barely spoke above a whisper. "You're not used to working with people of integrity."

The pull practically jerked me deeper into the corridor, past the opening of the door.

At that very moment, a *crack* sounded from inside the duke's rooms and the door opened out into the corridor. Georgiana fell to the stone floor, spilling out the open doorway, her back to me, her hand pressed to her scarlet red cheek.

"I must say, of all your assignments, I assumed this one would be the easiest." The open door offered just enough cover to hide me from the duke, but if Georgiana Kent turned, I had nowhere to hide.

The duke's shadow stretched long upon the floor, the light of his rooms framing him like an angel fallen from grace. He pretended to kick her side and she flinched so hard a sob escaped her perfectly painted lips.

I covered my gasp with both hands.

"Dangle the carrot in front of the horse's nose, Georgiana. I don't want him focused on anything but obtaining my blessing." The duke shut the door, leaving Lady Kent to pick herself off the ground.

"You don't know with whom you're dealing," she said under her breath. She gathered her skirts and ran into her own room, diagonal her father's, without a backward glance, blinded by her own tears.

The duke's door shut.

I held a hand over my heart, as if that would help stop its racing.

Footsteps echoed down the hallway of my intended escape. The occasional clink of metal convinced me they were soldiers. I looked around for a place to hide only to find Lord Kent's door, the sculpture, and a dead end.

The soldier's footsteps grew louder. I'd been lucky with Lady Kent, but soldiers would definitely notice me. The idea of walking into Lord Kent's room made my stomach roll. I turned a complete circle, hoping to find something, anything, to help me disappear besides Kent's door at the end of the hall.

The duke's doorknob turned and opened. His hand gripped the knob, his body angled back into the room. "I'll wear the gray tonight, Rolland. Make sure it's pressed." He began to turn back around…

Oh no!

I lunged for Lord Kent's door and yanked the handle just as the soldiers rounded the corner. Panic shot through me like a thousand arrows to my heart.

The door was locked.

CHAPTER TWENTY-NINE

A MAP AND MISSION

aught.

I leapt into the far corner at the end of the hall and pulled the cloak over my head. I was three years old again playing hide-and-seek with Gavin. Just because I closed my eyes didn't mean they wouldn't see me, especially only a few paces from the duke's door. The guards turned the corner, putting me directly in their line of sight just as the duke opened his door. I sat frozen with only my drawn cloak and the dim light and shadows for protection.

Please don't see me. Please don't see me.

I knew the ancestors were busy, but I hoped they might have time to help me out of this one. A thousand promises rushed through my head. I would even give up honeycakes if they would help me somehow blend into this wall. I pressed my body against the stone, peeking through the seams of my cloak, not daring to so much as exhale. The soldiers' laughter cut off at the sight of the duke.

"Report," the duke commanded.

"The apprentice has the ore in a clay crucible. Says he'll have to keep the bellows going for fourteen hours, Your Grace."

The duke nodded and glanced in my direction. This was it! He would see me and I would have to explain my reasons for hiding.

"Keep this quiet."

"Of course, my lord."

That's when Simon came bounding down the hall. He almost ran into the growing crowd of men stationed outside the duke's door. "I have a message for His Grace," he announced in a clearly forced baritone voice. His eyes flickered to me for the tiniest moment. The color drained from his young, plump cheeks.

"Well?" The duke thrust out his hand for the message. Simon handed it over.

"You're excused, page." The duke waved him off.

Simon didn't look at me again, but he also didn't move. I could sense a struggle taking place in his adolescent brain as he stared at a blank spot on the wall.

"You're excused, boy!"

Simon bowed, walked halfway down the corridor, and then did the craziest thing I'd ever seen: He dropped to the ground and started shaking and screaming. The guards rushed over to him. The duke took two lazy steps forward, seeming more interested in the spectacle than providing assistance. His valet stuck his head out, scowling, when Simon gave a particularly ear screeching wail. The duke impatiently nodded toward the boy, and the valet went to kneel by him as the soldiers stood uncertainly. The valet produced a vial of smelling salts, which seemed to quiet Simon. And that was when I took the only option I had, as suicidal as it was.

I bolted into the duke's chambers.

Inside, I turned three and a half circles looking—no, begging—for some place to hide. Desk. Table. Armchair. Voices outside, blocking my exit of this lion's den.

"Take him to the infirmary," the duke ordered.

"Yes, Your Grace."

Footsteps approached the door. Out of time, I tried to squeeze behind an armchair in the corner of the room but couldn't fit through the small space. I dove over the top of the chair, my arms barely able to slow the collision my head had with the stone floor. The door slammed shut and I tucked my legs, hoping they didn't show over the top of the thick armchair.

The duke sighed, like he was trying to relieve some amount of stress. I knew how he felt. In my upside-down perch I felt a little overwhelmed myself.

I held still until his steps carried him from the front room. Despite my best efforts, no amount of wiggling could turn me right. The space was just too small. I was stuck in the corner of the duke's front room with my skirts over my head and my backside in the air. My arms braced my aching head where it met the floor, the pain amplified by the blood rushing to it. If I didn't hurt so badly, and if my situation were less dire, I might have laughed. Hard. This was by far the most ridiculous pickle my sneaking had ever landed me in.

But now was hardly a time for laughing. I was in real trouble.

If I could just push the chair a few inches away from the wall, there was a chance I could flip around and right myself. Who knew how long the duke would stay in his chambers? If I was going to be stuck here all day, I might as well be comfortable.

I started by wiggling my legs—testing the chair to see how much noise it generated. The chair tipped back and forth with barely any sound. *Finally, something working in my favor.* Encouraged by my first experiment, I used my legs and arms to push a little harder. This proved tricky because it meant abandoning my head and using my back as leverage against the wall.

One... two... three...

I pushed too hard with my legs. Instead of moving the whole chair, the top tilted forward. I panicked and hooked the top of the chair with my foot as it balanced on two front legs. It required every meager muscle in my body to keep the chair from falling forward. Still, when I did swing back to the wall, the chair landed with a heavy *thud!*

I tucked my legs just as the duke came into the room. His feet moved straight to the door. "Hello?" he called to nobody.

After a moment, he shut the door and turned toward me. Again, I knew I was caught. Step. Step. Step. He stopped right in front of the chair. Just as I thought my life might end from suspense, his boots turned and he dropped into the chair, pinning me that much closer to the wall.

Perfect.

I don't know how long I waited. It felt like I'd been on my head long enough for my neck to snap in two. Without daring to move, I sat on my head as the duke puffed on his smoking pipe in complete relaxation. It wasn't his fault that I was stuck here, yet I couldn't help hating him in those long, painful minutes.

My salvation finally came with a knock at the door. A real knock.

I could tell this boy wasn't Simon, but he panted in a very Simon-like fashion as he delivered his message.

"Fire… in the lumber yard!"

The duke hurried around the room, gathering who knows what before slamming the door behind him and turning the lock.

Several moments passed before I felt it safe enough to push the chair out of the way. I readied my feet on top of the chair and braced for a quick escape once the chair knocked over.

I pushed once and only managed to rock the chair before it came back to smack me in the face. My muscles felt like the soles of well-worn shoes. The unnatural strain on my body along with the tax on my nerves had beaten me down to nothing. I considered the possibility that I might never leave this horrible corner—not alive and certainly not with any shred of dignity.

Father would be endlessly disappointed when the messenger arrived with the news.

"I'm sorry, Councilman Fields. She expired with her skirt over her head after breaking into the honorable duke's chambers."

Cringing, I placed my feet in the kicking place, and readied my legs for some serious shoving when I heard the sound of scraping metal and the click of the lock.

I would have cried—no wailed with all my voice—if I didn't think it would give me away. Instead, I whimpered and tucked my legs back behind that cursed chair.

"Ebby?" Wesley's voice never sounded so wonderful.

I went to call for him, but my voice caught in my throat as I remembered the status of my skirts. Wesley was the best and worst person to find me in this humiliating predicament.

"Ebby?" He traveled deeper into the duke's rooms, his calls growing more urgent as he went.

I sighed. "Over here, Wes."

His heavy working boots pivoted and advanced toward my corner. I abandoned my head and used my hands in a weak attempt to push up my skirts.

When my legs popped out from behind the chair, his feet slowed to a halt. "Ebby, are those your ankles?"

Was that humor in his voice?

"Just help me, blacksmith." I hoped he could hear my annoyance. "Or would you rather the duke found me?"

He crossed the remaining distance and grabbed the arms of the chair, pulling it away from the wall with an annoying amount of ease.

I fell flat on my face. My neck was so weak I lacked the energy to even turn my head. I barely managed to pull down my skirts.

"What were you doing, Ebby?" His voice rose in accusation, which automatically put me on the defensive.

"I had everything well in hand. I was just leaving when you barged in."

We looked at each other and our anger melted into smiles of relief. "We'll discuss how wrong you are as soon as we're clear of this wing of the fortress," he said, helping me to my feet.

I didn't argue. "How did you find me?" I grabbed my head, wishing the room would stop it's spinning. "I thought you were under guard in the smithy."

"Long story. Let's just say Simon has a gift with starting fires."

As Wesley set the chair back in the corner, I took a look around. In the middle of the room sat a square table with a giant map of the Southern Provinces laid out on it: Brennan, Sea Port, Vikehand, and Freeland, the island of Cyprian, and a number of the smaller territories. It was a beautiful drawing that reminded me of one of my father's illuminated books at home. Sweeping blue strokes depicted rivers and oceans, meticulously drawn small green trees represented forests, mountains—black as the coal we mined from them—stretched in elegant ranges dividing Freeland from the rest. Red dashed lines showed the traveling roads. *Red. Just like my warnings.*

Wesley tugged on her arm. "We need to leave," he said.

"Wait, Wes. Look at these red lines." I pointed to a road that cut through the mountain range dividing Sea Port from Freeland. "Does this road even exist?"

Wesley paused to look at the map, even though the shifting of his feet told me it pained him to take the moment to do so. "No. It must be a mistake. Only a mountain goat could travel that path."

"Look," I pointed to Brennan Pass, the same narrow pass we'd traveled weeks ago. "They've circled our pass in red. Why do you think—?"

"Please, Ebby. We need to get out of here before someone comes!"

That's when I noticed the wooden letterbox on the desk in the corner. It was beautifully carved, with a brass keyhole set at the front. Wesley's pleas for us to leave turned into background noise I drifted toward the box, the pull in my stomach telling me it was important.

As I expected, the box was locked.

"We need to open this, Wesley! Use your tools."

"There's no time for that now."

"Please." I took hold of his shirtfront and, for some reason, choked on my words. I couldn't sign that blood oath without evidence of a threat to Freeland. And if I didn't sign it, Wesley would be tortured for information he didn't have.

Wesley's eyes widened as he looked down at my hands in his shirt. I hadn't realized just how close we stood. If Wesley weren't so tall, we'd have been nose-to-nose. I carefully released my grasp on his shirt and patted down the wrinkles. "Sorry."

He sighed and said, "You're going to get yourself killed one day." He sidestepped me to get to the box. After only a half-minute or so of working his small iron instruments the lock clicked.

"You're a wizard!" I gushed.

Wesley shrugged and stepped aside, his cheeks red and startlingly adorable.

The box was filled with letters. I handed a small stack to Wesley and we both poured through them.

"Mine just look like supply lists," I complained. "Inventory on arms and food, men and other resources."

"That's strange."

"What is it?" I demanded.

Wesley scrunched his brow. *"Takes his breakfast at 6:00 am before morning ride,"* read Wesley. *"Spends most of his time in the fields, unprotected. Breaks at high noon and returns home for a meal with his son and daughter. Spends evenings at his desk handling affairs of his people. Sleeps without a lock on the door.*"

"That sounds like Father."

"We don't know for certain that it's—" Wesley began.

"Of course we do! What other leader works in the fields all day? Has a son and daughter?"

Wesley gathered the letters and jammed them back into the box. "We're leaving." He clamped his hand around my wrist and pulled me from the room.

CHAPTER THIRTY

WIND

Sitting at my writing desk with shaking hands, I composed a letter to Joe Ford explaining that I agreed to his terms. The only thing left was to sign it. In my own blood.

I stared down at the letter, building up the nerve to make such a drastic decision based on only the map for solid evidence. I cared for Wesley, and didn't want the rest of the Freelanders in Brennan to be in danger, but was I really prepared to commit my people to war?

A sharp knock sounded on my door. I startled, knocking over the inkwell.

"Miss Fields?" called Lord Kent through the door.

I snatched up the letter before it could be ruined and rushed to my bedside for a handkerchief to dab at the puddle of ink.

"You may enter."

Lord Kent carried a small bunch of flowers and a nervous grin. With some effort, I'd managed to avoid him since the night Wesley showed me the Purgo.

"Good day, Miss Fields." He handed me the flowers, and I accepted them with a nod. "I trust you're feeling better."

"They're beautiful." I held the flowers to my nose and inhaled the sweet aroma, but all I could think about was how the deep pink of the pedals reminded me of Wesley's blood after Lord Kent's men arrested and beat him. "What is the occasion?"

"I'm told apologies are always improved by flowers," he said, a hint of his striking smile teased the corner of his lips, just begging to emerge.

I liked Lord Kent, but how could he expect me to overlook what had happened to Wesley? How did I know that he wasn't involved with his father's plans?

As if reading my mind, he added, "I don't expect you to forgive me." He dug his toe into the floor. "I just wanted you to know that I never gave the order to harm Wesley. When he attacked my men, they responded. I'm sorry it happened, if that means anything to you."

I couldn't afford another enemy in Brennan right now, so I simply said, "The flowers are lovely." I smiled at him and he seemed to relax.

"I've missed you this past week. You haven't been to dinner or any of the evening parties." He cleared his throat. "But I suppose I know why."

Suddenly aware of my letter to Joe Ford, open and exposed in my hand, I casually tucked it behind my back.

"I'm hoping you might join me for cards this evening." Lord Kent reached for my free hand, and while keeping his eyes firmly locked on mine, raised it to his lips. "I can't stomach the thought of you holed up in your rooms for one more evening."

Cheeks blazing, I darted a quick glance back to the writing desk and the ink-soaked handkerchief. "You don't need to worry about me, my lord."

As he gently squeezed my hand, his voice grew soft and surprisingly sensual. "What if I told you my interest in your company wasn't entirely selfless?" He took a step closer, looking down at me with those handsome eyes that always shocked me with their clarity. "What if I told you that I missed you?" Another kiss to my hand.

I turned away before the heat in my cheeks fully betrayed me. But he followed, the warmth of his body at my back.

"I wish you wouldn't flatter me, sir."

His finger ran along the back of my arm from elbow to shoulder in slow trails that raised gooseflesh across the surface of my skin. "I only crave your company, my dear, and hope to put that pretty smile back on your face."

"I… I don't know—"

"I'm only asking for an evening." He paused. "Would you feel more comfortable if your friend Mr. Daily joined us? I know you like to play at cards with him."

The person I really want near me is Wesley.

I stepped away from Lord Kent's touch and gestured to the door. "If you don't mind giving me a moment to freshen up, I'll be right out." I tried to give him a courageous smile, but it felt wooden on my face.

He beamed at me, pausing just a moment to notice the letter in my hand. "To whom are you—?"

"I'll only be a moment!" I shut the door and ran over to the writing desk. My heart beat in my throat. Still uncertain that this was the right decision, I righted the empty inkwell, picked up the letter opener and muttered, "Don't let me down, Joe."

The blade was dull but effective. My own blood turned the crystal inkwell crimson as it rolled off the tip of my finger. I watched the droplets in fascination. If I delivered this letter, it was only fitting that mine should be the first blood spilt of my countrymen.

The quill soaked up the thick liquid and I signed *Ebrielle Ann Fields*.

I tucked the letter into my dress pocket, hoping I hadn't just made a terrible mistake.

Mr. Daily greeted us in the game room by taking both of my hands in his while kissing my cheeks. I'd seen enough of the Sea Port exchanges to know this was a common greeting.

"You have been missed." He glanced over at Lord Kent. "I'm sure I'm not the only one who feels that way."

Lord Kent laughed. "Am I that obvious?"

The duke's personal guard approached us and Lord Kent frowned. "Please excuse me. I won't be long."

Mr. Daily gestured to a table of chess. "Do you play?"

Images of Father stroking the whiskers on his chin while a fire crackled peacefully in the background came to mind. He always did that when we played chess together. If I closed my eyes, I could almost smell Hannah's warm bread baking only a few feet away. Home. I missed it like the fields miss the sun in winter.

"Miss Fields?" Mr. Daily raised a brow.

"Oh. Sorry. Yes, I'd love to play." The blood oath crinkled in my pocket as I sat.

"As ambassador of Sea Port, I have many ears in Brennan, my dear." He moved a pawn without taking his eyes from me. "I understand you have made some rather drastic friendships of late."

I might have panicked if there wasn't admiration in his eyes. There was no question he referred to my commitment to help the rebellion. "Do you think Father would disapprove?"

Mr. Daily crossed his arms and nodded. Around us bouts of laughter and lively conversation came from other tables. The sweet smell of wine and pipe tobacco filled the air.

"About your father." Daily leaned closer still, hesitating like he almost didn't want to tell me. "When I first arrived for the festival, one of my informants told me of a plot." He twisted one of the many rings on his fingers. A nervous habit, if I wasn't mistaken.

"I haven't wanted to say anything to you, but I fear it has now become my duty." He cleared his throat. "I've sent a man to deliver a warning to your father over the mountain. I knew the pass was dangerous, so he carried a pigeon along with him so he could send word when the message was delivered."

"My father?" My voice was dry. "What plot?"

All of his usual cheer was lost in the concerned lines on his forehead. "The pigeon hasn't returned, Miss Fields."

"What are you saying?" I spotted Lord Kent across the room, heading toward us.

"Your father's in trouble." His words came out in a rush. "My men have gathered supplies enough for a few of us to make the journey over the mountain. I will go myself this time."

"But the pass—?" I started, but my words died when the door to the game room flew open. Four armed soldiers marched toward Mr. Daily. They kicked the chair out from under him and grabbed him by both arms.

"Stop! Why are you taking him?" I yelled, digging my heels into the expensive rug as I hung onto a soldier's coat. He flicked me off his sleeve like a pesky fly.

I chased after them, this time grabbing Mr. Daily's arm and pulling him in the opposite direction.

"Don't fight them, child," Daily hissed under his breath. But I refused to let go. Clearly this was a tugging match I would not win, but I couldn't just let them take him.

"Halt!" shouted Lord Kent. He rushed to my side and pulled me away from Mr. Daily. My body shook. My skin flashed hot under his protective embrace. "What is the meaning of this?" he demanded of the guards.

"We have orders to arrest this man, my lord," said the lead soldier. "We have reason to believe he's trespassed on the duke's private quarters."

My face went cold.

Lord Kent looked around the crowded game room, at the faces of nobility all frozen in captivation at the scene. I saw resignation in his eyes as he waved his father's soldiers to continue. An ugly wail escaped my lips. He turned my head to face him, but I would not pull my gaze from Mr. Daily as they towed him away.

"I will look into the matter, Miss Fields. I'll talk to my father. He must have some reason for taking him."

He certainly did.

I gripped the letter in my pocket. I had to find Simon.

Freeland was going to war.

CHAPTER THIRTY-ONE

PREPARATIONS

Simon delivered my letter that night and returned with detailed instructions from Joe, including a plan for our escape. The next day I didn't even bother going to meet the duchess or her spoiled daughter in the pink wing. She would be furious, but I didn't plan to linger long enough for it to matter. Instead, I spent the morning visiting every Freeland craftsman, telling them of our plan and asking them to make quiet preparations to leave.

In all my running about, I couldn't stop thinking about Father. He was in trouble. Someone was going to harm him and there was absolutely nothing I could do about it. Meanwhile, Mr. Daily sat in some dungeon cell beneath the fortress, and Wesley faced an even worse fate if I couldn't get him out of here.

Once everything was in place, I approached the brazier of the Freeland tent and eyed the four guards stationed at each corner. Master Moorly greeted me with a kind smile, but when Wesley lifted his head, he had a fresh bruise around his eye and a pitiful frown on his face. With a set of metal tongs, he laid a glowing rectangle of ore on the anvil.

"I can't talk to you right now," Wesley called out to me. He lifted his hammer and started pounding. Master Moorly hit the oar with his own hammer in between every one of Wesley's blows.

I stepped to one of the guards, and asked, "Please, may I just speak to him."

The guard exchanged looks with the others, and then nodded.

"Thank you." I stepped past them, but their eyes didn't leave me.

"What are you doing?" I asked Wesley.

Wesley kept striking the metal. "They'll hurt you if I don't." His jaw was tight and his voice cold.

But Wesley didn't know the secrets of the Purgo. Was this just an act to buy us more time? The pull went wild within me. Frantic even.

"Everything will be all right," I whispered. I could almost feel the guards around us leaning in to hear our conversation. "I have a plan, and I need to borrow something."

I unfolded Joe's letter and held it before his eyes, not daring to say anything the guards could overhear.

Wesley's expression changed from sour to hopeful as he read.

"Hey!" one of the guards called. "Give me that letter!" He walked over with hand outstretched and I tossed it in the brazier.

"You little…" He lunged for me and I instinctively darted behind Wesley, like a coward.

"Don't you dare," Wesley's voice turned feral as he raised his hammer at my defense. "She hasn't done anything wrong."

The guard stopped just outside of Wesley's reach. "No more notes." He tried to sound threatening, but the tremor in his voice gave away the man's fear.

"Thank you, Wes," I whispered. For some reason, my cheeks felt as hot as the forges as I released my hold on Wesley's waist.

He lowered his hammer. "Everything will be fine. Just don't do anything foolish."

I scoffed. "Of course not."

MR. HOVEL. THE old gong farmer, wasn't by his tower. I combed through the heavy curtain of the throng, trying my hardest to blend in with the crowd.

"Are you looking for old man Hovel?"

The voice came from the mouth of the little girl standing on a stool stirring a pot of something. I barely heard her voice over the bustle of the crowd and the dickering of a nearby street vender.

"Uh, no, not at all. I was just…"

"He's not here." The girl didn't take her large, round eyes off the pot as she spoke. "Ma always complains about him passing on her stew. She never sells enough stew. Says if it's not good enough for a gong farmer it's not good enough for anyone."

The girl carried on with her stirring, tucking long dark hair behind her ear with her free hand before resting it on her hip. I would have wagered three bushels of barley that her mother stood the same way when she stirred the stew.

"How old are you?"

She counted five fingers on her hand and showed them to me.

"Five. That *is* old."

I knew I'd won her over because she looked me in the eyes for the first time and smiled. "And I can count to five, too. On my next birthday I'll learn to count one more number."

"Six. You'll be able to count to six."

She dropped her ladle and put both fists on her hips this time. "You ruined my surprise! Now I have to wait *forever* for another number."

I had to hold in the laugh that tickled my throat. "What do you do in kinder school? Plug your ears all day?" I giggled.

Her scowl softened to something less certain. "What is kinder school?"

They must've called it something different here. "It's where you learn your numbers, letters, writing, and reading."

The girl's mouth dropped in amazement. "Can I go?" she asked, hopping up and down on the wobbly stool.

"She's only teasing, child. There's no such thing as kinder school." Mr. Hovel came to stand at my side.

"You're mean." The girl bit her bottom lip to hold back a weak cry.

I walked away with Mr. Hovel, stunned.

"You shouldn't have spoken to that girl."

"I had no idea children in Brennan didn't go to school. How will she learn her letters? Will her parents teach her?"

"I'm sure they would if they knew them."

Oh.

I was such an idiot. It was like all the color in the world around me suddenly bled into a mass of gray ugliness. And I, the person who claimed to always know what was going on, was just a walking puddle of ignorance.

How could I have so much while that little girl was deprived of the numbers she seemed to cherish? It wasn't right!

"I assume you came to ask me something?" He looked sad, as if I had *his* pity. This whole place was just too confusing.

"If you don't mind, Mr. Hovel, I'm interested in locating the dungeon, and I'm afraid to ask anyone else for directions."

"Off to visit Mr. Daily, I assume?"

"How did you know?"

He pointed to his ear and shrugged. "It's a gift."

A gift indeed. "Mr. Daily was trying to tell me something before they took him. Something important."

Mr. Hovel studied me for a long moment before scooping up a shovel-load of delight. "I don't want to tell you, miss."

"Why ever not!" I'd anticipated his cooperation. Without it I was in trouble.

"Because it's no place for a lady, that's why not."

I gestured around us. "And this is?"

He grumbled something about tiresome females and went back to work on his pile.

"Please," I begged. I knew it was unbecoming, but compared to the last five minutes of my life it was close to singing a sonnet.

My pleading hung in the air along with the fumes of the alley for too long before he finally conceded. "All right, but if you must go, I'm going with you."

I didn't expect this. "I can't let you come. It would be too dangerous."

His bark of laughter startled me. "You need me, my lady. How else will you pass the guards?"

In truth I hadn't thought that far ahead.

"Meet me here just before sun-up tomorrow. That's when I usually go collect the buckets."

Buckets? Something told me I didn't want to know.

CHAPTER THIRTY-TWO

BUCKETS

I met Mr. Hovel by the west gate. The sky was gray and the earth around us officially dead or sleeping beneath the frost. Mr. Hovel didn't look happy to see me.

"I hoped you'd change your mind, Miss Fields," he said. White puffs of air escaped his lips as he spoke.

He handed me a heavy burlap cloak and hood. "Put this on. Keep your head down, and we might just get through this with our necks."

I nodded and donned the cloak. We traveled a portion of the fortress I'd never seen until this cold, dark morning. Several times I thought we were lost, until we found another door, another stairwell, taking us deeper into the belly of this stone beast.

"There's something I should tell you, Miss Fields."

"Is it happy?" I asked. I *really* needed some good news. A reprieve from the wildfire that seemed to surround me.

Mr. Hovel just gave one of his signature *humpfs*. By now I knew these were the sounds of a man who thought me crazy.

"You'll find no happy news while walking this part of Brennan."

"Tell me."

"I worked late last night. Some of the men coming out of the pub were a little too liberal with their tongues."

He wheezed a few times to catch his breath and I thought I might die from anticipation.

"I heard a man say something about a certain Freelander who was, and I quote, 'in for a deadly game of trouble'."

I gulped. "Did they say who?"

We reached the first guard and I bowed my head.

"Morning, dung man. Come to collect your prizes?" The guard slapped his knee and laughed. The sound echoed off the walls. I smelled the man's breath through my hood. *I wish burlap was a thicker fabric.*

"Who's the runt?" He walked over to me with a heavy swagger in his step. "I didn't think you had any help."

Mr. Hovel was just as ornery toward the guard as he was to everyone. "Newly assigned to me. Now get out of our way unless you want to find a shovel of *prizes* in your bed tonight."

The guard held his ground for a moment before stepping aside to let us pass.

"Watch out for the Sea Port bucket. I hear their bile is green as seaweed and will blister your nose if you whiff it directly," he said as we walked down what I hoped was the final set of stairs.

I was suddenly grateful for an empty stomach.

The smell had teeth. Sharp, sharp teeth that gnawed on my insides. Every jail cell was occupied, though many of the figures sprawled on the floor seemed inhuman, or just barely alive.

"Keep that hood down," Mr. Hovel ordered as he picked up bucket after bucket and emptied the contents into an even larger container strapped to his back. Several men and a few women sat huddled in the corner of their cells, rocking back and forth as they muttered to themselves.

"What's wrong with them?" I asked.

Mr. Hovel paused his work, and looked back at me, frowning. "They are lost to the Dark Ones."

"Who?"

"Dark spirits, miss. Terrible and vicious if they know how to reach your mind. Sprits of the damned don't move on from this life, so when they find someone who can hear them, someone who can commune with those beyond the grave, they attack. They break down their defenses, little by little, forcing them to do horrible things, until accessing the mind is easy. Almost like a dam breaking. It begins with a little leak and ends with a flood."

The dungeon grew colder. Mr. Hovel kept walking but a man who'd been pulling out his own hair in great chunks suddenly stopped his mumbled ranting and snapped his gaze from the ground to stare directly at me.

"We see you, girl. We see you." His wicked grin didn't match his sorrowful, bloodshot eyes.

Hovel raised a brow at me but kept pulling me along.

We came to the end of the long row of unfortunates before I had time to process what had just happened.

"You have two minutes." Mr. Hovel gestured to a disheveled figure sitting hunched over with arms folded in the corner of the last cell. Then he left me to finish his collection.

Mr. Daily raised his head like it weighed more than it should. "What do you want, farmer?" he asked.

I turned my back to the rest of the men and lifted my hood just enough to show him my face. He fell off the three-legged stool he'd been resting on. "What in the—"

"Shhhh. I don't have much time."

He crawled over to me and wrapped his fingers around the iron bars separating us. "You shouldn't have come here, Miss Fields."

I slipped him the iron tools Wesley had managed to give me the day before. The same tools he'd used to free me from the duke's chamber. "I don't know how to use them, but try to open your cell."

He accepted them with a frown. "In case I don't escape, I must tell you that as soon as Brennan can occupy Sea Port— something my people have been fighting for years—they're coming for Freeland. They're planning to build a road over the western mountain pass using explosives. Freeland's rich with resources, ore especially. But I think Brennan wants to bring Freeland to her knees for less noble reasons."

"Why?"

"Of all of us, Freeland's the most likely to oppose them. You're strong, and in ten years you could be even greater than Brennan. You represent defiance—a place for the rebellious and determined to find refuge. Brennan can't afford to lose any more of its workers to Freeland."

Mr. Hovel hobbled over to us, burdened by his newly acquired load. "It's time."

I placed my hands over Mr. Daily's and looked directly in his sad eyes. "What should I do?"

"Get Mr. Smith out of here. Find a way to warn your father. The duke has a man in Freeland now with orders to kill him just before first thaw."

"No." The full truth of the situation was a sledgehammer to my middle. It was too late in the year to trek over the pass to Freeland to warn my Father and traveling through Sea Port would take too long. Panic surged through me. Father murdered before spring. I had to warn him!

"You were going to travel the mountain pass. You have supplies and provisions to make the trip," I said.

He nodded. "The farm closest to the pass has an old shed with supplies. If I can escape this place, my men and I will leave directly."

"I'll go with you."

His voice flattened. "Not a chance. Your father would kill me if I let you do something so reckless."

"What else can I do?" I gasped as Mr. Hovel tried to pry my fingers away from Mr. Daily's.

"Travel with your friend, Joe Ford, and that blacksmith of yours. Tell him everything I've told you." He pulled a stubborn ring from his pinkie finger. "Give this to the first official you meet when you reach Sea Port. It's been in my family for years. They'll know what it means."

I accepted the ring, giving Mr. Hovel the chance to pull me from the bars.

"I'll save your father, Ebby," Daily called as I was dragged away. "Freeland needs him. We must stop Brennan from ruling us all."

My legs didn't work properly. I felt like my insides might boil if I didn't get some air. I followed Mr. Hovel until something occurred to me.

"Mr. Daily." I ran back to him. "Did you write the red letters?"

"Red letters?" he replied. "My dear, I have no idea what you're talking about."

Wesley, one year earlier

My parents are dead. Their loss is a crushing burden. One I'm not sure I can carry. It seems the whole town has come to pity me. If they really want to offer condolences, they'll leave me alone. Gavin, Stock, Marianna, Isa, and Ebby wait on the outskirts of the graveyard that has consumed my parents. They don't talk among themselves. Only watch me. Showing me they are there. Ready if I need them. They know me well enough to hold back, waiting. I'm grateful for that at least.

When the line of well-wishers dies, Master Moorly pats me on the back, bows his head, and walks away.

I eventually nod at them, and my friends trickle over to my side. Stock mutters something in such a deep voice I can't even discern his words. It doesn't matter. Isa and Gavin stand on either side of me, each resting a hand on one of my shoulders.

When they finally leave me, I decide I can't stand any longer but I also can't leave. The ground is cold when I sit. My mother hated the cold.

Clouds drift across the sky. I pick at the grass by my feet, then close my eyes and lie back. Exhaustion claims me, and I drift to sleep. It feels as though I've barely closed my eyes when I startle awake.

It's getting dark but I'm not ready to leave this spot. Leaving feels like the first step to forgetting. I will not do that. My parents may have left me, but I will not leave them.

Sitting with my hands clasped in front of my knees, I close my eyes and I can still smell the smoke. See the ash that floats down around me like a calm winter snow. I wonder if I'll think of my parents whenever I'm required to light the brazier and work the bellows. Fire. My father's life and now his death.

My stomach rolls and I don't know if I can be the smithy father raised me to be.

The sky purples like a sickly bruise. The first stars appear. It is difficult to believe so much time has passed without my consent.

I shiver and climb to my feet.

I consider abandoning my parents.

Movement on the fringe of the cemetery catches my attention.

It is just light enough to see Ebby's blond hair. She wears it down now.

It's easier walking away from my parents when I know I'm walking toward something. She stands when I approach. Her arms cross at her stomach. Her hands rove along her forearms, likely trying to create heat on this cool evening. Has she been here all day?

I don't even try to say anything. I don't have to with her.

Holding open my arms to her comes so naturally. It is always the pretending that is hard. Pretending she isn't important to me. Pretending I don't value her company. That is the lie I am too tired to tell right now.

She doesn't hesitate. Her arms slide around my waist. Mine fall around her in turn. She clings to me, burying her head into my chest as she cries. My chin rests on her head. God made her to fit in my arms.

Tears roll down my cheeks. The first I've been able to shed. A sob wracks my body, first hers, and then mine. Having her near me chases some of the despair away. The tightness in my chest relaxes.

This girl, in braids no longer, makes me feel as though I can have a second chance at a family. I swear I will protect her better than I did my mother. What is my world now but Ebrielle Ann Fields?

CHAPTER THIRTY-THREE

ESCAPE

The plan wasn't too complicated. Get Wesley outside the doors of the fortress at the appointed time and let the revolutionaries do the rest. Simple.

Even though I had everything in place, my time in the duchess's chambers stretched long and the lavender incense grew thick in my throat. I found myself stealing glances out the balcony window, embroidery in hand, hoping to see some of the Freeland craftsmen casually walking outside to find the meeting place.

No one would notice their absence among the throng of artists and craftsmen until we were well away from the fortress. At least that's what I told myself while stitching ugly flowers into a new sampler.

Everything would be fine.

But the truth was, I didn't know that for certain. I was just one girl. What right did I have to think I could thwart the great duke of Brennan? In all the stories I'd heard told, great heroes were constantly set against overwhelming odds. But there was always something in their character that made them victorious. Some redeeming quality that saved them from a doomed fate. I searched my heart for that something. Courage? No, I was terrified. Integrity? The work of eavesdropping was never considered honest. Talent? I looked down at my sampler and frowned. Did I have even one talent outside of my knack for finding trouble and disappointing my family?

I shook my head. There was too much that could go wrong with our plan. For instance, I might die of nerves before even having the chance to break Wesley out of his room tonight. Brennan was a gilded cage from which I couldn't wait to be free. The longer I stayed here, the less likely I'd be able to save my father. My home. Everything I cared for.

I just hoped I didn't mess it up, like I had everything else.

I WRUNG MY hands as I paced my rooms. A glance out the window confirmed the sun was only an hour or so from sinking below the horizon. Soon the guests of the fortress would congregate in the Great Hall to await the announcement of dinner. Since I had missed so many of these indulgent meals, I doubted my absence would raise suspicion.

Our plan depended upon it.

Where was Simon?

A sharp knock sounded on the door. "Thank goodness!" I said aloud to the empty room as I rushed to open the door.

But it wasn't Simon.

Lord Kent bowed with his usual confident smile. I only paused a moment before returning the gesture with a curtsy of my own.

"I believe I've startled you, my dear."

"Not at all, my lord."

"You will please call me Theodore. We're well past such formalities, don't you think?"

I got caught up in his eyes for a moment. He really was so handsome. But I blinked, seeing something beneath his good manners and kind attentions. Something I didn't trust.

"Is there something I can do for you," a pause, "Theodore? If you've come to escort me to dinner, I must decline the offer. I have a mind to stay in for the evening."

Lord Kent grinned. "I assumed you'd say that. No, I have something else planned for us. Something a Fields, of all people, must see."

I fought to mask my rising panic. Our plan tonight depended upon me reaching Wesley's rooms by sundown. "My lord—"

"Theodore." Lord Kent raised a hand. "I'm sorry, Ebby, but I really must insist you accompany me." He sidestepped me and walked into my room to the wardrobe to find a pair of warm gloves and my heavy cloak.

"Where are we going?" I asked. Perhaps if we hurried, I could be back to my rooms before Simon even missed me.

"It's a surprise." He winked at me, and practically pulled me from my chamber.

We crossed the courtyard in the brisk evening air and turned down a narrow, ivy-walled passage.

I saw the hothouses before he had the chance to point them out. I'd never seen so much glass in one concentrated area. It would cost Father a fortune to construct such a building. The rooftops domed with tiny chimneys released white smoke that reflected the light of the moon. The buildings glowed in the growing darkness, like excited lightning bugs, thanks to the white condensation of the walls and the flickering fire within.

"They're amazing," I said as we came to stand in front of the main structure.

"I'm glad you think so." He pulled open the door. "After you," he whispered with an amused smile playing about his lips.

There were plants I'd never seen before—vines with white star-shaped flowers that gave off the most seductive fragrance, exotic lilies, and so many others. In the center of the room stood a small flowering tree with waxy dark green leaves and fist-sized orange berries. Though I wasn't an artist, I longed for parchment and ink. I needed some means of capturing this beauty so my family could enjoy the miracle along with me.

"I'm beginning to think this was a bad idea."

I looked over to find Lord Kent holding out a chair next to a small table near the entrance. I hadn't even noticed the table set for two. "I'll never be able to compete for your attention in this room." He laughed.

For once my smile came naturally. I walked over and sat down. The light of a single candle flickered between us. "I'm sorry. I've just never seen such beauty in all my life."

"I know the feeling," he said, eyeing me like a starving man.

I looked at my hands and fiddled with a bead on my gloves. A small part of me felt bad for Lord Kent. There was a chance he had nothing to do with any of this mess, and here I was, leading him to believe I had romantic feelings for him.

The meal came in five courses, ending with a mug of spiced cider and cake. I let Lord Kent carry us through conversation, the whole time wishing he would hurry as I shot nervous glances to the darkening sky. Simon would definitely have come to my rooms by now. What would he do when he found them empty?

Lord Kent wanted to know more about my childhood. My parents. My brother. My home. My education. My everything. Every time I changed the subject, he found some way to bring the conversation back around to me. Back on the mountain, I'd considered his inquiries a sign of his desired friendship. I'd been happy to answer all of his questions. Now, I questioned his motives, wondering if he'd help his father use this information to hurt my family.

After dinner, the full moon helped to guide our silent stroll back to my rooms. I held on to Lord Kent's arm, resisting the urge to tug him along and increase our pace.

I was late. Wesley would be in a panic.

Dark, long shadows played tricks on me, distorted wisps of carts, crates, and bodies, some moving in sharp lines, others standing still like long fingers reaching out to grab me.

We stopped just outside the door of my room. I used my back to block the latch. The last thing I wanted was Lord Kent on the other side of this door without a chaperone at this time of night. "Thank you for taking me to the hothouses. They were incredible."

Lord Kent pushed the hood of my cloak back and used the backside of his fingers to brush my cheek. "Good heavens, Ebby, why didn't you tell me you were so cold?"

I told him I was fine, but my assurances fell on deaf ears. He took my waist and moved me aside—like I was a piece of furniture blocking his path—and let himself into my room.

"Let me build up your fire before I leave."

I rolled my eyes. I didn't know what kind of girls he was used to, but I was perfectly capable of throwing a log on the fire.

"Then again," he stood, dusting his fingers after completing the task, "a fire can only do so much to warm you."

My back met the wall with an ungraceful bump as Lord Kent pressed close to me. He reached up and stroked my cheek with the back of his hand. His fingers ran along my jaw and brushed down the length of my neck with feather softness. Then they followed the curve of my collar bone, tracing the too-low neckline of my dress.

"You're so tense, dearest. Try to relax." He took my wrist and placed my arms around his neck.

I quickly pulled it away. "Lord Kent, I think you should leave."

He kissed me hard. If I didn't know better, I would have thought he was trying to tear open my lips and lick up my blood.

I pulled away with a groan that he misinterpreted as passion. His lips moved to my neck.

As my breathing increased, my limbs stiffened and a sob issued from somewhere within my chest. Suppressing the sound only added to the pain I felt. I didn't move. I couldn't move. I was a statue, frozen in fear of what might come if I didn't find some way to stop him.

I was in trouble.

If only Wesley or Father or Gavin were here. They would protect me from this predator.

Is that how it's going to be with you, Ebby? Are you really so weak to need man around to save you? Determined not to be helpless, I found movement in my arms and used them to push Lord Kent away. He resisted for a moment, and then seemed to come to his senses.

"What's wrong, my dear?" His words were gentlemanly but came out like the pant of a hungry wolf.

"You need to leave, my lord." I studied my hands in an attempt to look bashful. Though I didn't look up at him, I could sense his anger. He'd gone far enough down the road of intimacy to feel put out. I stole a glance at him and tried to smile.

His lips were forced up into what I assumed to be a grin. If I was being honest with myself, he looked insane, like he wanted to make me pay for stopping him from getting what he was after.

After what seemed like an endless stretch of time, his smile became less forced and his hands rubbed up and down my arms. "Are you warm now, Ebby?"

I must have been holding my breath because my words came with a good amount of wind behind them. "Yes, thank you."

He bent to kiss my cheek and left the room.

I closed the door behind him, fighting to breathe. I'd wanted my first kiss to be special. Instead, I felt robbed of something that I could never get back. I bit my lip to keep it from trembling.

Another knock sounded.

I cleared my throat and took a deep breath, but still my voice shook as I said, "Who is it?"

"It's me!" Simon. Thank goodness!

"It's about time!" Simon slipped into my room carrying a bundle of brown clothing. "You were supposed to be at Wesley's door an hour ago. The guard change has already happened. Your opportunity has passed!"

I took the bundle from Simon. "We don't have a choice."

"I don't think you understand." He threw up his hands. "Even with the key, it's not going to work."

"I can't see a better option."

"I can think of five right now," said Simon.

"Any that don't involve you putting yourself in danger?" I perched a hand on my hip, knowing I looked just like my mother when I did. Simon had done so much already. I couldn't ask more from him.

"I can help…"

"No." I walked around a changing curtain and shivered out of my dress and into the trousers. The itchy fabric formed to my legs in odd places, showing every curve. The tunic wasn't as bad, but, even though it was large, you could still see the slight shape of my figure beneath the fabric. Thank goodness I wasn't endowed like Lady Kent! I twisted my hair up and shoved it under a felt cap then used the ash of the fireplace to tint my fair colored eyebrows.

"Thanks for the words of comfort, Simon."

"Anytime, page boy." His banter fell as flat as his smile. Carefree Simon was really worried for me, and that more than anything made me scared.

"Whatever you do, don't get caught." Simon's expression had turned from concern to misery as he realized I was actually going through with my plans. "Once the duke sees you as an enemy, you don't have a chance."

I pulled on a little pack that held my Freeland clothes and a few other essentials, but froze at the subtle tugging of my stomach. The pull brought me over to the leather-bound journal on my writing desk. My little stolen piece of Brennan. I reached for the book and was overwhelmed with the clear impression that I should take it with me, even though doing so defied all reason. Without hesitation, I picked up the red sash I'd kept on my dressing table—the sash I never did give to Lord Kent after the hunt—and wrapped it around the journal for protection. After adding it to my pack with the other possessions I'd be taking with me on my journey, I carefully pocketed Mr. Daily's ring.

"See you at the Talk About." I ruffled Simon's hair and gave him a hug.

Simon left to go about his duties in the servant's wing and I, dressed like a skinny pip of a boy, headed toward the Great Hall—the only access to the west wing. To Wesley.

THE HALL WAS full of ladies wearing lavish dresses. Some wore peacock feathers in their hair, others wore elaborate hats and sashes spun with golden thread. It seemed every noble in the fortress, including the duke, had just finished dinner and now mingled as musicians played the lyre and pipes in the corner.

I approached the scene from the shadows of the east corridor with my back pressed against the stone wall. The corridor to Wesley's room opened at the other end of the Great Hall. Now that dinner was out, what was meant to be a quick pass through the hall was now a veritable gauntlet. Guards lined the walls and the duke himself stood between me and my destination. I slowed in fear.

If I didn't get Wesley out tonight, we'd lose our only chance for escape. Cowering in my room to wait for a better opportunity simply wasn't an option. Still, my feet felt like they were cast in mortar bricks and only the sound of approaching footsteps from behind propelled me to action.

I left the shadows and rushed to the curtain near the thick wooden trusses that held up the ceiling in a giant arc. I was only ten feet from the nearest guard, but he'd been too busy scanning the crowd to notice me.

The base of the massive truss was high above and an idea formed. A crazy thought that made me wonder if the evil spirits were back to haunt me. But this necessary madness was mine alone. Hidden inside the draperies, like a mouse in a cloth tunnel, I tested the fabric to see if it would hold my weight. When it didn't tear from its attachment to the ceiling, I gripped the fabric and pulled myself up. My legs swung wildly below me, my arms shaking from supporting my weight.

Halfway up, I peeked around to the outside of the curtain to find the nearest guard staring at the bottom. He elbowed the guard next to him and pointed to the drapery. I held perfectly still. *Please don't come over. Please don't come over.* The second guard nodded for his friend to investigate.

Tears of frustration swelled in my eyes. In spite of all of the trees I'd climbed, without any help from my legs, I knew I would soon fall, killing the hope of helping Wesley. Of saving my father. Of ever being proud to use the name Fields again.

The guard crossed the distance between us. My hands slipped an inch on the fabric. More tears accompanied the physical pain of supporting my weight with only my arms.

The guard took hold of the curtain.

Please, no. My fingers ached.

Just then, Georgiana 's voice rose above the others. I never thought I would be so happy to hear her voice.

"Peter, is it not?" she said to the guard.

Though I couldn't see him, I could hear the young guard's bewilderment. It was no small privilege to be singled out by the duke's pretty daughter.

"Yes, my lady?" the guard responded.

"I wanted to congratulate you on the fine way you wear your uniform. I would that every soldier of my father's employ looked so regal in Brennan red."

I didn't wait around to listen to the man's bumbling thanks. Instead, I prayed for strength that I didn't have and pulled myself up the last few feet of drapery to the trusses above. The rough wood was heaven in my hands. I collapsed face down on the truss. It was as wide as my shoulders, offering some comfort that no one could see me while I collected my breath.

Arms shaking, I eventually pushed up onto my hands and knees and began my crawl over the arching truss. The farther I moved along the wood, the higher I climbed—higher than any tree I'd ever scaled back home. Dust and dirt turned my hands black. But dust wasn't the only thing that had set up residency in the open ceiling. Dead beetles and other dried insects littered the beam. Spider webs clung to my forearms like sticky lace.

I crossed the highest point of the beam, careful not to glance down at the height separating me from the unforgiving marble floor. Below me, the duke's laugh carried above the rest of the crowd. It was the sound of a man full of confidence. He had the world at his fingertips and would never, ever imagine a lowly Freeland girl taking away his one chance at uncontested dominance in the region.

The closer I got to the other side of the room, the faster I crawled. Never stopping to worry about dodging bugs and wiping dust, I dared a peek over the edge of the wood to find Theodore talking to an elderly woman. She held a teacup in her hand and a pair of spectacles on a chain around her neck. The general buzz of the room kept me from hearing what they said. I planted another hand on the truss and felt something squishy and... furry.

I choked on a scream and flailed to get away from the now oozing dead mouse. One knee slipped beneath me, and before I knew it, both of my legs dangled from the wooden beam only twenty or so feet from the floor.

Someone would see me, if they hadn't already.

I scrambled back up to the safety of my perch but knocked something down in the process.

The dead furry creature turned two flips in the air before it plunked into the old woman's teacup. Lord Kent was talking to someone else now, and the old woman, who surely must have felt the jostle and splash of drink, didn't seem to notice.

She lifted the cup to her lips.

Then took a sip.

The woman shrieked. My stomach lurched, but I forced myself forward, my heart pumping with the speed of a hummingbird's wing. Ladies took the arm of their escorts, and I used their distraction to grab hold of the drapery. I landed on the marble floor and darted to the corridor of the west wing. To Wesley.

I pulled out the key and ran to Wesley's door. Simon had said dinner was the only possible time to get him. That's when most of the guards were either assisting in the banquet room or catching their own bite to eat. I didn't know what I'd find now other than a locked door. A lock to which I had a key! We would make it. I would find some way to get to my father and save my people from the Brennan's lies of peace and friendship.

I sprinted around the corner and collided with a red clad soldier standing guard outside Wesley's door. The force of the contact knocked me off my feet.

"Watch where you're going, you little rat!" the soldier snarled. Then he stopped, his eyes wide and his mouth hanging open. I glanced over and spotted my cap on the ground exposing my long blonde hair. For a moment the soldier and I just looked at each other. The moment passed, and I snatched my hat and ran for Wesley's door. "Wesley!" I jammed the key into the lock, but arms yanked me back before I could turn it and the key clattered to the floor.

Wesley called my name as I fought against the soldier. I scratched at the guard's cheek. He cried out as blood bloomed from the trails of my nails.

"Why you little…"

The guard grabbed my throat with both hands and squeezed. My air passage closed. I pulled at his arms and thrashed in panic. I was already so exhausted from my trip through the great hall that I didn't even budge him.

Black spots darkened the edges of my vision. *Please.* I mouthed my plea, lacking the air to speak the words. I remembered the key clattering to the ground next to me and used my heel to feel for the bit of metal that was meant to bring freedom instead of my own undoing.

"Ebby!" Wesley's pounded on his side of the door.

I let my arms fall and kicked one final time. The tinkling of metal on stone as the key slid under the door was the last thing I heard before I felt myself begin to slide into unconsciousness.

Then the pressure on my neck released, and I sank to the floor, blinking, as my vision and hearing returned. Above me, the guard turned in time for Wesley's fist to connect with his chin. I massaged my neck, beyond grateful for the air that rushed back into my panicked lungs.

Wesley stood over the unconscious guard with his chest rising and falling as though he'd been running. He turned to me, a storm passing across his face. "He hurt you," he said, reaching down to help me stand. Pulling me to him, my feet barely touching the ground in his urgent embrace.

I couldn't control the tremors that wracked my body.

"I have you now, Ebby." He smoothed the hair from my face with one hand and touched the tender parts of my neck that would surely bruise. "I have you."

A door shut somewhere down the long corridor, startling us both back to action.

Wesley dragged the limp body back into his room while I found my cap and tucked away my hair.

"Your message said sundown." Wesley shoved a sock in the man's mouth and tied it in place with a strip of cloth. "Bind his ankles." He tossed me a leather belt while he tied the guard's hands behind his back and to the bedpost. "I was worried when you didn't come." He doubled the knot on the man's bindings and then helped me to my feet.

"I was… detained by Lord Kent." I couldn't meet his gaze.

Wesley froze. Likely sensing what I wasn't saying, he took me by the shoulders. "Something happened." He stated it as fact, his face darkening by even the suggestion of what he could not say. "If he tried anything… Did he touch you?"

I could see the monster lurking behind Wesley's eyes. I'd seen variations of that look throughout our childhood. The most memorable being the day the Prickett brothers picked a fight with Gavin.

Wesley hadn't even let my brother take the first punch before attacking both brothers in a violent rage. I shuddered to think what he would do to Lord Kent if he learned the details of the evening.

I looked up at Wesley and gently, cautiously rested my hands upon his muscled chest. "My honor is intact, Wes." I let my hands travel the length of his shoulders, down his arms, until they reached his balled fists. I nudged them open and he relaxed his hands enough for me to thread my fingers between his. "Can we please get out of here?"

Wesley stared down at me, his gaze shifting from my eyes to my lips. He leaned down just a fraction and paused. Testing me or perhaps doubting himself. His brow wrinkled while his lips set in apparent frustration.

Without thought or permission, I rested my hands on his shoulders and pushed up on my toes, closing the charged distance between us. My fingers threaded through the thick locks of hair at the nape of his neck. The sudden and soft warmth of his hands met my waist. Gentle, as though he was afraid of breaking me somehow.

"Ebby." And then the distance between us vanished. His lips brushed mine once, twice, and then captured them completely. The arms that had been hardened from years of work tightened around me. Locking me in his embrace, he brought our bodies closer, but not close enough. Nothing could have prepared me for the need I felt. My lips moved against his and my hands moved to frame his whiskered cheeks.

The door flew open.

Wesley's lips tore away from mine, and I was suddenly shoved behind his back in time to spot Stock and Isa peering into the room.

"What happened to sundown—"

Whatever Isa had planned to say died on his tongue.

I appreciated the wall of privacy Wesley's back provided, as I labored to catch my breath and slow my beating heart.

"We're ready," said Wesley, and without another word, we locked Wesley's door behind us and ran the short distance to a servant's entrance.

We followed the route Simon gave me through a lesser-known servants' door through the outer wall of the fortress, avoiding the heavily guarded main gate and portcullis. Just like he promised, we didn't find any other guards. I held fast to Wesley's hand as we navigated the winding back streets of Brennan and tried to commit the feeling of his lips against mine to memory as we fled into the heart of the city.

CHAPTER THIRTY-FOUR

FACING THE MOUNTAIN

S tock, Isa, Wesley and I stood before the red door of the Talk About. I used Joe's special series of long and short knocks, and for the first time, noticed three narrow holes in a line on the door before me. The holes were covered on the backside to keep unwelcome eyes from peeking in.

Was it possible that this was the door the writer of the leather journal had skewered with a pitchfork so many years ago when he was starting his own rebellion and his own escape from Brennan? I felt a strange connection to the mysterious writer. Every time I read his words the *pull* in my stomach flared with life.

Perhaps it was because I related to him. I was trying to save my father just like he hoped to save Charlotte so many years ago.

Joe threw open the door and pulled us through. "Finally!"

Men for the rebellion clapped Wesley on the back and passed along welcome as though it were cake at a party. These were the same men who'd seriously considered killing Wesley if they couldn't break him out alive. I held onto the tail of Wesley's coat, eyeing everyone around me with wary gratitude. Nothing felt safe anymore.

Joe laid out a giant map and showed Wesley, Isa, and Stock the plans for our escape to Sea Port. As young as he was, they all looked to Wesley like he was a god capable of saving them in their fight against the duke of Brennan. Would they be angry when they discovered he couldn't help them make a Purgo blade?

The plan was to sleep until an hour before sunrise because the guards at the gate of Brennan's outer wall would ask too many questions otherwise. If everything went well, they'd leave Brennan with a few hours head start on the duke, using hideouts along the road to Sea Port to keep the duke off their trail. Everyone and everything was in place. It was a good plan, but all I could think about was my father.

A knock sounded again on the red door of the Talk About and every conversation died while everyone held their breath. "Who could it be? We're all here," one of the men mumbled as Joe Ford walked to answer the door.

Wesley took my hand and squeezed. I stepped closer to him, gripping his arm as we both followed Joe with our eyes.

The door opened, and a man with several earrings filled the doorway, speaking to Joe in whispers. The man's head hung and Joe's posture seemed to droop by the second. The two shook hands and the door shut again.

"What's happened?" asked Wesley.

Joe tried on a smile, but couldn't quite pull it off. "There is good news and bad." He took a breath and released an audible sigh. "The good news is the alarm hasn't been raised by your escape. Brennan guards still think you're locked in your room for the night."

"And the bad?" I asked.

"Kilsome Daily, the Sea Port ambassador friendly to our cause, was killed while trying to escape the dungeons tonight."

Joe looked to me. "A new acquaintance of yours, if I'm not mistaken, Miss Fields."

Blood drained from my face.

As much as Mr. Daily's death devastated me, my very first thoughts went to Father. Mr. Daily had been so certain he could make the trek over the mountain to warn him, but now…

The pull in my gut whirled in frenzy.

"Ebby?" Wesley took hold of my elbow and led me to a chair. My hands shook and the heat of my body seemed to drain from head to feet.

I vaguely heard Wesley make demands of the men around us and was soon handed a mug of cider. "Drink, Ebby." His voice tickled my ear as he wrapped a blanket around my shoulders. Obeying, I struggled to swallow the tangy liquid.

"I encouraged Daily's escape. I gave him the tools to make it possible."

Guilt washed through me as I pulled Kilsome's ring from the pocket of my trousers. My throat closed up and I barely managed, "We were to deliver this to a Sea Port official."

Joe stepped to my side and accepted the ring I held out for him. "His death will not be in vain, Miss Fields. We will avenge him."

I nodded, tears invading my shock, blurring my vision. Father's face was all I could see in my mind's eye. Who would warn him now?

Then I remembered the shed of supplies and provisions. Wiping my tears, I mentally told them to cease. Nothing could be gained from my breakdown. Father needed me before the first thaw. If I traveled on to Sea Port with Joe and the others, we wouldn't warn him in time.

In a way, I think some part of me always knew I'd travel that mountain pass again.

I considered asking Wesley to accompany me but abandoned the idea immediately. If he didn't cooperate with the rebels, Joe made it very clear they would come after him with as much energy as the duke himself. I wouldn't be responsible for another man's life. Especially his. I just hoped he'd forgive me.

As men wandered back to the map, I handed Wesley the mug and pulled the blanket tight around me. "Go with them, Wes." I gestured to Joe and the others. "You'll be missed."

"Hang them."

"Shhh." I reached out and placed my fingers over his warm lips. The connection made us both startle and I was suddenly back in the fortress kissing Wesley. I dropped both my hand and my eyes, afraid to look at him in case my thoughts were obvious. "They're your way home. Don't make them your enemies."

Wesley crouched in front of me, taking my hands and turning his intense gaze up to meet mine. Heat rushed back to my cheeks. "I care about very few people in this world. These men will wait." He brought my hand to his lips. "We'll be in Freeland before you know it."

Wesley Smith cared for me.

If there was ever a mantra that might help me survive my fate with the mountain, it was those beautiful five words. My lie would feel like betrayal to him, but I had to believe he'd forgive me once we were both safely back in Freeland. It was for his own protection.

I froze, paralyzed by the thread of my own thoughts. Hadn't those words been the very same my mother had used the day she finally admitted to her illness?

I didn't want to spoil our final months, Ebby Ann. If a mother can spare her child from pain, it is her duty to do so. I did it for your protection.

"Wesley?" Joe Ford called to him from across the room, awakening me from the memory I'd just relived. A memory as real to me as this room.

My blacksmith rolled his eyes, a gesture that reminded me of our childhood.

"Go to them. I'm fine." His brows rose, as though asking if I was sure.

I answered him with a gentle shove. "Go be the hero. I'd like some time to myself." I certainly had plenty to think about.

Mother had asked for my forgiveness. She'd been so sick and wanted me by her bedside, but I was hurt and needed to lick my wounds alone. Looking back at my fifteen-year-old self, I could see my actions had been selfish. Her dying wish had been for my happiness and forgiveness, but I hadn't given it to her. We were told that our ancestors watch us from the stars. Maybe that was the real reason for my obsession with the ruin stones. It was my way of sitting near her, even with my feelings of betrayal. All this time, I'd held on to that anger.

I could only hope Wesley would be more forgiving than I had been.

Wesley reluctantly left my side and a minute later I jumped and spun to find Mr. Hovel standing behind me holding a carved stick with a knapsack tied to one end. "What are you doing here?" I looked around. Most of the men had gone back to their business. Wesley examined the map with Joe, murmuring quietly.

"I heard about Daily and came straight here. I know what you're about, missy, and I've come to save you from yourself."

"What are you talking about?" I whispered. I didn't want Wesley to know my plans. It was the only way to keep him from joining me. The only way to keep him safe.

Mr. Hovel tapped his nose twice. "The mountain's not safe, Miss Fields. Dying's not going to save your father. I've heard he's a big man. He'll manage fine without your recklessness."

I was both impressed and offended that he'd read me so well. "You don't know what you're talking about." I huffed.

"Don't do it." He studied me for a bit, then walked to the door of the Talk About and left.

OF COURSE. WESLEY made sure my bedroll was safely spread in a corner of the Talk About where he and Master Moorly could plant themselves beside me. I kept a candle by my bedside, telling Wesley that I wanted to read the leather journal I'd stolen from the duke by its light.

"You need your sleep, Ebby." Wesley watched Master Moorly from the corner of his eye. The old man had been muttering worriedly to himself ever since we left the fortress.

"I just need the distraction." It wasn't a complete lie. But the candle's real purpose didn't come into play until the fire in the Talk About's hearth burned low and the smell of ale and revolution had simmered. By the light of my tiny, flickering flame, I pulled out a charcoal pencil and slip of parchment I'd nicked from the map table and scratched out a note.

Joe,

I need to beg another favor and ask you to tell one last story for me. One that will convince Wesley that I left while he slept—something that will persuade him that the sudden departure was for my safety. He'll be angry you didn't wake him, and I'm sorry for that.

I've enclosed a separate letter for him, but you must promise not to give it to him until you board the ship in Sea Port.

And Joe, please take care of him.

Thanks for everything,

Ebby

I tore the page and stared at the blank space I wasn't sure how to fill. My hands trembled and the marks of the pencil were joined by one of my tears.

Dear Wesley,

I know you often blamed yourself for not being there to save your parents from that fire. You had no way of knowing what would happen to them while you were hunting. At our last meeting, Daily confirmed that there is an assassination plot against Father. Before his death, Daily ordered supplies to be readied and stashed in a barn on the outskirts of Brennan.

I took a fortifying breath, willing my writing hand to stop shaking.

I am going in Daily's place. How can I live with myself if I don't try to warn Father? How can I sit by and do nothing when there is even a small chance I can save him? Please don't be angry. I would have told you my plans sooner, but I know you. You'd risk the wrath of the revolution to help me if I did. That or prevent me from going by tying me to that packhorse of yours.

I smiled through my tears at the thought.

I'm sorry for the things I said to you in the smithy. You're going to make a great councilman someday. Your father would have been proud.

With hope that we will see each other again in Freeland,

Ebby

The letter wasn't meant to be a goodbye. But it certainly felt like one. I stared at the page, hovering in the place below my name, contemplating a postscript, daring myself to write the words that had been trapped inside me for too long.

The feel of Wesley's strong arms pulling our bodies together. His warmth. His absolute protection. The moment of our kiss in the fortress. The history we shared…

Dozens of Wesley's traits and quirks and memories rushed through me.

Filled me.

Knowing it might be my final opportunity to tell him exactly how I felt, and even knowing Joe Ford would likely read the letter, I wrote the greatest truth I'd ever known.

P.S. I've loved you my whole life.

I creased the paper and tucked it into Joe's shoe while he slept with the rest of the men. Thankfully, no one stood guard at the door in the small hours of the night. I stole a pack and some rations, doubled up a bedroll, and walked over to where Wesley slept. I sank to my knees and, after the slightest hesitation, kissed his forehead.

I swallowed a lump in my throat, but the gentle pull guided me to the door, validating my decision. Bundled in every layer of clothing I could get my hands on, I lifted the latch of the Talk About and stole into the night, answering the call of the pull and wishing I didn't have to leave my heart here.

THE WALK TO the mouth of the canyon took most of the night. I avoided the major streets, weaving in and out of alleyways, the whole time trusting the needle and thread of my gut to tug me along. The mountain pass loomed on the horizon, the white peaks reflecting the light of the moon. Self-preservation compelled me to turn back, but my stomach pulled me and the wind pushed me onward—urging me toward the bleached mountain that would determine my fate.

The homes on the outskirts of Brennan belonged to farming families with too much sense to be caught out in the brisk weather. Still, whenever a sharp gust assaulted my back, I wondered if someone was on my trail, watching me.

The road grew rocky, the mountain looming ever closer. If not for the moonlight I would never have seen the old farmhouse and shed standing alone, nestled only a few hundred yards from the canyon opening.

Though the home appeared abandoned, I took care to avoid it as I crept to the barn. The front door hung slanted on a broken hinge, missing one plank. It cried like a screeching cat when I forced it open. Standing in the damp, dark space with the smell of molding hay curling in my nostrils reminded me of the last time I sneaked into a barn at night. I could only hope this would end better than my last experience.

After stumbling about in the dark, I found several of Mr. Daily's packs hidden beneath a burlap cloth near the back corner of the barn. I dragged one outside by the strap and examined it under the light of the moon. Though I wore the clothing and boots I'd used to cross the mountain while coming to Brennan, I appreciated the extra pair of woolen stockings, as well as the thick outer cloak and gloves I discovered in the pack. Together with the food rations, I could only hope it was enough to get me over the mountain. I abandoned my own bedroll in exchange for the one already tied to the base of the pack, transferred my journal wrapped in the Brennan red shawl, and hefted the large pack onto my back with a pathetic grunt.

Were there rocks in the bottom?

I took a few steps along the path. How would I manage this load for eight or more days? The bedroll bounced against the back of my knees. I focused on putting one foot in front of another, and I eventually found a rhythm to the process.

Run to the mountain.

The mountain is safe.

Father needs me.

The pack isn't that heavy.

Hurry!

I froze mid-stride, chills crawling along my skin, coldness seeping into my bones.

Voices in my head. Mine… and yet somehow not.

Go!

Run!

Save him!

Don't delay!

The whispers caught me off guard, playing at my fears. I didn't feel the pull. Had it left or simply been overpowered? The moment I gave ear to the strange whispers and took a step in the direction of the mountain, they tackled my mind. Demanding. Hungry. Forcing away everything but the need to move forward.

Without giving my feet permission, I stepped once, twice, and then commanded my body to hold. Though I dragged gulps of air into my lungs, I couldn't catch my breath. This was the madness I'd see in the dungeons. The spirits knew I could hear them and devoured the chance to be heard.

When I couldn't fight them any longer, I had no choice but to turn myself over to them and ran to the mountain pass.

CHAPTER THIRTY-FIVE

MOUNT BRENNAN

Whispers in my head propelled me onward as I approached a large outcropping of rock that marked the canyon entrance. The frantic rush both exhilarated and terrified me, as though I was a boulder tipped into motion on a hill. My body was mine no longer, and I couldn't stop. It simply wasn't an option. I rounded the bend where the darkness deepened within the shadows of the high canyon walls and nearly collided with a man standing guard on the other side.

The whispers vanished. My body my own again as I screeched in surprise and tried to run away.

Two hands came down on my shoulders, yanking me back. "Look what I found," said a gruff voice at my neck. The guard pinned my arms to my sides. I jumped, kicked, and flailed like a fish pulled from its home, but nothing loosened those arms. My energy ran out after a pathetically short amount of time.

Another soldier guarding the trail ran toward us and I went limp in my captor's arms, letting him support my weight. My pack dropped from my shoulders and hit the ground with a thud.

The second man was tall, with oars for arms and low-drooping eyes that made him look sleepy.

"Never thought we'd actually nab one," said the winded runner. I could tell he was in charge just by his chin-raised demeanor. "And here you thought guarding the pass was punishment for missing drills last week."

"Let go of me!" I demanded. "You've no right to hold me here."

"That's just it, miss," said the droopy-eyed leader. "By order of the duke we have every right to hold you and anyone else who tries to enter. The pass is closed until spring. Only a fool or a vagrant would try to cross now."

There was no use arguing with these men. They thought I was mad. But I hoped a subtle threat might help. "I am a friend of Lord Kent. He wouldn't be happy seeing me tethered and tied like a regular prisoner."

The arms around my waist slackened some. I seized the opportunity, jumping on his toe while thrusting my elbow up into my captor's nose. If there was one thing I was good at, it was running. I think I spent half my childhood running away from my brother and Wesley. Back then I knew once I got away from them, I'd be safe if I reached the folds of my mother's skirt. Only this was no game, and there was no skirt in which I could hide.

Abandoning my pack, I sprinted toward the canyon. My boots slipped in the snow. I fell but scrambled up again. I didn't dare look back, and there wasn't a need. Heavy footfalls gained ground behind me and I sensed hands reaching out to grab me. The wind whistled by. I tasted a metallic flavor in my mouth—blood from biting my tongue.

I turned a sharp corner. A guard yanked the back of my cloak so hard both feet flew out from under me. I fell and rolled out of his grasp, gasping as the path dropped steeply into a dry riverbed off the side of the trail. Coming to a painful rest at the bottom, I immediately got to my feet.

I didn't remember picking up the fist-sized rock as the tall guard scrambled down the hill toward me, but I did remember throwing it. The river stone struck the guard square in the temple. He crumpled to the ground just before his shorter companion turned the corner. I ducked back into the riverbed, taking cover behind a snow laden patch of bushes.

Had I just killed a man?

Crunching boots on snow only amplified my fear. And my heart rate. I closed my eyes and forced myself to breathe, silently tapping an even rhythm on my chest for my heart to match. My free hand searched blindly through the snow for another rock.

The boots came closer.

I tapped my heart.

Rocks and snow slid down the bank as the guard approached.

My fingers closed around another rock and I was suddenly in the field with Gavin. We were clearing rocks again—Father's favorite punishment when we'd been fighting. "Every Fields should know how to throw a rock," Gavin had said.

My heart calmed. I opened my eyes and my vision stilled. Gavin's instruction filled me, blocking out everything and everyone else. I turned, took aim, and threw with all my strength.

As fast as it happened, I still managed to see the surprise in my victim's eyes before he slunk to the ground. He wasn't expecting me to be dangerous.

It was as if I stood next to the scene before me, watching it as a terrified spectator. Blood drained from the gash on the side of the second guard's head. I crawled over to the first man and felt for a pulse. I saw his chest rise and fall, but I still wanted to feel the rhythm of his heart. I needed to know he was alive. I needed to feel it. I wanted that knowledge to warm the ice that had settled into my bones.

Satisfied, I forced myself to my wobbly feet and tried to keep balance while stumbling back to the boulder just outside the canyon entrance to retrieve my pack. I passed the broken men on the trail and hoped I could put a good amount of distance between us before they awoke. I don't know how far I traveled before I collapsed. It could have been five miles or fifteen. I just knew the sun had risen, reached its height in the sky, and dipped below the western canyon wall before I slumped to the side of the trail in total exhaustion. After a full day of walking on no sleep, I was too far away from my senses to judge distance.

However, there were things of which I was very aware. I was aware of night's approach. I was aware of the hard ground and the sensation of snowmelt seeping through my clothes. I was aware of the cold because it caused my jaw to shake. And I was aware of the spirits, laughing in the wind over my lifeless form and celebrating my fall. Knowing that they could overtake me at any moment, I had no choice but to continue forward or they would be the literal death of me.

They were the masters of this mountain, and just like Mr. Hovel warned, they'd grown stronger. Unless I found a way to block them from my mind, they would consume me before I had a chance to save my father and warn my homeland.

THE FIRE BURNED me. Or at least my skin felt the burning pain of its warmth as the flames dispelled the cold from my cheeks and fingertips.

"You're a ruddy fool, girl."

I sat up too fast at the sound of Mr. Hovel's rough voice. He tucked the blankets around me. "You should have died," he continued. "No one ever listens to Derby Hovel. They think I don't know sense just because I get a little dung on my boot every day. Well, I know better than to run off into a murderous mountain pass in the middle of winter. Alone!"

I didn't hear the rest of his rant. It came out as one long stream of ornery mumblings and curses. Such a beautiful sound.

"How did you find me?" I asked, daring to push up to my elbows.

"It's not like you were hiding in some bush. A dying girl lying smack in the middle of the only trail in this pass is a little hard to miss, even at night. You're lucky I got to you before the wolves. Or worse."

The frost of early morning turned everything more than five feet from our fire to ice. I couldn't believe I'd slept all night. "The guards at the mouth of the canyon. Were they still there?"

Mr. Hovel's brows dipped in concern. He felt my forehead and said, "There weren't any guards. Did you hit your head when you fell?"

I pushed his hand aside. "There were two. They tried to take me back to Brennan."

"How did you escape?" he asked.

I didn't want to relive the fear of being chased by those men or the thud of the rocks connecting with their skulls, but I did. I told him every last detail as if I were confessing my sins to an unsympathetic priest. When I finished, Mr. Hovel was the one who had to sit.

"Oh, what a mess you've created for yourself, child." He pulled out his dirty handkerchief and wiped his brow with one long sweep. "I'm afraid you'll have to get moving, and soon. How are you feeling?"

I wanted to curl up in a ball and sleep until spring. If it weren't for Father, I might have done just that. "I feel like moving."

Mr. Hovel gathered up his things and stood with his stick and knapsack resting on his stooped shoulder. The gloves on his hands were patched and threadbare, his nose red with cold.

"Thank you for saving my life." I offered him my hand in farewell and he threw his head back and released a gargled laugh that turned into a wheezing cough. He adjusted the cap on his head and started walking toward Freeland.

"You can't come. Don't do this for me, Mr. Hovel."

I quickly gathered my things to follow him just as the orange light of morning kissed the brim of the horizon.

Mr. Hovel ignored me and started walking up the steep trail.

The moment we left the fire, I wanted to return. I felt naked to the sharp, stinging air that penetrated every seam and pore of my clothing. It was as though my cloak was made of air and my boots were icy blocks with the sole purpose of weighing me down.

I studied the sky for some kind of reprieve from the freeze that had settled into my bones. There was nothing but a dull haze, trapping the cold air like a stubborn net cast over the sky. At least there would be no snow today.

By noon, Mr. Hovel still wouldn't answer my pleas for him to return to Brennan. By evening I stopped asking him to leave. There was something about the lightness of his mood, despite our dreary situation, that made me wonder if he wanted to come with me to Freeland and freedom.

By the time we stopped, Mr. Hovel didn't seem tired at all. He busied himself with kindling and even found a few dry pieces of wood to start a fire.

"You look exhausted, Miss Fields." I was. But I was also antsy to keep moving. It seemed every moment spent resting was one moment longer I'd be away from home. From Father and the man hired to kill him.

"I like my friends to call me Ebby," I said.

"What would that giant friend of yours think if he knew I was using your first name?"

I frowned and looked away, not wanting to think of Wesley.

"Are you worried for him?" Mr. Hovel paused in his gathering to glance over his shoulder at me.

I bit on my lower lip and gave a curt nod, even though I wasn't sure if he referred to Father or Wesley.

"Well, you shouldn't be. He's protected by an army of revolutionaries. I'd spend my time worrying about this mountain if I were you."

Or the spirits on it.

I worked to sound more confident than I felt. "The mountain pass can't be much worse than it was a month ago."

Derby Hovel stopped and looked at me, eyes hard. "We are likely walking to our deaths."

I swallowed his words and nodded. "Then why won't you turn around?" My chin shook. Mr. Hovel chewed on my question like a cow on cud, the folds of his elderly face bending and stretching with the movement. Finally, he said, "I'd rather die walking toward somethin' I believe in than live knowin' I didn't try."

Mr. Hovel was escaping, too. Just like the man from the journal. Just like me.

Why couldn't life be more like planting a field of crops? Plow the field, seed it, water it, till it, and watch it grow. There was such a peaceful sort of justice that came with gardening.

But life wasn't that simple. The words of the journal filled my head like air passing lazily through one of Father's wheat fields. *"I am convinced life is nothing more than a string of choices. In the end, our intentions do not mean much, but our actions… they define us."*

AS WE STARTED hiking the next day, I was still caught up in my thoughts. I had never truly appreciated my own freedom until it was almost taken from me while trying to leave Brennan. The man from the journal was selfless in his search for freedom, just as Father was selfless in his commitment to feeding our people. These men were so many things that I was not. I'd never claimed to be brave and never enjoyed hard work or sacrifice, but there was one thing I had going for me—one fact that provided a little grain of hope.

I was a Fields. And just as Father repeatedly told me as a child, doing hard things was in my blood.

I was so absorbed in my fate that the snow caught me by complete surprise—something that never happened. Low, moist clouds covered the entire horizon, and the weight of the air was such that it felt like the sky pushed against my pack. The snow would likely carry us into the next day. Storms meant delays, and delays meant hunger.

"We need to find some shelter before this gets too bad," I called ahead to Mr. Hovel.

He didn't turn around. "It's just a little snow, Miss Fields." The trail had a frozen layer of snow that slowed us down but still made the crossing passable if we walked close to the canyon wall and avoided the cliff's edge that dropped into the deep ravine.

"If we don't find a place soon, we'll get stuck in the storm. Trust me, I know the weather like you know the business of Brennan. We see and hear things that others miss."

He looked back and grimaced, but since he regularly had that expression on his face, I had no idea what he was thinking. "We need to cover more ground, Miss Fields. Our food—"

"Will serve us no purpose if we die from exposure."

His jaw relaxed and his eyes drooped to concern. "How long do you think we have before it gets bad?"

"I'd say anywhere from thirty minutes to an hour."

He nodded with one crisp movement. "How well do you remember the trail?"

When we traveled this stretch on our way to Brennan, I was on Wesley's supply horse. I was too annoyed with him at the time to pay proper attention to the surroundings. Fool girl, I was.

"Not well. The road narrows after a few days travel, but I'm not so sure of this area."

"Keep your eyes open. With luck, we might have time to set a few snares and get a fire going before the weather gets bad."

By the time we found the cave, the snow came down like a thick, heavy curtain. We were lucky Mr. Hovel spotted it, for it was nothing more than a barrel-sized gap in the stone. We had gathered what firewood we could along the trail, but it was too wet to burn. Mr. Hovel and I shivered together in a space barely tall enough for us to crouch. He worked the flint for sparks, and I just tried not to freeze to death.

I was exhausted. The shivers that ran along my joints and spine were cruel little demons, intent on robbing me of the meager energy I had left. My jaw rattled, my teeth smacked together, and I couldn't undo the fists my hands had made.

A wolf's howl pulled my focus away from the cold. Another wolf joined in to make an eerie harmony. Then another.

I exchanged a look with Mr. Hovel and hurried over to help with the fire building. I used the few dry areas of the skirt of my dress to absorb what water I could from the wood as Mr. Hovel swore over his flint stones. The howling grew louder. The echo bounced off the walls of our shelter, making it seem as if the beasts were right there with us.

"Catch, you worthless pile of—"

"Here!" I handed him still damp sticks from my skirt. But they were too thick to truly catch. We needed dry kindling to help the flames take to the larger pieces of wood. Mr. Hovel's hands shook as he used an old knife to whittle away at the sticks. I pulled Wesley's knife from my pack and joined in the effort of shaving away the damp wood. Progress was slow and the hungry howls outside had us both too anxious to be productive. If we could just defend our little opening, there was a chance we could survive the night.

Mr. Hovel's knife slipped and sliced deep into his hand. He dropped the blade and stared as the blood dripped black into the white snow. Everything happened so slowly, though I'm sure only a few beats of my heart passed before the pull nudged me toward the bottom of my pack. I hadn't felt the pull since my run in with the guards. Snatching up the journal, I irreverently tore out a few empty pages from the back.

The wolves howled again. My hands wouldn't move fast enough.

After only two strikes, a spark caught the crumpled paper and fire licked at the smaller pieces of wood.

The howls grew louder.

Eventually, bright flames filled the space at the mouth of the cave. Only then did I turn to Mr. Hovel. He cradled his hand, still seeping blood, and stared into the flames as if bewitched by some trance. I stripped some fabric from my slip and bandaged his wound, turning in time to see a dark creature pace on the other side of the fire.

The meager pile of wood might buy us an hour or two—no more.

I had a feeling the wolves would wait.

CHAPTER THIRTY-SIX

THUNDER

"Sleep," said Mr. Hovel as he placed one more log on the hungry fire. Some of the wood was still moist, filling the cave with a heavy smoke as it burned. Every time the fire dwindled, the wolves grew more anxious. Their eager whimpers sounded over the cracks and hisses. They were hungry, just like the fire was hungry for more wood. How could I sleep?

I scooted closer to Mr. Hovel, and he wrapped his thin arm around me for comfort. Only the fire breathed. We didn't have long. Maybe another hour before the fire died and…

We didn't have long.

In an instant, comfort of Mr. Hovel's company shrived into something drastically different.

Panic.

I'm going to be eaten alive.

We should kill each other now.

Less suffering.

I pulled away from him and scratched at my cheeks, trying to force away the whispered thoughts by imagining one perfect day back home, a day from another time, when Mother was still alive and things were as they should have been in Freeland.

Take up the knife.

Plunge it in deep.

It will be quick.

Hurt less than the wolves' teeth.

I felt my body rocking and cut off a scream as my hands clasped my skirts with white knuckles, my will fighting the demanding urge to pick up Wesley's knife. Shaking with effort.

I spoke aloud, praying that my words would drown out the voices combating in my mind. "A perfect day in Freeland," I said, gasping. "I wake up. Put on a simple dress—something Hannah wouldn't kill me for getting soiled."

Do it.

I need to do it.

More rocking. The words hard to push past my lips. "After morning chores, I find Father and Gavin mending the fence that keeps animals out of the berries. I kiss Father on the cheek, and he says how proud he is of me."

Running out of time.

Must hurry.

Wolves.

Teeth.

"Gavin tugs on my braid. Tells me again that I am far too pretty. Father's wheat fields." My voice came as a strangled sob. "I lose the world and find myself in the fields."

Take the knife. End this pain!

It's the only way to save us!

Tears rolled down my cheeks. The hilt of the knife is cold in my hands. How did it get there?

"Wesley and I at the ruin stones. T-together." Two hands on the hilt. Eyes clamped shut. "My head resting against his shoulder. Trees sway. So many stars."

Kill!

Something struck me hard in the back of my head. Stars exploded behind my eyes and the spirits and I faded to blackness.

"THANK GOODNESS." Mr. Hovel gripped my hand and frowned as I blinked awake. Wolves whined outside the small cave entrance. The fire burned hot as he added the last log to the fire.

"A weapon to fight off both spirit and beast," he said, gesturing to the log.

I sat up slowly. The back of my head had its own heartbeat. "You hit me with a stick." A statement, not a question.

The old man nodded. "I knew the spirits would leave you if your mind turned off for long enough." Light from the fire reflected off the whites of his eyes. "I've seen it before. They go frantic without a host and are likely searching for ya somewhere back in Brennan as we speak."

"How can you know this?"

Mr. Hovel offered a dark chuckle. "Because I've seen it, Miss Fields. Not only in the dungeons of Brennan, but by my tower. Others think they're crazy, but I've seen when the spirits come and when they leave a person. Good people change in the blink of an eye. Once a man begged me to take him to Brennan guards so he could be thrown in the duke's dungeons. Said he didn't trust himself to be around his family anymore."

"Why don't they affect you? Why are only some their target?"

Mr. Hovel shook his head. His head dropped to his curved, wrinkled hands. "I don't know, child."

We grew quiet. Mr. Hovel stared at the flames as they greedily devoured the final log of the fire. The wolves paced outside. Waiting. Hungry.

I thumbed through the pages of the journal with shaking hands, wishing I knew the end of the writer's story. Had the duke discovered the author's actions? Whatever happened to Charlotte? Had his *gift* led him to his destruction, like mine?

The fire snapped and sparks flew as Mr. Hovel broke the silence. "I want to thank you for helping me leave Brennan, Miss Fields."

A lump rose in my throat about as cleanly as the heavy bucket from the well back home. It hurt to swallow. "Please, Mr. Hovel. You shouldn't be thanking me. I should never have let you come with me. You said it was just too dangerous, and I didn't listen."

"Nonsense," he snapped. "Today I was a free man, Ebby. Today I lived." After a moment he sighed. "Fight them, Miss Fields. Find a way."

"Fight who?" The wolves outside yapped in frustration.

"The Dark Ones. Don't let them overtake you. Don't trust them, no matter what they offer." He spoke fast, his jaw tight, barely allowing the words to pass.

I didn't know what to say to that. The evil spirits seemed less threatening than the wolves outside the cave at the moment.

"I want you to do somethin' for me," he continued.

"Anything."

"Do everythin' in your power to keep your home a refuge for people like me."

I pushed up to my knees. "Of course, but stop talking like we're not going to get out of this." Knots of dread tied in my stomach.

"And tell that blacksmith to keep you well, Miss Fields. It was a true honor to know you."

Suddenly, Mr. Hovel sprang to his feet and ran through the fire and out of the cave before I could stop him.

The wolves hollered and snapped, the sounds growing fainter as he led them away from my hole in the mountain. Not far enough. Mr. Hovel's anguished cries filled the night. The cave walls seemed to close in around me. I curled in a ball covering my ears, rocking back and forth, not daring to make a sound, not wanting to remind the wolves of my presence and make vain my dear friend's sacrifice.

I hated myself in those moments.

I hated him for leaving me.

I hated us both.

I SAT LOCKED in a ball until I lost the battle with consciousness. I slept, shivering in two blankets instead of one. Thunder woke me in the weak light of the morning. Of course, I knew it couldn't be thunder—not during the peak of winter. The sound shook the mountain. Sheets of white snow fell in front of the cave. I gathered my pack and bedroll and dashed out.

Outside, everything was still. I looked to the sky to explain the noise but saw only a general haze. My boots sunk deep in the fresh snow. I trudged forward, numbed but motivated by Mr. Hovel's sacrifice and my desperate desire to reach Father. I kept my head down as I pushed against the wind.

Trails of blood passed beneath my vision. The snow had melted some around the bright red. I suppose I should have expected to see some sign of Mr. Hovel's struggle with the wolves. My mind was past internalizing what my eyes saw. I sidestepped the blood and kept moving.

The cold saved my life. Without it I might have simply sat down and grieved to death. But the cold kept me moving, forcing me to place one frozen foot in front of the other. I didn't hear another sound of thunder as I hiked that trail. Could it have been another avalanche? Part of me wondered if it had all been in my head, but then I remembered the shaking and the snow that fell in front of the mouth of the cave.

There was a good chance the duke had sent guards after me. They could be close given my pathetic pace, but I just couldn't push myself any faster. By evening I couldn't feel my fingers as I searched for wood to build a fire. When I grasped the flint stones, I had to watch my numb hands to make sure they were doing what I told them to.

I gave up on creating fire out of the damp wood once it was too dark to see my hands in front of me. I stumbled over to a small crevasse in the mountain's rock wall and huddled under the blankets, head and all. Fear as sharp as daggers pressed against me. I removed my boots and rubbed my dead toes with shaking hands. It felt like I had wooden blocks connected to the stumps of my arms and legs. I couldn't tell what I was doing but kept trying to rub some sort of feeling into them.

I was too cold to care about wolves. That is, until I heard them come for me.

Their pace was steady and sure. Crunching steps in an even rhythm. They were tracking me—hugging the trail what sounded like a mere twenty yards away. I didn't dare lift the blankets covering my head, hoping—no, praying—the covers might hide some of my scent.

Please let them keep walking. Please let them keep walking.

I imagined their teeth in my flesh. In one of his stories, Joe had described that when a wolf killed, it started with your neck and ripped out your throat until you stopped fighting. As fast as my heart was working, the anticipation might have killed me before the wolves ever had the chance. The crunching continued. For a moment I thought the predator might keep going. Maybe they traveled the trail just out of habit. Maybe they weren't tracking me after all. With every crunch a small dose of hope leaked into my mind. I might live for another night! I might survive! I might save Father!

Then the crunching stopped. I listened for more paws in the snow but heard nothing for a few seconds. When the crunching started again the steps were deliberate, quick, and heading right for me. They'd found where I left the trail.

In my last moments I thought of my Father as I grabbed a knife Wesley had given me in one hand and Mr. Hovel's dull dagger in the other. They would be my teeth. I held them blade down, ready to kill. I might die tonight, but I wouldn't go without a fight.

As the beasts grabbed my blanket, I yelled and jumped to attack.

But there were no beasts. Instead, a cloaked man took hold of my wrists. My battle cry turned into a wail. I didn't drop the weapons until I recognized the hands holding me.

I melted into Wesley.

He gathered me up in his arms and sunk to his knees, cradling me to his chest. I'd not seen him cry since the day in the graveyard after his parents' burial, but we wept together on the mountain that night. He kept moving the mess of hair from my face saying things like "How could you?" and "The most foolish thing you've ever done." I should have been worried for him. The revolutionaries would be furious. But at that moment, I let myself be relieved.

"Where are you hurt?" he asked.

"What do you mean?"

"We saw blood on the trail."

I tensed from the thought of Mr. Hovel, not ready to relive that nightmare. "I'm not hurt."

Wesley pulled my chin up to look into his eyes. I don't know what he saw in mine, but he didn't push me for answers.

"Let's get a fire going," Wesley called to someone over his shoulder.

"Who's there?" I didn't want to pull away to look.

Joe Ford crouched next to us. "Glad you're safe, Miss Fields. You've had us worried."

"I told you not to tell him—"

"And risk the lad's anger when he found out I knew where you were?" He laughed darkly. "I have a stronger sense of self-preservation than that, Miss Fields."

Wesley gripped me under the arms and pulled me to my feet, supporting most of my weight. "We'll explain everything as soon as we get a fire going. You're frozen."

"Good luck." I gestured to the pile of wood I'd gathered. "It's too wet to burn."

Wesley chuckled. "I'm a blacksmith, Ebby. Fire is what I do."

Sure enough, Wesley had a fire going in less than a few minutes. I should have been thrilled, but a small part of me was irritated by how easy he made the job appear. As easy for him as carrying my water buckets back in Freeland. I had to smile at the memory.

Some things never changed.

I wanted to jump into the flames. I was that cold. Once my feet and hands began to defrost, the heat stung. Wesley hung my damp outerwear on a tree branch while I stayed huddled beneath a quilt wearing nothing more than my underclothes. He blushed as he worked.

"Something wrong, Smith?" Joe mused.

Wesley's face reddened even more. He cleared his throat and smiled sheepishly, like a little boy caught doing something he knew he shouldn't. "I'm fine, Storyteller."

"I bet you are," said Joe with a fox-like grin as he tossed some loose bark into the fire.

Wesley sat down at my other side and tugged at his boot. "Are you ready to explain that blood, Ebby?" he asked once his toes were exposed to the fire.

I stared at the flame for a while, trying to find the courage in my weakened soul to dig up the memory. "I… it… it was Mr. Hovel's blood."

"Who's Mr. Hovel?" asked Joe.

"Mr. Hovel was an old man I met in Brennan. When he found out about Daily's passing, he knew I'd attempt the mountain and followed me." I gulped. "He was a friend."

"What happened?" Wesley put a comforting hand on my back. I opened my mouth to explain how Mr. Hovel had sacrificed his life for mine even after the Dark Ones had tried to have me kill us both… and felt the rest of my truth die on the tip of my tongue. How could I tell Wesley evil spirits could possess me at any time? How no one would ever truly be safe around me. I couldn't bear to hear those words spoken aloud, even though I knew Wesley should hear them.

So, I just sat there and fought the overwhelming urge to weep. There was no way of telling how long the three of us sat staring at the fire. Joe surprised me by being the one to break the deafening silence.

"I suppose you want to know what happened after you left the Talk About?"

I nodded, grateful to have something else to think about besides fangs and fires and evil spirits.

"I convinced the rebellion that if we wanted the blood oath to be honored by your dear old dad, we'd better produce his daughter alive."

"I might have sworn not to help them if they didn't let me go after you." Wesley's smile pulled the corner of his mouth on one side.

Joe, ever the storyteller, took back control of the tale. "We convinced them to continue on as planned and draw the duke's eye to Sea Port while we took the pass in secret."

"Do you think they know you're here?" I asked.

Joe and Wesley shared a knowing glance. "We should have reached you sooner, but we were delayed. We came across a pair of scouts not two miles back and made them talk. I guess two of the duke's men were found unconscious by the canyon entrance the day before we left. We could only assume it was you, though how you bested two trained guards is beyond me."

I was too embarrassed to look at either of them. "Rocks," I whispered as I used a small stick to draw a shape in the soggy ground.

When I looked up from my picture, both men had wide eyes. "Rocks?" Joe asked in awe.

A baritone laugh bubbled in Wesley's chest. "Only Gavin's sister could fell two grown men with rocks."

Joe was too stunned to continue, so Wesley picked up the story. "The duke assembled a group of soldiers to come after you, and we left just before them. Joe here has connections with an alchemist who owed him a favor. We set off powder bombs at a narrow point in the trail a while back. Hopefully it slows them until we can reach Freeland's defenses."

"You made the thunder?" I asked. "I had to leave the cave because I was afraid the snow would trap me in."

"The cave?"

There we were—right back to Mr. Hovel and that awful cave. I rested my head in my hands and decided to get it over with. "Mr. Hovel died a free man yesterday. He ended his life to save my own."

I told them everything: from how he'd found me half dead in the snow to how he died. I couldn't help but become emotional when I talked about my dear friend. I told them about his dreams of going to Freeland and living life as a free man.

"By all the ships at port, child. You've been through it, haven't you?" said Joe. "I don't recall all women of Freeland being this resilient."

"Freeland raises strong daughters, Storyteller, but Ebby is special."

"Please stop speaking like I'm not right here. I didn't do anything courageous, just sat there while a friend sacrificed himself for me!" Burying my face in the blanket, I tried to mask the prickling self-loathing that pulsed through me. "I just waited to die." It didn't seem the right time to mention that the Dark Ones had wanted to me to end my own life, as well.

"Forgive me for upsetting you, Miss Fields. But you were prepared to fight us tonight."

"My father needs me." I looked up and shrugged. The simple gesture took far more effort than it should. "I have to protect my family."

We went to bed that night in somber spirits. There was no need to speak openly about the threat of wolves. Wesley tucked his dry shirt under his head. I stretched out on my tattered bedroll beside him. Then, without pretense or apology, he reached up and hooked me by the waist, tugging me back to his chest. My heart pounded in double-time as I allowed my head to relax on his shoulder, already warm wherever our bodies connected. It occurred to me that I should probably at least pretend to be scandalized by his forward gesture.

"Sleep well, my Ebby. I won't let so much as a flea touch you while you dream." He hesitated then kissed the top of my head.

"Thanks for coming after me."

"We're family. I'll always come for you, as long as I'm welcome," he whispered.

If I were any kind of family to Wesley, I would have told him about the spirits. But like a coward, I closed my eyes and relished his warmth, leaving the hard confession for tomorrow.

CHAPTER THIRTY-SEVEN

AROUND EVERY CORNER

Wesley kept his steps small to accommodate my pace. "When we were kids, I always liked you best in winter, Ebby. Your fair hair caught the light reflected off the snow. It made you look like a snow angel."

Joe was on yet another scouting excursion up ahead. To be honest, I thought it was because he was tired of our banter.

"Did you notice my hair before or after you smeared snow in my face?" I asked.

Wesley's smile leapt from the corners of his mouth and wrinkled his nose. "Both, I suppose."

"If I had the energy, I'd kick you."

He threw back his head and laughed. "If you had the energy, I wouldn't say such things."

"Yes, but you'd think them."

He nodded. "That I would."

As much as our banter lightened my mood, my smile slipped when thoughts of yesterday emerged. I couldn't pretend my predicament with the Dark Ones away. I'd almost killed myself in that cave with Mr. Hovel. Killed us both. Chills spread up and down my arms and I rubbed them away. Wesley's safety and the success of our efforts to get home and warn my father were more important than his good opinion of me.

I cleared my throat, knowing if I didn't start talking, I'd lose my nerve. "Wes, there's something I need to tell you. Something that might be hard to believe." I started from the beginning, telling him about the strange urges that led me into trouble back home. I told of Joe's story about the Dark Ones on our first night and the difference between the pulls and the whispers. I even told him about the journal and the young man who called his promptings a gift. Not once did I look at Wesley, but his stride never faltered beside me, and that steadiness helped me continue. When I finally described what happened in the cave, he stopped walking.

"I was going to listen to them. I didn't have a choice. Had Mr. Hovel not managed to break the Dark Ones' hold over me, we would have died in that cave."

I looked at him, needing to gauge his reaction.

He stood like a statue in the snow, from his dark eyes to the hard lines of his jaw and the protruding veins of his neck. Only the light falling snow around us and the billow of his cloak in the wind proved that time hadn't frozen still.

I searched his tense expression for some sign of disgust or fear. Needing him to know this was serious, I wanted to drive the point across that I was damaged and potentially dangerous. "Say something," I said finally. "Tell me you understand and will use caution around me. You have to understand that as long as they can invade my thoughts, I'm not safe to be with."

That seemed to awaken him from whatever trance held him captive. He crossed to me in two strides and used no caution whatsoever as he wrapped me in his arms and pulled me into the warmth of his chest.

"You'll always be my safe place, Ebrielle Fields," he said in my ear. "Nothing can change that." The sudden, intense kindness stole my breath and triggered tears. He pulled me back to meet my eyes with his. "We'll find a way to shut them out."

The fear that had been building ever since my near suicide seemed to dissipate with his words. I didn't know how Wesley would help, but I didn't have to carry this monstrous secret alone anymore. Wesley let his hands run down my arms to squeeze my hands before letting go completely. I missed him the moment our connection broke but knew we had to keep moving. I felt lighter than I had in days.

As the day progressed, the red skies plotted something terrible. Under normal circumstances I would insist we find shelter, and fast. But with a small army of Brennan soldiers at our backs we didn't dare stop. Although we were still three days outside of Freeland, according to Wesley and Joe's calculations, the blocked trail would buy us a day's head start if we were lucky. With my slow pace, the soldiers could be as little as a half day behind us. I felt a constant pressure at my back, a pressure as real as the ever-growing wind.

We came to the narrowest part of the trail—the part where I'd lost my sweet horse Millie in the avalanche on the way to Brennan. "Wesley, do you see that sky?"

"Just tell me. Good or bad?"

"As bad as the last time we walked this narrow stretch."

Joe rejoined us looking nervous. "We have to move faster. If Brennan catches up there's nowhere to go but down." He pointed to the snowy abyss at the bottom of the ravine.

Wesley looked at me, but I had a feeling he didn't see me at all. "The last time we crossed this stretch we found shelter in a hidden cavern. If we hurry, we could get there by night fall."

"What about the storm?" I said.

"What storm?" asked Joe.

"The one Ebby says is coming." Wesley removed his cap and ran a hand through his dark hair. "We don't have a choice. We've got to brave the storm and hope Brennan waits it out. It might be the only way to put distance between us."

Without asking my permission, Wesley reached over and took my pack and bedroll and strapped it to his chest. "Let's pick up the pace."

The further we hiked, the harder the wind blew. "Don't you think the Brennan group will be looking for the gap in the wall, too?" I asked.

"What?" he called over the wind.

I yanked him down by the arm so I could cup his ear with my hands. This time he heard me and nodded. "I've considered that. But there are many places like that in this pass. The chance of them finding our camp is remote at best."

The snow flew sideways. We traveled in a straight line: Wesley first, then me, then Joe. I held onto Wesley's pack. My other hand brushed faithfully along the rock wall, convinced we'd walk right off the cliff without it for an anchor. The storm brought back too many memories of avalanches and horses falling off the sides of mountains.

I didn't trust this wind. Stories of evil winds and mountain spirits jumped to the forefront of my mind. A shrill panic began at my gut and wormed through my body. My muscles tensed into rigid knots. I placed a hand on my stomach, searching for the pull that guided me to the mountain and then abandoned me since entering the pass. Had I made a wrong choice coming here, or was the constant buzz of whispers growing too strong for me to feel the familiar tug?

Where are you?

The dark sky turned darker as day gave way to night. There were no stars, only wind and snow to push us closer and closer to our graves. Eventually Wesley shifted the pack he carried on his back to one shoulder. He lifted the back of his travel cloak and gestured for me to find shelter underneath it.

I didn't hesitate to accept the offer. His blind hand found mine and guided me to hold onto his belt. I did so with both hands. He all but dragged me along. I tripped over his feet, my feet, and his again. Exhaustion crippled my movements but at least I was somewhat warm and out of the wind. Poor Wesley and Joe weren't so lucky.

When Wesley stopped suddenly, I didn't have the energy to catch myself. I dropped to the snow and rolled onto my back. Wesley knelt next to me. "Are you all right?" He brushed the collecting flakes from my face.

In the dim light of dusk, I had a sudden, powerful impression. "This place is important," I said. The stirring in my gut confirmed it.

It took a surprising amount of effort for Wesley to help me off the ground. "You're exhausted, Ebby. You're not thinking clearly."

"No... I... I..." If it were just Wesley, I would have told him about the pull. Not wanting Joe to think me crazy, I just gestured toward the familiar gap in the wall. If I wasn't mistaken, it was the same gap that opened up to the cavern our company had used less than two months prior. "Are we stopping?"

"I don't believe we have a choice," said Joe.

"What about the Brennan soldiers?" I asked, getting to my feet.

"Let's just hope they rest, too."

As I looked to the narrowed gap of the pass again, the pull dissipated, replaced by peace. I shook my head and followed the men through the crevice in the mountain. Without the wind, our voices sounded loud and clear against the three overhanging walls of the cavern.

"Wood!" Wesley dropped his pack and staggered to a small pile of wood stored in the corner of the cavern. "Dry wood!" It had been let over from our last visit to the cave.

Joe and Wesley went right to work building a fire while I worked on clearing the snow from our packs and laying out our soaked bedrolls. Joe was right; we were all shivering so hard we might have bitten off our tongues just trying to speak. We couldn't keep moving in these conditions.

When the fire gained heavy flame, an audible sigh escaped each one of our lips. We huddled together in not much more than our underclothes while our packs, cloaks, and supplies dried. Normally I would have been embarrassed with two men seeing me in no more than a shift and a quilt, but we were all past caring.

I found myself drawing in the dirt again, just like I had the first time we took refuge in this cave. The simple design of my Freeland home took shape in the rudimentary lines.

Home.

Seeing this glimpse of home was like tasting the first crop of gooseberries in summer. It had been a long time, but just as gooseberries would always taste like gooseberries, my home would always be a symbol of peace. Now it was the fruit just a branch too high for my grasp. A tease.

I suddenly wanted to remember everything. I needed to.

"Wesley, what will happen when we get home?"

Sparks drifted upward as he poked at the fire. "We'll warn your father about Brennan's assassin. He'll hang me for allowing you to travel the mountain pass at this time of year. Then Freeland will prepare for war in the spring."

I paled.

Wesley shrugged. "It's what will happen. Minus the hanging. But the war will happen, Ebby."

I pulled the quilt closer to me while staring into the fire. Wesley would always tell me the truth, without sparing my feelings.

But he was wrong.

"If we survive this mountain, Father will kiss you for bringing me home and Brennan will back down once they learn of the alliance between us and Sea Port."

"Whatever helps you sleep tonight, Ebby."

A subtle stirring at the entrance of the cavern had us all turning, eyes wide. The hem of a dark cape billowed as what must have been a Brennan scout ran off into the wintry night. Wesley and Joe yanked on their boots and ran after him.

"Wait!" I screamed.

"Stay here!" Joe turned around and pointed at me as if his fingertip could freeze me to the ground.

I didn't listen to him. How could he expect me to?

I fumbled with my clothes for a moment before abandoning them all together. My heavy cloak and boots would have to do.

The storm had died some, but under the curtain of night I still couldn't see much beyond the tip of my nose. I followed the direction of the shouts, keeping a sure hand on the rock wall so I wouldn't run off the edge of the cliff.

"Ahh!" It was the distinct sound of a man in pain. Running faster, I saw the faint outline of one man standing and one crouched on the ground. As I got closer, I recognized the man kneeling as Joe. He reached down and yanked a knife out of the back of the scout. Wesley stepped in front of me to block my view. "Don't look." He held me so tight my breath was even harder coming than before.

"Help me with him, Smith!"

Wesley helped Joe roll the dead Brennan scout off the cliff. No one would hear his body hit the ground.

When we got to the cave everything happened fast. We packed what provisions we had and killed the fire. My dress was still soaked, so I tied the sleeves around my neck so it draped down my back like a second cloak. "We have to get rid of this ash and wood. They can't know we were here," said Joe. We kicked the hot coals to every corner of the cavern. I used my boot to move around the remaining ash. When we were finished, there was nothing left but a smoking piece of earth.

"Our tracks are the biggest problem," said Wesley. "They'll know they're close when they see the cave."

Joe seemed doubtful. "I'll cover the tracks leading into the cave. You get her moving."

If the winds hadn't died, I never would have heard the crunch of snow as the Brennan company moved through the pass behind us. The echo of men's voices bounced off the narrow rock walls.

For a long moment we all just stared in the direction of our pursuers—shocked that our best efforts for survival would not be enough. I thought of Mr. Hovel. His dying wish churned around and around in my head.

Do everything in your power to keep your home a refuge for people like me.

I yanked my arm out of Wesley's grasp and turned to Joe. "You need to run ahead. Your tracks might lead them on."

Joe shook his head, as if awakened from a trance.

"Wesley and I are going to hide. When you reach my father, tell him everything."

Wesley grabbed my arm. "You're not staying here. We'll outrun them!"

I placed my hand on his chest and looked into his eyes. "I can't, Wes. My body is exhausted."

His face fell. We both knew he couldn't carry me and still outpace the Brennan soldiers.

"Run, Joe!" I begged.

He looked from me to Wesley, searching for an alternate solution. "I'll sprint the whole way to Freeland. We'll come for you." With that, he left us at a dead run.

CHAPTER THIRTY-EIGHT

AN ARROW OF HOPE

I turned on Wesley. "You cover the tracks. I've got to find us a place to hide."

He gawked at me, but I couldn't wait for him to tell me the hopelessness of our situation. I had a job to do.

The cave wasn't safe. Of that much I was certain. I could just see those Brennan men, as diligent in their search for us as the wolves had been. They would look under every rock to find us. I stared around me at the bleak surroundings. All I could see was a vertical rock wall and a trail five feet wide.

Think, Ebby. Think!

The sound of Brennan soldiers traveling the winding trail made me dizzy. Closer and closer they came. Their hurried crunch-crunching beat out the rhythm of my pounding heart.

Come on, come on, come on… I thought back to every hiding place I'd ever used for my eavesdropping: the barn loft, the haystacks, the climbing trees, the hen houses, and when I was especially desperate, the outhouses. I'd hidden behind boulders and in tall grasses. I could do this! I might lack sewing skills and dining etiquette, but if there was one thing I could do, it was hide.

I searched from every angle. I even tried scaling the rock wall. Short of jumping off the cliff, there was no place to hide.

Then it came. The faint pull in my stomach that I had come to trust—a feeling similar but opposite the cold possession of the Dark Ones. It brought me gently to the edge of the cliff, beckoning me to take one more step into oblivion.

I frowned. Ever since leading me to the journal in the duke's library, this inexplicable feeling, this spirit, had become my greatest ally. Yes, it put me in dangerous situations, but it had also inspired me to trust Joe and saved me in a number of other instances. Everything had happened for a reason. This force, this spirit, was on our side.

So why would it bring me to the edge of a cliff?

The Brennan soldiers were close now. We had only a few final moments before they rounded the bend and spotted us. I looked up at the narrow patch of sky, praying to heaven for some kind of miracle. Though most of the sky was still clouded, a gap in the cloud cover revealed a swirl of color.

Sky dancers, like those I'd seen at the ruin stones lit up the sky, a light blue more vivid than the pinks and greens. The pull beckoned me forward, and this time I didn't doubt. I looked down to take that final step into oblivion.

There was no way to prepare myself for that sight—not in a hundred years—no, not a thousand.

I ran for Wesley. He was busy scattering the last couple feet of tracks leading into the cavern.

"Grab the packs and follow me!"

He didn't argue. I led him to the edge of the cliff and jumped.

"Ebby!" he yelled.

I landed hard. The fall was farther than the sneaky darkness suggested. I struggled to my feet just as Wesley dropped next to me. He teetered on the edge of a little shelf of rock, waving his arms like a new gosling before I pulled him back.

"I can't believe you just did that!" he said, too loud. Even from our little ledge I could tell the soldiers had turned the final corner. They were with us now.

I put my hand over his mouth and held a finger to my dry, cracked lips. I pointed upward to indicate our company. Couldn't he hear them tromping through the snow like they owned the mountain? The noises from above quickened until they halted just above our heads. I pulled Wesley back so our bodies pressed against the wall.

They'd found the cavern.

"The tracks are jumbled, sir. They stopped here."

"How long ago?" The voice of the leader made the hair on the back of my neck stand tall. Theodore Kent.

"Twenty minutes to an hour at most. The ground is still warm from fire."

"Explain these tracks leading on," Lord Kent ordered. His voice sounded different. Older and harder than he'd sounded before.

There was a long pause before the tracker spoke. "They're fresh. No new snow in the prints. I'd narrow the time by half. It only stopped snowing twenty minutes ago. And then there's the obvious…"

"The obvious?" Lord Kent sounded annoyed.

"Just one set, sir."

Again, the pause that followed kept me holding my breath.

"They're close. I can sense it," Theodore said. "Search the cave! I need twenty men to follow these tracks. It can't be the blacksmith. He and Miss Fields would stay together."

Wesley pulled my attention from the sound of busy men above. I didn't realize I'd been shivering until he moved his hands up and down my arms. *Your clothes.* He mouthed the words, looking me over with mild surprise.

I motioned to the dress tied around my neck. "I'll be fine." I shivered, effectively contradicting my assurance.

He pulled me under his cloak then took a quilt from the bedroll and draped it around us both. We sat on the ground with Wesley's back pressed to the cliff face and mine pressed into Wesley's firm chest. There was barely enough room to extend our legs. With so many people talking and rushing about up on the trail, I wasn't too afraid to whisper.

"How far down are we?" I asked, hoping the conversation would calm me down some. A stiff wind had picked up, muting the voices above.

"I'd guess about ten to twelve feet. Far enough that climbing out will prove challenging," he whispered.

I hadn't considered that.

He shook me out of my thoughts. "What you did was really brave, Ebby. I doubt I would have jumped if you hadn't flown over the edge first."

"You are a little girly when it comes to these types of things." I nudged him with my elbow, doing my best to make light of our predicament.

He chest shook with silent laughter. "Being called girly by a girl. Would you really belittle your own gender?"

"Good point."

Slowly, carefully, Wesley draped his arm around my waist, pulling me even closer to him. I held my breath at the feel of his arms around me. Terrified that any sudden movement on my part might frighten him away.

Because I wanted him near me. Craved his touch.

I let my head roll back to his chest. Of course, this was ridiculous. If there was ever a time to panic, this was it. Being trapped on a shelf of rock on a freezing cold night with our foes blocking our only exit could hardly be considered ideal. But I think Wesley and I were both too exhausted to do anything but lean on each other and hope for a miracle.

After a minute of his blissful embrace, he squeezed me tighter to him and whispered in my ear. "Are you warm?"

"Mmm," I purred, hugging his forearms.

"Ebby?" he whispered again.

"Yes, Wesley?"

"I... I... Do you think you would ever... I mean, could you..."

I repositioned until I knelt in front of him, eye to eye. "What is it?"

His gentle fingertips trailed along my cheek, brushing my ear, and sliding down my neck. I closed my eyes and nuzzled into the touch. It was suddenly summer on this cold mountain. His hand cupped behind my neck as he carefully pulled me to him until our breaths formed one cloud between us. He stared at my lips and paused, as if giving me the chance to stop him.

I didn't.

His warm, soft lips gently pressed against mine. He pulled away too soon. His eyebrows rose as if to ask, *Is this all right?* I took hold of his shirtfront and pressed into him until the warmth of his lips burned as they moved with mine. His hands traveled up and down my back... in my hair... at my neck.

And then our kisses slowed. Moving together in tender synchronization.

Wesley turned his head, breaking our connection. The labor of his breathing rocked me.

"What's wrong?" I asked when he turned away. I was new to this. Had I done it wrong?

Wesley wouldn't look at me. "That was a mistake."

I felt small. So small. And there was nowhere for me to run. I tried to pull away from him, but he tightened his hold on me, demanding to be heard.

"Since we were kids, I've planned to kiss you. Sitting here, knowing this might be our last night together, I don't want to say goodbye without showing you how I feel. How I've always felt."

Hope combated with fear. "Then why am I a mistake?"

"Now, when I'm chained to a brazier in Brennan, I'll live the rest of my life knowing what it felt like to hold you. To kiss you." His lips found my forehead. "Losing you will absolutely destroy me, Ebby."

Was this even possible? Could he really care for me as much as I cared for him?

I jabbed my finger into his chest. "You will not give up on us yet. I won't let you."

"I can make the Purgo, Ebby. I lied to you in the fortress. I wanted to protect you."

I jolted in his embrace. Was he serious?

A man's voice from above silenced our whispered conversation.

"They're not here, my lord."

"How could they just disappear?"

There was silence a while and then Lord Kent raised his voice so it echoed off the rock walls. "Did Ebby tell you about the good times we had in Brennan, Wesley?"

Wesley went very still.

"Did you know her lips taste like strawberries?" His shout echoed around us.

The men in the Brennan camp laughed, but Lord Kent shushed them.

He wouldn't be able to hear us if they didn't keep quiet. He was playing to Wesley's greatest weakness—his temper, especially where my honor was concerned.

The wind had died, and without the men moving around above, it wasn't safe to talk. I forced Wesley to look at me as I shook my head. *Don't you do anything, Wesley Smith. Don't you dare!*

"Have you held her close enough to smell the sweet lilac of her hair? Have you felt the fine curves of her body?"

Wesley trembled beneath me. I shook my head, begging him to block out the sound of Lord Kent's voice. This was an entirely different kind of wolf—the kind that slashed with words and bit with lies.

"Of all the women I've ever had, she was…"

In less than a second, Wesley had dumped me from his lap and began to climb the wall. I swiftly crawled onto his back as though he were a tree. "Get down!" I ordered in my softest, angriest whisper.

We hung there, Wesley supporting my weight while he tried to gain control over himself. He was a fool to let his emotions best him in this situation.

"Did you hear that, my lord?" asked one of the soldiers.

"Where?" said Lord Kent.

All was quiet while Wesley and I hung from the wall like bats in a cave. "It's impossible, my lord, but I thought it came from the other side of the ravine."

I could imagine the soldier pointing across the dark expanse.

I pulled the hood of my cloak forward. My light hair would be too easy to spot, even on a night as dark as this. Wesley and I froze as a new sprinkling of snow drifted past us. Someone must have disturbed the snow on the ledge up above. Poor Wesley's arms shook from having to support us both.

Just when I was sure we were caught, shouts echoed off the rock walls. Clashing swords rang out somewhere in the darkness above. Using the commotion as cover, we dropped back down to our ledge and huddled together underneath Wesley's cloak.

Men yelled things impossible to decipher. Even though we couldn't hear the words, the anger behind the noise reminded me again of those snarling wolves.

Will they never leave me?

Somewhere a man cried, "No, no! Please don't! I beg you!" Then the screams turned hysterical as the man dropped past us to his death.

Wesley pulled me closer to him. I bit the back of my hand to hold back my own screams. What were we doing here on the top of this horrible mountain? Who was attacking the Brennan men, and were they friend or foe? How had things gotten so bad?

"I'm sorry, Ebby. I shouldn't have let him get to me," said Wesley.

No, you shouldn't have! I wanted to say, but I didn't want to make him feel worse than he already did. "You didn't believe him, did you?" I asked.

He didn't answer right away. "All that talk about your lips and your hair, well, it's true. I don't doubt your character, but I couldn't bear to hear him go on. I'll kill that man. I swear I will."

WHATEVER BATTLE HAD raged on the ledge above them had quieted just as quickly as it began. Wesley and I kept the cloak over our heads for the rest of the night. The Brennan camp settled to dull murmurings and then to nothing at all, leaving Wesley and I to await our fate.

I couldn't stop thinking of the red letters back at the fortress and the blood oath I'd signed, committing my people to war. It made me wonder if Father ever questioned his decisions. I'd heard so many stories about young heroes defying impossible odds. They always seemed so confident, like perhaps they already knew the happy ending of their story. For all I knew, I'd sentenced my people to their deaths and dragged Wesley along with me to die on this mountain.

My head nodded forward and whipped back as I drifted in and out of sleep. We needed to do something before the sun came up and gave away our "perfect" hiding place.

Just as these thoughts shivered through me, I fell into a restless sleep laden with a horrible chain of dreams. I was caught in a well with no rope to help me out. Then Simon Right turned into a wolf and tried to talk me out of going home. Worse still, I saw Mr. Hovel shoveling snow off the mountain trail to ease our journey.

I awoke with hot tears burning my frozen cheeks.

"Are you awake?" Wesley's deep whisper tickled my ear and sent chills throughout my body.

I nodded. "We can't stay here."

He took my hand and helped me to my feet. "I have a plan." His voice wavered enough that I could tell he wasn't exactly sold on his own idea. "I'll climb out and take care of the soldiers on watch. When I give you the signal, you start climbing."

"And what if they alert the rest before you can 'take care of them?'"

"They won't."

As large as Wesley was, I doubted his ability to sneak up on a blind pig, let alone a night watchman. They would spot him before he had two feet on the ground.

"They'll catch you."

"What other options do we have?" he asked.

I had an idea, but Wesley wasn't going to like it. "What if I went first? Maybe I could talk to them." I clutched a rock at my side. It would be a little more involved than just talking.

Wesley's arms tightened around me. "No."

"What if I told you I didn't think I could climb out of here without help?"

He rolled his eyes. "You'd be lying. You're not going up there alone. We'll just have to think of something else." There was doubt in his voice again.

Just then, a soft thud hit the ground right next to us. There, sticking out of the white snow, was a familiar-looking arrow.

We were caught.

I cringed waiting for a volley of arrows to follow before remembering they needed us alive: Wesley for the Purgo blade, and me to keep Wesley in line. A second arrow parted the thin air and struck the snow just next to the first.

Wesley reached for the arrow and pulled off a folded piece of parchment that had been tightly wrapped around the shaft. I leaned over him as we both tried to decipher the words written on the page. It was too dark to see anything, so Wesley pulled out his flint and tried to shoot a spark to the page. When it caught, the red letters burned just after I read them.

Come up.

CHAPTER THIRTY-NINE

UNEXPECTED ALLY

Wesley frowned. "Did you see the red ink?"

I nodded. "Let's go."

Wesley grabbed my arm, as if to stop me, but then slowly let go. He knew as well as I did that this was our only card, so we might as well play it. Whoever waited for us at the top of this wall could be friend or enemy. But at least we were moving toward something.

When I reached the top, a hooded figure stretched out a gloved hand to help me. The hand was smaller than I'd expected. The person didn't waste words or wait for Wesley to scale the rest of the wall before walking off in the direction of Brennan. With a wave, the small man beckoned us to follow.

Three men lay dead in the snow, each with an arrow to the heart. Aside from those three guards, the path was completely clear. Light from a dying fire glowed inside the cavern we'd taken shelter in, but no one stirred. I could only assume Lord Kent slept with at least a portion of his company inside.

Wesley took care of the bodies and caught up to me. Once we rounded the second turn, our rescuer turned on us. He pulled back the hood of his cloak and a long tumble of dark hair dropped past his shoulders. With his face cast in shadow, I still couldn't make out his face.

"Hello, Miss Fields." Georgiana Kent stepped into the light of the moon. She held her bow loosely at her side, her usual pompous demeanor gone.

I gaped. "How did you… you… you wrote the red letters?"

She nodded. "I did." She looked past me to Wesley. "I tried to get you to leave the moment I discovered Wesley's gift."

"How?" asked Wesley.

Lady Kent lifted a finger to her lips to quiet him and glanced over her shoulder to check that the way was clear. "The first night you arrived in Brennan, I intercepted the message you sent to an arms dealer saying you were looking for a buyer."

Wesley raked a hand through his thick, dark hair. "Why not just turn me over to your father?"

A muscle in her neck leaped. She seemed to battle her next words. "I've been planning to run away for years. If Freeland is destroyed, where will I go to escape my father?"

If what she said was true, Lady Kent had learned about the *Purgo* long before the duke and I had.

Her father had underestimated her.

In my mind I saw Lady Kent lying on the floor outside the duke's room as he pretended to kick her, using her to seduce Wesley. What else had he made her do?

I'd want to escape, too.

"Why all the letters?" I whispered. "Why the secrecy?" It didn't make sense.

Her smile sunk into chagrin. "I didn't know if I could trust you." She shrugged. "I knew Wesley wouldn't leave without you, and without the *Purgo*, my family might just get what's coming to them." She regained her snobby air and brushed a clump of flowing hair from her eyes. But I could still see the scared little girl hiding behind the mask, a girl as desperate for freedom as Mr. Hovel had been. Perhaps more so.

Wesley stepped forward. "We have to get moving. How long before the next watch?"

"Unless someone wakes them, I doubt they'll get up on their own." She gestured down the trail in the direction of Brennan. "The other half of the camp is holed up in another cavern a quarter of a mile back."

Wesley glanced in both directions. His fists were clenched and his stance tense, as though prepared to charge against a foe in either direction. "How many men in total?" he asked.

"An even hundred. Eighty camped here and twenty that went on ahead after your friend." Georgiana turned and walked up the trail toward Brennan, effectively sandwiching them between two enemies. "I'll take you to my camp."

Wesley took me by my arm, unwilling to let me follow. "Shouldn't we get moving toward Freeland?" he whispered.

"If we trail them, we can travel at our own pace." By that I had to assume she meant her pace. No matter her skill with a bow, Georgiana hadn't lived a life of work and manual labor like Wesley and I had.

When Wesley opened his mouth to argue, she winked at him. "You're just going to have to trust me, blacksmith."

Though I hated to side with Lady Kent, the familiar pull in my gut suggested we follow her. "We've no other option," I said to Wesley. "We can't stay ahead of them."

His grip on me relaxed enough for his hand to slide down my arm, catching my hand and bringing it to his cold lips. "After you." With hands still clasped, we walked together in the direction of our enemy.

I had to admit, Lady Kent's camp was impressive. She had taken my idea the night I was lost in the woods and improved upon it. Hers was a perch about fifteen feet above the trail that she'd managed to climb with her pack of supplies. We struggled to the top where I was pleased to find a shelf large enough for the three of us.

"Rest until it's safe to continue on," she said, taking up a position where she could watch the trail.

From this angle, no one could see us if we stayed low to the ground. I puzzled through the unlikelihood of working with Georgiana Kent. I'd despised the women. Now I questioned every moment of our acquaintance, examining it with new perspective as Wesley slept at my back with one arm draped protectively around my middle under our shared blanket.

WHEN THE SUN broke the horizon there was an hour of chaos. With so many tracks from the Brennan camp, no one deciphered ours from the rest. Though I didn't see Lord Kent's face when he learned of his missing night watchmen, I could imagine his anger. We'd escaped him, and he had no choice but to continue the pursuit toward Freeland or turn around and go home like a beaten pup with his tail between his legs.

Lord Kent wasn't the type to accept defeat with any sort of grace, so I wasn't surprised to see him continue his trek toward Freeland. We rested for another hour before packing up.

Georgiana walked ahead of us. She wore men's trousers and a bow strapped to her back. Everything touching her skin was crafted out of fine leather. Her cloak was as white as the snow lightly falling around us, and with her hood up, she blended into the wintry mountain. I was too jealous to admit to her genius. No wonder she was able to follow the Brennan camp without detection. We could barely see her as she walked five feet in front of us.

For two days we traveled this way. Georgiana kept mostly to herself, and Wesley and I didn't bother engaging her in conversation. I knew we owed her a great debt, but I still wasn't convinced I trusted her.

The closer we came to Freeland, the faster we traveled. The walls of the pass opened up. Our steps sloped downward, and the snow seemed less deep.

I awoke on the morning of the third day with Wesley's arm wrapped around my middle, pinning me tight to his chest. We'd slept in this position every night since he'd found me. I would miss his solid warmth when we were off the mountain, and I wondered what our lives would look like when this ordeal passed and we didn't have the excuse of a cold mountain to keep us together.

"I'm going to scout ahead." Wesley's words tickled my ear as he held me. The sun hadn't fully risen, but a pair of winter finches flitted and chirped from one branch to another overhead.

"Let me go with you."

I felt more than saw the shake of his head. He kissed my hair and mumbled, "Too dangerous," against my scalp, effectively sending a thousand chills up and down my spine. I unpeeled his arm and lifted his palm to my lips. "Don't be long." Another kiss. "Be careful."

The moment he left, I felt the full brunt of the cold mountain air and shivered.

Georgiana lay with her back only a few feet away from me. Though her body lay still and I couldn't see her face, I sensed that she was awake.

"Are you cold?" I asked. She didn't have another body near to keep her warm.

Georgiana didn't answer for several long moments. When she did speak, her voice was deep and hollow. "Wesley was the first to refuse me. Did you know that?" she said, not turning around. "Before he came along, I thought all men were the same."

I pushed up onto one hand, still clutching the wool blanket around me.

"I wondered what was so special about you," Georgiana continued in a whisper, her words carried away on the morning breeze. "I thought maybe you knew something I didn't—something I could use on a different man to be more effective for my father. Men are animals, Ebrielle Fields. Simple creatures who never bother adapting for the people around them the way women are trained to do from birth. So, when Wesley didn't respond to my advances, I watched you. Studied you. You were pretty. Your manners were acceptable. But you didn't know how to flirt and were an even worse dancer." At that she chuckled.

I was too caught up in her experience, her view, to be offended. And I *was* a terrible dancer. "What are you going to do now?" I asked.

Georgiana rolled onto her back, staring up at the gray morning sky. "I suppose I don't know, Miss Fields." She held her glazed expression for an uncomfortable amount of time. When she finally looked at me there was something different in her eyes. Something softer. "You feel things for Wesley and your father and I suspect your brother—things I haven't felt in a very long time. I don't remember what it's like to be loved, or to love someone in return…" She trailed off.

I wanted to reach out and take her hand, to squeeze away some of her pain. With all her wiles, with all her hidden abilities, there was a little wounded girl peeking around the rim of those dark eyes. Frightened and alone, but daring to emerge, desperate but terrified to let someone know her.

"You'll be welcome in Freeland, Georgiana." I was surprised to find that I meant those words, that I liked calling her by her given name. It made the idea of us eventually burying old differences seem possible.

She frowned. "I'm sorry I was so awful to you in Brennan." She swallowed hard and looked away. "I had a part to play with Wesley, and I didn't want anyone to know I was secretly trying to warn you."

"You don't really care for Wesley, do you?" I chewed on my bottom lip.

She smiled, the expression capturing her whole face. "He's a little too noble for me." Another short laugh. "But even if I did, that man is undeniably yours, Ebrielle Fields."

WESLEY RETURNED AN hour later, announcing the way was clear. A light rain drizzled around us as we shouldered our packs and set off again. Though cold, wet, and hungry, we were also less than a day away from home. As thrilled as I was to get off this mountain, somewhere between here and Freeland were one hundred trained Brennan soldiers.

"They're not foolish enough to challenge Freeland," said Wesley as we walked. "Joe should be there by now with the alarm raised. I'm surprised we haven't run into a rescue party yet."

"Agreed," said Lady Kent, just before I had the chance to agree myself.

Giant evergreens stood alone here and there along the rocky trail. They seemed to grow out of pure rock—defiant and beautiful. As we moved closer to Freeland, the ground changed from rock to soil and the giant redwoods grew thick and wonderful.

"I think we should get off the trail. The trees can provide us a little cover," I said.

Wesley agreed and hummed an old smithy song that his father always sang as he pounded away in the forges. I fingered my mother's necklace. The leather journal weighed heavy in my otherwise light pack. Wesley and I seemed to both be thinking of home because we shared a smile.

Then something behind him caught my attention.

Shadows are wily things. I remember following my shadow to run errands in the morning, then following it home late at night. A shadow could make me tall and lean in the morning and then disappear completely by midday. When I was very young, Mother used to take me to the fields to play while she helped Father and the rest of the men bring in the yields. Because I liked to wander, Father taught me how to read the shadows to find home if I was ever lost. *The shade of a tree can do a lot more than cool your brow,* he'd said.

There was something else I knew about the shadows of trees: they didn't change form in front of your eyes.

"Wesley, don't panic, but there's a man standing behind a tree back there."

Wesley's smile dropped and his body became noticeably rigid, but he didn't stop walking. "If there's one there's a hundred," he spoke out of the side of his mouth. "They must have sent scouts to double back once they approached Freeland."

We didn't have time to think of a plan, let alone carry one out. Men from every direction stepped out of their hiding places with bows drawn and swords in hand.

Wesley drew his sword, a paltry piece of metal the revolutionaries gifted him back at the Talk About.

Lord Kent walked through the front line of his men, holding his own sword as casually as a walking stick. Judging by the intricate design of the hilt, I guessed it was one of Wesley's blades. Not the *Purgo* but still very valuable. He strolled up to our group, careful to keep good distance from Wesley. "I told you, men. The best way to catch a fox is to wait by its hole. It always comes home." The men around him snickered. Lord Kent cut them off with a small wave of his hand. I had the distinct impression that he was flaunting his power, enjoying the moment.

"Hello, sister." He lunged at Georgiana and grabbed her by the hair. She cried out in pain. Wesley stepped forward to fight him off, but four Brennan soldiers thrust swords at his chest, prepared to run him through if he took another step.

Lord Kent wrenched back Georgiana's head and growled, "I'll deal with you later," before throwing her to the ground.

She didn't rise.

Wesley grabbed my wrist and placed himself between Lord Kent and me, as if he could do anything against all these men.

"You don't need them, Kent. I'll give you what you want."

Lord Kent stared at me like he had the other night in my room: hungry and hot. "I have no doubt you will give me what I want, blacksmith, especially with our little cornflower under my personal protection."

I flinched, involuntarily remembering his rough touch, his teeth on my lips. I knew exactly what kind of "protection" I would find with Lord Kent.

We were so close!

Wesley let out a string of curses. "Touch her, and I'll kill you." There was no hesitation in his threat. His tone completely even, as though the statement were as true as grass was green.

"Now, now. Let's not get dramatic. I'm sure there's no need to fear for Miss Fields. She'll be fine, so long as you do what we ask."

Lord Kent took a step closer. "Let's start right now. Drop your sword, let my men bind your wrists, and I'll spare Ebby the same degradation."

Wesley looked around the group, as if sizing up his competition.

"Perhaps an arrow to Ebby's knee might expedite your decision." Lord Kent lifted his hand to ready one of his archers.

"I'm dropping it!" Wesley yelled as he set down his blade.

"See. This won't be so bad." Lord Kent sounded like he was reassuring a five-year-old.

Ten men swarmed Wesley, forcing him to the ground as they tied him. Lord Kent walked up to me with a sad smile. "I could have given you everything you ever wanted. Together we could produce posterity to rule the provinces." He let his finger trail down my cheek. "It's not too late for us, you know. Our lives could be perfect."

Just like Gavin taught me, I arched my neck and spat right in Lord Kent's face. He used a handkerchief and wiped the face that I used to think was so handsome. After tucking the cloth back into his shirt pocket with all the grace of a courtly gentleman, he struck me hard across the face with the back of his hand. The force of his blow knocked me off my feet. Wesley bucked and rolled like a wild horse on a halter.

"Don't, Wes. I'm fine. Don't fight them."

Lord Kent stood over me with a brutish grin on his face, no doubt enjoying the sight of me in the mud. Part of me wanted to just fall asleep right there on the wet ground surrounded by scores of Brennan soldiers. My body begged for rest. It was Lord Kent's smug expression that motivated me. I pushed up to my knees and gathered my balance to stand. Lord Kent pressed his boot to my side and knocked me down again. The men laughed, though some with less mirth than others.

This was not the Lord Kent who'd sent me flowers and escorted me to dinner. This man was as cold and calloused as his father.

I didn't have the energy to get up right away. I panted like a lame horse on the ground. Lord Kent bent down, resting his forearms on his knees. He whispered so no one else could hear him. "Ebby, my love. Soon you'll know what it's like to beg forgiveness." He used his finger to lift up my chin. "With the proper persuasion, I can be very forgiving, you know."

As I contemplated biting his fingers off, a rough-cut arrow whistled through the air and penetrated deep into Lord Kent's thigh.

CHAPTER FORTY

A BATTLE OF WILLS

The arrow was so sudden I had to blink to make sure it wasn't my imagination. Red seeped from around where it had lodged in Lord Kent's thigh.

The proud Theodore Kent cried out as he dropped to the ground.

I looked up to see Joe Ford along with what had to be every man in Freeland lining the surrounding trees. Every family of Freeland had at least one good hunting bow in the house. At that moment, every single one was carefully aimed at a Brennan heart. I scanned the familiar crowd for Father and heard his voice before I found his face.

"Kent!" Even I flinched under the commanding, deep bellow of my father.

He stepped forward with his giant shovel resting on his shoulder. "Release them!"

Lord Kent wept where he lay on the ground. I couldn't be sure, but it looked as though he'd pissed himself. For all his time spent as a soldier, he'd apparently never been injured. The Brennan soldiers looked to each other, lost without their leader.

Father roared, "Release them!" He took another step forward, and without orders, a Brennan archer let fly an arrow. It struck my father's shoulder with a deep thump sound. My brother appeared beside him, ready to help, but Father raised his hand to stop him. He studied the arrow like he might study a plant to determine if it was a weed or a wildflower and then, without ceremony, broke the shaft and tossed it on the ground.

I'm not exactly sure what happened after that. It could have been a frightened Brennan who fired the next arrow. It could have been an angry Freelander defending my father. It didn't matter. Arrows flew. I dropped flat to the ground and covered my head. A part of me thought if I lifted my gaze, I might find my father on the ground with a hundred arrows piercing his body.

"Ebby!" Wesley called.

A man grabbed me by the back of the neck and forced me up to my knees. I cried out, shocked by the force. Suddenly, he gasped and his body jerked. I wrenched away from him as he fell. On all fours, I scrambled toward the still trussed Wesley. A glance back showed me a man slumped to the ground, an arrow in his back.

Arrows flew around my head, cutting the air with whistles and screams. I crouched over Wesley's bound hands and pulled my knife.

"Run for the trees," Wesley said as I sawed through the ropes binding his wrists. "Climb the tallest one you can find and stay up there until I come for you."

Not another tree! But I knew better than to argue.

Wesley snatched up his dropped sword and I ran for a tree as he charged a Brennan man with a primal yell. Wesley's battle cry diverted enough Brennan attention that the volley of arrows subsided, giving the men in the trees the window they needed. They swarmed past me into the fray. Like Father, most of his field workers held nothing but a spade or rake. Others held hammers, flails, and picks—the tools of their trades. They were masters of these tools and could wield them better than any sword or mace. Despite their rag-tag weapons, their eyes held a fire that could burn through any advantage the trained Brennan soldiers possessed.

I reached a tall tree whose branches spiraled above me like a ladder and tucked the knife back in my belt. I climbed as quickly as possible and positioned myself on a branch twenty feet above the ground.

The tree swayed as Lady Kent scrambled up to join me, bow in hand. She settled into a neighboring branch and looked out on the meadow, seeming more numb than alive. "You shouldn't watch," she said.

But how could I not when so many I loved fought below me? I scanned the field for Father, Gavin, and Wesley. Shouts of pain and war cries filled the air.

Marianna's father fought a Brennan soldier who had to be half his age. The soldier dodged a blow from the old councilman's hammer, spun, and dragged a sword across the back of his knees. Councilman Miller crumpled to the ground. Just as the soldier raised his sword for a killing blow, Gavin rushed up and tackled him. They rolled around on the ground, their movements too difficult to see from where I sat, until Gavin thrust what seemed like a knife into the soldier's chest and the man lay still.

What was I doing sitting like a useless bystander in this tree? I couldn't stand to watch any longer.

"Where are you going?" Miss Kent shouted at me. "You'll only make it worse!"

But I was already halfway down the tree, with no intention of stopping. I'd made this journey to save my family. I wasn't about to lose them now!

I gathered about a dozen fist-sized rocks in my skirt—the process taking far too long—and sprinted with my clattering ammunition into the clearing.

Wesley and Gavin fought back-to-back against three Brennan soldiers, the swordplay they practiced in their childhood poor preparation for facing this enemy. If it weren't for Wesley's size, I might not have recognized him under the mask of blood and sweat.

No one seemed to notice me as I dropped my load of rocks, picked one up, and took aim at one of the three soldiers attacking the men I loved.

"Please, please, please." I reared back and threw.

The rock struck the soldier on the arm, distracting him long enough for Wesley to cut the man down like a felled tree.

I threw another rock, this time connecting hard with a soldier's back. The man cried out, and Gavin finished him.

The look both men cast in my direction would have made a grown warrior flee, but I wasn't leaving. Two more soldiers came in to take the others' place, preventing Wesley and Gavin from doing anything to stop my intervention.

Again and again, I connected with my targets, helping in the only way I knew how.

And I was helping! Distracted by my rocks, the Brennan soldiers lost focus just long enough for the Freelanders to gain the advantage. If a soldier ran at me, a Freelander cut him down from behind. One Brennan soldier leapt for me, but I dodged away just as an arrow caught him in the side. I grew numb to the gore, mentally distancing myself from the reality of lives lost. Of pain. Of tragedy. In my mind, none of it was real.

I lifted my last stone and cocked my arm back to throw, but a large hand grabbed my wrist and twisted until something popped. I cried out, dropping the rock. "No more," the man growled, hooking his arm around my middle and dragging me from the field.

Wesley's shouts followed me, but my captor sprinted on.

"I'll be rewarded handsomely for you, girl." He wheezed. "Just you—

Whatever he planned to say died with the *thunk* of an arrow buried into his chest.

I looked around to find Georgiana Kent lowering her bow and stepping back behind a tree to conceal herself from the soldiers. If the woman knew one thing, it was self-preservation.

My right hand was completely numb when I finally made it back to the tree.

Shouts of surrender rang out around the field. Under Father's command, Wesley and Gavin helped corral the remaining Brennan into a tight group while other Freelanders ran around answering the panicked cries of the wounded. Georgiana joined me by the tree and together we scanned the clearing for Lord Kent.

"I'm going to head toward the pass. We can't let him get back over the mountain," she said, not waiting for a reply before taking off with bow in hand.

I stretched up onto my toes to look around, gingerly cradling my wrist to my chest. Lord Kent was wounded. He couldn't have gone far.

A warm prickling sensation spread down my spine and into my gut.

A pull that led me deeper into the forest, toward a flicker of moment.

I looked back to the center of the clearing where Father and Gavin worked to aid the wounded Freelanders, and in a quick decision, stepped deeper into the woods to follow the gift that had spared me time and again.

The pull amplified, racing through my veins like an angry river current. Even though jogging jostled my wrist, I picked up my pace like a hound who'd caught its scent. The foothills of Freeland were a maze of trees that extended for miles. If the pull was leading me to Lord Kent, I wasn't foolhardy enough to think I could stop him, but I could follow him and learn of his hiding place so others might.

I eventually found a game trail and followed it down the mountain. After two minutes, a chorus of whispers slithered through my thoughts and a cold chill wrapped around my arms and legs until it filled every part of me.

Stop.

I'm going the wrong way.

I should head back to the mountain.

Now.

I stood panting on the trail, searching the path behind me. A rational part of my mind knew I should ignore the whispers circulating in my head, while a stronger, more urgent side felt certain I must follow their command.

I'm a fool to chase what I can't see.

I'm a failure.

I'll never be enough.

I sat on the forest floor, uncertain when I'd given my legs permission to bend. I gripped my hands in my hair, tugging until several strains came loose. Not feeling pain in wrist or scalp, I gripped harder, terrified, crying out as a battle waged within me. The whispers turned to shouts.

Surrender.

Surrender and be free.

The pendant around my neck grew warm and I gripped it as though it were a lifeline. If I was going to lose my mind to this madness and give up this body to the dark spirits, I couldn't meet my mother in the next life without speaking my heart in this one. "I understand now," I said, gritting my teeth, fighting back the Dark Ones with gasps of pain and lanced my mind. "I don't blame you. I just miss you." The whispers doubled their pressing efforts and I cried out. "So ashamed for leaving."

A single thread of thought, as thin and frail as a blade of grass, nagged at my middle. A female voice I knew well entered my thoughts. The voice vibrated in my core, stirring the place within me where the needle and thread of the pull usually resided.

I understood now. It was the needle and thread of my mother. *"You are a Fields, my love. Beat them back."*

I mentally anchored myself, drawing on the pull with every last ounce of my strength. The Dark Ones inside me resisted, their poisonous consciousness dragging through me, commanding and insisting I give myself over to them. Sweat beaded along my forehead, every muscle in my body strained as I closed my eyes.

I found myself standing again. Without lifting my legs, my feet dragged along the path, back toward the mountain.

"No," I cried. "I don't belong to you."

But my body was no match for the Dark Ones. As long as my mind was open to them, they would never let me go again. I knew it as surely as I knew the sun would rise in the morning.

The Dark Ones lifted my foot to step, but I fought them, causing my body to crumple to the ground. Stabs of pain sprayed from wrist to elbow as I crawled, like a beast, toward the mountain under the ugly control of my enemy.

Lord Kent, or whomever the pull guided me to, would soon be lost to the forest. My family needed me. Freeland needed me.

The pull flickered within, the final efforts of a dying fire.

"I… I'm sorry!" I sobbed. "I shouldn't have left. I love you!" Calling upon my mother's help with all the will left in my control, I focused on its little, dying flame that was her pull. I remembered the author of the journal. The gift that aided the Brennan scribe to help the women he loved.

"Please. Help me." My jaw locked. I couldn't form another word. I lost feeling in my hands, arms, legs and feet. A sense of numbness worked its way from my limbs to my core. Shoulders. Hips. Chest. Just as the hollowness threatened to take over my middle, a thin thread of the pull fought its way back from oblivion. I clung to that thread, mentally tugging with all that remained of my strength.

With each tug, a glimmer of energy filled me, feeling returned to my limbs, the shouts in my head muted. And then, as quickly as it came, the darkness inside me vanished completely.

I sat panting, hugging my knees to my chest, wiping away tears.

"I beat them," I said aloud. The pull warmed within me and I climbed to my feet.

"*We* beat them." My mother and I both. We'd mended our connection, and I could feel it now, filling all of the empty spaces left by her passing. The bonds that tied us whole.

But I couldn't celebrate my victory over the Dark Ones forever.

I still had a job to do.

THE FOOTHILLS WERE vast, and I knew how easy it would be for someone to hide. My gift might be our only hope of finding Lord Kent.

I tucked my throbbing wrist to my chest again and ran. It wasn't long before I approached the ancient temple ground littered with the ruin stones. The pull within me seemed to relax just by being near this site that so many in Freeland avoided. Ducking behind a fallen log, I peered over the edge to see the small clearing around the stones.

One of Father's field workers shifted from foot to foot as Lord Kent stretched back on one of the black ruins.

"You're sure it's safe to rest here?" asked Lord Kent.

The Freelander stood with concave shoulders. His Adam's apple protruded from his thin neck, and his head hung forward, as though he were a vulture. Not a trace of blood stained his clothing. No limp or sign of injury. The man must have avoided the battle all together.

"We're safe for now. No one comes here. The ruins make people nervous."

Lord Kent frowned as he glanced around at the old stone monuments. "I don't blame them."

Suddenly the nagging pieces to the puzzle came together. This worker had only lived in Freeland a year. He'd been quiet. I couldn't even recall his name, just his friendly smile as he thanked me for the water I carried for the field workers on hot summer days. But I did recall which province he'd lived in before Freeland.

Brennan's spy and assassin—the man contracted to kill my father.

"I want a full update." Lord Kent grunted as he eased his injured leg onto the stone.

"They know everything about the apprentice's ability, about Sea Port, and the new pass the duke is planning to build. Even the planned assassination," the Freeland traitor said.

Lord Kent groaned, whether pained by his leg or the news I could not tell. "How is that possible? Do they suspect you?"

"They will if I don't return soon."

Lord Kent shook his head. "You'll have to help me back over the pass. The duke needs to know what we're up against."

Shouts rang out in the distance. "Ebby! Ebby!" Gavin's voice, or maybe Wesley's. I'd decided long ago that when boys grow up together their shouts sound the same.

Father's field worker all but dragged Lord Kent from the clearing and behind a grouping of thick pines not more than fifteen feet from where I crouched, then rushed in the other direction. "Miss Fields!" he called out, like he too was searching for me. I had to admit it was a genius move.

I stayed hidden near Lord Kent, determined he would not slink away from me unnoticed. The sound of hurried steps and whipping tree branches traveled toward us. "Ebby!" Wesley called again, emerging in the distance, placing Lord Kent between us.

"Mr. Smith!" The field worker ran to Wesley then dropped his hands to his knees and panted like he'd been running for hours. "I've searched this whole area. Maybe we should go back toward the pass." He took Wesley's arm to guide him in the other direction.

I couldn't wait any longer. "Don't listen to him!" I jumped up from my hiding place even though help was still more than fifty feet away. "He's a traitor!"

Wesley must not have understood, because he didn't bother grabbing the man before barreling through the trees in my direction.

Lord Kent struggled to his feet and turned to face me, grinning from his hiding place as he drew a dagger from his belt and cocked his arm back to throw it at Wesley.

I was no warrior. I could barely see over a half-grown crop of corn, and dripping wet I was a fraction of Lord Kent's weight. But simple logistics didn't matter when the world was about to crumble on top of you. I put my head down and charged Lord Kent from behind before the knife left his hand. We hit the ground hard. I scrambled to my knees, but he grabbed me by the hair, wrenched me back to his chest, and pressed the knife to my neck.

My scream stopped Wesley's advance.

"There's no way out of this for you, Kent. Let her go," Wesley shouted. My brother, Gavin, broke through the trees at a sprint and halted at Wesley's side. His face went from red to purple like it always did when he was really, really angry. He balled his fists and his whole body shook. He looked like a man. He looked like Father.

As Kent's knife dug into my neck, I realized I might never see Gavin marry Marianna. I'd never hug my father again, never having the chance to tell him about the gift. I let my body go limp, sinking deeper into Lord Kent's shoulder. With his bad leg he couldn't support my weight. We slumped to the ground together, but he kept the knife pressed at my throat. The sharp blade broke skin.

"Stay where you are, or I'll finish her."

"You're a dead man, Kent. This will only make it worse for you," said Wesley, a shaky pleading entered his voice. Desperation.

I thought of the conversation I'd overheard between the duke and Lord Kent so many nights ago. The duke had threatened Lord Kent that if he didn't secure the maker of the *Purgo*, he'd lose his inheritance.

As the cold blade of the knife bit into the skin of my neck, I carefully brushed my hand along the wet ground. Searching. Asking my mother's spirit to be my eyes.

"I'm already dead, boys. At least I'll go knowing you lost as well."

I closed my eyes, bracing for the end. Kent tightened his hold on my shoulders for leverage to drag the blade across my throat.

I love you, Gavin. Tell Father I'm sorry for all the trouble I caused him. Tell him I think I finally know what it means to be a Fields.

My fingers brushed something solid. I snatched up the fist-sized stone and jammed it into Lord Kent's wounded thigh. His cry filled my ears. His grip on me slackened enough for me to lean away from him.

The thump of a knife struck right next to my face. Lord Kent fell on top of me, limp. I cried out as our combined weight fell on my bad wrist.

Then a hundred things happened at once: shouts from every direction, Gavin retrieving his knife, hands lifting me out of the snow, pressure applied to my neck, a splint on my wrist, my heart racing like a tadpole upstream, and running. Lots of running.

CHAPTER FORTY-ONE

NEW BEGINNINGS

I found the dark leather book in Father's office only two days later. The pull had guided me, of course. I'd come to the office the moment Hannah had let me leave my bed, compelled by a suspicion that was completely my own.

It didn't take long to find the book. The hand-sewn bindings were old, the pages yellowing. But the tight clean script matched the brown leather journal I'd found in the duke of Brennan's library perfectly.

April 5th

I begin this account on some parchment salvaged in the market on our way out of Brennan. I write now less for my own musings, and more to provide a proper record if we are to die on this mountain and our bodies are recovered.

The mountain spirits are aggressive and evil. My ability to channel the spirits of the dead allows them access to my

*mind. Were it not for the protection of my ancestral guardi-
an, they would easily overtake me.*

*Wolves are a constant threat. There is no way of knowing
what dangers await us on the other side of the mountain,
but the gift continues to confirm this is the right course of
action. We will deal with the consequences as they come.
All I can trust is the urgency of my heart and the power of
my hands. Even if it takes our company a year to cross this
mountain, we will reach the valley on the other side.*

May 2nd

*This morning the entire company stood overlooking the val-
ley before us. Our future. There are thick forests and two
main rivers that cut through the land. Charlotte is determined to make a farmer out of me. I can't say I mind the
idea, especially if she is by my side.*

*We are still wary of the duke's power. The new leaders of
our settlement have changed their names to match our respective trades. We set up a council and are well organized.
After our company's first official vote, I have been appointed Governor, to serve for a span of ten years, unless God
should see fit to take me from this life sooner. As Charlotte
and I have the seed and supplies to manage the planting, we
have taken on the name of Fields. It is a name we look forward to passing on to our own children. Know me
forevermore as Anthony Abbott Fields.*

We are calling our new home Freeland.

Great-grandfather? I dropped the book and covered my
mouth with both hands.

A calming, true knowing settled over me. I thought back to my experiences with the pull and the crazy circumstances surrounding my exodus to Brennan and back. From my mishap in Father's barn to tracking down Lord Kent and his hired assassin. Was it possible great-grandfather and my mother had been working together to help me? He'd mentioned in his journal that his gift was inherited. Had it found its way down to me?

I could only assume.

I set the journal back on the shelf and turned, my eyes focusing on Father's lockbox key that had been left on his desk. It seemed to call to me, and instead of fighting the guilt I usually might have felt, I trusted the needle that pierced my core, the thread that pulled me toward it.

I turned the key in the lockbox and reached to the back until my fingers grazed a padded fabric container. Perhaps I should have asked father before invading this private space. But as sure as I knew the clouds, the moment I closed my fingers around the soft fabric, I knew these items belonged to me.

I sucked in a breath at the sight of blue fabric folded and sewn into pouch with a leather tie securing the contents in place. I settled back into Father's chair and reverently removed the tie. Inside were three letters labeled *Coming Out*, *Marriage*, and *Motherhood*. The script belonged to my mother. They were each closed with the family seal.

I placed a hand over my mouth, physically hoping to hold in a sob.

The pull nudged me to open the envelope entitled *Coming Out*. I set the others on the desk and broke the seal.

My Dearest Ebby,

Today I write three letters that a mother should never have to write. If you are reading this first letter, the illness has won, and you are left without a mother to guide you through this world. My darling, I am so sorry that I didn't tell you I wasn't well. You have always had such an appetite for life, and I didn't have the heart to dampen your spirit.

It is your wild spirit and your curious knack for eavesdropping that have always made me wonder if you possess the same gift that has assisted our line for generations. I hoped you did! My aunt had the gift, and her father before her. It is the same gift that led a blacksmith to the sacred oar of the mountain and taught him how to craft the Hundred Swords of history.

If my suspicions are correct, the strength of your abilities will not settle with you until you are of age. But the signs are there, Ebby dearest.

I will not be there to pass along what I know in person, but I can write this much (if you will excuse my shaking hand). My aunt told me the gift is granted to many of us, but few feel it on a physical level. If you are one of those people, my darling, you must trust the guidance you receive. Trust that it will grow from simple curiosity into a tool that may help your family and Freeland. When I pressed her, my aunt also told me her promptings felt like they came from your great-grandfather. I'm hoping that when I go, I can be that for you. It would bring me such peace knowing my spirit could be with you even after my body fails me.

As for your Coming Out—enjoy yourself. Don't feel the need to make a hasty match. I have certain predictions, but I'll leave those for my next letter.

All my love,

Mama

A peaceful blanket seemed to wrap me up and I was enveloped in a love that refused to bow to time and death. *I love you, Mama.*

THAT NIGHT FATHER sat in his high-backed chair. Hannah stood nearby, offering support. The flickering candlelight cast shadows about his face, emphasizing his furrowed features.

"I can't believe I sent you to Brennan." He massaged his temples.

I smiled despite myself. This might have been his first headache not caused by my eavesdropping. "Everything will work out, Father. The Brennan spy may have escaped but at least now we know who our enemies are."

A smile cracked Father's hard demeanor. "We wouldn't if it weren't for you, Ebby." He took hold of my uninjured hand. "I'm so proud of you."

I scrunched up my nose. "You might not be when you hear everything that happened."

Father's face took on a hard line. "Wesley told me about the deal you struck with those revolutionaries."

I winced. "I shouldn't have committed us to something so drastic—"

"Wesley also told me about the *Purgo*. Once word reaches the other provinces that we're harboring the secret of the famous blade, most of the region will be willing to join our side. I've already sent word to one of Kilsom's old friends in Sea Port, a man with strong political connections." I'd told Father about Mr. Daily passing and he'd taken the news hard.

"So Freeland will join the fight against Brennan?"

Father's features dipped, but he nodded. "We represent something important to the region, Ebby."

"What is that?" I asked, even though I was certain I knew the answer.

"Freedom."

Gavin stood from his chair in the corner of the room. "Father, there's a rather famous blacksmith pacing on our front porch. He's likely to break down the front door if he isn't allowed to see Ebby soon."

Father sat back in his armchair, staring at a charcoal sketch of my mother. "I think I'd rather like to keep the boy waiting a little longer." A light danced in his eyes, and he turned a devious grin in my direction. It was a smile that harkened back to the years when mother was with us.

"I have something for you, Father." I handed him Great-grandfather's journal. "I found this in the duke's library in Brennan. I don't think I could have survived without it."

He studied me for a moment then placed the book on the shelf with tender respect next to the journal's brother. "Do you know your name now, child?"

I looked him in the eyes, and for a moment, imagined I saw my great-grandfather sitting in my father's chair. Chills rolled over my skin.

"Yes, Father. I believe I do."

This was peace. I had found it. And even though there were inevitable storms ahead for me and my beloved Freeland, I was whole in this perfect, delicious moment. I was Ebrielle, granddaughter of Ebrielle. I was Ann, daughter of Ann. Above all...

I was a Fields.

EPILOGUE

Spring came early. After assuring Hannah three times that I was able, I set off to the well. Father's workers would be thirsty preparing the fields for seed. I lowered the bucket and waited for the bristled rope to get heavy. When I felt that familiar tug, I placed both feet on the wall of the well and pulled with my whole body to bring up the bucket. My wrist had healed. It felt good to use my muscles this way. It'd been too long.

Once I had the bucket high enough, I took one foot off the well and nudged the bucket until it swung over to rest on the lip of the well. I had to smile at the accomplishment.

That's when I heard the laugh. It wasn't a snickering, nor was it too boisterous. It was the deep rumbling sound of contentment.

"May I carry your bucket, Miss Fields?" Wesley leaned against his usual maple tree with arms crossed and the brim of his hat low over his eyes.

I hefted my bucket off the side of the well—splashing a good amount onto my dress. "No, thank you." I walked past him and let out a lazy sort of sigh.

Of course he came up behind me and snatched the bucket out of my hands. He set both the bucket and a parcel he'd been holding to the ground in such a hurry, half of the water spilled onto the newly thawed earth. He threw my hands around his neck and lifted me off the ground. I laughed out loud as we spun in circles. "Wesley, I've got to get this water to the fields."

But I didn't really care about the water, and he knew it. He set me down and carefully traced the pink scar that ran along my neck with his fingers. Hannah had done a fine job stitching me up after Lord Kent's blade, but the thin scar remained.

He pulled away, looking around to make sure we weren't being watched. "Fields would kill me if he—"

I pushed onto my toes. His words dissolved into a kiss that, like Wesley, was both strong and tender. His hands found my waist and I was flying in a place that seemed more dream than reality. Wesley slowly lowered me back to my feet.

"I have something for you," he said, reaching down for the brown-paper parcel with a vibrant blue ribbon.

I accepted the package and shot him a side-long glance. "Should I be worried? There's not a dead raccoon in here, is there?"

He threw his head back and laughed. "I've graduated from dead raccoons."

I knelt on a patch of grass, tugged free the ribbon, and pulled back the wrapping. The shock of blue fabric turned me instantly weepy. I couldn't wipe my tears fast enough. "Wesley, what have you done?"

I lifted my mother's creation from the wrapping to find it clean, the many tears from the night of the flood mended.

"Hannah thought I was crazy when I told her I wanted to mend it."

"You did this?"

Wesley shrugged. "My mother taught me to sew before she passed. I'm slow but my stitches are straight and even. I guess my time in the smithy has taught these hands more than just how to hit things."

I reverently laid the dress down in the wrappings, careful to retie the ribbon before gaining my feet.

Wesley eyed me with the look of a man completely satisfied with himself.

I reached for his hands and he readily offered them to me.

One by one, I lifted his palms to my lips. "These hands mean a great deal to me."

His smile slipped into something more intense and slightly less certain. "They belong to you, you know," he whispered. "They always have."

We walked to the fields with hands interlocked.

And Wesley carried my bucket.

ACKNOWLEDGEMENTS

This book was inspired by a lecture I used to receive from my father about the importance of the names we bear. When I was younger, I loved to let my wild imagination "improve" the truth from time to time. My parents were constantly sitting me down to discuss the importance of integrity and of honoring my family name. As a child, it always struck me that names are something that must be carried. And as I wrote this book, I considered the idea that names are also something that can lift us. I'm grateful for all of the names in my life that have encouraged me through the decade-long process of writing this book and seeing it through to publication.

First, I must thank my agent, Amy Jameson, for seeing something in this story from the beginning and for my publisher, Emma Nelson, for shaping it into such a beautiful book. Sincere thanks to Hannah, Olivia, and the rest of the Owl Hollow Press team. You are a mighty force and I'm honored to do this second book with you and be included among your talented flock.

Special thanks to early readers such as Tahsha Wilson, Lois Brown, Jo Layton, James Lewis, and Margie Jordan. You played a massive role in the development of this story and I'm forever grateful. I'm also very grateful to later readers such as Amy Beatty, Nichole Van, Brad Walker, Greta Bradford, Stacy Jenkins, Whitnee Jenkins, Barb Adamson, and Angela Jacobson. Some of these amazing people have read this book more than once. You deserve all of the honeycakes this world has to offer.

My family is the "why" behind everything that I am and do. I feel so much support from the Jenkins and Eldredge Clans. I'm grateful for parents who taught me that the only boundaries of my success are those of my own making and for Julie and Glayd who constantly "show up" in my life. I'm proud to carry your name, too! Thank you to Casey, Liberty, Boston, and the love of my life, Clint. You define support and I love you.

With her degree in History and Secondary Education, Jennifer Jenkins had every intention of teaching teens to love George Washington, the Napoleonic Wars, and Ancient Sparta ... until the writing began. She is the author of the Nameless trilogy (2015-2018), *To Kill a Curse* (2019), *Of Blood and Fire* (2020), *The Order of Chaos* (2021), and *Teen Writer's Guide: Your Road Map to Writing* (2020). She is also the co-founder and Executive Director of Teen Author Boot Camp, a federal non-profit organization dedicated to promoting teen literacy and authorship.

She divides her free time between teaching creative writing classes at Utah Valley University, reading, taking spontaneous trips, researching random events from the past, and fostering her adrenaline junkie addictions. You can learn more about the adventures that inspire her writing on her blog, *The Bucket List Writer*.

WWW.AUTHORJENNIFERJENKINS.COM

Instagram: @jenniferajenkins
Instagram: @thebucketlistwriter
Facebook: @authorjenniferjenkins

OTHER BOOKS BY JENNIFER JENKINS

Non-Fiction:
Teen Writer's Guide: Your Road Map to Writing

Nameless Trilogy:
Nameless
Clanless
Fearless

Lingering Sea Novels:
To Kill a Curse
Of Blood and Fire
The Order of Chaos